The POISONER'S ENEMY

THE POISONER OF KINGFOUNTAIN

JEFF WHEELER

All rights reserved.

No part of this publication may be sold, copied, distributed, reproduced or transmitted in any form or by any means, mechanical or digital, including photocopying and recording or by any information storage and retrieval system without the prior written permission of both the publisher, Oliver Heber Books and the author, Jeff Wheeler, except in the case of brief quotations embodied in critical articles and reviews.

PUBLISHER'S NOTE: This is a work of fiction. Names, characters, places, and incidents either are the product of the author's imagination or are used fictitiously. Any resemblance to actual persons, living or dead, business establishments, events, or locales is entirely coincidental.

Text copyright © 2017 Jeff Wheeler

Cover Art by Covermint Design

Published by Oliver-Heber Books

0 9 8 7 6 5 4 3 2 1

To Professor VanBeek

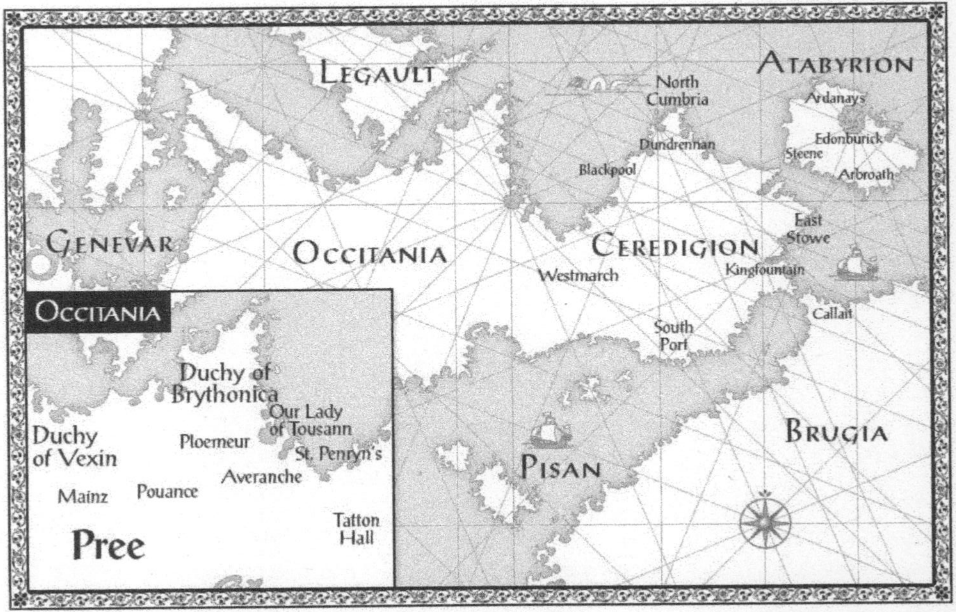
Legault
North Cumbria
Atabyrion
Ardanays
Edonburick
Steene
Arbroath
Dundrennan
Blackpool
Genevar
Occitania
Ceredigion
East Stowe
Kingfountain
Westmarch
Callait
South Port
Brugia
Pisan
Occitania
Duchy of Brythonica
Our Lady of Tousann
St. Penryn's
Duchy of Vexin
Ploemeur
Averanche
Mainz
Pouance
Tatton Hall
Pree

REALMS & CHARACTERS
MONARCHIES

Ceredigion: Eredur (House of Argentine): after his father was killed in an attempted insurrection, Eredur managed to wrest control of Ceredigion from his cousin, the mad king Henricus Argentine, son of the famous king who defeated Occitania at the Battle of Azinkeep. Eredur, a handsome and capable soldier, has consolidated his power while the mad king and his Occitanian queen (Morvared) have abandoned the realm to seek refuge in Edonburick. They still seek allies to restore the hollow crown to its "rightful" owner.

Occitania: Lewis XI (House of Vertus): Lewis, known as the Spider King for his cunning, is delighted that the factions within Ceredigion have been brutally at war with each other. He has signed a treaty with Eredur, promising to withhold support from Ceredigion's enemies in return for peace between the realms.

Brugia: Philip (House of Temaire): the kingdoms of Brugia and Occitania are constantly at war. The port city of Callait is still held by Kingfountain and is maintained by Duke Warrewik with a large army as a means of preventing Brugia or Occitania from claiming this strategic location that offers many military advantages to Kingfountain.

LORDS OF CEREDIGION

Lord Warrewik: Duke of North Cumbria, governor of Callait, master of the Espion
    Severn Argentine: Duke of Glosstyr
    Dunsdworth Argentine: Duke of Clare
    Lord Kiskaddon: Duke of Westmarch
    Lord Pogue: Duke of East Stowe
    Lord Lovel: Duke of Southport

I was born the year it all started. The year that the Duke of Yuork, Eyric Argentine, and his brother-in-law the Duke of North Cumbria, Nevin Warrewik, realized their king was truly, inescapably mad and utterly incapable of ruling. Queen Morvared summoned the two dukes to Kingfountain to answer charges of breaking the peace. They refused to obey, fearing for their lives, and were branded traitors to the crown. If caught, they would be executed for treason by being bound in boats and thrown into the river leading to the falls. Only someone who was Fountain-blessed could survive such a fate. An idea my father scoffed at.

We lived in Yuork. My childhood was spent living in fear of the armed knights from both sides marauding the land, threatening to kill any who did not support their cause. My father was raised in Atabyrion and had left that land to study law. He still had a rich accent that I adored, and he often grew quite animated while explaining the intricacies of the conflict. As a child, I would listen to his stories of betrayal and sedition for hours. My mother would sit and listen too, always with needlework in her lap, and though I would begin to annoy my father with all my questions before long, she never said a word.

I thought she was very boring when I was young—the way she'd do her needlework so quietly and patiently, listening but not speaking—but the constant needlework helped her dexterity. It made it easier for her to suture wounds.

Mother was a midwife. I was her only child.

By the time I was eleven, Eyric had been killed in an ambush, but his son Eredur rose to power. With his uncle Warrewik's help, he defeated the mad king's army and ascended the Argentine throne. The war was over, but we had all paid a price. My father, though not a soldier, had been killed for his support of Eredur.

No matter how much we wished to believe otherwise, none of us believed the peace would last.

— ANKARETTE TRYNEOWY

PART ONE
THE MIDWIFE'S DAUGHTER

CHAPTER 1
THE KINGMAKER'S SUMMONS

Ankarette had been up all night and had seen a babe safely delivered into a bloody world. The healthy cries had been a relief, both to the mother and father *and* to Ankarette. She had often attended her mother in deliveries, but she was only a girl of twelve. This was one of the first birthings she'd handled alone. From her experiences with her mother, she'd learned birth was an ordeal of pain and suffering that could bring exquisite joy or crushing grief, and she was grateful this difficult night had ended in joy. She was exhausted, relieved, and excited to share her success with her mother.

The streets of Yuork were bustling with life. The air was filled with the noises of squawking chickens, the panting and yapping of dogs, the rattling of cart wheels, and the grumbling of voices thick with the accent of the North—all melodies she had listened to her entire life. Something jarred within the normal chorus, however—the heavy bootfalls and the slight jangle of spurs of someone walking behind her. It was those spurs that had pricked her attention, making the noise memorable and out of place.

Ankarette was wrapped in a thin cloak and the morning air was just chilly enough to make her breath come out in a puff. The dress beneath her cloak was begrimed from the birthing process. She needed to wash the dress before she slept so that the bloodstains wouldn't linger. She turned the corner, heading toward her mother's small home, and the sound of the spurs followed her.

She had noticed the noise before, but it hadn't alarmed her. There were plenty of people on the street, and there'd been no reason to believe the footsteps were following her. Now, it was undeniable. The clink of the spurs continued at a steady rate, and the man—for it *was* a man, the tread was heavy enough—did not attempt to pass her. He was deliberately keeping his pace to match hers.

A spike of unease pierced her chest, but she attempted to ignore it. She was near her home and there were others on the street. No one would accost her in daylight. In fact, most of the people of Yuork recognized the midwife's daughter and would come to her aid if she called for help.

Ankarette risked a backward glance, just a brief one, and saw that her pursuer was a soldier wearing a badge. The man carried a sword and made no attempt to hide his martial insignia: a lumpy tree with a muzzled bear. The Bear and Ragged Staff. That was the emblem of the Duke of Warrewik, the richest lord in all of Ceredigion. What would one of his soldiers be doing in Yuork?

She quickened her stride, her fatigue from the long night melting away with the threat. Her mind began to work furiously, trying to decide on a strategy. In the horrible years of civil war, she had grown accustomed to dangers and threats. As the kingdom tottered between the control of various nobles, the citizens had borne much grief and heartache. Her own city, Yuork, had played a decisive role in the success of Eredur's kingship.

And her father's murder.

The jangle of the spurs didn't increase with her new pace, and she felt a spurt of relief. Perhaps it had been foolish to assume the worst. She turned the corner of the crowded street and her mother's dwelling came into sight—a narrow two-story home wedged in between the apothecary shop and Mickle the Barber. Her mother had cleverly chosen to move next to the apothecary to save time in fetching the various herbs used for remedies during childbirth. And Mickle had come because he sought to woo Ankarette's mother, who was still a handsome woman. His attentions were treated with kindness, but the midwife had no intention of remarrying.

Through the crowd, Ankarette noticed there were horses tied up in front of all three stores and soldiers were milling around. Soldiers who also wore the badge of the Bear and Ragged Staff.

Ankarette's stomach squeezed in on itself and she stopped in her tracks. Why were Warrewik's soldiers there? It was possible they had come to see Mickle the Barber, but Ankarette felt a queer sensation that they had come instead for *her*.

But why? She was twelve years old, a girl of significance to no one apart from the families she helped...

There was no time to think. The subtle clink of the spurs came up behind her. The beat of her pulse in her temples was deafening. Her mouth was so dry she was afraid she'd choke. Her eyes were fixed on the guards stationed outside her home. One of them had already noticed her, and she watched as he leaned in and said something to the others. All their heads turned toward her as one.

"It's all right, lass," said a voice in a Northern brogue behind her. "Don't be alarmed. You should feel honored to have gained the notice of such a powerful lord. Your mother awaits you at home and can tell you the news first, as is proper."

She turned fully around, getting a good look at him for the first time. He had eyes that were gray or green—she wasn't sure which—a knight's swagger, and a precocious smile. His thumbs hooked in a broad leather belt that boasted the nicked and scarred sheath of a sword that had clearly seen battle. His knuckles had been battered, there was a scar on his brow, and the little flat part on his nose indicated a healed break. His hair was dark brown, thick around his ears and shorn above his collar. There was a ring on his finger—not a wedding band, for it was on his littlest finger. He wore a chain hauberk beneath his tunic. If she were to guess, the man was five or six years her senior.

"Who are you?" she asked him, staring at his face. He was handsome, despite his scars.

"Sir Thomas," he answered with a courteous nod. "Do you recognize my badge, lass?"

She nodded, her throat slowly unloosing as she tried to force her thoughts to be calm. "You serve the Duke of Warrewik."

"Aye, lass. I do. You look weary. You've been up all night."

She noticed his eyes were bleary. He did not look well rested either.

"Go," he bid her. "My men will wait out here while you speak to your mother. I came to fetch you, lass. I don't like to keep my master waiting."

~

ANKARETTE SHUT the door behind her. Her mother was pacing the small space anxiously, and as soon as the door thumped shut, her gaze snapped to Ankarette.

"Did you see the soldiers?" she asked, striding quickly to the door.

Ankarette trembled. "They are Warrewik's men. Is this about Father?"

Her mother shook her head no. "It's about you."

Ankarette tried to unhook the clasp of her cloak, but her fingers were trembling too much. Her mother, so swift with her fingers, did it for her. "You must change. You can't go to Dundrennan like this."

"Dundrennan?" Ankarette gasped.

Her mother looked worried, anxious. "Yes, child. You've been summoned by the duke."

"But why?" She was completely baffled.

Her mother stroked her golden brown hair—a feature they shared—and hugged her close, squeezing her hard enough to hurt. Then she pulled back, shaking her head. "Listen to me, Daughter. Neither of us have any say in this. Not really. Powerful men like the duke must be obeyed." She bit her lip and shook her head. "Too soon, too soon. You must grow up too soon." She hugged her again, tears falling down her cheeks. Ankarette started to cry softly, hugging her mother close.

"Tell me, please!"

"Daughter." Her mother stepped back and knelt, gripping her shoulders. "The duke seeks a companion for his eldest daughter, Isybelle. A friend. He's chosen you." She cupped Ankarette's chin. "Only the Fountain knows why you were chosen. I had hoped to train you more, to prepare you to serve a noble household someday." She shook her head. "I haven't had enough time. You'll be taken from me. And somehow I must bear being alone."

Ankarette hugged her mother tightly, her mind whirling with the new information. Dundrennan was the chief castle in the North. Part of her thrilled at the sudden opportunity, but she felt guilty for the corresponding excitement. She didn't wish to leave her mother.

"There is much I still need to learn," Ankarette said, shaking her head.

"Aye, and you will!" her mother said tearfully. "The duke can afford the best of schools. He is always thinking ahead, that one. He's a cunning, ambitious man. You remember what Father used to call him?"

That was her mother's way—she'd never participated in Ankarette's father's conversations about politics, but she'd listened and learned.

"The kingmaker," Ankarette said softly, realizing that she would be part of the duke's household. The magnitude of it overwhelmed her.

"Aye," her mother whispered. "The most powerful man in the kingdom. Even more powerful than the king himself. Be obedient to him, Daughter. He rewards those who serve him faithfully."

"I will, Mother," Ankarette promised, wiping tears from her cheeks.

The door was jostled open and Sir Thomas barged into the space, his bulk instantly making the room feel smaller. "Daylight is wasting, lass," he said. "I need to get you to Dundrennan before nightfall. I don't think you would feel comfortable bedding down for the night in the heath surrounded by soldiers. No one would harm you, lass, so no need to fear that. But I'd rather avoid the temptation altogether since some of these men are rough. Now, kiss your mother's cheek and we'll be off."

Ankarette blinked quickly, realizing she hadn't yet changed out of her bloody dress. "Can I put on a new dress first?"

He sighed and stamped his boot, jangling the spur. "I don't see what difference a new one will make," he complained. "You'll be wearing one of the duke's gowns ere you see him. The faster we get there, the better. On our way, then."

She felt a gentle pinch on her arm. Turning, she saw her mother's insistent look. *Obey the duke . . . obey his men.* Ankarette hesitated, unsure of what to do. She had no idea what her future held and how this moment would affect her. Looking back at Sir Thomas, she saw the impatient look in his eyes. He was impatient, yes, but was he trustworthy?

A little ripple came into her heart as she continued to stare at him. A calming feeling. It was there one moment, gone the next, but it was enough to guide her.

Ankarette kissed her mother's cheek. "The babe was a son. All went well."

"I'll check on the mother later today. Good-bye, child. Go with all my love." She returned Ankarette's kiss.

Ankarette turned and followed the knight out of the house.

The other soldiers were all mounted now, and the beasts snorted and groaned, anxious to be on their way. One of the horses was in the act of plopping a steaming pile of manure on the street when they emerged, and the soldiers guffawed and booed at the horse's sense of timing.

Sir Thomas wrinkled his nose. There were just enough horses for the number of soldiers. There wasn't one for her, and she stood in the street, confused and astonished by this sudden reversal in her fortune. Her companion, exuding confidence, sauntered up to his horse and dug his boot into the stirrup before hoisting himself up onto the back of the broad mount. The horse nickered and stamped and he led it around in a short circle as Ankarette stared up at him. *What next?*

He reached his hand down to her. "You'll be riding with me, lass." He smiled in a comforting way, as if realizing that she was unsure of herself.

She reached up to grip his hand, but he caught her by the forearm instead and, leaning out of the saddle, pulled her up behind him. The horse's rump was so big it felt like straddling an over-large barrel. She had never ridden horseback before and instantly felt like she was going to fall off.

"Hold on to me tightly, lass," he said over his shoulder. "It'll get a bit bouncy, but you'll get the feeling of it soon enough. Lady Isybelle loves to ride. She enjoys falconry too. You will do things you've never done before and bless the Fountain for the good fortune. Now, be of good courage, Angarad."

She felt strange wrapping her arms around his

waist. He was a soldier, as hard as stone. "My name is Ankarette," she corrected softly, deferentially.

"Aye, but if this were Atabyrion, it would be pronounced the proper way. It's your family stock. Tryneowy isn't a name you find in Kingfountain. But whatever suits you. I'll not object. My name is Sir Thomas, as I told you. Sir Thomas Mortimer."

CHAPTER 2
THE EARL'S SECOND SON

It was midday when Sir Thomas finally called a halt so they could rest and feed their mounts. Ankarette was so saddle sore she could hardly stand. Her arms felt like stretched-out ropes from clutching the soldier for so long. She hadn't slackened her grip once, fearful that she would tumble out of the saddle and get trampled by the other riders.

She had never traveled so far before, and the vastness of the land around them was astounding. The mountains were capped in snow and the air was brisk and chill. She stumbled around, wincing from the pain in her legs, and listened to the rough language of the soldiers. One of whom was relieving himself noisily against a tree.

"Oy!" Sir Thomas snapped as he secured a bag of provender to the bridle of their shared steed. "Go in the trees over yonder. You're making the poor lass blush. Seethin' idiot, mind the company."

The soldier, chagrined, obeyed, and the others snorted and chuckled and tamed their rough language. Sir Thomas shook his head in disbelief, then stroked his horse's neck and coddled it with clucks. "Good old Pent.

You've ridden well so far. She's barely a burden, eh? Good beast." He quickly patted down the horse's withers, followed by the legs, and then inspected the horseshoes for pebbles and stones. Finding one, he produced his dagger, which earned him a grumbling snort from the horse. "Oh, shush . . . I'll not prick ya."

Ankarette needed to relieve herself, but she wouldn't dare mention it now, after seeing how the other man had been shamed. She certainly didn't wish to say anything in front of all the soldiers. Her hair had tugged loose from its braid during the windy ride and she debated trying to tame it again. Her dress smelled awful, which embarrassed her, but Sir Thomas had not commented on it.

"Lass," he said with a grunt, after loosing the stone from his horse's shoe. "I have some bread and cheese in the saddlebag." He nodded with his head.

"Any ale, my lord?" one of the soldiers asked.

"Just river water," he countered. "You'll not be addling your wits on this journey. But I'll buy you each a flagon if we make good time."

There was a chorus of assent. The soldiers were all expert animal handlers and Ankarette watched them care for their horses first before meeting their own needs. She went to the saddlebag and opened it. On top was a letter, sealed with red wax, and it tumbled out when she tried to reach for the loaf. Guiltily, she reached down to snatch it and put it back, but Sir Thomas seized it first. Their hands touched, and she flinched and drew back, frightened.

"Don't be skittish," he said with a chuckle. "You have nothing to fear from any of us, lass. The duke of the North is a fair master and doesn't punish his underlings for trifles. You can judge a man by the way he treats those beneath him." He tapped his nose with the folded letter. "Ask any servant in Dundrennan. Now, where is that loaf? My stomach is complaining."

She reached into the saddlebag, pulled out the loaf, and handed it to him. He took it and wrenched it in half with a quick motion. She saw he was about to offer the larger portion to her, but she reached for the smaller. "I'm not that hungry, but thank you."

He shrugged and took a big mouthful, walking around the horse once again and continuing his inspection. "Old Pent isn't the fastest or the meanest, but he's seen me through my troubles well enough. A gift from my father, may the Fountain bless him."

"Your father," Ankarette said, teasing a bit of bread loose with her fingers. "The Earl of Sur?"

"Aye, he *was* the Earl of Sur." He checked the girth straps next. "He died at the Battle of Mortimer's Cross."

Ankarette flinched, biting her lip. "I'm . . . I'm sorry." She had also lost her father after that battle, just six months previously. Her father had advocated for young Eredur's right to be their king—and he'd died for it.

The knight shrugged, his countenance altering slightly, but his tone remained easygoing. "Many died at that battle. He fought bravely; that's what matters. My brother was made earl to take his place, and I was knighted and sent to serve the duke of the North. There are worse posts, I can assure you. Keep walking around while you eat, lass. Else your legs will freeze up and you won't be able to move for days. You will be an expert rider in a fortnight." He patted old Pent one more time and chewed on his bread.

Ankarette took his advice and kept walking, looking covertly at the other soldiers, who were mumbling amongst themselves.

"My lord!" one of them called. Another tried to shush him, but the man shoved the other fellow back. "Is it true the mad king wears his wife's dresses?" Some snickers and guffaws broke out at the question, and she saw that Sir Thomas's eyes turned as gray as steel. His face hardened with anger at the impertinence. She watched him chew on a piece of bread, slowly, deliberately, calming himself down.

"No, Bradford," he said at last, his kindly smile belying the cooling anger in his eyes. "You can't believe all the rumors you hear, man."

"Yates was the one that said it," the man chuffed.

"Yates believes that pigs can fly," Sir Thomas quipped. "Speak no ill of the mad king. Let him alone."

Interesting . . . he had fought for King Eredur, but he was not without sympathy for the other side. Ankarette listened to their talk and nibbled on the bread the knight had given her. Since her father's death, there hadn't been anyone to explain the politics to her anymore. It occurred to her that she was traveling with an earl's son to a duke's castle. Suddenly, she wasn't hungry for the bread, but for information.

Sir Thomas paced around with restless energy, examining the crooked roots of the nearby trees, checking the saddlebags again. She watched him slip the note back into the bag before fetching the cheese. With his dagger, which he wiped quickly on his leg, he sliced it in half evenly and gave her a portion.

"Thank you," she said as she took it, feeling self-conscious.

"You've been ill fed in Yuork," he said with a half smile. "You're nothing but sticks and skin, lass. There is plenty to eat in the duke's household. Mind his butler,

Berwick. He has a nasty temper when he's feeling the gout."

"What can you tell me about Lady Isybelle?" Ankarette asked, feeling shy, but determined to overcome it.

Sir Thomas tore off a hunk of bread with his teeth and walked around the road, kicking some dry grass. "She has a pleasant disposition. All the virtues that a nobleman's daughter should possess." He frowned. "She has an . . . instinct to please, you could say."

Though it seemed there was more he was not saying, she didn't press.

Sir Thomas whistled through his teeth—a loud, surprisingly harsh sound that roused the other soldiers. "Mount up. We don't want to arrive at Dundrennan in the dark." His command brought the other soldiers to their feet with a bit of grumbling.

Turning back to Ankarette, the knight gave her an arch look. "The king has secured our borders from threats these last two years. He's managed to keep his enemy confined in a powerless kingdom that can only bark at us but not bite. Do you know the game of Wizr? Can you play?"

"M-my father taught me," she stuttered, feeling her cheeks flush.

"There is still a queen piece on the board," he said, his voice serious. "Even though the game has ended, she's *still* playing. The former queen has a son, you see. Why, he's only a little younger than you, lass. The mother and her cub are skulking in Occitania presently, looking for a way to rejoin her husband in Edonburick. Lewis claims they are *prisoners*, so as not to default on the treaty he signed with Eredur." He clucked his tongue. "So the game isn't over yet after all. What does our king need? A queen. And who has he commissioned to secure one for him? Your new master, Duke Warrewik."

There was some hidden knowledge behind his words. Some secret that he didn't plan to share.

Ankarette wanted to know what it was.

～

Shadows had begun to shroud them by the time they reached the mountain valley where Dundrennan lay. Sir Thomas reined in and turned the horse so that Ankarette faced the breathtaking view. The giant stone cliffs were dotted with bright splotches of snow that looked purple in the fading light, and the woods beneath them bristled with ancient pines. She could see the castle nestled in the valley and the town gathered without it, the small cottages as bright as a swarm of fireflies. An enormous waterfall tumbled from the cliffs behind the castle, and even from a distance, she could hear the distant rumble of it, which awakened a strange, giddy murmuring in her heart. She'd never seen anything quite so splendid.

"It's quite a view, lass," Sir Thomas said. "We'll be down there ere long. Hold on tighter. The road can be bumpy."

She'd relaxed her death grip, she realized, and pressed her palms against his muscular chest. Cheeks flushed, she gripped her wrists again, joints aching, as the company rode down into the valley. The chill air was sweetened with the fragrant scent of the pines, but the glorious view became dark as the sun disappeared. It would be a while yet before the moon made its presence known, and she found her cheek bumping on the knight's shoulder blades as she blinked and tried, unsuccessfully, to stave off sleep.

When Ankarette awoke, they were already inside the castle bailey. Bright torches flared against her tender eyes and she felt herself falling from the saddle. In a panic, she gripped Sir Thomas's cloak.

"It's all right, lass," he said. "Let go. They've got you."

She realized that some of the grooms had been trying to pull her down from the saddle. Disoriented, she hearkened to his voice and released her white-knuckled grip. Soon she was on her feet, swaying as the soldiers—Sir Thomas, included—dismounted around her. Dogs from the interior of the castle snuffled around her shoes and skirts.

"Go on, get away," Sir Thomas said, gripping her arm with one hand and waving the dogs away with the other. He marched her to the massive doors of the fortress and she craned her neck to look at the tower that seemed high enough to conquer the sky. She could see a few stars glimmering amidst the haze of chimney smoke. Her legs felt like they belonged to a puppet with broken strings, but she forced herself to walk against the pain, digging her nails into her palms.

A man stood in the open doorway of the castle. He was an older fellow with silver in his hair and a goatee. He wore the badge of the Bear and Ragged Staff as well and looked stern and somber, almost like the cliffs outside the castle. Was this the duke?

"Here she is, Lord Horwath," Sir Thomas said. "Lady Isybelle's maid."

"You're late," the man responded in a stiff brogue. "Did you drag her here behind the horse? Look at all that blood."

Sir Thomas scowled. "She needs a bath and a lady's gown. This one's fit to be burned. Can you see to it? I've a message for the duke."

Horwath frowned. "The duke wanted to see her right away. He must away to Occitania tomorrow."

Not like this, Ankarette thought in a panic.

Sir Thomas uttered a curse. "Already? Did an answer come from King Lewis's court?"

"How should I know?" Horwath answered. "I'm not Espion like you."

"Shut it!" Sir Thomas said angrily, glaring at the older man. Ankarette had no idea what the word meant —*Espion*—but the knight was obviously furious if he would speak thus to an earl. His cheek twitched and she could see he wished to give Lord Horwath another rebuke.

Instead, Sir Thomas ground his jaw, waited a moment, and then turned to Ankarette. "You were not supposed to hear that part, lass," he said with seething patience. "I beg you to keep that knowledge to yourself."

She blinked up at him. "I will," she said sincerely, looking into his steely eyes. She'd keep his secret, but that didn't mean she wouldn't try to find out what it meant.

Her promise mollified him. "Good, lass. My lord, the lass was up all night helping with the birthing of a babe and then in the saddle all day from Yuork. That's why she is as you see her. I promised her a change in gowns when we got here. Can you see that she is brought to the duke when she is suitable?"

"Aye, lad," the earl said with a grunt. "My daughter will help her get ready."

"Thank you," Sir Thomas said, suddenly agitated.

"How is . . . never mind. It seems I may be going to Occitania with the duke. Have a care with the lass, my lord." He turned to Ankarette and bowed stiffly.

But as he straightened and she curtsied, she saw a flash in his eyes. They looked very green in that moment, in the wavering light from the wall torches. "You notice things. People." He paused, hesitating. "That will serve you well here. Watch and learn, Angarad Tryneowy."

CHAPTER 3
WARREWIK

The castellan's daughter, Lady Elysabeth Horwath, was Ankarette's elder by several years. Her long dark hair was arranged in an elegant Northern style, partially held up in braids, something that made Ankarette feel more conscious of her own hair's disarray. She took Ankarette in with civility, but not warmth, and looked too tired to be performing the duties of hospitality. She asked no questions about where Ankarette had come from and offered no sympathy.

"Do you fancy the red or the silver?" Elysabeth asked with an air of boredom, holding up two different silk gowns. Both had a damask pattern and were trimmed with beads, and they were finer than anything she had ever worn. "The coloring of both would suit you, I should think."

Ankarette had already dried off from her bath and was wearing a clean white shift. "The silver one, if you please. It's beautiful."

"It's Occitanian," Elysabeth said, stifling a yawn. "The duke always orders the latest fashions for his two daughters. The court of King Lewis is exceptionally fine.

Or so I am *told*." That last bit was uttered with a tone of longing and a little resentment. "I think it should fit you. It can be altered in the morning. The duke has several maids for such work usually . . . but they are all abed."

Ankarette could easily sense that Elysabeth wished she were there herself. She didn't want to be a nuisance, so she kept quiet and hurriedly changed into the silver gown. It was tight, meant for a younger girl, but she didn't complain. After Elysabeth helped her with the long row of buttons on the back, Ankarette hurried to the brazier and knelt by it, running her fingers through her hair to try to dry it faster.

"No time for that," Elysabeth said with a cough. "Duke Warrewik will be waiting for you. Here, let me braid it for you. Quickly now."

A few moments later, Ankarette was declared ready. She squeezed her feet into a set of shoes that pinched and followed the older girl into the depths of the vast castle of Dundrennan. Ankarette's eyes lingered on the tapestries and pennants showing the standard of the Bear and Ragged Staff, which were displayed prominently throughout the halls. There were not many servants around, but the shadows within the corridors were shoved back by flaming torches. They turned a sharp corner, and Elysabeth nearly collided with a tall man with a fringe of gray hair around his balding top.

"Watch yerself, lass!" the man grumbled with an ornery air. "Why ye be skulking in the halls at night? I thought I heard footsteps and came *rickon* to see who was 'bout."

"This is Lady Isybelle's new maid," Elysabeth said, gesturing toward Ankarette. "The duke wanted to see her when she arrived, Berwick."

THE POISONER'S ENEMY

The man hocked but didn't spit. "Indeed." He gave Ankarette a baleful look before shifting his attention to the older girl. "The duke and his daughter are in the solar with your father and Sir Thomas. Off with ye both, then."

"Sir Thomas is with them?" Elysabeth said with an interested air that had been previously uncharacteristic of her. Her blue eyes lit up with a secret smile.

"Aye, lass. Now go. We'd all like to be abed. Your young charge looks like she'll fall asleep standin'."

Elysabeth curtsied and then swept forward with more vim in her stride than before. When they reached the solar, the older girl knocked, and her father, Lord Horwath, opened the door. He looked Ankarette over by way of inspection and nodded curtly without saying a word before letting them in.

They had walked into the middle of an animated conversation. "And so who *are* you going to station in Callait, my lord?" Sir Thomas asked, his voice throbbing with anger.

"Captain Vauclair, of course—an excellent man and an ideal choice to lead the garrison at Callait," replied a man whose authoritative air marked him as the duke. The man was tall and powerfully built. His wife was an Argentine, Ankarette knew, a wealthy heiress who had helped bring him the bulk of his fortune prior to the civil war, and he had been handsomely rewarded for his services to King Eredur. Everyone said he was the one who'd put his nephew on the throne. He had thick golden hair with streaks of gray at his temples and a handsome face. Warrewik spoke with his whole body, not just his words, and had a commanding voice that was deep and penetrating. He was older than her father had been at the time of his death.

Sir Thomas and the duke were standing on opposite sides of a large wooden table covered in various maps and scrolls. The hearth was spacious, but no one had tended to it for a while and it was thick with smoking, sizzling red coals. The chamber was cozy, but it featured all the trappings of a man of exalted rank, from high-quality furniture to tasteful—though extravagant—statues and urns and tapestries.

"Vauclair," Sir Thomas said with contempt, his eyes flashing like steel. He had not shifted his attention from the duke. "You're trusting an Occitanian to be loyal?"

"The man's not to blame for his place of birth. He served the king's interests in the duchy of Vexin, though it earned him the hatred of his own people. He needs a new assignment."

"He *lost* Vexin," Sir Thomas said pointedly.

Warrewik batted away the comment with a calm wave of his hand. "That's not his fault, Thomas. I don't punish a man for failure unless he is disobedient. He was given the impossible task of holding King Lewis's army with only two thousand men. Hardly sufficient against the might of Occitania. And now that we have the opportunity for a more lasting peace with Lewis, I need someone I can trust in Callait while I begin the negotiations for a . . . a *suitable* marriage partner for the king." He glanced across the room, and Ankarette noticed a young woman sitting meekly on the window seat. She'd been so quiet and unobtrusive Ankarette had missed seeing her before. The resemblance between the girl and the duke marked her as his daughter, as Isybelle.

A look passed between father and daughter, and Isybelle bowed her head, her cheeks flaming. Interesting . . .

"If I had been commanded to hold Vexin," Sir Thomas said confidently, "I would have held it despite the odds."

Warrewik chuckled. "I like your brashness, Thomas. You're ambitious, and I know you wanted the post of Callait yourself. Be patient. I need you here in Dundrennan while I am gone to Pree. It could take many months to negotiate this."

"Dundrennan?" Sir Thomas asked in disbelief. "But Lord Horwath is already here."

"Aye, and he's a wise and competent man. You could learn a lot from him. I want you to look after my daughters while I'm gone."

Ankarette could see the news infuriated the knight. His fingers clenched into fists on the tabletop and he looked as if he'd fly into a rage. Warrewik stared him down with calm composure and a patient smile, as if the young man were merely an overanxious hunting dog.

"As you wish, my lord," Sir Thomas finally muttered, pushing away from the table. He stormed out of the solar, passing Ankarette and Elysabeth without looking at either of them. Elysabeth's smile looked haughty.

When the door closed, Warrewik chuckled. "I'm sorry to leave you with a problem, Stiev. But it would be best if he doesn't come with me to Occitania. He's too hot-blooded."

"He's young," the earl said with a shrug.

"And he's a second son," Warrewik said thoughtfully, walking around the table and wagging his finger. He used his arms expansively as he spoke. "Thwarting a man's ambition once in a while helps stoke the forge. My father did that to me routinely.

Thomas will serve me twice as hard now to prove himself. You'll see."

Horwath nodded solemnly and said nothing.

The duke shifted his gaze to the young ladies at the door. Studying Ankarette with interest, he said, "Thank you, Lady Elysabeth. You may go."

"If you please, my lord," she responded with a polite curtsy and left.

Ankarette felt uncomfortable under the man's scrutiny. Her hair was damp and braided, and she was exhausted from the long ride and the night she'd spent ushering in a new life. She had heard and witnessed so much in this place . . . and couldn't help but wonder what kind of world she had entered. Although tempted to fidget, she kept her hands still.

"You have great composure," the duke complimented after the silence started to become unbearable. "A natural poise. I study people, you know." He turned toward a Wizr set arranged at the end of the table and touched one of the pieces. The tower piece. "Do you play Wizr, Ankarette Tryneowy?"

Her throat constricted, so she bobbed her head up and down.

"Your father taught you, I suppose?"

"Yes, my lord."

"He was very good at the game," Warrewik said, watching her eyes, watching her reaction. Ankarette felt a little gushing feeling, a little trickling sensation. She knew what the duke would say just before he said it.

"Your father was part of the Espion."

The words startled her. How had she known what he would say beforehand? She hadn't even heard that word before tonight, and she still didn't understand what it meant.

THE POISONER'S ENEMY

She bit her lip, feeling unsure of herself but struggling not to show it. "He ... he never told me."

Warrewik smiled reassuringly. "No, you're still very young Ankarette. Do you know what the Espion is?"

She shook her head no. She wanted desperately to know.

"Every ruler keeps a network of spies. The Espion are the men and *women* who are paid to inform us what is going on in different kingdoms. And here within our own realm. Your father was one of our agents in Atabyrion. He studied the law and became an excellent lawyer." He spread his hands expansively. "He was murdered because he was doing his duty to the true king. I have had my eye on your family for quite some time, but it was my will that you be trained as a midwife. If it weren't for that, I would have summoned you to Dundrennan years ago. I have plans for you Ankarette."

Ankarette blinked in astonishment and the duke chuckled.

"Oh yes! I see I've surprised you." He reached for the tower piece again and moved it across the board to another square. "One of the reasons I love Wizr is that you have to plan your moves well in advance. To think three or four moves ahead of your enemy. To put your pieces in position so that they will serve you best later." He turned and made a subtle gesture, and Isybelle obediently rose from the window seat to join him at the table.

She was a pretty girl, though her demeanor and looks were both very demure. The girl's hair was more red than gold, and a smattering of freckles crested her nose. Her pale complexion had faded from its earlier blush. She gave Ankarette a shy, encouraging smile.

"This is my eldest daughter," the duke said, putting

his hands on her shoulders. He towered over her. "She will inherit this vast fortress and its many estates. My other daughter, Nanette, will also inherit expansive properties. The Fountain only blessed my wife and I with two children, Ankarette. Only two, and both pregnancies were very difficult. I look ahead, as I told you. Both of my daughters are fit to marry kings, and they will not lack for suitors." He said this with power and conviction, his eyes blazing with certainty.

"Your duty, child, is to be Isybelle's friend and companion, and in so doing, to protect her reputation. You will sleep in the same room, even in the same bed! No one will be able to accuse her of being anything but chaste. As you can imagine, there will be some who would seek to win her fortunes against my wishes or my will. She is a dutiful daughter. But some men are unscrupulous." His voice hinted at a lingering fury from something that had happened in the past. "They would use flowery words and gallant promises to steal her heart from me. You must be observant and vigilant, Ankarette. You must interfere with any attempts a paramour might make to seduce her. Notify Thomas at once if you have even the slightest suspicion that someone is trifling with my daughter. Before I leave for Occitania, I will instruct Thomas to train you in the ways of the Espion. There are certain signals and gestures, a secret language, if you will. You need to know this to be effective in your role."

He patted Isybelle's shoulders, either unmoved by or unaware of the fiery blush on the girl's cheeks, and then closed some of the distance between himself and Ankarette. Even though he smiled at her benevolently, she felt physically intimidated by his height. "Now, let me be clear. You will hear many things said in Dundrennan. You will become privy to secrets that should not and ought not be shared outside this household. I am choosing to trust you, Ankarette, and I demand loyalty and obedience from you in return. If you serve me faithfully, you will be greatly rewarded.

"Your father died in my service. I have not forgotten that. Your mother will be cared for while you serve me here. And then, when your duties are fulfilled, you will live in comfort and peace on one of my estates."

He stepped closer. "Let me be frank, child. I am asking that you sacrifice part of your life in your service to the hollow crown. You will need to live beyond reproach yourself, or many ill-intentioned men will seek *your* favor. You will care for the children of my heirs. To be a midwife and companion in a noble household is a position of incomparable trust and confidence. My trust and confidence in you must be absolute. What say you, Ankarette Tryneowy? Do you recognize the honor you have been chosen for?"

She had listened to his words and felt a niggling of doubt in her mind. Was he asking her to serve his interests or the king's? Was it his intention to marry Isybelle to Eredur?

Something was going on that she didn't understand. She felt completely out of her depth, struggling to break to the surface of a dark pool.

"It is a great honor, my lord," Ankarette said, trying not to stammer. "Am I to understand that I shall serve you as well as the king? King Eredur?"

"Yes, yes, of course," the duke said, giving her a patient smile. There was something in his eyes, though... A smug look. "Eredur *wears* the hollow crown. He *is* the rightful king. Of course you will serve him. And you will, no doubt, get the opportunity to meet him someday. When you are ready. When you have been trained in all the formalities of court." He scratched his smooth cheek with a well-trimmed nail. Everything about him was decorous and polished. "Your accent, for example. You speak the brogue of the North, but they will look down on you for that in Kingfountain. My daughter has been working on changing her accent. You must as well, if you choose to accept this great honor. How proud your father would be if he knew you were given this chance! Will you serve?"

"I will," Ankarette said, bending her knee in a curtsy.

CHAPTER 4
THE DUKE'S DAUGHTER

Ankarette didn't remember falling asleep, but she awoke on a small couch. A chambermaid was stealthily sweeping ashes and cinders into a metal pail, and it was the soft scraping sounds that had roused her. She blinked, utterly confused, and then memories of the previous day came crashing down on her and she sat up in startled surprise.

The blanket that had covered her fell to her lap. It was made of soft fur, a winter animal's pelt of some kind. The curtains were drawn across the closest window, but judging by the faint rays gleaming through the crack, it was just past dawn.

"Pardon, miss, if I woke you," said the chambermaid in her sweet Northern accent. She was a drudge with smudges of soot on her nose and cheek, probably eight years old.

"It's all right," Ankarette replied, giving her a comforting smile. She looked around and spied a spacious bed. A veil of gauzy fabric was draped over the top of the bed from an iron ring in the ceiling, the fabric attached to each of the four large posts, and pillows were scattered hither and yon.

When Ankarette sat up, she saw Isybelle and another, younger, girl slumbering on the vast mattress. The younger girl had a mass of dark hair that completely hid her face.

The chambermaid finished sweeping out the hearth in front of Ankarette's couch and added some more logs from the stack. On her hands and knees, she blew on the coals, causing them to sizzle and the logs to catch. Soon, a fire began to crackle as it was revived from the snowy ashes. Ankarette slipped off the couch and approached the bed. The other girl could only be Isybelle's sister, though Ankarette could not remember her name.

Her legs ached from the long ride. Memories of riding behind Sir Thomas, clinging to him, struck her forcefully and her cheeks started to burn. Ankarette shoved the thoughts aside and maneuvered to the curtained window like a newborn colt. Pushing apart the folds of fabric, she stared outside.

Her breath caught at the splendor of the scene. This set of windows faced north, away from the town, and she had an unobstructed view of the massive waterfall spilling down the jagged face of the cliff. The sunlight bathed the stone in golden light, and the beauty of it snatched her heart like a fisherman's hook. Tears pricked her eyes at the thought of seeing such a view every day. Her good fortune, the change that had come into her life, was simply beyond belief. And her mother would not be left alone and struggling. The duke had promised to provide for her, which settled a nagging concern Ankarette had harbored since leaving Yuork.

"Is there anything you'll be needing, miss?" asked the chambermaid with a quick bob and awkward curtsy. Ankarette was a fellow servant. She didn't deserve such a display of respect.

"What's your name?" she asked the girl, giving her a friendly smile.

"Kamryn," said the girl with pleasure.

"How long does Lady Isybelle usually sleep?"

The waif glanced at the bed. "She's been known to sleep for a good while, miss." She paused, then added, "I'd heard someone was coming, but I didn't know it would be last night, miss. I'll try not to wake you tomorrow."

Ankarette shook her head. "I don't like to sleep late. If I'm not awake before you come in the morning, would you wake me?"

Kamryn's eyes widened. "Yes, miss."

"Thank you." Ankarette asked her some more questions to get an understanding for how the daughters of the duke spent their days. There were lessons in language, history, and mathematics. Rides in the valley accompanied by protectors. Lady Isybelle enjoyed falconry as well. The waif was a fount of information, and judging from Iysbelle's lack of movement, the duke's daughter was a deep sleeper.

After the brief chat, the chambermaid left. Ankarette explored the room, looking at the various combs, mirrors, and jewelry boxes in a state of disarray. There were gowns strewn over the floor as well, marking Lady Isybelle's preference for a state of untidiness. She walked around the room, examining it from different angles, admiring the cut of the stone in the walls and the decorative trim above the doorway.

Embroidery was something Ankarette's mother had taught her to love, and she was thrilled to find a basket crowded with hoops and thread and needles and half-finished works. There was a partially done rose, a bird's beak and eyes, the trim of vines and leaves—all tossed aside unfinished. Nestling back down on the couch, Ankarette began to work on the flower. As she worked, her mind sorted through the events of the preceding day. Embroidery helped her open the door to her thoughts and sort through them in a deep, satisfying way. As she made the tiny, precise stitches, she felt better equipped to judge the truth of whatever was vexing or confusing her. Something about it helped her reason through her feelings and solve problems.

"I was asleep when you came last night," said a voice at her elbow, startling her.

It was the dark-haired girl, Isybelle's sister. Ankarette hadn't heard the child slip out of bed and pad up to her. "I didn't hear you."

"Sometimes I sleep in Belle's bed." She was looking at Ankarette in an almost accusatory way.

"I see," she answered, setting down her needlework. She had a natural way with children. Some people were afraid of children because their behavior was erratic and hard to predict, but Ankarette found them adorable. "Does your papa know?"

The girl shook her head slowly, a small frown twisting her mouth.

"Ah, I see. Are you worried that I'll tell him?"

The girl stared daggers at Ankarette.

"Are you Isybelle's sister?"

"I am. I'm Nanette."

"I thought you were." Ankarette gave her a warm smile. "Nanette, I am very good at keeping secrets. I won't tell your papa. If he asks me, I will be truthful. You should always be truthful. But I will not mention it to him."

Nanette surprised her with a kiss on the cheek.

"Thank you, Karette! I like your name. It's close to mine."

Ankarette smiled and saw that Isybelle was sitting up, rubbing her bleary eyes.

"Go back to your room, Nanette," she said. "The governess will be looking for you by now."

The younger girl obeyed and slipped quietly out of the room.

Ankarette pushed aside the hoop and needlework and rose. "I'm sorry I fell asleep on you last night, my lady. I was very weary."

Isybelle smiled and waved off the apology. "No need, Ankarette." She slid her legs off the bed and rose, then grabbed a blanket as a shawl and wrapped it around her nightdress. "Sir Thomas mentioned that you'd been up the entire night before helping with the birthing of a child. I've never witnessed something like that. I'm afraid I'd be shocked and faint. They say there is a lot of blood." Her skin took on a greenish cast.

"Sometimes," Ankarette replied. "You were kind to put a blanket on me. Thank you."

Isybelle walked up to her, giving her a pleased and friendly smile. She took Ankarette's hands and stroked them with her thumbs. "I'm grateful you agreed to come. I have many acquaintances, but I've never had my own particular friend. Well, except for Nanette, but she likes to be with Cousin Severn more than me." She smiled wryly.

"The king's brother is here?"

"Severn is, yes. Dunsdworth used to be, but he's the Duke of Clare, so he spends more time at that estate now. I thought he would stay until he was of age, sixteen, but Cousin Eredur sent him away." Her countenance fell.

Ankarette gave her a curious look. "When did that happen?"

Isybelle turned away sharply, concealing her face. "Not long ago." Then she looked back and tried to smile, though it failed to mask her inner anguish. "But I'm glad you are here now. I need a friend."

"I'm grateful to be here."

"Do you like Dundrennan, Ankarette? It is the most beautiful castle in all the realm. Well, maybe not as beautiful as Kingfountain, I'll admit, but it is so peaceful here in the North. I *hope* you will be happy here."

Ankarette wasn't sure what she had expected, but Isybelle was clearly starving for friendship. There was a huge gap between their stations in life, but the duke's eldest daughter treated Ankarette like an equal. The lady was highborn, not haughty.

"I'm very pleased to be able to serve you, my lady," she said.

Isybelle shook her head and gave her a conspiratorial smile. "Please. In private, call me Belle."

∼

A NEW WORLD had opened before Ankarette Tryneowy like a chest of glittering treasure. The only portions of the castle forbidden to her were the duke and duchess's personal chambers and the treasury, and within the first few days, she had visited the entire fortress and knew her way around. The palace was full of servants and those seeking the duke's patronage. While he was gone, his wife ruled in his stead. The duchess of the North, a wealthy heiress in her own right, was a stately woman with honey-brown hair and only a few streaks of gray. She was prim and proper and gave Ankarette the condescending looks she'd expected from Isybelle.

In addition to the taciturn castellan, Stiev Horwath, Ankarette had also been introduced to Severn Argentine, the king's youngest brother, who spent his days in the training yard practicing to become a knight. He was about Ankarette's age, although his brooding looks and crooked back made him seem older. His vigilant training was impressive, but she avoided him because he had a gift for sarcasm and biting words.

The duke had departed for Occitania within a day or two of Ankarette's arrival, to commence negotiations for a bride for the king. It was suspected that he would be away for months, yet still the Espion came to bring the duchess tidings of his travels. The duke and duchess seemed to genuinely care for each other, and the household staff respected their masters—though they had exacting standards, they were never malicious.

Ankarette loved the daily rides with Isybelle and she benefitted from the education that the duke provided to his daughters. The castle boasted an extensive library, and Ankarette was encouraged to read, though she didn't need any coaxing to pick up books. Taught by her father to read, she loved all manner of histories, especially about the long line of Argentine kings. Isybelle, she discovered, preferred the legends about the Fountain-blessed. Ankarette's father had always been skeptical about those ancient stories. He hadn't believed in magic. In the stories, the Fountain-blessed were capable of such impossible feats as divining the future, swaying others' thoughts, changing appearance at will, and immense prowess in battle. People whispered that there were *still* Fountain-blessed, but he'd never believed it.

Her favorite part of her new life, undoubtedly, was her Espion training with Sir Thomas. These lessons coincided with Isybelle's singing lessons, and they marked the only time Ankarette spent away from the duke's daughter. Sir Thomas taught her how to handle and throw a blade, how to wrestle a man to the ground, and how to quickly incapacitate someone by attacking his or her vulnerable spots. He showed her the Espion ring on his finger, which startled her at first because she had remembered seeing one like it on her father's hand. She'd always assumed it was a trifle, an outward sign of his prosperity. Sir Thomas promised that she would earn a ring of her own after she had completed her training, which would take at least a year.

She asked many questions. He never hesitated in answering them, except for one.

"Did something happen between Eredur and Lady Isybelle?" she had asked him one day while attempting to pick a lock with a wire and dagger. She was a quick study, so he had taken her to the dungeon to work on a harder kind of lock. The low light added to the difficulty, and he had refused her request to bring the torch closer. She struggled, lips pursed, trying to feel the latching mechanism with the wire.

"Ach, Ankarette," he said with a sigh. "You can't ask me that."

"Why not?" she replied, keeping her gaze fixed on the lock. She squinted, bringing her face so close that her nose touched the metal. "It's obvious something did."

"Obvious, you say?"

"She blushes every time his name is mentioned. Almost every time. Duke Dunsdworth was sent away recently. And Duke Warrewik seems more intent on delaying negotiations for a foreign bride than he is on finding one. I think he wants his daughter to be Eredur's queen."

The lock snicked and Ankarette stood and opened the cell door.

"Clever lass," he said, nodding toward the lock.

She felt her cheeks flush with his praise. "What happened, Sir Thomas?"

He folded his arms. "I can't tell you, lass. Nor should I. Did the duke ask you to find out from me? Is this one of his tests of loyalty?"

"No one asked me, Sir Thomas. I like to figure things out for myself. But the clues are all very cryptic. I can see why the king *wouldn't* want to marry Lady Isybelle."

Sir Thomas wrinkled his brow. "And how would *you* know *that*? You're acquainted with the king, are you?"

"I know very little about him or his character. But the duke of the North is very powerful. I don't think the king would want to give him any more power."

Sir Thomas chuckled softly. "Oh, I think we'll make an Espion out of you yet, lass. You're more thoughtful than I'd given you credit for, and I'm not the type to flatter. I cannot say whether anything happened between the king and the duke's daughter or not. Loyalty binds me. You'll have to take the king's measure yourself. See how he strikes you."

"I hope to do that," Ankarette said, feeling pleased. "Someday."

Sir Thomas chuckled again. "Someday. Aye. Tomorrow. He's on the way to Dundrennan now. A *hunting* trip." He gave her a wry smile.

CHAPTER 5
THE MISTY FALLS

One of Ankarette's favorite places in the valley was near the base of the massive waterfall. The spray of the plummeting water came down in clouds of mist that roiled and churned and fed the huge river that wound all the way to the city of Kingfountain. The base of the waterfall was a large bowl-shaped pond and the ground around it was sandy and flat, free of towering, moss-covered pines, although those majestic sentinels stood nearby. The castle loomed farther down the mountainside.

The air was cool from the mist and the cacophonous waterfall was so loud, one practically had to shout to be heard over it.

That afternoon, the afternoon before the king was due to arrive, Isybelle, Ankarette, and Sir Thomas had made their way to the pond for an outing. Isybelle had brought her favorite falcon, a creature she had named Spark, to hunt, and they'd watched it soar over the wide expanse of the valley, majestic and fearsome, and then plummet down with a shriek to catch a hare. Sir Thomas had skinned the animal and provided the victorious hunter with strips of bloody meat.

THE POISONER'S ENEMY

"She's an admirable bird, Lady Isybelle," Sir Thomas said, tossing the hunter another scrap of meat.

Spark seemed to sense the compliment and uttered a loud squawk.

Isybelle laughed mildly. "She's a *he*, Sir Thomas. I think you offended him."

He laughed. "A thousand pardons. Here are the gizzards and other tripe for him to feast on next. He made quick work of that hare."

"Indeed," Isybelle said, scrunching her nose. She looked squeamish at the sight of the hare's entrails, but Ankarette found them fascinating. Being a midwife's apprentice, she had a naturally strong stomach and an insatiable curiosity about how bodies were formed. "So did you. Your hands are very bloody."

Ankarette watched for signs of affection between Isybelle and the knight, but all she had seen was friendship. He always treated them both with respect.

"That does happen when butchering an animal," he conceded. "I was about to wash them in the river by yonder boulder. The one the size of a cottage. Would that I could have seen it come tumbling down from the heights above. For all we know, there's a skeleton smashed beneath it!"

Ankarette smiled at his humor and studied the boulder. It was indeed as tall as a cottage. It hulked partway into the river, but that boulder was not going to budge regardless of the current. How many generations had it sat there, all misshapen and bulky? It was fascinating to think about all the things it must have seen—the people who had come and gone.

Sir Thomas tossed the final scraps of meat to Spark and then rose with his hands dripping. "When I was a lad of twelve, my brother and I used to clamber onto that boulder and jump into the river."

"You did not!" Lady Isybelle chided. "That water is freshly melted snow!"

"Aye, it is a bit cold," he admitted with a chuckle. "But if you don't stay in the river long, your teeth will chatter a bit, nothing more. No, the hard part is mustering the courage to jump. It looks even larger when you're standing atop it, I assure you."

"I dare you to jump in right now," Isybelle said. "Before we ride back to the castle."

He chuffed. "Now where is the fun in that, my lady? I've jumped in a dozen times at least."

"I don't believe you," she said. "He's toying with us, Ankarette. Seeing how gullible we are. The river is too fast—you'd be swept away."

He cocked his head at her. "I see what you're doing, lass. Trying to goad me into making a spectacle of myself. The river is swift, but not around the boulder. The bulk of it slows down the river. Come closer, and you'll see what I mean."

He sauntered over to the river's edge and squatted by it, washing his hands clean.

"Do you think he's telling the truth?" Isybelle asked.

Ankarette nodded. "He doesn't seem the kind of man who tells stories."

"Now look at him," Isybelle sighed. "He's going to make his way to that boulder, you mark my words. There he goes! I was right."

"You teased him into doing it," Ankarette pointed out.

"I didn't think he actually would. Do you think he will climb up and jump?"

THE POISONER'S ENEMY

Ankarette saw Thomas craning his neck as he patrolled around the boulder. He massaged the rough hide of the rock. Then he unbuckled his sword belt and dropped it and his dagger to the earth.

"Your strategy worked," Ankarette said.

The back side of the boulder was broken and had a little shelf on it, and in a few minutes, Sir Thomas had clawed his way to the top. He stood there, hands on his hips, gazing up at the falls as the mist swirled around him. He shouted something down to them, but neither of them could hear him.

"Let's go closer," Isybelle said. "Spark is devouring the hare. He's tethered and won't fly away."

Ankarette rose and followed her to the boulder where Sir Thomas was still strutting around, arms folded. She felt a prick of uneasiness and hoped he didn't fall. A man could break his neck from that height.

"Have you ever climbed up here, Lady Isybelle?" he asked her.

"Of course not," she said.

He dropped down, squatting on his haunches. "Why not? It isn't a difficult climb. The view of the falls is most impressive. See the water down there?" He pointed to a spot at the base. "Toss in a tree branch and you'll see it doesn't go fast. The water is quite calm right there. It's safe to jump. I wouldn't lie about an adventure. Ankarette believes me. Don't you, lass?"

She was gazing up at him, feeling an eager desire to be up there with him, but she shifted her gaze as soon as he said her name.

"How do you get up?" Isybelle asked, walking around the base.

"It's easier to climb from right there," he said, rising

and walking over to where the broken part had formed a makeshift step. "Are you going to climb up, my lady?"

"If Ankarette helps me," she answered, her eyes gleaming with the adventure. "Come on."

It was her own heart's desire, so she easily succumbed. Sir Thomas scuttled down and met them on the broken side of the boulder, on the step halfway down. He reached down with one hand, gripping a knobby bit of stone with the other.

"Come on, lass. Reach up."

Isybelle approached the rock and Ankarette stood behind her, ready to help push her up . . . only she found herself imagining what the duke would say if he found out about their adventure.

"Is this wise?" she asked.

Isybelle turned her head, looking confused. "Of course it isn't. I might tear my dress. I don't think I could jump down into the water, but I do want to see the view."

"You'll be fine, lass." Sir Thomas smiled confidently down at them. "Grab my hand."

Lady Isybelle readied herself again and Ankarette prepared to push her. In a trice, the duke's daughter was up on the boulder and gazing down wonderingly. "My goodness, it is beautiful. I feel like the wind could knock me down."

Ankarette stepped back, craning her neck to see them. Isybelle's arms were tightly folded as she stared down at the river. Then she turned and beckoned for Ankarette to join them.

So she did. Stepping up to the rock, she caught hold of a ridge of stone.

"Grab my hand, lass. I'll pull you up to the ledge."

There was the proffered hand again.

"I can manage it, Sir Thomas," she said with determination.

He chuckled. "Aye. I know you could, Ankarette. But it's just a little help."

A sudden lump in her throat made it difficult to swallow. She pushed against the discomfort and reached up for his hand. His grip was firm and she scrabbled up the side of the boulder to join him on the small ledge. Then, as he had done with Isybelle, he put his hands on her waist and hoisted her up the rest of the way.

"There we are," he said, mounting the apex of the boulder behind them. "Not as much room with three, I'll daresay. Make way." The three of them stood there, looking out at the water as the mist continued to fall in never-ending plumes from the roaring falls. In the brightness of the day, a rainbow glimmered in the mist. The boulder thrummed with the commotion.

"Are you going to jump, Sir Thomas?" Isybelle asked worriedly. "It *does* look much farther down from here." She swayed a little and caught herself.

He stood, arms akimbo, and shrugged. "Only if one of you will jump with me."

"I couldn't," Isybelle said resolutely, trembling with fear. Her eyes were wide as she gazed off the edge. "Get me down, Sir Thomas. I think I might faint." Ankarette, worried, caught hold of Isybelle's arm to steady her.

Sir Thomas nodded and took hold of her other arm. "That happens to some folks, lass. They get dizzy when they get up on heights. There is a bridge atop the falls. Haven't you been there?"

"I have," Isybelle said. "But I can never stay on it for long. I feel dizzy when I'm up there, and I need to get down."

"Very well. Let's go back the way we came." Sir Thomas shuffled off to the lower portion and Ankarette helped the other girl down to him. From there, the knight helped lower her all the way to the ground.

Isybelle reached the bottom and stumbled, but didn't fall. She got up and brushed her hands together. "That is much better," she said. "I don't care for that boulder, Sir Thomas. You can have it all to yourself."

Laughing at her comment, he turned and gazed up at Ankarette. "So. Would *you* like to jump down to the river, lass?"

A thrill of excitement ran through her.

"I would," she said.

"Good girl. You have spirit."

Ankarette turned and walked to the edge of the boulder. Looking down, she felt a spasm of utter terror. The water was indeed sluggish, but it looked cold. Isybelle stood at the water's edge, hands clasped by her mouth, staring at Ankarette with a strange mix of hope and misery.

Sir Thomas came up behind her. "It's not as far as it looks," he said coaxingly. "You can do this."

Ankarette realized she was breathing quickly, her pulse racing. She blinked, wondering absently what utter madness had driven her to stand at the edge of a boulder. Her stomach was clenching and she worried for a moment she would vomit.

With the noise of the falls bellowing in her ears, she felt very small, very vulnerable. Fear locked her legs. She tried to breathe slower, but the air was coming in and out too fast. Spots began to dance in her eyes.

"I can jump with you?" Sir Thomas offered, holding out his hand.

Her heart took another jolt, although not from fear

this time, and resolution filled her to the brim. She would do this without his help. A man had to face his fears on the eve of his first battle. Sir Thomas had already faced his. A jump off a rock was nothing compared with the prospect of imminent slaughter. And Ankarette had faced her fears too, the fear that an infant would die while she was performing her charge.

"I can do this," she said with conviction. Then she turned and stepped off the rock.

It took entirely too long for her to hit the water, and then she was sheathed in liquid ice that seemed to stab through her gown, through her skin, and freeze her very marrow. Where was the surface? Had she screamed on the way down? Thoughts jumbled in her mind. Images of her life came in rapid succession. The trees. The falls. The boulder. Sir Thomas's bloody hands.

Her head popped above the surface, her muscles hardening from the cold. Isybelle was shouting for her, but the water was in Ankarette's ears, in her nose. She saw the duke's daughter waving for her, looking so proud of her for the accomplishment. She saw Spark, claws tethered with leather thongs, flapping wildly, but firmly attached to a dead log. Why was the bird so frantic?

Ankarette sensed the presence of another person.

Part of her mind opened, and despite the violence of the waterfall, the unrelenting thunder of water in her ears, and her freezing limbs, she was aware of another presence. The impression was as forceful as if a spike of silver had been driven into her mind. There, hidden in the woods beyond where they'd settled, swathed in the shadows and mist . . . someone was waiting and watching.

Ankarette pumped her arms and legs, her dress

weighing her down. The current was not difficult to fight, as Sir Thomas had said, and she reached the bank where found him waiting to seize her arm and pull her free of the water's grasp. Her mind was in a fog from the chill, and she wondered why he hadn't jumped in himself. His clothes weren't wet. Had he abandoned the idea at the last minute? But her thoughts were soon pulled away by the strong sensation that all was not right. She still sensed someone and felt a pulse of danger and warning.

"You did it!" Isybelle said with wild joy. "Your skin is blue. You can wear my cloak for warmth. Here, let's wring some of this water out of your gown." Her hands gathered up bunches of Ankarette's dress and she squeezed them unselfconsciously, twisting the water free.

Ankarette tried to speak, but her words were slurred. She babbled incoherently.

"I told you it was cold," Sir Thomas said, kneeling next to her. "Not one man in twenty has the courage to actually jump. I've seen lads older than you quail and climb back down. Well done, lass!"

She tried to speak again, but her jaw was chattering too much. Looking past them both, she gazed into the woods, expecting to see someone there.

"Should we build her a fire, Sir Thomas?"

"Best to get her back down to the castle," he answered with confidence.

Ankarette grabbed his tunic front and jerked it hard.

"What is it?" he asked in surprise.

"Th-th-there is s-someone. O-o-ver there."

She raised a trembling arm and pointed.

"Spark is going wild," Isybelle said worriedly, suddenly noticing.

THE POISONER'S ENEMY

Sir Thomas gripped Ankarette's arms, his fingers firm and powerful. "Did you see someone, lass?"

She hadn't. But she could sense them moving away now. Moving away quickly. "I thought I did," she answered. It was a half-truth, but she could think of no better way to explain it. While working as a midwife, she'd occasionally experienced flashes of insight related to the birthing process—the notion that a babe would come early or that a birth would go easier if the mother paced during labor. Since coming to Dundrennan, the insights she'd experienced had all been related to political machinations. This was the first one that had warned of danger.

Her words were enough to get Sir Thomas moving. He quickly scooped up his sword belt and buckled it on. He drew his sword from its sheath as he marched toward the woods.

"Strange," Isybelle said. "These lands are forbidden from hunters, save the king and the nobles. It might have been a poacher."

The feeling was gone. While Sir Thomas scouted the woods, always staying within sight, Isybelle helped Ankarette back to the small camp where Sir Thomas dressed the falcon's kill. Spark was preening, no longer squawking and trying to escape.

After a few more moments, Sir Thomas came back looking concerned. "We'll not be hunting here with the king tomorrow," he said plainly. "In fact, it's best if we head back quickly. Don't cover the falcon, my lady. We might need him to get back safely."

"What's wrong?" Lady Isybelle asked fearfully. "Was it man or beast?"

He shook his head. "I thought it might be a bear or wolf at first. But I found tracks by that tree over there.

Footprints of a man. They're heading deeper into the woods. I'll send some Espion to follow the tracks when we get back." He stood, arms folded, and gazed at Ankarette with deep respect. "Good eyes, lass. Someone followed us out here. And I believe they meant us harm."

I did not realize, when I was summoned to Dundrennan, what would unfold in my life. The duke was an impressive leader, both in temperament and wealth. The game of Wizr was his favorite, and he thought of the world in terms of strategies and movement on the board. Little did I know what complex machinations were at work inside his mind. He knew how to make a man do something against his own interests—and be happy for it. He had a mighty reputation throughout all the realms. Everyone wanted to treat with him, to earn his favor or condescension. But there were others who sought his downfall.

It was while I was living in the duke's household that I began to hone my own intuition. I began to see the difference between what people said and what they meant. At the time, I didn't really understand what those stirring thoughts really meant. I came to realize that later.

It was during those innocent days in Dundrennan that I was first exposed to what lay concealed in the shadow of politics. I met my first poisoner without even realizing it. A man whose shadow crossed mine often in those early days. And I didn't know it until it was too late.

— ANKARETTE TRYNEOWY

CHAPTER 6
THE KING

When they returned to the castle, Ankarette was no longer dripping wet, but she was cold and uncomfortable and they found the castle in commotion. A page shouted in passing that King Eredur had arrived earlier than expected, accompanied by the Deconeus of Ely.

Ankarette watched as Isybelle's expression shifted in reaction to the news. Her face flushed, but then her mood turned somber and she started fidgeting. She gave the falcon to the hunting master to secure in the mews.

Sir Thomas was approached by one of the Espion, who bent his head low and began talking to him in an urgent undertone. Ankarette noticed this, but she wasn't close enough to hear what they were discussing. Then she felt a tug on her sleeve.

"Let's go back to my rooms and get you into something dry," Isybelle said. "Mother will be furious if you come to the great hall like this."

The two quickly slipped into the castle, although Ankarette glanced back at Sir Thomas before following her friend inside. The troubled look on his face seemed a bad portent.

After stripping away her sodden garments, Ankarette dressed in a blue-and-silver gown—the colors of the duke's servants—and with Isybelle's help, her damp tresses were tamed and braided in the Northern style.

"That will do nicely," Isybelle said, smiling at her in the mirror. "Best if we get this over with now."

"Are you nervous about seeing the king?"

Isybelle smoothed her dress and feigned a composed look. "Why should I be nervous? I've known Eredur my whole life." But she was still fidgeting with her dress. "Did you hear what the page said? The Deconeus of Ely is also here. John Tunmore. I didn't know he was coming. He and Father have long been allies. I think he's going to be invested soon as the deconeus of Our Lady in Kingfountain."

Ankarette knew nothing about the deconeus and didn't care to. She was far more interested in learning about the king and Isybelle.

The two young women hurried to the audience hall. The duke was still in Occitania, so the duchess was duty bound to provide hospitality to the king and his companions in her husband's absence.

The state of the hall was boisterous. Servants were bustling in and out, providing trays of meat, nuts, and cheese and flagons of wine in abundance. The duchess was attentive to the king's whims, standing nearby and watching him closely to try to anticipate his every need.

The king had bright flaxen hair and skin that had been darkened by the sun over countless hours in the saddle. A man of twenty-two, he was strong and bulky but surprisingly light on his feet, able to snatch a goblet from a passing serving girl without sloshing a drop on the floor. The king was bantering with his youngest brother, Severn. They were about as opposite as a hawk and a crow, but there was no mistaking the camaraderie between them.

A tall man in ceremonial robes stood near the brothers, at a somewhat awkward distance. Deconeus Tunmore, then. It had to be.

Isybelle suddenly squeezed Ankarette's hand, her eyes fixed on the king. She seemed to be steeling herself, building up her courage. Then she released her grip and walked deliberately toward her mother, who had finally noticed their arrival. Someone else had noticed them as well, a man who was a stranger to Dundrennan. Or at least, he had not darkened the castle's halls since Ankarette's arrival. The man wore a fashionable tunic from Occitania and combed his hair forward in their style. He was speaking to the castellan, Lord Horwath, but his gaze had found and followed Ankarette and Isybelle. He was probably thirty, judging from the creases around his eyes, and had a bright, easygoing manner. This was definitely a man who used his hands to speak. She made a mental reminder to ask about him later.

"There you are," the duchess said, meeting them partway. She examined Isybelle's dress and frowned. "I thought you changed before coming down. It looks like you just came from the woods."

They were close enough to the king for Ankarette to hear Nanette's voice. "Severn caught three rings on his spear," the girl boasted. "But then the quintain hit him on the fourth try and knocked him off!"

Ankarette was struggling to observe everything at once—the conversation underway between the king, his brother, and the girl; the intent deconeus; the duchess's displeased look; and the tension between the mother and her elder daughter.

"There wasn't time, Maman," Isybelle whispered, flushing slightly.

The duchess gave her daughter an icy look, promising they would have words later, but her anger melted away as she turned her attention back to the king. Giving him a beaming smile, she nodded as if she'd been paying attention all along. He didn't appear to notice.

"Three rings?" Eredur said, impressed. "I've been knocked down my share of times." He gripped Severn's shoulder and gave him a friendly shake. "But it makes it that much harder to have girls around to laugh at you. Admit it, Cousin," he said, winking at Nanette, "that was your favorite part."

"No, my lord!" Nanette said sincerely. She sidled closer to Severn. "I was ever so proud of my cousin when he took the rings on the spear."

"I'm just jesting with you, lass," the king said, mussing up her dark brown hair. The familiar gesture brought on another icy look from the duchess.

"Pray, my lord," the duchess said, interrupting. "Did you see Lord Warrewik before he departed for Pree?"

The king turned and caught sight of the new arrivals at last. "I did indeed. We consulted very closely on his upcoming negotiations, and I saw him to his ship in person. The new deconeus of Our Lady was also with us."

"Indeed, my lord," Deconeus Tunmore said graciously, taking a step forward.

Severn's voice always had a sarcastic edge to it. "Aye, and they immediately made plans to come hunt in the duke's lands while he was gone, no doubt."

There was a double meaning in his words that Ankarette caught. She saw the duchess stiffen, her smile wilting.

Eredur looked abashed for a moment, as if the comment pained him, but he wrestled down any resentment he might have felt and then turned and put his arm around Severn's neck, not altogether gently. "With that tongue of yours, Brother, you never need carry a whip to urge your horse faster. Now, all the world knows the best game is in the North, so it shouldn't create too much of fuss that I felt compelled to follow it. And I *did*," he added with a warning glare at his brother, "seek my uncle's permission ere I came."

The duchess looked nervous. "You never need ask, my lord king. You are welcome to come whenever it suits you, of course." She bowed formally.

The king gave her a polite nod but he clearly wasn't interested in talking with her further. He shifted his gaze to his cousin, Lady Isybelle. "A pleasure to see you again, *Cousin*." He took her hand and kissed her knuckles. It was a respectful gesture, not a lover's kiss. His words seemed carefully chosen and fraught with meaning. "Is this your new maid?" he asked, shifting his gaze to Ankarette. "The one your father mentioned? The midwife's daughter?"

It took every ounce of composure within Ankarette not to buckle under the weight of his gaze. He was perhaps the most handsome man she'd ever met. She'd seen him before, riding through the streets of Yuork in his glistering armor, his knights parading behind him with banners displaying the Sun and Rose.

The king knew of her. She would not embarrass herself. She dropped into a deferential curtsy.

"Yes," Isybelle said with warmth in her voice. "This is Ankarette Tryneowy, my new companion."

"An interesting name," Tunmore said with a look of interest. "Atabyrion, is it not?"

"Indeed, Your Grace," Ankarette said, then coughed, her throat suddenly very dry. "My father was from Edonburick."

The conversation shifted as the king turned his attention back to his young brother and Nanette, who continually tried to vie for everyone's notice. The girl was only nine and prone to chatting. As she listened to the ebb and flow of the conversation, Ankarette found some nuts on a tray and began to eat them, trying to remain aware of the room and what was going on. But she stayed near Isybelle, keeping especially sensitive to her looks and how they might reveal her feelings. The duke's daughter continued to cast glances at the king, mostly covertly, and with eyes that were sad and regretful. Ankarette noticed the deconeus was also paying close attention to the people in the room.

Eventually the Occitanian man separated from Lord Horwath and approached the duchess. His accent was smooth and refined, and it bore the marked accent of his Occitanian heritage. "If you will permit me, Duchess, to introduce myself again. I am Lord Hux, the herald of His Majesty King Lewis of Occitania." He bowed deeply. He wasn't tall, but he was stately and had the elegant manners of a man quite accustomed to the privileges of rank.

"Yes, I do recall you. Welcome once again to Dundrennan. I know that you have been greatly involved in the correspondence between my husband and your king."

"But of course!" he said with a cheerful smile and another bow. "I saw him immediately upon his arrival on our fair shores, and since I was bound already for Dundrennan, I promised I would deliver to you, on his behalf, the assurance that he arrived safely, thanks be to the Fountain."

"Thank you, it is most welcome news. Do you plan to stay long in the North? Visitors often come from distance kingdoms to enjoy the pleasant views of our valley."

"They are most exquisite, Duchess!" His hands moved as he spoke, the gestures conveying his ardor and wonder. "With your permission, I may linger a day longer than my charge. Perhaps even join the king on his hunting expedition, if it is permitted?"

"You are indeed welcome to stay," the duchess said.

The king interrupted them. "I won't be hunting after all," he said. Ankarette noticed Sir Thomas had joined the company. "On the journey here, I found a quaint little village along the road to Kingfountain. I was tempted to stay there for the night and hunt in those woods, but didn't wish to risk offense by not coming here as I had originally planned. I won't trespass on your hospitality for more than a day, my lady. I had thought to hike up beyond the cliffs and see Mount Helvellyn closer, but perhaps another time."

"What village was that?" the duchess asked with curiosity.

The king shrugged and looked baffled. "I cannot remember the name."

"Was it Huntstanton?" the duchess offered.

The king snapped his fingers. "That's the one! Sometimes the crowd at court can get overwhelming. I never go hunting, but I so enjoy spending time out in nature."

"You will be missed," the duchess said politely.

"Not likely," Severn muttered under his breath, his eyes glinting with pleasure at his remark. He'd spoken it just loud enough for the duchess to hear it and her smile wilted again.

"If I told you to behave, Severn, would it do any good? I highly doubt it." The king shook his head and laughed ruefully. "'Tis a pity to come all this way and not spear a boar, eh my lord duke of Glosstyr?"

Severn frowned but he knew the barb was intended for him. His badge was the White Boar. "It is illegal in my duchy to hunt them."

"I don't make hunting roses illegal. To each his own," the king replied. He grabbed another wine cup and tipped it toward his brother, wagging his eyebrows playfully.

~

AFTER THE EVENING MEAL, the telling of tales by the hearth, and an easing of tensions, it was time for everyone to retire for the night. Ankarette helped brush loose Isybelle's hair after they'd both changed into nightgowns. The duke's daughter sat on a chair in front of her vanity. The angle of the mirror showed the night sky, and judging by the slant of the moon, it was not yet midnight.

There was a subtle, gentle knock on the door. Isybelle stiffened, her hand gripping the handle of the small mirror she'd been using to examine blemishes on her chin. She set it down, her hands trembling to the point that it rattled as she released it. Ankarette quickly strode to the door.

"Who is it?" she whispered loudly enough to be heard on the other side.

"Sir Thomas," he replied, his voice muffled.

Ankarette pulled the latch and tugged the heavy door open enough to see Sir Thomas standing beyond it, a long stripe of light across his face. Behind him, barely visible in the gloom of the corridor, was the king.

Her heart began to hammer wildly. She started to push the door closed, but Sir Thomas resisted and used his greater size and strength to shove it open.

"Ankarette, who is—?" Isybelle's voice cut off as she turned in the chair. All the color drained from her face, replaced by a chalky pallor.

Ankarette gave Sir Thomas a demanding glare. She was now in a very uncomfortable position. She'd been warned of her duty by the duke, yet how was a woman of her status supposed to tell the king no? And the duke had warned her to tell Sir Thomas if anything untoward happened.

The knight saw her anguished look and pursed his lips into an amused frown. "Be quick, Eredur. You're frightening the lasses out of their wits."

"I will, Tom," the king said.

With that, the knight shut and bolted the door behind them. Now she and Isybelle were alone in a room with two men, something the duke assuredly would not like.

Eredur's tunic collar was open and he looked more like a knight than a king. He was heavily muscled and gave off an aura of power. He carried a dagger and a sword, which struck Ankarette as inappropriate under the circumstances.

"I have kept my promise, Isybelle," the king said, giving her a serious, compassionate look. "I keep my promises." His words conveyed meaning, but Ankarette was ignorant of what that meaning could be.

"W-why are you here, my lord?" Isybelle said, stumbling a little over her words in confusion.

"I need to speak to your maid. To Ankarette." He turned the brunt of his gaze on her, and though she felt her body weaken, she stiffened her resolve to be firm, unmoved.

"Yes, my lord?" she asked him softly.

"I find that you really do not get to know a person until you've looked into their eyes," he said, stepping toward her. "You did me a great service today, Ankarette Tryneowy. Although I wonder if you know what you did?"

She was abashed. "M-my lord?"

"I'll be blunt, for I'm a soldier. Tom told me that you spotted someone in the woods today. You told him straightaway and he discovered prints in the dirt. Prints that the intruder didn't have time to conceal, thanks to you. The Espion tracked those prints back to Dundrennan. There is a poisoner in the castle right now."

A shadow of fear passed over Ankarette's heart. Everyone knew the stories about poisoners. They were the secret tools kings and queens used to do away with enemies, to accomplish a mission when diplomacy failed. Each was highly skilled and deadly.

Isybelle gasped. "Truly?"

The king nodded. "That's why I can't stay. Your timely warning, lass, has probably saved a life. Mine . . . or someone else's. I couldn't thank you in the great hall, now could I?" He gave her a disarming smile.

She still felt the awkwardness of being in her nightdress before the two men. Not knowing what to say, she simply curtsied.

"Tom says you are discreet," the king continued, stepping forward. Sir Thomas gave her a little nod of encouragement. "Your father was part of the Espion as well. Some of the Espion, like your father—like Tom—were loyal to my father when he ran the service. But now many are loyal to Duke Warrewik."

Isybelle bristled. "My father is loyal to you, Cousin."

He looked at her, doubt obvious in his narrowed eyes. "I wish I could believe that, lass. But I think we *both* know that the interests he serves most are his own."

Isybelle looked down, her cheeks flaming.

The king addressed Ankarette again. "The duke told me about you. In passing. Said he's brought on a maid for his daughters, one he intends to groom as a midwife. He always thinks several moves ahead." He scratched his neck, sighing. "Thomas believes the duke is going to ask me, eventually, to send you to study at Pisan." He gave her a knowing look. "Has he mentioned this to you?"

Ankarette shook her head no. "Why the kingdom of Pisan?" she asked him, trying not to let any emotion bleed into her voice.

"Because that is where the poisoner school is," Sir Thomas answered bluntly. "He wants you to be the very best midwife money can buy, which they'll teach you, and they'll also teach you other things he would have you know."

Eredur stepped closer. His eyes were fixed on her face. "I am not going to ask you for your loyalty, Ankarette. One cannot pay money for that. Loyalty must be earned through trust and respect. What I demand of you is something different. Tom thinks you are special. He has been watching you and studying you. I trust his judgment, but I had to meet you in person.

"If you feel you are asked to do anything amiss or untoward by anyone in this kingdom, please send word to me, Ankarette. Some kings train poisoners to murder their rivals and enemies. Some use them to defend their thrones. If I give my uncle permission to send you to Pisan, I want it understood plainly between us that I am asking you to defend *my* throne. No deceptions." He gave Isybelle a pleading look. "I've trusted him and rewarded my uncle. But he is not the king. He does not bear the burden of the hollow crown."

There was an urgent knock on the door.

Sir Thomas sighed and gritted his teeth. "*That* was not supposed to happen," he grumbled.

Ankarette felt a jolt of panic. What if it was the duchess? Isybelle sank back in her chair, her eyes filling with tears.

"Hide behind the changing screen," Ankarette whispered, pointing to it. They quickly reacted and slipped behind the concealment. She walked to the door and tried to calm and steady herself. "Who is it?" she whispered.

"Message for Sir Thomas," came the harsh, hoarse reply. "Dunsdworth just arrived and is coming up the stairs."

CHAPTER 7
THE KING'S BROTHER

Moments later, the noise of boots coming up the stairwell hearkened the arrival of the king's brother. The sound of garbled voices leaked into the room, followed by an insistent rapping noise and the jiggling of the door handle.

Ankarette tried to remain calm despite the current of emotions that had caught her in its grip. Her mind whirled with all the king had just told her, of poisoners and schools and misguided loyalty.

"Who is it?" she asked.

"Open the door." The words were spoken in a commanding tone, by a voice she didn't recognize.

"Who is it?" Ankarette repeated, eyeing the changing screen. The king and Sir Thomas had ably concealed themselves.

A heavy weight jostled the door.

"Let him in," Isybelle said anxiously. She was pacing, wringing her hands.

Ankarette slid open the latch bar and then the door. The Duke of Clare, Dunsdworth, looked very much like his elder brother, but his hair was rust-colored and wavy instead of blond and he had eyes as blue as seawater. He was a handsome man and, despite having traveled to Dundrennan in the middle of the night, looked refreshed, eager, and full of energy.

"Hello, Cousin," Isybelle said, her voice trembling slightly.

Dunsdworth gave Ankarette a sharp look. "Who are you?"

"That is my new maid, Ankarette Tryneowy," Isybelle said. Her cheeks flushed as she came closer to the new arrival. Her features were animating quickly, full of regard and warmth—none of the posture of guilt she'd demonstrated with Eredur.

"Ankarette," Dunsdworth said in an offhanded manner. He had a stern look and a natural wariness that made him doubtful of everything, everyone. His gaze shot around the room in an almost violent fashion, going from the various pieces of furniture to the bed that was still tidily made up. It was as if he expected to find someone there in the room.

"This is untoward, coming to my chamber at night," Isybelle said. "Father is gone."

"I know he's gone," Dunsdworth said, stepping around in a circle. "And I know my *brother* came here as soon as your father left." His voice practically vibrated with the tinny sound of jealousy.

"Yes, he came to hunt," Isybelle said. "He isn't going to stay long."

"Yes, but hunt *what*," he replied with suspicion. "I came as soon as I heard he was en route. I couldn't bear the thought . . ." His words trailed off. Ankarette watched him squeeze his hand into a fist.

"Sshhh," Isybelle soothed. "He's not interested in me, Dunne. I told you."

There was a look of dark brooding and anger in his eyes. "I wish I could be sure of that."

"You can. My father went to Occitania to negotiate a marriage for Eredur with one of their princesses."

"But none of them are half as rich as your father," he said tellingly. "You and Nanette stand to inherit all his vast domains. Surely my brother might want them for himself?"

His challenging tone belied his utter distrust of his elder brother. Dunsdworth had the bearing and demeanor of a king, and his ambition was almost brazenly on display. Yes, he cared for the duke's eldest daughter. He looked at her with an almost hungry anticipation as she stood there in her nightgown. But it was equally clear that he coveted her fortune.

"He is the king," Isybelle said, casting a nervous glance at the changing screen. Ankarette winced, biting her lip. She had deliberately avoided looking that way. "He can marry whomever he wishes. He doesn't want me."

Unspoken words passed between them.

Dunsdworth looked mollified by her statement. "If he ever touches you," he said with a threatening barb in his voice, his jaw clenched with barely bridled rage.

"He hasn't," she said firmly, resolutely.

Dunsdworth breathed in through his nose and then took her hand and pressed a kiss against her knuckles. "I will go. I shouldn't be here, but I'd heard rumors . . . I won't mention them. No lady should hear such talk."

Isybelle flushed crimson and looked down. "People talk, Dunne. It doesn't make it true."

He brushed the back of his hand across his forehead. "I should go. I just wanted to be sure you were . . . you were safe." He turned to Ankarette, his pale blue eyes riveting. "You're a pretty thing," he said, eyes narrowing. "Where do you hail from?"

"Yuork, my lord," she answered with a small curtsy.

He gave her an approving nod. "Our father's duchy. Well and good. You are Lady Isybelle's new companion, then? I see. Bar the door when I am gone. I don't care if the king himself comes at midnight. You bar the door. The next time *I* come, you open it at once."

"I do as my lady commands me," Ankarette said, discomfited by the way he was ordering her around.

Dunsdworth eyed Isybelle with a possessive look. "Well, you do that, Ingrid. And don't try to hide my visit from the duke, her father. You can tell him that I was here. I know one of his little Espion slaves will report it, anyway." He sneered with disdain. "I did nothing untoward to my cousin." He gave Isybelle a bow and strode out of the room. Before shutting the door, he looked at Ankarette again. "Don't forget to lock it."

She was only too grateful to do as he said.

Her palms were sweating, but she'd managed to keep her calm—or at least appear as if she had—and didn't feel more than a little dampness on her brow. She exchanged a glance with Isybelle now that the door was shut. It was clear that her friend's life was more complicated than she had first supposed. A few moments later, there was a small rap on the door and a voice muttered, "He's gone."

Sir Thomas and the king emerged from behind the changing screen. Eredur had an amused look on his face as he gazed at the door.

"That was quick thinking, lass," Sir Thomas told Ankarette. "Thank you."

She bowed her head and said nothing in reply.

"Your brother is suspicious by nature," Sir Thomas

said to the king, folding his arms. "For a moment, I thought he might search the room."

The king put his arm around the other man's shoulder. "No, I didn't think that likely. Well played, Cousin. Well spoken, *Ingrid*." He chuckled at the way her name had been butchered. "I think our nocturnal interview is at an end. Now that my brother is here, I'm in an even greater hurry to leave Dundrennan. We're like a blacksmith and a pair of burning tongs. There's always a shower of sparks whenever we meet. Severn's tongue can slice through steel, but at least I know he's on my side. I'd trust him with my life. Dunsdworth, I'm afraid, wishes I'd catch the plague and die."

Isybelle flushed. "He does not mean you ill, my lord."

Eredur gave her a knowing smile. "You keep thinking that, lass. But let me be clear—I have no intention of letting the two of you marry. He craves power like a drunken man craves his ale. He's already a duke, but that isn't enough to sate him. And he's more loyal to your father than he is to me. I'm not a hard-hearted man. I know you care for him." His eyes narrowed and his jaw was firm. "But letting the two of you wed would only end in disaster . . . and in heartache for *you*. I've seen the way my brother treats the people around him." He shook his head. "He's not a patient man."

Isybelle looked down. "I could change him, my lord," she whispered.

Eredur's lips pressed together. Ankarette could see he didn't agree, but he was too kind to say so.

~

ANKARETTE AWOKE with a start from a vivid dream, her heart pounding wildly in her chest. Something was wrong. The feeling was as strong now as it had been earlier near the river. The room was dark but for a weak glow of light streaming through the window. There was no moon out, only a fleece of stars. Isybelle lay on her side, her head nestled on a pillow. She was fast asleep.

What had awakened Ankarette? Had she heard a noise? She listened, holding her breath, straining to hear a sound. The castle was deathly still, and yet her heart throbbed in warning. As her mind cleared from the fog of her dream, she sensed a presence. There was someone standing outside the door of the bedchamber —and her intuition told her it was not the Espion who was supposed to be standing guard.

The poisoner.

The thought pierced her with knife-sharp certainty. These strange feelings she'd begun to have baffled her, but something told her to trust them. This was the same presence she had sensed by the boulder. The man who had skulked in the woods.

Her throat instantly went dry. Sitting up in bed, she fidgeted with fear, wondering if she should cry out for help.

A small noise rattled the lock, making her jump.

Her mind nearly went blank white with terror. She bit her lip, staring at the door, too young and experienced to know what to do. When Isybelle mumbled in her sleep and turned over, Ankarette nearly screamed.

Despite her fear, there was a queer giddiness inside her, the sensation of water flowing, like the lapping of a fountain.

Then Ankarette felt the presence back away from the door. Had her thoughts repelled the poisoner in some inexplicable way? She sensed the person retreating down the stairs, the presence fading until she could no longer feel it.

What could any of it mean?

~

THE NEXT MORNING, the family and household visitors gathered in the audience hall for the morning meal. There was plenty of banter, some of it good-natured, some of it revealing a deep rift in the Argentine family. The Duchess of Warrewik tried to steer the boats away from the turbulent waters, but even her commanding presence wasn't enough to soothe the brothers' tempers.

"And why won't you tell me where you plan to hunt next?" Dunsdworth asked Eredur angrily. "What if you decide to go to Clare? Shouldn't I know so I can be prepared to greet you?"

"Trust me, Brother," Eredur said, trying to keep his tone civil, "that is the *last* place I intend to hunt."

"Then why not tell me?"

"Why should I?" Eredur asked flippantly, his eyes beginning to burn with anger. "What business is it of yours?"

"I could come with you," Dunsdworth suggested. "We haven't hunted together in years. Not since Edmund died."

His words struck a nerve, a powerful one, and Ankarette watched as Eredur's composure went up in flames. He held his tongue, but raw feelings surged across his face.

Severn spoke up, forcing himself into the conversation. "I can understand why Eredur doesn't care to hunt with you, Brother—you talk too much. You'd frighten away the game."

Dunsdworth glowered with fury and turned his anger on his younger brother. "Who asked for your thoughts, Severn?"

"Who asked you for yours?" came the immediate reply. Severn seemed eager to debate. "Were you even invited to Dundrennan?"

"Was Eredur invited?" Dunsdworth shot back impetuously.

"I spoke to our uncle ere coming," Eredur said. He'd mastered himself again. "Did you?"

"This is such a jade's trick," Dunsdworth snarled, shoving away from the table with a loud squeal of his chair. "You two are constantly flapping about, aiding each other against me."

He wasn't altogether wrong. The youngest and eldest Argentine shared a much closer relationship. It reminded Ankarette of a street game she had seen children play with an apple, tossing it back and forth to prevent a third from snatching it. The game usually ended with the apple smashed in the commotion.

"Sit down," Eredur said, sighing with exasperation. "Don't ruin the meal. It's all in jest."

The stifling atmosphere in the room did not fit his words. Eredur and Severn seemed to share an equal amount of disdain for their brother, but Dunsdworth provoked them both needlessly.

The brother obeyed the king, but she saw resentment in his eyes as he slumped back down into his chair. He grabbed his chalice of wine and brought it to his lips. Finding it empty, he thumped it on the table several times, attracting a servant, who came to refill it.

"Can I come hunting with you instead?" Severn

asked. The question was intended for Eredur, but he said it while smiling slyly at Dunsdworth. He enjoyed goading him.

The question had been timed for effect, and Dunsdworth started choking on his drink. Severn chuckled coldly as he spluttered and coughed.

"Severn!" Eredur moaned with only feigned anger.

"It's just a question," the young man said innocently.

Dunsdworth grabbed a linen napkin from the table and began mopping the flecks of wine from his tunic.

"No, you may *not*," Eredur said, chastening him. "I didn't come all this way for a family gathering. I came to bloody hunt! While you both are sitting idle here and in Clare, I'm beset by problems and intrigues and worries back at the palace. I need a break from squabbling, and yet I get more from the pair of you than I could ever want. I expect more civility the next time we meet. Aunt, forgive this sordid scene at breakfast, but as you can see, it was none of my doing!"

Dunsdworth glowered at Severn, dabbing his chin with the napkin. Severn had already known he wasn't invited on the hunting trip, which seemed odd to Ankarette.

As she ate her meal, she wondered at the relationship between the Argentine brothers. Had it always been this way? Their father was dead, killed in the same civil war that had also taken the life of a fourth brother. Perhaps their dynamic had been different before the war?

The chief butler, Berwick, came into the room and stamped his staff on the floor. It was the signal he made prior to announcements, and the hall quickly quieted.

"Lord Hux, the herald, seeks to bid ye farewell before he departs for Pree, my lady. He will be escorted by the deconeus."

The duchess waved in acknowledgment and the butler turned to face the doorway. The Occitanian walked in, smiling pleasantly at all who were present. The deconeus followed him into the room, but he lingered by the door.

"Before I depart the splendors of Dundrennan," Lord Hux said, bowing gallantly, "I wished to ask if my lady the duchess had any communication to deliver to your lord husband, the Duke of Warrewik? I should be seeing him in a few days' time."

"Please tell my lord husband that his wife and daughters miss him," the duchess replied sincerely. "That the king and his brothers were our welcome guests at the castle and displayed great brotherly amity. Thank you."

"The pleasure, my lady, is indeed mine," Lord Hux said, bowing deeply and with a flourish.

Ankarette felt a tingle in her heart as she heard him speak. The sensation of warning and mistrust seemed to well up inside her, unbidden and uncontrollable. Something loosened it, and the unseen energy came spilling out. It was like she'd toppled a goblet of water onto her dress. The fear from the night before came rushing back into her chest. In her embarrassment, she fumbled the spoon she'd been holding and it clattered noisily onto her plate.

The sound drew the herald's eyes to hers. They were full of cunning.

CHAPTER 8
QUEEN OF CEREDIGION

Time passed quickly in Dundrennan. Within a few months of her arrival, Ankarette had become thoroughly integrated into the household and its traditions. She and Isybelle had become close, although the secret about Eredur still loomed between them. The young woman had given her heart to the king's brother and spoke of him often, wondering when they would next meet. The affection between them had started while Dunsdworth was the ward of the Duke of Warrewik, and it was clearly mutual.

The shadowy presence of the Occitanian herald soon became a distant memory. She never told Sir Thomas about her experience. It would have embarrassed her to try to explain the inexplicable feelings. Besides, those feelings did not repeat themselves after the herald left.

Her favorite activity was sitting in the solar and doing needlework, and she discovered she had a gift for finishing the birds, flowers, and comforting scenes that Isybelle had begun. Even the duchess praised her handiwork and would marvel at how quickly she worked. For Ankarette, an afternoon could expire in a moment, and she'd discover herself holding a finished project with hardly the recollection of having worked on it. Sometimes she'd become too lost in thought to take note of what was going on around her—even if someone was calling out her name. It made her smile and blush, but there wasn't anything she could do to stop.

After one such moment, Isybelle poked her in the ribs to rouse her.

"My goodness, Ankarette," she said laughingly, "I've called your name several times. Did you not hear Sir Thomas's news?"

Not only had she *not* heard the news, she also hadn't noticed him enter the solar. He was standing in front of the duchess, hands clasped behind his back. His fingers looked taut and hard, and there was a restless energy about him. Whatever he'd come to say, he was very attached to the duchess's reaction.

"What is it?" Ankarette asked softly, keeping her voice low.

Sir Thomas heard the comment and rocked on his heels. "The duke is returning from his negotiations in Occitania. He'll be at Kingfountain on the morrow or the day after, after he stops by Callait to inspect the defenses. He's traveling by ship. News just arrived by an Espion courier that he'd like to see his family at the palace when he arrives."

This was grand news indeed. Ankarette had never been to the capital city before, let alone the palace. Her stomach flipped over with excitement and she understood Isybelle's enthusiasm. In all likelihood, Dunsdworth would join them in Kingfountain.

The duchess rose from her seat and set the letter down beneath her. She looked thrilled by the news and more than eager to see her husband again. "These negotiations have dragged on for months. Do you know who they settled on for Eredur's bride, Sir Thomas?"

There was a look in Sir Thomas's eyes that defied description. A little wrinkle in his lips, almost a sneer. "I believe King Lewis's sister is the lady who was chosen."

"Aymonette," the duchess said with surety. "She's not too young. A good choice for a queen."

Sir Thomas pursed his lips and rocked on his heels. "We will need to depart in all haste, my lady." He looked brooding, ill at ease.

"Indeed we must," the duchess replied. "We'll prepare the carriage and bring an escort to the palace. Twenty men will be enough, I should think."

"The duke asked for fifty," Sir Thomas said pointedly.

The duchess's brow furrowed. "That seems an excessive expense, does it not?"

"My opinion hardly matters, my lady," Sir Thomas said affably.

The pronouncement of the journey sent an immediate uproar through the castle. Ankarette was in charge of helping Isybelle choose gowns that put her in the best possible light. Nanette was positively beside herself with enthusiasm and kept exclaiming to Severn how thrilled she was to see her papa again and visit the palace.

After her duties were done, Ankarette sought out Sir Thomas, only to learn that he was already out in the bailey, preparing to leave. She had thought the knight would escort them and was a little disappointed he would not be keeping them company. When she found Sir Thomas, he was deep in conversation with the castellan, Lord Horwath. She lingered by the huge palace doors, gazing up at the fangs of the portcullis. After a few moments, Lord Horwath marched past her, deep in thought, and she hurried out to the crowded and noisy yard. Servants were already loading the carriage.

Sir Thomas gazed up at the high tower of the castle, lost in thought, until she arrived next to the stirrup of his horse.

His brow wrinkled. "What is it, Ankarette?" he asked, speaking with just a hint of impatience. He cast his eyes at the rampway leading to the town.

"Is everything well?" she asked him.

He flinched, something he quickly masked.

"Why shouldn't it be well?" he asked her lightly, but the tone belied the look in his eyes.

"You seem . . . distracted, Sir Thomas," she said, keeping her voice low. There was a burden he was carrying. She wished she knew what it was.

"Are you practicing your skills on me, lass?" he asked her, arching his eyebrows accusingly but with good grace.

She flushed because he had read her right. "Is there something wrong with the match, Sir Thomas? With Princess Aymonette?"

He smiled ruefully. "You could say that, lass. The rooster crows in its own time, though. Not when we want it to."

In other words, she realized, he would say no more.

~

THE PEOPLE of Kingfountain had gathered in the streets to watch the Duchess of Warrewik's carriage pass. Nanette waved through the window, her cheeks pink with flushed excitement. Ankarette was mystified by the show of respect and acclaim given to the knights wearing the badge of the Bear and Ragged Staff.

The wheels of the carriage clacked on the cobblestones, and Ankarette found herself wishing she and Isybelle were on horseback instead of enduring the bone-jarring carriage ride.

Ahead, the impressive river reached its abrupt end and churned over the cliff in a remarkable display of frothing white water. The roar of the falls grew louder as the carriage and its entourage approached the stone bridge that connected the mainland to the island of the sanctuary of Our Lady of the Fountain. Ankarette gripped the edge of the window, staring breathlessly at the huge spire that rose ahead of them, gleaming like a spike of sunlight. There were birds in the sky, along with sparse clouds that made the heavens a deep, wondrous blue.

Hawkers and merchants cleared the way for them, and soon they were on the bridge. The gates of the sanctuary were thronged with people, most wearing ragged clothes. A motley array of hands and hats waved at them from the crowd and a few jeers and whistles followed them too.

Ankarette covered her eyes, wincing at the enormous grandeur of the place. Something rustled inside her heart, and she felt her throat thicken with emotion. *Power* emanated from the sanctuary, like the hearth at Dundrennan where she would warm her hands after spending a day hunting with Isybelle's falcon. A feeling of peace and tranquility flowed from the structure, and she felt the urge to toss a coin into one of the fountains later and say a prayer for her mother who was so far away.

"We're almost to the gate," the duchess said primly, ignoring the rabble flocking the carriage. After crossing the wooden bridge, they reached the opposite side of the river, where the palace of Kingfountain soared in its unrivaled splendor. Ankarette gazed at it hungrily, taking in the tall turrets that seemed high enough to stab the clouds and the rings of walls that covered the hill leading up to the palace. Who was she, a young girl from Yuork, to be visiting such a grand place? It was like a dream and she didn't want to wake up.

Their arrival sparked a commotion in the bailey. When the carriage lurched to a stop in front of the castle, grooms quickly emerged from the stables and began caring for the steeds. The duchess emerged from the carriage, smiling brightly, and Ankarette noticed it was Sir Thomas who had helped her out. He gallantly assisted each of the girls, and when he touched Ankarette, she felt a tingle shoot through her hand. It was just as she'd suspected—something was wrong.

She searched his face for a sign of trouble, but he gave her a carefully neutral expression. He winked at her playfully after helping her to the ground, flashed her a knowing smile, and then offered the crook of his arm to the duchess. There was Severn beside the carriage, dismounting his horse and gazing up at the battlements with a scrutinizing frown that seemed to notice the pock marks more than the roses in bloom.

Ankarette followed the others into the castle, gawking at the wide corridors and the decorative suits of armor that stood at attention on either side. The banner of the king hung from tapestry poles and fluttered with the breeze of them passing. As she walked, she began to notice the servants were all hushed, heads bent low in consternation. She couldn't understand their demeanor, but she noticed that very few would meet their gazes. There was a chill from the castle inhabitants they hadn't experienced in the streets outside the castle, and the other ladies in her party seemed to feel it too. None of them spoke as they swept through the halls.

When they reached the throne room, Ankarette was on her guard and her eyes shifted feverishly to take everything in. Her gaze found the Duke of Warrewik instantly—and one look at him confirmed that something was very wrong indeed. His cheeks were mottled with pent-up fury, and further evidence of his rage could be seen in his eyes, his clenched jaw, and the firm grip of his hands behind his back. Sir Thomas had removed himself to a discreet distance but stood by the duke, his master.

Eredur, who sat on the throne, was barely recognizable as the lighthearted man she'd met at Dundrennan, and his brother Dunsdworth was pacing the throne room. The royal brother glanced up at their arrival, and his eyes offered additional proof they'd walked in on a squall. Severn frowned upon seeing Dunsdworth and his demeanor didn't brighten after his gaze shifted to his eldest brother.

"My lady!" Eredur boomed with a good-natured smile that temporarily banished the gloom. "Arrived safely from Dundrennan! Welcome to Kingfountain. I don't think you have been here since my coronation ceremony, I believe."

"Indeed so, my lord," the duchess said in a firm voice, but her eyes were shooting worried darts at her husband.

"I'm so grateful that you came," Eredur said, rising from the throne. He closed the distance to his aunt and

THE POISONER'S ENEMY

embraced her, kissing her purposefully on each cheek. "Your help will be needed for the coming event."

"I would be honored to help in any way that I can," the duchess demurred. "When do you expect your bride to arrive?"

Eredur smiled at her words. "Later this afternoon, if all goes well," he said respectfully.

The duchess wrinkled her brow. "So soon? I heard the negotiations were finished, but surely she—"

"I hate to disrupt your speech, Aunt," Eredur said with a sigh. "Your husband knows already, so best to get it out in the open quickly."

Her face went as gray as ash. "W-what, m-my lord?"

Eredur held her hand and patted it gently. "I will not be marrying Princess Aymonette after all. The truth is, I am married already and have been since I last saw you in Dundrennan. I had just come from the nuptials."

His words were like thunder. It explained the nearly purple complexion of the Duke of Warrewik, who had negotiated in good faith for months with the King of Occitania. This was not just a snub. This was a political nightmare, an outrage of colossal proportions.

A deliberate move on the Wizr board that would have far-reaching consequences.

The duchess was so dumbfounded she could not speak. Her pallor was startling. She glanced at her husband with new understanding.

Eredur patted her hands gently, as if they were the greatest of friends. "So, as I said, I will need your help for my wife's coronation ceremony. You must have a place of honor, Aunt. I insist on it. I know this news is surprising. It had to be kept in the greatest secrecy until today."

"B-b-but who?" the duchess stammered. "I'm beside myself. You are already married?"

"Yes, Aunt. She's a wonderful woman. Her name is Lady Elyse Degriy, daughter of the Dowager Duchess of Westmarch. She comes from a very noble line."

The duchess's eyes widened with horror. "M-my lord, she was married before. She had two sons through her first husband. Her people were enemies of your . . . your father!"

"I know this," Eredur said reassuringly, his eyes flashing with confidence. "And now she is to be the Queen of Ceredigion."

CHAPTER 9
DISCRETION

The duke's state room at Kingfountain palace was lavish in decoration and ornamented with costly Genevese rugs and a myriad of fetching decor showing his rank and status. Tall white tapers were lit atop elegantly wrought stands, but there was little need for them. The room was suffused with light due to the gauzy curtains tied back to reveal the afternoon light.

The duke had returned from his journey to Occitania with chests full of fabric, gowns, jewels, and books he had acquired during his long ambassadorship to that country, and Isybelle and Nanette were huddled by some of the open ones, gazing at the various treasures and grinning at the evidence of their father's generosity.

Ankarette sat on a closed chest nearby, but her eyes were focused on the duke, his wife, and Dunsdworth, who were railing animatedly about the shameful way Warrewik had been treated by his nephew the king.

Dunsdworth was particularly vehement. "And what kind of woman is Lady Degriy? A widow? And we're to welcome *her* as our queen? Her husband died at the

Battle of Mortimer's Cross fighting *against* Eredur." He threw up his hands and glowered with fury.

"Patience, patience," Warrewik said, shaking his head, but he was clearly flustered himself. Ankarette could tell he was chafing from the indignity he had endured in the great hall. He wagged his finger. "Your brother intends to provoke a reaction out of me. I'll not give in to it."

"Are you not affronted?" Dunsdworth demanded.

The duchess looked worriedly at her husband. "What are we going to do, Nevin?"

The duke raised his hands, as if trying to quiet a crowd. "Patience! Give me time to think!" He gritted his teeth and paced with anxiety. Then he spied a Wizr board and stopped, gazing down at it. His fingers fondled some of the pieces. "It's a provocation. Clearly. He wants me to be hasty in my response. To reveal the depth of my discontent."

"He had no right to treat you that way," Dunsdworth snarled, his blue eyes menacing.

"He's the king; of course he has the right," Warrewik snapped. "He's trying to humble me. The Fountain knows it. I'm not daft." He stroked his chin, still studying the board. "He expects me to be rash. I will not be. I will bide my time. I will wait until he is distracted by something else on the board. Do you have any idea how angry King Lewis will be? Your brother has not just offended me, he has offended the powerful and *very* wealthy ruler of a kingdom who still hates us because of Azinkeep fifty years ago." He snorted. "This decision of his, this offense, may just provoke Lewis into starting another war with us."

"Do you think so?" the duke's wife asked with concern.

"I hope it does," Dunsdworth glowered. Ankarette saw that he was itching to prove himself. He had been too young to fight in the battles that had won his brother the crown. He was now of an age to win honor for himself in battle. Perhaps he was too eager, Ankarette thought.

"I do not," Warrewik said as he shifted his intent gaze between his wife and nephew. "Listen, Anne. Dunsdworth. King Lewis is far wiser and craftier than our stripling king. He is a master of the game of Wizr. I played him often during my stay there. He has a keen mind, but I always beat him. He knows that invading Ceredigion would do nothing but rally the people to Eredur. We don't want that, do we? No, we must delay. Bide our time. I am smarting at the deception and trickery of the king, but we are not the only ones angered by this decision. He hadn't even told his privy council!" He shook his head in bafflement.

Isybelle nudged Ankarette's arm. "Do you like this one?" she asked, holding out a folded ream of cloth. Ankarette was much more interested in the conversation happening across the room, but she turned an appreciative eye to the fabric and nodded enthusiastically. The last thing she wished to do was draw undue attention to herself.

"How can you bear it?" Dunsdworth sniped.

"Because we must," the duchess said. "You must as well."

Dunsdworth scowled and shook his head. "If I were king, I would never have treated you so poorly. You are the wisest and most capable man in Ceredigion. You are the king's greatest supporter. Without you, he never would have worn the hollow crown. Now that he has it, he's gone blind to the past."

Ankarette suspected that Dunsdworth was stroking the duke's ego deliberately, but it was obvious Warrewik relished the praise.

"That is often the case with power, lad. It does blind you." The duke reached out and put his hand on the younger man's shoulder. "I know you would never betray me. You know I'm fond of you. I'm fond of all my nephews, even Severn."

"He's a goad," Dunsdworth said acidly.

"He can be very convincing in his reasoning," the duke countered. "But yes, his sarcasm must be endured. Patience, lad." He squeezed Dunsdworth's shoulder. "How many times have I told you that your thoughts create your destiny? Does a boulder stop the river from flowing? No, water finds its way around it. The Fountain delivers to us that which we secretly want. With perseverance and commitment, we may achieve all that we desire. Remember that, lad." He gave him a piercing look, his words fraught with meaning.

Ambition burned nakedly in Dunsdworth's eyes, just as it had that night in Dundrennan. Ankarette could see the fires there. Moreover, she could see how the duke was fanning them—how, indeed, they were encouraging each other. It made her feel uneasy.

Her attention was snagged when a panel on the wall suddenly swung open and Sir Thomas entered the room. The implication astonished her: there were tunnels behind the walls. There was so much she didn't know about life in the palace. She hoped Sir Thomas would teach her everything.

Dunsdworth's gaze shifted from the newcomer to Warrewik, and he gave the duke a telling nod.

Warrewik turned and clapped his hands together. "Sir Thomas, that took longer than expected. What in-

THE POISONER'S ENEMY

formation have you gathered about our new queen? How did they meet? She's from Westmarch, correct? I need to speak to Lord Kiskaddon about her."

"Greetings, my lord," Sir Thomas said, walking up to them quickly. "Welcome back from your journey."

"Thank you. But I want news."

"Of course," Sir Thomas said. "I've not had much time to seek it out, but—"

The duke sighed. "Sir Thomas, you're at court. You should really try to conquer the Northern brogue."

"Pardon, my lord. It slipped out in my enthusiasm to share the news." His voice changed subtly, but Ankarette could tell he had to work to keep the inflection subtle. "Elyse Degriy is the daughter of Duke Deford's wife through her second husband. Her blood is noble and still holds influence in Westmarch, which as you recall, used to be a duchy of Occitania."

"Skip the history lesson," the duke said archly. "How did they meet?"

"Apparently, the king took a mild detour to Hutton Manor on his way to the North when he came to visit us. He spent the afternoon at the manor, and his visit with the duchess's daughter intrigued him. He stayed the night and then came to Dundrennan. Apparently, he and the lady were married in the early morning by the Deconeus of St. Penryn, who was summoned for the occasion."

"St. Penryn?" the duke said, baffled. "This makes no sense. I thought Tunmore would have been involved, surely."

Sir Thomas shook his head. "The Deconeus of Ely was ambushed by the news like the rest of us. No one knows whether the king met Lady Elyse prior to that occasion or not. I have the court historians searching the records for any petitions she may have made to the crown or any decisions levied against her husband during the Assizes after the Battle of Mortimer's Cross. That will take some time."

The duke's brow furrowed. "This makes no sense. By your tale, Sir Thomas, you'd have me believe that the king happened upon the manor after losing his way, fell in a great passion for the widow, then decided to marry her against all common sense and decorum in such a hasty manner out of . . . out of lust? Is she a water sprite to have such power over a man?"

"The reports I have say she is pretty but not exotic. They say her mother is the more handsome of the two. By all accounts, it does seem rather . . . rash."

Warrewik looked at Dunsdworth. "What do you make of it?"

Ankarette was grateful that she wouldn't be asked any questions. It was obvious to her that Sir Thomas knew much more about the situation than he was letting on. He was playing a part, a role. Something told her the meeting of Eredur and Elyse had been no coincidence. It had been thoughtfully and deliberately planned—perhaps by Sir Thomas. And this first move on the board would be followed by others calculated to reduce the duke's power and Eredur's dependence on him. Ankarette knew these things were true as they flashed through her mind. But she said nothing.

Then Sir Thomas met her gaze and something unspoken passed between them—a little quirk of his mouth, the tug of a half smile, gone so quickly she may have imagined it.

"Did not the first Argentine king Henricus take another man's wife?" Dunsdworth said. "Was that not the founding of the dynasty? She already has two sons. He's confident she'll beget more. I've not seen the girl to comment on whether her beauty distracted him. It's probably so. He's always had an eye for a fair damsel." He folded his arms, his expression brooding. "The sooner he gets her with child, the sooner they might have a son." He gave the duke a pointed look.

The duke gave him a subtle gesture to say no more. That Dunsdworth wanted to be king was emblazoned for all to see. A son would mean an heir, which would put a huge obstacle in the brother's path to the throne.

The duke turned to Sir Thomas. "Find out more. I think Eredur will control access to her, so it may be impossible to gain useful information from the source. The Espion will continue to uncover facts about how they met and wed. It could be no more than the impetuousness of youth. But I don't trust that the answer is so simple. Go, and bring word to me as soon as you learn more."

"Aye, my lord," Sir Thomas said, and departed through the secret panel by which he had entered.

"I will see you in the great hall for dinner," the duke told Dunsdworth, squeezing his shoulder again and then patting his back. It occurred to Ankarette, not for the first time, that Warrewik had fashioned himself as a replacement father for the Argentine brothers. Only Eredur hadn't accepted him in that role.

Dunsdworth nodded and crossed over to the ladies' side of the room. Isybelle held up a beautiful Occitanian gown and displayed it for him.

"I like that one better," he said, gesturing to another dress, one that was more extreme in style and cost. "It suits you." He took her hand and pressed a quick kiss to her knuckles. Isybelle shivered in pleasure, watching him as he strode out the main door.

"Ankarette," the duke called, startling her. He had walked to the open window and stood at the edge of the balcony. He gestured for her to come to him and she obeyed, her stomach twisting with nerves.

"Yes, my lord?"

He gave her a stern but gentle look. "Have you enjoyed your life in Dundrennan so far?"

"I have indeed, my lord." She wanted to say more but thought better of it.

"While I was gone, I received reports about you from Sir Thomas. He said you noticed an intruder in the woods. He's impressed by how quickly you've learned the Espion ways. He said you were discreet and observant. Those are excellent qualities. Sir Thomas is a very good judge of character. It's one of his gifts."

She flushed at the praise.

The duke clasped his hands behind his back and gazed out the balcony at the gardens below. Some young magnolia trees were still in bloom. She felt her nerves tightening.

"Did anyone attempt to visit Isybelle in her room at night?" he asked her softly, still not looking at her. His gaze was far away, but she sensed he was listening very closely. She also sensed that he already had an answer to the question he'd asked her. He was testing her loyalty.

Her mouth went dry. Isybelle had entertained only two nocturnal visitors in the months Ankarette had lived in Dundrennan. Both had paid her a visit on the same night.

She knew that if she hesitated too long, it would impair the duke's trust of her.

"Yes, my lord. The Duke of Clare came one night. It was the day the king arrived."

She waited, holding her breath, studying his reaction. She left out the part about Eredur visiting first, believing that it would compromise Sir Thomas if she said anything. It would reveal his role as Eredur's friend and confidante. She could see the duke wasn't truly loyal to the king, so she wasn't sure how he would react to that.

Warrewik pursed his lips. "Thank you for being honest. Did anything ... untoward happen?"

"No, my lord, I assure you," she answered. "The interview was very short. There was a guard at the door—"

"I know," he interrupted. He still didn't look at her. "Is there anything else?"

She hesitated, feeling the danger of her situation vividly. Was he testing her still? Did he know about Sir Thomas and the king? There was no way she could know his thoughts, no way to tell whether his words were a trap. What should she say?

The strange feeling came inside her again, like the rippling of waters. It bid her to hold her tongue and say nothing.

She looked down at the ground.

Only a few seconds passed before the duke spoke again. "Very well," he said jovially. "Thank you for your honesty, Ankarette. Anne and I will be staying in the state rooms here. Rooms adjoining ours have been provided by the chamberlain for you and my daughters. Here is a ring that I would like to give you. It is an Espion ring and will give you authority that few of your age or rank have. Sir Thomas will show you its proper use." He reached into his pocket and then handed her the ring. It glimmered in her palm and she stared at it with fascination. "We will stay in Kingfountain for several weeks. I must show the king that he has not upset me. So must we all." She glanced up, and he gave her a pleased, indulgent smile. "Anne tells me that you and Isybelle have formed a close bond. You are a good influence on her and she on you."

She was about to back away from the balcony, but he gestured for her to stop.

"After we return to Dundrennan," he said in an offhanded manner, "we may have cause to discuss some additional . . . training." He shrugged. "You never know, Ankarette. The queen may need your midwifery services before my daughter does."

The cunning look he gave her made her throat tighten with dread.

CHAPTER 10
LADY ELYSE

Ankarette was awakened in the black of night by the noise of a tripping latch and the soft whoosh of wind. Fear rose to choke her, for the noises were stealthy, it was well past midnight, and an intruder had entered the room. Since her experience months before when the poisoner had come to the door in the night, she had always put a dagger in an easy place to reach before retiring to bed. She groped in the dark, finding the handle of the weapon just as Sir Thomas's face appeared above a burning taper candle from the secret door in the room.

She let out her breath in a relieved exhale and eased off the bed, trying not to awaken Isybelle.

He held up the light, and an amused smile flashed across his face when he saw Ankarette's dagger. "You're not intending to use that against me, are you, lass?" he whispered with a chuckle.

"Why are you here, Sir Thomas?" she asked, putting the dagger behind her.

"To fetch you," he said, nodding for her to follow him into the darkness.

Excitement began to dance within her bosom. Ever

since he'd exited one of those secret doors earlier, she'd been anxious to explore. She came closer but glanced back at her sleeping friend. "What if she awakens?"

Sir Thomas shrugged. "We won't be long. Besides, don't you want to see the Espion tunnels? Leave the dagger here."

She nodded, unable to hide her eagerness, and he gestured once again for her to follow him. After she restored the dagger to its hiding place, she did follow him into the labyrinthine secret corridors. He shut the door behind her and showed her the latch he'd used to release it.

"There aren't many of us who use the corridors at night," he explained over his shoulder, keeping his voice low. "It's too dark to wander them without a candle. Someone could get lost in here for hours. And with the noise of the wind and the creaking beams, it's like as not to frighten someone out of their wits." He looked back and gave her a crooked smile. "These secret corridors encircle the palace and provide the Espion with private access to most of the major rooms. It allows us to bypass the sentries posted at the doors."

"I thought the Espion ring would handle that?" she said.

"Yes," he acknowledged, "but our presence wouldn't go unnoticed. These corridors also allow us to eavesdrop on guests and visitors. You can learn much about someone when they do not know you are watching. But at night, most people are abed and there is very little to witness, so the tunnels are typically unused. I made sure that I was assigned to wander the passages on this night."

"Where are we going, Sir Thomas?" she asked.

"To the queen. She wants to meet you."

The words sent a startled thrill through Ankarette. The height of the corridor was variable—sometimes she could feel drafts wafting down from above, and on other occasions they almost needed to crouch to make it beneath the angle of the stone steps above. The air was musty and stale and it tickled her throat and made her want to cough, but she suppressed the urge with her hand.

"That one leads to one of the towers," he said, gesturing with the candle. "There are so many in this palace."

Onward they went, weaving their way through the corridors. She tried to keep her sense of direction, but he took different byways, and despite knowing that the castle was a circular design, she couldn't keep track. Without him, she would have unable to find her way back.

"During the day, some light comes in through arrow slits. It's a little easier to traverse the tunnels then. Most of the main rooms come with spy holes. Like this one." He stopped and slid one open, motioning her forward. The spy hole opened to a darkened room, but she could make out a few chairs. "Where is this?" she asked him.

"The privy council chamber," he said, wagging his eyebrows. "This is why Eredur had to keep his marriage a secret for so long. Even if he'd discussed the matter in private with his council, my lord duke would have found out about it."

Ankarette turned to Sir Thomas, her expression serious. "Running the Espion is a powerful position."

He pursed his lips and nodded in agreement. "We have spies in nearly every kingdom and the letters arrive in heaps and stacks. The duke has a special room here called the Star Chamber. He was there until midnight tonight, crafting messages and dispatching them. I waited until he was asleep before coming to get you. This way."

Together they continued through a serpentine passage that became increasingly narrow. It ended suddenly, no further way to go. Ankarette gazed at the bricks and wondered if there was a secret door hidden there, allowing further passage, but Sir Thomas turned to the left and indicated the spy hole and latch in front of him. He gazed into the room through the spy hole, nodded, and then opened his palm and gestured for her to open the door. She did.

She realized with some shock that she had entered the king's private bedroom. There was a crackling fire in the hearth and it was pleasantly warm. The stale smell of the corridor had been replaced by the pleasant fragrances of flowers and tea. There was a mantel above the fireplace. A Wizr board sat near the bed, a game in play, and a scabbard and sword dangled from a chair peg by a sturdy leather belt. Eredur had tossed his clothes onto the floor for a servant to pick up later.

As Ankarette's eyes followed the trail of clothes, she spied the king at a desk, quill in hand, wearing a nightshirt and breeches. Candles, a few wax sticks, and a gold signet ring sat on the desk. His shoulders were broad and powerful and his neck drooped with fatigue. He raked his fingers through his hair almost as if he were trying to claw himself awake.

"Ahem," Sir Thomas coughed into his hand.

Eredur turned quickly, alerted to their presence by the noise, and quickly came to his feet.

"Tom!" he said, suddenly beaming. The smile didn't leave his eyes when he noticed Ankarette.

"Hello again, lass. You're in your nightrobe once

more, I see, although this time I'm in my nightshirt too. We have to stop meeting at such awkward hours."

She flushed with the attention and started to fidget.

"No need to blush, lass. I'm only jesting. My lady wished to meet you. She fell asleep, but let me rouse her." It was a mountain of a bed, heaped with so many sheets and blankets and pillows Ankarette hadn't noticed it was occupied. She wondered how it was even possible she was standing in the king's bedroom in the middle of the night. Had her father ever had experiences like this in his time with the Espion?

"Love? Elyse?" the king crooned soothingly as he approached the bed.

Ankarette waited, fingers tangled together behind her back. The king's wife rose and Ankarette was grateful the lady was also covered with a robe. She had long blonde hair, very straight, that fell down her back as she sat up. She was older than her husband, maybe by a four or five years, but she was handsome and striking in her look of maturity. Eredur was all easygoing and friendly, but his wife was guarded—careful. Taking her hand, Eredur helped her dismount the colossal bed onto a portable footstool.

There was no crown, no diadem, no outward symbol of rank. But she had a regal look and a self-confident bearing that suggested dignity and demanded respect.

Ankarette felt very young and vulnerable in comparison. She was probably half the queen's age and felt in awe of her.

"So you are Ankarette Tryneowy," the king's wife said seriously. Then she smiled. It started slow and spread across her face like a sunrise, setting her face aglow. The effect was so stunning, Ankarette nearly took a step back.

Ankarette felt a blush rise on her cheeks and she belatedly remembered to curtsy, which made Sir Thomas and Eredur chuckle.

The queen gave her husband a scolding look that instantly squelched his mirth. "Please, dear. You shouldn't tease like that." She approached Ankarette and took both of her hands. "You are so young, child. How old are you?"

"I turned thirteen this past month," Ankarette replied.

"I would have guessed fifteen," the queen said generously. "You may call me Elyse when we are alone like this. Sir Thomas has told me so much about you and I've longed to meet you in person. Look at you, nearly a woman grown at thirteen."

Ankarette blushed again, wishing she were wearing more than a nightgown.

The queen kissed her cheek and then put an arm around her and guided her to a nearby sofa. Eredur took Sir Thomas over to the desk where he had been working before their arrival.

"I think we will be great friends," Elyse said, taking Ankarette's hands into her lap. "I will need a confidante in the palace. So many intrigues and rumors already. I'm very nervous about how the people will receive me." She sighed and shook her head. "I am not exactly a welcome addition to the court. Not yet."

"It's a pleasure to meet you," Ankarette said. She wondered at the familiarity between them since the queen was a stranger to her.

"Likewise. I understand your father was a lawyer *and* an Espion. That is true? Good, I've always had a fair memory for details. And I never forget a face. You are uncommonly pretty, Ankarette."

"Thank you, my lady," Ankarette said, flushing.

"No. Elyse," the queen corrected. "Titles can get in the way sometimes. They create distance. You and I are going to be acquainted rather intimately, I think. Childbearing is a rather vulnerable process. I'm so impressed that at your age, you have already learned the craft of midwifery. You've survived the battlefield of the birthing chamber. Are you squeamish?"

Ankarette shrugged. "Perhaps I was the first few times. But I think it's one of the most beautiful things in the world. I love babies."

Elyse stroked Ankarette's hair over her ear. "Sir Thomas is an excellent judge of character. He told me that I would like you." She paused, then said, "Of course, maybe he's simply good at influencing people, because one likes what one expects to like. Is that not true?"

"I like you, Elyse," Ankarette said, feeling a shy smile spread on her face.

The queen gave her a pointed, serious look, and then that smile came again—that wonderful flower of a smile. "Bless you, dearest," she said, kissing Ankarette's forehead. "I think we will get along very well. I've had two children already by my late husband. They are in wardship with my elder brother at present. I miss them very much. The eldest is ten and the younger is eight, so it has been a while since I've given birth. But I'm not afraid of the pain of childbirth. Many women are. I hope," she added, rubbing her abdomen, "that Eredur and I will be blessed to have more. We are quite compatible, he and I." She gazed lovingly across the room at her husband. "He has so much energy, so much passion.

He just needs to pour it in the right direction. He can accomplish so much in his reign if he does." She patted Ankarette's hands again. "Now, if I am right, he is telling Sir Thomas about our plans to usurp control away from Lord Warrewik."

"Indeed, I am, my dear," said Eredur. He turned and gestured for them to approach the desk.

Ankarette felt a thrill of excitement as she and Elyse joined the others.

"These documents," the king said to Ankarette, wagging a quill at her, "make Elyse's father a major lord of the realm."

"The Duke of East Stowe to be exact," Sir Thomas said.

"That is Lord Pogue, currently," Ankarette said, hoping she remembered correctly.

"Good memory, lass," Eredur said. "And he is loyal to . . . ?"

"The Duke of Warrewik," Ankarette answered.

"Very loyal," Sir Thomas said. "And so Pogue controls the shipping to Brugia and defends the coast. No one is going to invade Ceredigion from the North except Atabyrion." He rolled his eyes. "I don't think the threat of *that* is very great. No, the dangers are from Brugia and Occitania."

"But doesn't Warrewik still control Callait?" the queen said.

"He does," Eredur said broodingly. "I need to wrest it away from him. Our biggest garrison is stationed there and he commands it." He squinted his eyes and shook his head. "Who did he assign there, Tom? Do you recall?"

"Captain Vauclair," Sir Thomas answered with a hint of anger in his voice. Ankarette remembered the conversation she'd walked in on upon first arriving at Dundrennan. Ah, yes—Thomas had wanted that position.

"By the Fathoms, you're right," Eredur said. "He's very loyal."

"True, but he may come to your side in time," Sir Thomas said. "All you need to do is give him a reason, Eredur. You can't allow Warrewik to control Callait forever, but you won't break his grip all at once. Finger by finger is the way of it."

The king looked at Ankarette closely. "You arrived just after the duke found out about Elyse. He wasn't happy was he?"

Ankarette shook her head. "He's biding his time."

"Of course he is," Elyse said, taking her husband's arm. "There will be another civil war, I fear."

Eredur shook his head. "No, I think I can prevent that. I don't want to destroy my own uncle, but I no longer trust him. Not after . . ." He sighed and shook his head. Elyse rubbed his arm comfortingly.

Sir Thomas shot him a glare to say no more, and while Ankarette could not divine the meaning of that, she thought it might have something to do with Isybelle.

"Well, that is no matter," the king said with good nature. "Back to bed, lass. I can tell you rather enjoy staying up discussing politics to the wee hours. As does she"—he kissed his wife's neck—"so I agreed to set your meeting for tonight. We think Warrewik is going to ask you to go to Pisan soon, Ankarette. You may be gone from court for a year. Maybe two. But what you learn over there will be immeasurably helpful to us. The most clever and cunning minds are trained in the poisoner school in Pisan. Other skills are taught there as well. At thirteen, you won't be the youngest student. Some go as early as ten. But I think you're ready, Ankarette. And you will do us proud."

"Thank you," Ankarette said, dropping to a curtsy again.

"Take her back, Tom," the king said, giving her a wink and a genuine smile.

"Good night, my dear," Elyse said, kissing her cheek and giving her another radiant smile.

They were young and ambitious. And she could see they were determined to remake their world. Just like the first Argentine king and his bride. But only if they survived the coming trouble.

I was educated at the poisoner school in Pisan when I was thirteen years old. Every day for two years, I was grateful to my mother for the kindness of teaching me not only skills as a midwife, but also the ability to observe people. I was grateful too for the training of Thomas Mortimer, who had prepared me in so many subtle ways to become a poisoner.

How can I describe what I learned? There were lessons in herbs and plants, of course. I earned my share of bruises in the practicable study of fighting and was the best in the school at throwing a dagger with precision. I particularly enjoyed learning the court dances from various realms and the manners of speech and customs of other nations, from Atabyrion to Genevar. We studied history, languages, feigning accents, and disguise. I learned how to impersonate someone much older by adopting subtle mannerisms that usually come with age and confidence. I learned how to gain the trust of children, pets, and servants.

I think the study came easily to me because of my experiences living in Dundrennan and my brief exposure to the intricacies of life in Kingfountain. I was able to take every concept taught to me and apply it in some way to the people that I actually knew. It made the concepts stick in my mind, like tiles in a mosaic that revealed a grand picture.

One of the most important pieces of knowledge I learned was the identity of other poisoners and their reputations. The most mysterious poisoner of all, I

***

learned, was in the employ of the King of Occitania. He was one of the nobility, sent to the school of Pisan in disguise to train. Only the masters of the school knew his true identity. Everyone else knew someone who believed they had once seen him, and my fellow students never tired of guessing at his role in this or that political mishap.

They all agreed that Lewis's poisoner was probably the deadliest man in any realm. There were stories of those who tried to cross him and how he could kill a man from miles away with little more than a charming smile. In the school, we learned the true name of every poisoner. Except his.

No one ever said that he was King Lewis's herald, so I kept that knowledge to myself. Sometimes it can be difficult keeping a secret. They want to worm free. It is the temptation of most to boast about themselves, but I have always been good at keeping secrets.

— ANKARETTE TRYNEOWY

PART TWO
THE DUKE'S POISONER

PART TWO

THE DUKE'S POISONER

CHAPTER II
REUNION

The summons back to Kingfountain by the Duke of Warrewik did not come as a surprise. Yes, he was the man who had paid the exorbitant cost of the exclusive school. But Ankarette also knew it had to do with Elyse's upcoming confinement. The time drew near for the queen to deliver her child, and Ankarette's midwifery skills would be put to the test. She had the suspicion that her loyalties would be as well.

An Espion courier had delivered the note of the summons and specified the day of departure, so she had plenty of time to be nervous and worried. On the morning of the day she was to leave, she checked her traveling trunk to ensure she hadn't forgotten anything. It had a false bottom that concealed the implements of her new trade.

She secretly hoped Sir Thomas would be sent to retrieve her. In the two years of her training, she had thought of him often and fondly. She missed him and missed Isybelle, with whom she'd corresponded. It would be wonderful to rekindle her friendships in person. Of course, the duke could have sent anyone to fetch her.

A knock sounded at the door and when she opened it, one of the pages of the school told her in a hurried accent that the duke's ship had been spotted and would be in the harbor within the hour. She thanked the young man and felt the nervous flutter in her stomach once again. When he left, she turned to look at her small room, barely more than a cell. The school was ancient and the amenities sparse and it smelled of must and the grit of the ages. The window glass was so thick with marbling it was only good for telling the time of day. But she would miss it all the same, and the thought of leaving forever tugged at her heart. There were some she might even have called friends. In a place where ambition reigned supreme, it was difficult to judge whether affection was real or feigned, but Ankarette felt she was a good judge of character and had avoided the more obvious dissemblers.

It was then that she sensed an undercurrent—a preternatural warning the likes of which she had not experienced very often in Pisan. She stared at the door, a shiver starting at the base of her spine. Memories from a dark night long ago rushed into her mind.

Someone was walking toward the room. There was no sound of footfalls, but she didn't need her ears to tell her what her heart already knew. The faint trickling noise of a distant fountain seemed to fill her ears. It was a warning. There was a slit in the fold of her gown and she drew a small dirk and concealed it behind her.

Another knock came on the door, this one much softer, less urgent.

The feeling of unease grew into a pit in her stomach. She knew the effects of fear. Knew how it impaired a person's judgment—and yet she could not prevent it from unfurling inside her. But she had also been taught that fear would pass. Action would help dispel it.

"Who is it?" she called, staring at the handle of the door. She had not bothered to lock it after the page left.

She already knew who stood behind that door. Something about this man had lingered with her ever since the afternoon she'd sensed him lurking in the woods in Dundrennan.

The handle pressed down and the door pushed open slightly, just enough to reveal a man standing there. She only saw one of his eyes. After two years of poisoner school, she understood why. He was using the door as a shield in case she threw a dagger at him.

"Ah, here you are, damoselle," he said, pushing the door the rest of the way open, keeping it wide. He gave her a charming smile, the crinkles around his eyes showing he was genuinely eager to talk with her. He had a disarming manner that no doubt served him well in his profession. "I had hoped to catch you before you left for Kingfountain." His gallant Occitanian court accent was on full display.

Catch indeed, like a fly in a spider's web.

"It's an honor to meet you, Lord Hux," she said, careful not to stammer. She was terrified of him. He probably knew that just from looking at her, but she tried to project calm and confidence. If his intention was to murder her on the day she was departing for Kingfountain, she'd not be killed without a fight. Her hand gripped the dirk tightly.

"But we've met *before*," he said with a secret smile. "In Dundrennan! Have we not?"

She inclined her head in acknowledgment.

"I've heard such good things about the school's new

protégé," he said with eagerness. "The headmaster is most impressed. You are a capable poisoner, they say. And look at you—so beautiful and refined." He folded his arms and clucked his tongue, tapping his chin in an almost flirtatious manner. She saw both of his hands. That was an indication he did not mean to attack her ... *yet*. "Be at ease, damoselle. I merely came to deliver a message from my master to yours, since you are due to return to court this day. It saves me an unnecessary journey, and I have many other duties for my master. Will you be so kind as to deliver it?"

Her mouth was dry, but she quickly moistened it. "A message, you say?" Would it be poisoned?

"Yes, damoselle!" He slowly unfolded his arms and there was a letter suddenly in his hand. She hadn't seen him draw it out. His sleight of hand was impressive. "It was written in the formian cipher, naturally."

"Naturally," Ankarette replied. She did not trust him. Not one whit.

"I will let you read it before we seal it, eh? You should know the message in case something befalls the letter. It is common for us poisoners to know our masters' secrets. Such is the way of Pisan. My master seeks to warn the duke that the king will next force Callait from his hands. See for yourself." He opened the letter gingerly and shook it out. "No dust. No poison ink." He smiled warmly, then blew on the pages and rubbed his own hands across them. "No tricks, damoselle. Just a warning to the duke from his friend, my master. Read it."

He handed her the note and gestured for her to peruse the contents. It was just as he'd said—the information he'd conveyed in the cipher he had mentioned. In the two years she had been away, Eredur had made multiple attempts to wrest Callait and its massive garrison from Warrewik. But each time the duke had strategically sidestepped the issue.

There had also been a recent insurrection attempt led by the deposed mad king and his cunning wife. It had ended with the mad king locked up in Holistern Tower and Queen Morvared and her son back in her father's lands in Occitania.

Ankarette had wondered if the rebellion was just a decoy, if the duke might have something to do with it.

"Are you satisfied?" Lord Hux asked her with a smile. "Will you deliver this message to the duke?"

She nodded quickly and he took it back. He produced a stub of wax, held it over the burning candle on her table, and pressed it on the fold of the letter. Then he twisted off a signet ring, the royal seal of Occitania, and pressed it into the wax to finalize it.

"Ah, there we are." As soon as the wax was set, he handed it to her. "I am obliged to you, damoselle. I owe you a favor. Do not hesitate to seek my aid in any matter. My residence, when I'm not at court, is the royal castle of Shynom. A generous gift from a generous king." His eyes locked on hers, and she once again felt that strange churning sensation in her gut. He was staring at her, but it felt almost as if his hands were touching her body. She was unable to repress a shudder.

The feeling stopped.

"What is it, damoselle?" he asked, his brows furrowing. "Are you unwell?"

She blinked rapidly, trying to calm her swimming mind. "I am well. Thank you."

He took a step closer. "Did you . . . *feel* something, damoselle?" he asked in a whisper, his eyes still locked on hers. The feeling struck her again, even more forcefully this time. It was as if he were now looking inside her soul, laying bare her secrets.

"I'm more than a little intimidated," she said, trying to feign lightness. "You have such a reputation, Lord Hux."

He smiled, pleased, and the feelings abated once again. He bowed. "I have deep respect for the Duke of Warrewik," he said. "My master considers him a friend. It was not his fault your king reneged on his promise to marry my master's sister. She was devastated, I assure you. Well, damoselle. I am certain our paths will cross again in the future. Ceredigion and Occitania have been enemies for a great number of years. That shall provide us with ample opportunity to discuss affairs of state." He paused, weighing his words more carefully. "If you ever find that your master's... prospects... have diminished... How can I put this delicately? Should his ambitions and plans not come to fruition and you find yourself in need of friendly advice, then I adjure you, damoselle, to seek out my master. You have skills, I think, that you are ... as yet ... unaware of. I believe my master would value them highly."

Leaving the letter in her hand and the offering lingering in the air between them, he bowed once again and abandoned her room. Her wrist was sore from squeezing the handle of the dirk so hard.

∼

ANKARETTE HAD DROPPED a coin into the fountain earlier out of superstition, and it would seem her prayer had been granted. The servants and pages were carrying her chest up the gangway of Duke Warrewik's ship when

Sir Thomas appeared at the railing. He waited for them to clear the path before he came strutting down it himself.

The two years had changed him, but she would have recognized his face anywhere, even with his unshaven appearance. He was broader in the shoulders and had a more confident bearing. She had changed too—she had become a woman since they'd last met—and he gave her a startled look as he approached.

Her studies at the school had trained her to notice the many small things that revealed someone before they even spoke. His slightly raised eyebrows showed he was admiring her.

"Well met, Ankarette," he said in his waning Northern brogue. "Look at you, lass." He shook his head in bewilderment. "Has it really been two years? May it have been longer? My, what a pretty lass you've become. How are you? I asked for this assignment and am glad the duke granted it."

"I am well, Sir Thomas," she answered, careful not to flush. She kept herself calm and poised. There was no hint of an accent in her voice now.

He gave her a playful butt with his elbow as he came to stand next to her. Then he held out his arm, silently offering to escort her up the gangplank. He wore the duke's badge on his tunic.

In short order, they were underway. He said they'd reach Kingfountain by dawn if not sooner. The sailors crawled through the nest of ropes and sails, and she watched with fascination as they went about their work. Her luggage was stowed in her room near the captain's quarters, and soon they were off. She felt melancholy again as she stood alone at the side of the ship, watching the island kingdom pass into the distance.

The sound of his boots announced him. She would have recognized his tread anywhere.

"You'll have returned to Ceredigion just in time," Thomas said, planting his hands on the railing. "The queen is ripe as a melon."

"How has she handled the pregnancy so far?" Ankarette asked, trying to keep the conversation in calm waters, although she was anxious to learn as much as she could before arriving home. She had many questions she wished to ask about the gossip she had heard.

"Patiently, for her part," he answered with a look. "I think Eredur is more anxious than she is. But the queen's had a very calming influence on him. She's very deliberate."

"Should we be seen talking like this?" she asked him, noticing some of the sailors were motioning at them and grinning. It didn't take much imagination to suspect the nature of their thoughts.

Thomas looked over his shoulder and flashed the sailors a scowl. They quickly went back to work. "We both work for the same men, do we not?" he answered with a quiet chuckle. "I'm sure you'll be wanting news?"

"I would be grateful, yes."

He shook his head and chuckled. "Always curious. Always thinking. That's what I like about you, lass. These last two years have been difficult. As you know, Eredur promoted his father-in-law as a duke of the realm. He's also done things for other members of his lady's family, much to the wrath of Warrewik and Dunsdworth. One of her sisters married Lord Bletchley, for example. Warrewik was furious. Each move has increased Eredur and Elyse's power and diminished the duke's influence. The two are hardly civil to each other right now. It's getting bad, Ankarette."

She sighed. "I can imagine so. I heard the old king was arrested and put in the tower?"

"Aye," he replied, a distant look in his eyes. "I put him there myself."

"You did?" she said, surprised.

He snorted. "He's daft, he is. May the Fountain bless him. Nearly every word he speaks is gibberish. I don't see how any man could swear to serve someone so incapable of kingly duties. He's a puppet. And yet, as long as he lives, there will be men who will fight to put him back on the throne. Eredur is the true king. But there's still Morvared and her plotting and treason to contend with. She's not content to linger in Occitania with her boy. The Espion are watching her closely. Visitors come often to her estate." He shook his head. "It's not over yet. Let's see, what else. You missed the war with Genevar while you were gone."

"The trade war?" Ankarette asked.

"Aye. Hardly worth talking about." He scratched his scruffy chin. "The biggest news, though, is the row between Eredur and his brother."

"Not Severn, surely?"

He wrinkled his nose. "No, Eredur and Severn are tight as drums. The lad's only fifteen, but he's every bit a man grown. Severn is trusted and he's loyal. He's watching the North for his brother. No, I'm talking about Dunsdworth. He asked to marry Isybelle again. Demanded it, actually."

Ankarette had not heard any gossip about that, nor had Isybelle said anything in her periodic letters.

"Eredur said no, surely?" she assumed.

"Aye. How could the king say yes? It would give Warrewik everything he wants and legitimize Dunsdworth as a rival to the throne. The situation is coming to a head, Ankarette. And it all hinges on you." He gave her a pointed look. "If the queen has a son, there could be war. It isn't happenchance that the duke has summoned you to the palace, lass. We both know that. He's got it fixed in his mind that Dunsdworth should be king. And he's got it fixed in Dunsdworth's mind as well." His look was dark and serious. "Are you ready for this, lass? I know this river and see where it's headed. It goes straight toward the falls."

CHAPTER 12
THE DECONEUS

When Ankarette arrived at Kingfountain palace with Sir Thomas, she did not come through the main doors as she had done with the duchess's retinue. There were no crowds thronging the streets this time, no one gawking at the duke's badge. They entered the grounds through a porter door along the lower wall of the palace grounds and then marched up the hillside trail to the next defenses. They spoke unceasingly as they made the journey—Ankarette was hungry to know everything he would tell her, and Sir Thomas did not hesitate to answer her questions.

The knight led the way to the duke's chamber through the Espion tunnels, and Ankarette, whose prodigious memory had been trained to be even sharper in Pisan, set her mind to the task of memorizing the way, noticing little markers to help distinguish the paths.

When they reached a certain spot, she stopped him. "Isn't this the way to the king's chamber?"

He craned his neck and then nodded. "The duke's chamber is along the same path. You remembered?"

"It seemed familiar," she replied, storing away the memory. Because it was daytime, they encountered other Espion in the tunnels. But the other men knew Sir Thomas on sight and no one challenged them or asked for an explanation for her presence.

As they approached the duke's chamber, she felt the subtle flow of Fountain waters. It put her on her guard immediately. There was no change in Sir Thomas's demeanor at all. If he heard the sound or felt it, he showed no indication. The closer they got to his chambers, the more the feeling intensified. Would they find the duke with the Occitanian herald? She still carried his note in a pocket sewn into her gown.

"Is the duke alone?" she asked, touching Sir Thomas's shoulder.

He gave her a baffled look. "Likely not. It's midmorning. Why?"

She shook her head but could not escape the foreboding feeling in her heart. There was an Espion slouched near the spy hole outside the duke's room, arms folded with a bored look on his face. He squinted as they approached.

"Sir Thomas?" he asked.

"Aye, Bennet," the other replied. "Is the duke here?"

"He's meeting with the deconeus," the Espion said, jabbing his thumb toward the room. He turned and gazed into the spy hole.

"That's no matter," Sir Thomas said with a shrug. "Tunmore knows about the Espion tunnels. Come on, lass. Warrewik will be grateful to know you've returned home."

The Espion on guard duty tripped the latch and swung open the door. Sir Thomas ducked his head before entering the chamber. Ankarette followed, her stomach roiling with nerves. The years had not done much to change the deconeus of Our Lady—he wore his dark hair in the same shorn style, and his posture and demeanor seemed haughty. The duke was bent over a table, quill in hand, signing a paper. The deconeus's eyes were riveted on the paper, and Ankarette sensed the rippling feeling growing more pronounced now that she was inside the room.

"There, that should conclude the matter," the duke said, setting down the quill. The feeling of power instantly evaporated.

"Thank you for your time, my lord," the deconeus said smoothly. He bowed his head in respect.

"We've known each other for years, John," the duke said amiably. "You know I'm always willing to do another favor for a friend."

"Indeed. I knew I could count on you." The deconeus bowed again before his gaze shifted to the new arrivals.

The duke took notice of them too. "Welcome back, Sir Thomas! Another successful mission. Our little midwife has blossomed into a rose. Look at you, Ankarette!" He smiled with pleasure, as if relishing the gleaming new possession his knight had brought home from Pisan.

"My, you've grown." He rubbed his mouth, nodding in satisfaction. "The reports from the school were very good. You've worked hard there and with distinction. You may not know this, but even the noble deconeus here recommended that I send you to Pisan after I first met you in Dundrennan. He saw potential in you. As did I."

"Excuse me, if you would," the deconeus said curtly.

He gathered up the paper and stowed it away. "I must return to the sanctuary. Good day."

"As you will, John. Never too busy for a friend." He waved with disinterest, his eyes still keenly studying Ankarette. She felt abashed by his scrutiny, but her intuition told her there was some bond they shared—a communion with the Fountain's power. She was determined to learn more.

"Sir Thomas, would you notify the queen that Ankarette has returned?" Warrewik asked. "It's important that they get to know each other at long last."

Sir Thomas nodded, gave Ankarette a wary look, and then disappeared back into the secret passage. She had a suspicion he and Bennet would linger at the spy hole to watch them.

The duke riffled through some papers on the desk. "I trust the journey was without incident?" he asked.

"Indeed, my lord. The weather was calm."

"My ships from Callait patrol the waters along the coast. I made certain there would be no disruptions. You're a valuable prize now, Ankarette." He glanced up from his papers, his eyes full of meaning. "Very valuable."

"I am grateful for the opportunity you have given me, my lord."

He nodded, pleased by her answer. "I was going to ask Sir Thomas to escort you to the manor at Marshaw. You deserve a chance to see your mother. She has her own ladies and servants now. A very respectable widow in the county. I've spared no expense." His look was not difficult to interpret. He was impressing on her that her mother was under his power. That he controlled the fate of both Tryneowy women. She'd learned the subtle arts of politics in Pisan. Never shout when a firm voice will do. Never a firm voice when a whisper suffices. Never a whisper if a sigh says it all. And sometimes a glance is powerful enough to convey the true meaning.

She received his unspoken message. "You've been very generous, my lord. I'm aware of everything you've done for my mother and me. I've tried to express my gratitude in my letters to you, but the words feel too small."

He smiled smugly. Her groveling was not totally insincere, but people tended not to balk from a sweet, regardless of the giver's intentions.

"Before I left Pisan, I was given a message from Lord Hux to deliver to your hand."

"Indeed?" the duke said with relish, eagerness brightening his eyes. She produced the sealed letter and handed it to him. After breaking the seal, he quickly perused the document, his lips moving quietly as he decoded the cipher. He rubbed his mouth and stuffed the letter into his pocket. "Good, very well."

"My lord, you *are* aware that Lord Hux is a poisoner?" Ankarette asked.

"Yes, of course," the duke replied with conviction. "Probably tried to recruit you to Lewis's side, hmmm?"

Ankarette controlled her expression, giving off an air of unconcern. "You know King Lewis well," she replied with a bow. "Yes, he did."

"And I knew you would tell me he did," the duke said with satisfaction. "It's the height of bad manners to try stealing what someone else has paid for. Of course, Lewis would never do that. We are friends. I have his full support and confidence. He's a great ally." Again, his words implied more than what he was saying.

He rubbed his mouth and leaned back against the

desk. "Come closer," he bid her. She felt her anxiety grow. He was purposefully positioning her so that she blocked the spy hole. His voice was very low.

"I'm grateful you are back, Ankarette. The queen is worried about her pregnancy. I'd like you to visit with her. To *befriend* her. She needs to have confidence in your skills. You know the dangers that come in the birthing chamber. Every woman must face them with bravery. You have all the skills needed to ensure the babe arrives safely into this world." His eyes crinkled. "But alas, many do not survive the first few hours. The mother is weakened by the ordeal. She is vulnerable to sickness and languishing. Many babies, through no fault of anyone, simply are not robust enough to thrive." He gave her a pointed look and shook his head. "It would be such a pity if that happened to the king's babe. Especially a *son*." His eyes bore into hers, his gaze fiercely intense and deliberate. She knew what he was asking, and it made her blood run cold.

Without saying the words, he was ordering her to kill the babe if it were a boy. He had impressed on her the sense of duty and obligation she owed him. He had made a point of reminding her that her mother was under his control. Part of her shriveled inside.

"Go see the queen," he said coaxingly, touching her arm in a fatherly way. "Then you can see Isybelle. She's anxious to be reunited with you. Every letter you sent her, she shared with me."

In other words, he'd made sure to spy on Ankarette's correspondence. Of course, she'd expected as much.

"I am eager to see her as well," Ankarette said. "Thank you for providing this opportunity, my lord."

She met his gaze with her own. "The king might be disappointed, though. The babe might be a girl."

Warrewik shrugged. "If it please the Fountain."

~

THE DAY WAS WANING when Ankarette entered the gates of the sanctuary of Our Lady. Her heart was heavy with conflict. She had enjoyed her visit with Elyse. She had shared with the queen and the king the implied order to kill their son if the babe was a boy. The queen's face had gone pale, but she had not overreacted. She'd squeezed her husband's hands while Eredur's eyes smoldered with rage and the desire for vengeance. But Warrewik was canny. He had not given her the order directly. There was no evidence other than her word and training. He could not be brought to the Assizes and tried for treason, for he had not said anything worthy of death. Everything had been implied.

The queen had asked for Ankarette's opinion, following the examination, as to whether she was carrying a boy. There were all sorts of rumors and superstitions about how a woman carried differently if the babe was a boy or a girl, but Ankarette didn't subscribe to any of them. Only the Fountain knew the sex of the child. And that knowledge would not be revealed until the birthing chamber.

Eredur knew Ankarette was in a tenuous position. If the babe was a boy and the poisoner did nothing, it would show her true allegiance. The king had promised to protect her from Warrewik's wrath.

She walked across the grounds and climbed the steps to the sanctuary. The white and black marble tiles were arranged in an alternating pattern like a giant

Wizr board. There were families gathered around the edge of the largest fountain. Little children tossed coins into the water, each small piece of metal accompanied by wishes and prayers.

She stood alone by the edge of the bubbling pool, listening to the sound of the waters. What could she do? The situation was a thorny problem. She couldn't kill a babe. The very idea sickened her.

In the poisoner school, she had learned that most nobles killed each other for rank and power. Very few poisoners were ever asked to dispatch infants, although she had been trained in the best ways to accomplish it. She closed her eyes a moment, listening to the sound of the water, falling deeper into her thoughts. How could she protect the queen's babe without betraying Warrewik? If she thought about it hard enough, she was sure she could come up with a solution.

As her mind wrestled with the dilemma, she felt the stirrings of something inside her. There it was again, that strange mercurial feeling that seemed to come and go of its own volition. She worried that recognizing its presence might frighten it away, so she kept her eyes closed and held perfectly still, trying to understand what was happening inside of her. The feeling swelled, expanding like a soap bubble on the verge of popping. There were others standing nearby, but she lost sense of them, almost as if the world had hushed around her, drawing her deeper into herself. A feeling of warmth and happiness trembled in her breast, and she sensed rather than saw color and light behind her closed eyes.

All will be well.

They were not so much whispered words as a surge of feelings of relief. Her eyes blinked open, and she looked around to see if someone was standing nearby. She was still alone. But someone had spoken to her.

No, she realized—not a person. The feelings had come from the bubbling waters.

Then she sensed the power she had felt earlier, in the duke's chamber, emanating from an alcove of the inner sanctum. She turned her head and spied the deconeus standing in the shadows, gazing down at her. She sensed his presence and recognized it from earlier that morning. And she knew, instinctively, that he sensed her as well.

Tunmore walked across the tiles, hands clasped behind his back. He bowed his head to one family and offered a banal benediction to them. But she sensed he was crossing the room toward *her*, and she kept still and waited for him to arrive. He did not look threatening. He looked intrigued.

He came to stand beside her at the fountain's edge, his head bowed as if in prayer. "Many find solace here," he said to her in a low, confidential voice.

"Yes, I can see that," Ankarette answered. She turned and gazed up at him.

"You're Warrewik's girl," he said offhandedly. "The one returned from school."

"I am," she answered. "I didn't know you had recommended me. We never spoke when you came to Dundrennan."

The deconeus's lips pursed. He did not look at her, just at the waters. "Does the duke know?"

That question baffled her. Certainly, she could try to reason through it to divine his meaning, but she decided it would be better to just ask. "Know what, sir?"

He sniffed, still not meeting her gaze. "That you are Fountain-blessed."

Her first instinct was to toss it aside as a jest. Her father had been her teacher and her hero. She'd trusted his word in all things. So, while she'd heard all the stories of Fountain-blessed heroes like the Maid of Donremy, the mighty king Henricus, and the Wizr called Myrddin, she'd believed they were merely stories. That there was no magic connected to the mysteries of the Deep Fathoms. And yet . . . she felt the sudden veracity of the deconeus's words throb deep inside her. She *was* Fountain-blessed.

The realization sent a tremor down from her head to her ankles. Her intuition, which she had long since learned to follow and trust, had always seemed a little different, a little keener than other people's. Now she knew why.

"How old are you?" he asked her simply.

"Fifteen."

He nodded. "How old were you when the Fountain began speaking to you?"

She bit her lip. "Until this very moment, I didn't believe it was real. I think it happened a few times when I was younger. But when I was twelve and living in Dundrennan—that's when I started to notice it more."

Tunmore rocked on his heels. "It's rare for very young children to exhibit the traits. For most, it begins in adolescence. I am Fountain-blessed as well," he confided. "Though it is a secret I choose to keep. So I ask again. Does your master know? He usually brags about his accomplishments. He's never mentioned it, although I've suspected it after sensing you use the power on Lord Hux in the great hall of Dundrennan."

Ankarette shook her head. "I didn't *use* it on Lord Hux deliberately. If I used the . . . power on him, it slipped out, you could say. And no, I haven't told the duke. Do you think I should? I only just found out myself."

"No, child," he said seriously. "Not yet. The magic is very . . . elusive. It takes training and discipline. It is a sign from the Fountain that it has chosen you to be one of its pawns on the earth. If Warrewik knew, he would exploit you."

She turned and faced him, her voice very serious. "As you did to him today? I did not just come here for solace, Deconeus. I sensed *you* using the power on the duke. What did you make him sign?"

The deconeus looked surprised by her accusation. Then pleased. "That was rather clever, girl. You caught me in a trap." His smile broadened. "I think you will enjoy playing this game of secrets and favors. But like any game, there are multiple sides. And any number of rules."

"And whose side are you on, Deconeus?" she asked him pointedly.

He grinned. "The Fountain's."

CHAPTER 13
FOUNTAIN-BLESSED

The deconeus showed Ankarette to his private chambers within the majestic sanctuary. The room was locked and he produced the key from a set of rings belted at his waist. The smell of incense was particularly strong and she noticed an assortment of thuribles of various styles hanging from pegs on the wall. More incense sticks poked out from various urns, many of which bore the marks of antiquity. The room was a treasure trove of artifacts.

Her gaze lingered on a vase carved with the symbol of a raven. It was riddled with chips and cracks, yet there was something about it that held the eye . . . that made her *feel* something. She couldn't remember seeing that symbol in any of her studies in Pisan.

Tunmore locked the door and went to his desk. There were heaps of coins there, most of them blotched with rust and grime.

"Who made this?" she asked, not daring to touch the vase. She committed the symbol to her memory, determined to embroider it later.

"I bought it from a Genevese trader who does business in Ploemeur," he answered, easing into the stuffed chair at the end of the desk. He leaned forward, elbows on the desk, his fingers steepled over his mouth.

"Brythonica?"

"Yes indeed," he answered. "I collect artifacts, as you can see." He gestured expansively at the room and its treasures. There were several chests and locked boxes in addition to the various vases and the coins piled atop his desk. "But I do not keep my best treasures here in my chambers. There are too many thieves wandering around. There is a way to hide such things within the Deep Fathoms itself."

She stared at him with surprise and curiosity. He smiled back in a cunning way.

"I propose a truce between us," he said, his voice firm but deliberate. "I will give you knowledge that would otherwise take you years to discover on your own. I will loan you books to read about the tradition of the Fountain-blessed. In return, you will keep my secret and I will keep yours."

Tunmore had a commanding presence. She had heard he was an able diplomat and had quickly worked his way up the hierarchy of the religion. It seemed likely his gift from the Fountain had much to do with it.

"You said you were on the Fountain's side," Ankarette said, stepping toward him and coming close enough to see the beads of sweat on his brow. He was a powerful man, but it would seem he was also nervous. The poisoner school of Pisan had a reputation. He knew that she could kill him. He swallowed, then reached for a goblet of wine and took a sip, wincing at the flavor. It was a common reaction that someone who was afraid would find their favorite food or drink to be off-putting.

"I am," he answered hesitantly. He was trying to

read her posture, looking to see what kind of danger he was in.

"I'm not going to hurt you unless you do something foolish," she said seriously. "Show me the letter you had the duke sign."

He nodded in acquiescence and withdrew something from the stack on his desk. "This is the one. You'll recognize his signature."

He handed it to her and she cautiously took it. As she began to unfold it, she felt the strange flowing sensation in her gut. She stopped and looked at him accusingly.

"What's in this letter?" she demanded.

Tunmore frowned. There was sweat on his lip now. "Read it and see for yourself."

She shook her head warily.

"Come now," he said. "You want answers. Read it."

Walking forward until her gown swished against his desk, she stared at him coldly. "Don't play games with me, Deconeus."

"It is a game, and as I said, there are rules. Rule number one—someone who is Fountain-blessed can discern the presence of someone else who shares the power, and we can sense when that person is using their ability. Rule number two—each is blessed with a different gift or gifts. You will need to learn what yours is. But the best way to teach someone how to use their gift is to allow them to experience yours. My gift from the Fountain is manifested in my writing. Hence, the letter. Read it so I can explain how it works. You are going to have to trust me, my dear, for this arrangement to work."

The paper quivered in her hand. She did not trust him. She had only just met him. Any number of things could go wrong. Looking intently into his eyes, she wondered what secrets he was hiding. Having someone with his experience and knowledge as an ally would be very useful to her. Though she had sensed the Fountain magic inside her, she lacked training.

"Well?" he asked challengingly, a smug look on his face.

She wished there was a way she could gauge his trustworthiness, but her instincts clashed with each other when it came to this man. And so, just as she had jumped from the boulder into the river, she plunged ahead.

As she opened the letter, she felt the churn of the magic surround her. Her eyes darted quickly to the duke's signature and she recognized that it had indeed been signed by his hand. As she quickly scanned the content, she saw that it was a license to procure wine at a discount from Brugian merchants and store them in Callait before sale in Kingfountain. As she read, her mind became numb with fatigue. It was a boring contract, with little strategic value. The deconeus enjoyed his wine and it was ultimately a selfish endeavor on his part. She nearly tossed the letter aside, but something inside her made her persist. She clenched her jaw and stared at the words, reading them again and again, until the words on the page began to jumble.

The bearer of this letter is authorized to command the Espion stationed in Callait.

The words jolted her. The whisper was almost faint enough to be inaudible, but the words pierced down to her heart. She broke her gaze away from the letter and saw the deconeus staring at her in surprise.

"Did you hear it?" he asked anxiously.

"I heard . . . something," she hedged.

He stood, planting his hands on the desk, his eyes feverish with interest. "You heard the voice of the Fountain. You began to see the true words I had written. My gift from the Fountain, my *blessing*, is the ability to persuade with the written word. I can embed secret meanings within my messages. Someone reading it might see a list, a deposition, a cargo manifest. But there are those who can divine the true meaning, not through the words themselves but through the power of the Fountain."

He gazed at her eagerly. "The duke's strongest asset is his rule of Callait. With this letter, I can command the Espion in that city. The captain's name is Vauclair. He is a greedy, self-serving man. If you want anything there, you must pay him a bribe.

"The duke believes he has given me something of very little value. The best wines are from Occitania, after all, not Brugia. But I seek to write books, to harness this gift from the Fountain for the betterment of the world, and the best book printers are in Brugia. Importing those books would be very expensive. Vauclair sees to that. But when I finish writing my book I will be able to produce it for much less in Brugia and ship it without tax throughout the kingdoms. This letter prepares the way."

He seated himself again. "You have caught me in my trap. You could show the duke the letter, of course, but he will only see what was written there, not the true meaning. I do not fear that. What I do fear is the possibility that you could expose my gift to common knowledge. If it were known that I was Fountain-blessed, you can imagine how many people would come flocking to the sanctuary to beseech me to use my gift on their behalf or to seek my blessing."

She looked at him in bafflement. "Isn't that your role, Deconeus?" She could see he was, at heart, a self-serving man.

"You are not so naive as that," he replied, then shook his head firmly. "It would be a living torture to me. I would not be able to fulfill the work the Fountain has asked me to do. So in return for you silence, I will teach you the secrets of harnessing the magic for yourself."

He might be selfish, but it was likely their needs intersected.

"When will you teach me?" she asked. His words had ignited her excitement and imagination. She felt the budding gifts inside of her. If she could learn to use them...

"Now. I will start teaching you now. And I will teach you further after you have practiced what you learn. In return, you will safeguard my secret and not use it against me."

"But what if our aims are counter to each other's?" she asked. "I have loyalties that I must maintain." She did not wish to tell him that she was truly loyal to the king.

"My aim is the preservation of the kingdom of Ceredigion," he stated. "There must be an Argentine king on the throne." He looked emphatic.

"There is one now," she said. "And the mad king locked in the tower is also one. Who do you support?"

Tunmore shook his head. "It doesn't matter which. This game has its rules, my dear. There must be a king. If Eredur dies without a male heir, then I will support another taking his stead. The line must be preserved. It is imperative."

"For what?" she challenged.

He shook his head. "You cannot handle the full truth yet. You are only just discovering who you really are. Your role in all of this. Tell me, my dear. Do you have any habits that you do routinely? That bring you comfort and solace and allow your mind to wander free? Everyone who is Fountain-blessed must feed their power somehow. This would be something you've done since you were a child. Something that helps you think clearly, something—"

"There is," she said, interrupting him. "My mother taught me to stitch and sew. I like to do embroidery, to make things that are pleasing."

Tunmore looked exultant. "I thought so. Everyone who manifests power in the Fountain has something. This is the source of your power. This is a ritual you must safeguard throughout your life. It will replenish you. Imagine that the Fountain's power is like a well of water. Use too much and you will be bereft of your powers for a time. You must continue to practice your stitching, every day."

"But how will I know what gift I have?" she asked him.

Tunmore shrugged. "It will manifest itself in due time, my dear. The powers of the Fountain-blessed are limitless. The Wizr Myrddin could see the future. Read the stories and you will begin to see the various manifestations that are possible. You will need to try and understand your gift."

She felt confused and a little frustrated. "But how will I know?"

"Practice. That is the key. You may have the potential for multiple gifts. My advice is to practice your embroidery until you feel the power swelling inside you. Then . . . see where it takes you. Let it carry you away.

THE POISONER'S ENEMY

Water always makes its own path. Sometimes it stays in the known riverbanks. Sometimes it runs amok and carves new ground. Water is always changing. Practice your embroidery and see if you can sense the power building up inside you. Then come see me again and I will teach you how to unleash it."

He rose from the table and went to a bookshelf. He perused several titles before choosing one. "Start with this one. On the surface, it is a book of stories about our great King Andrew, but there are precepts in here that will teach you more about the power. As you read, listen for the Fountain. It will help you find the parts that will guide you. There are powerful words in this book, though only a Wizr could discover all of them." He handed it to her and she accepted it gratefully.

"Thank you, Deconeus," she said.

"Until we meet anew, Ankarette. It is my hope that we can remain allies through what happens next."

"What do you mean?"

He gave her an incisive look. "It's obvious to me that Warrewik is about to make his next move."

~

When Ankarette had left her home in Yuork as a child, she had ridden to Dundrennan behind Sir Thomas and clung to him the entire way. Now that she was older and skilled in riding, she had her own steed, but he was once again her companion. This time, however, they rode alone, and they traveled toward her mother rather than away from her. The ride to Marshaw was long enough that they would need to spend the night in Blackpool, and the long hours in the saddle gave Ankarette plenty of time to think. Though she and her mother had corresponded, this would be their first visit in years. So much had changed since they'd last seen each other...

Sir Thomas kept quiet for a time, leaving her to her thoughts, but as they neared Blackpool he struck up a conversation about the current affairs in Kingfountain. She found herself telling him about Warrewik's implied directive that she should murder the queen's offspring if it were a boy.

"What a burden to put on you," he said with disgust. "That man has no conscience left. There's no room for one anymore. His ambition has crowded out all else." They rode at a companionable gait, but Sir Thomas was always one to push on and make the horses suffer for the pace.

"He seems more eager than ever to put Dunsdworth on the throne," Ankarette said.

"Aye, you're right, especially with how he's pestering Eredur to let Dunsdworth marry Isybelle. How was your reunion with her?"

"All we talked about was Dunsdworth," Ankarette said sadly. "She's very devoted to him. I saw him in court. He does look more regal now. The elder Argentines are too handsome for their own good."

"You haven't taken a fancy to him yourself, have you?" he teased.

No, she wanted to say. *I have my eye on a man with a much lower station.*

She didn't deign to reply to his banter.

Sir Thomas cleared his throat. "There will be war soon, Ankarette. Just like I can see those clouds yonder and deduce we'll be soaked before reaching Blackpool, I can see the land will be drenched with blood ere long. If the queen has a boy, there won't even be time for the water rite before the duke unfurls his banners." He gave her an arch look. "And fighting against Warrewik means fighting the Espion as well. I'm glad you're on Eredur's side. You have a heart, Ankarette. I could tell that about you from the start. I still can."

So why do you keep trampling on it with your smiles, Sir Knight? she thought wistfully.

"Have you been back to Dundrennan often?" she asked, changing the subject.

"Oh, the duke has me riding hither and yon," he complained. "But yes, I try to steal there as often as I can. I'm more at home in the North than in Kingfountain."

A rumble of thunder sounded in the distance. The wind was picking up and blew her hair across her face.

"I hate being right so often," he said jokingly. "Best if we hurry, lass, before the roads turn to muck. Blackpool is just over that rise. Shall we race?"

"Do you think you can win?" she asked him brazenly, then stamped her horse's flanks.

CHAPTER 14
AMBITION

It was reckless, thrilling, and Ankarette won. By the time they reached Blackpool, they were soaked through and muddy from the mad dash. After they caught their breath, she commented on the smear of mud on his face kicked up from her stallion, and he wiped at it, smearing it more, and then flung some of it at her. It didn't matter—she was already stained.

Sir Thomas was gracious in defeat, although she could tell her victory had wounded his pride.

"Did they teach you riding in Pisan as well?" he asked her, chuffing.

"Of course," she said with a smile. "Escaping is a poisoner's specialty."

The pocked cobblestones were pooled with water from the deluge. She wiped strands of wet hair from her face, gazing around the gray-shrouded town for any sign of an inn. She had never been to this town before. It looked empty, but she knew the villagers were no doubt hunkered indoors, waiting out the winds and the torrent.

"If you're looking for a place to stay, do not trouble yourself," Sir Thomas said. "We'll be staying at the

Arthington. The owner is part of the Espion. He'll make sure we have a room. I've stayed there many times on my journeys."

Grateful for his knowledge, she held back and followed him to the inn. The Arthington was a two-story dwelling; the second story was constructed from square-cut timbers and plastered walls, and the bottom half was made of stone. There was a raised dais before the sturdy door, and a wooden sign announced the name of the place. The gutters were swollen with rain and overflowed all along the front, splashing noisily in the street. A few vines decorated the walls, but none of them appeared sturdy enough to climb. Her eyes were always searching for such details now. She imagined there were twenty to thirty rooms for patrons. A central chimney rose from the back and not even the steady rain could squelch the smoke pouring from it.

As they reached the main door and dismounted into the streets with a splash, the door opened and a youth of around twelve, head covered in a leather cap, hurried out and took their mounts for them.

"I'll give you a crown if you carry our saddlebags inside," Sir Thomas offered the boy—a commission the lad cheerfully accepted.

The door was wooden with iron bars across it. As they entered, the warmth from the common room greeted them, along with the yeasty smell of ale and buttered bread, and Ankarette's mouth began to water. Her hands were frigid and she chafed them together, trying to restore sensation to them.

The innkeeper, a man in his early thirties with a copper-colored beard and a receding hairline, greeted them warmly. "Sir Thomas! I see you got caught in the storm. Look at you both. Wet and muddy as dogs." He looked at her hand, saw the Espion ring there, and gave her a surreptitious nod. "Welcome, welcome. My stableboy Nicholas will tend to your horses and bring in your bags. Darcy will draw a bath for ye, and we'll get you warmed up fast and fed." He approached Ankarette and smiled warmly. "There are private rooms for the duke's men. And women. This is your first time at the Arthington. You'll be treated well."

"That's why we came," Sir Thomas said wearily.

An hour later, after cleaning off the mud and changing in their separate rooms, they sat cozily by the fireplace that fed the kitchen on the other side of the wall. The clatter of pots and squeak of a spit wheel provided a steady source of background noise, but music from the common room was tamped by the thick walls. The room was decorated with pleasing ornaments, showing a woman's caring touch.

The innkeeper, Miles, and his family joined them for a simple repast of meat and bread. He was garrulous, but his wife, Darcy, was very quiet and subdued, and Ankarette noticed a persistent cough that was worrisome. The two had a child, a sprightly little girl, and Darcy was clearly pregnant with the second.

Ankarette enjoyed both the food and the company. After their hosts went off to bed, she found herself watching Sir Thomas as he gazed into the crackling fire, lost in thought. He'd been more quiet than usual over dinner.

"Where are you tonight?" she asked him. They sat side by side on a couch, and she'd felt the growing urge to reach out and touch him. She finally did, intent on capturing his attention. Her fingers tingled at the contact.

He looked surprised, blinking quickly. Then he gave

her a sheepish smile and replied, "I do that often, unfortunately. What did you say?"

"You were lost in your thoughts. Where were you?"

He picked at his beard, gazing back at the fire. "Wishing, waiting, hoping," he answered in a jumble, shrugging. "I'm weary of racing from one end of the kingdom to the other, Ankarette. When I was a little younger, I thought the Espion was perfect for me. I never slept in the same bed twice, always moving with the duke and his company. I've been to many places and seen many things. I've fought in many battles. Enough for a lifetime. Tonight, I am weary of it." He sighed and set his hand down in his lap. She felt a deep longing to hold it, but fought the impulse.

"You have seen too much war," she said softly, trying to coax him to speak more. "Ceredigion is a violent land."

"Aye, that it is," he said, chuffing. "I look at Miles and Darcy and part of me just blazes with jealousy." He looked up at the ceiling rafters. "I would almost be content to be an innkeeper, to live in a warm, comfortable home like this one." Then he smiled self-deprecatingly. "*Almost*. Sadly, I have too much ambition. Or maybe it's the desire to live in the beehive rather than wander the fields looking for flowers. It's my greatest weakness. I have to be in the thick of it."

She kept silent, looking at him with keen interest. She had learned in the poisoner school that most people craved attention. Showing someone the smallest bit of interest could get them to reveal much about themselves. He glanced at her, found her a willing listener, and did just that.

"I'm tired of being someone else's man," Sir Thomas said in a low voice. "I have no doubt Warrewik appreciates me and my abilities. I have no doubt the king does as well. But I long to be someone in my own right." His eyes flashed with inner fire. "To give commands instead of only *obeying* them. I have no title of my own, nor will I. Being a second son is a curse. My brother will gain the earldom, and I don't think he appreciates the freedom it gives him. Being denied something makes you all the keener to have it." He shook his head. "I'm talking too much."

"I don't mind listening," Ankarette replied.

"You're a good friend," he said, smiling at her. "And I'm acting boorish. How many men would be jealous of what I have? My life is thrilling. There is always the promise of more excitement. I shouldn't complain. What about you, Ankarette? What is your ambition? You cannot say you do not have any. That would be a lie and we both know it. The reports from the school all said you did exceptionally well."

She blushed modestly and looked away. She did not like it when others focused on her. Especially him. "I've never had your ambition," she said, "and I could never become a lady, no matter how well I served the duke or the king."

"But...?" he encouraged.

"I suppose my ambition lies in creating a reputation for myself. When I lived back in Yuork, other girls my age talked about catching a husband one day. I felt a measure of pride in the work my mother trained me to do . . . and in being helpful to her, something she praised me for. I suppose I would like to win respect from those much older than me. That's my ambition, Sir Thomas."

He stared at her seriously, his eyes full of kindness. It made her squirm inside. "You did earn a reputation, even as a girl of twelve. It was part of what brought you to the duke's attention. And when I spied on you in Yuork, I agreed. I do have a knack for recognizing talent." He winked at her. "We are alike in many ways, Ankarette. We both serve two masters, although our true allegiance is to one. It is a dangerous walk. The suspense is brutal. How are you enduring it?"

"I endure it day by day, like you do," she said, folding her hands in her lap. "At the school, we were taught to kill with poison, but we were also taught to keep others alive. To protect. That is the aspect of the training I enjoyed best. How to recognize the symptoms of poison and administer a cure before the victim dies, how to heal wounds, and how to safely deliver a baby when the birth goes awry. I will try to save lives whenever possible, Sir Thomas, that's what I've promised myself. That's how I'll endure it." She was quiet for a moment, then she added, "There was a man spoken of quite a bit at the school. King Lewis's poisoner."

Sir Thomas's eyebrows lifted. "You know who it is? The Espion have tried to learn who he is for years."

She nodded. "His herald. Warrewik knows, though he clearly hasn't seen fit to tell anyone."

"Lord Hux?" Sir Thomas was dumbfounded.

"The very one. He has a fearsome reputation at the school, but his identity is cloaked in secrecy. Only the masters know who he is in truth. I guessed after his visit to Dundrennan, though, and he came to see me before I left Pisan."

"Did he try to recruit you?"

"Of course. I said no. But he made it clear that I'd be welcome in Occitania."

Sir Thomas nodded his head wonderingly. "You

didn't have to tell me this," he said. "It's dangerous that you did."

She smiled and shrugged. "I trust you."

He reached over and patted her hand. His touch felt very warm. "Dangerous for me, that is. But thank you, lass."

Her cheeks started to flush. She needed to shift the conversation, or her feelings would start to run away with her. "I'm grateful you're taking me to Marshaw. I miss my mother very much. But I must be honest with you, Sir Thomas, I'm worried about what will become of her. Duke Warrewik made it very clear, in his way, that her fate depended on my cooperation. What if the queen does have a son?"

He looked at her seriously. "I will make certain your mother is protected, Ankarette. You need not fear that."

"Yes, but how?" She wrung her hands. "Marshaw is far away from Kingfountain. Maybe Warrewik left orders..."

The door opened and another man walked in, his clothes dripping wet. Ankarette reached for her dagger out of reflex. The man's gaze landed on them for a moment, but he walked past their couch to the fire and crouched there to warm himself. Ankarette kept watch on him. His clothing didn't mark him as a man of importance, but he carried himself with confidence and skill. He was tall, weathered, and well-built, with close-shorn hair and a wide black mustache.

"What brings you so far north, Robert?" Sir Thomas asked, clearly recognizing the man. By the way he shifted on the couch, moving a little farther away from Ankarette, he did not trust him. She felt a pang of self-consciousness at this subtle distancing from her.

"The duke's business, of course," he replied in a

gravelly voice. He glanced at the two of them, his eyes mocking. "Thought you were loyal to Horwath's daughter."

Sir Thomas's eyes flared with anger and Ankarette experienced her own flush of heat from the man's rude comment. *Oh.*

"I am," Sir Thomas said tightly.

The man chuckled to himself, warming his hands. "Makes no difference to me," Robert said. "She's a pretty thing." He gave Ankarette a sly look. "A bit young, though."

Sir Thomas rose off the sofa, his eyes charged with rage. "Watch your words, man," he said threateningly.

The newcomer didn't look concerned at all. He sized up Sir Thomas and rose to his feet. He was taller. There was a look in his eye that told her he enjoyed goading Thomas. That, indeed, he was trying to goad him into a fight.

Rising from the sofa herself, she twisted her Espion ring in a nervous gesture and released the poisoned tip. "I've not met you before, Sir Robert," Ankarette said, touching his arm in a kindly way. "Where are you from?"

He looked startled, having felt the pain on his arm, the subtle sting of the needle. He looked at her, his eyes narrowing. And then he slumped onto the floor in a wet heap.

∽

AFTER RIFLING THROUGH HIS CLOTHES, they discovered his orders, written in the formian cipher. Sir Thomas crouched by his body, wagging the paper in his hand.

"What does it say?" Ankarette asked him.

He handed it to her. "See for yourself."

She quickly gazed at the document. The comatose Robert was snoring in a pool of drool by the fire. Sir Thomas stared down at the body and chuckled. "That poison worked very fast. What was it?"

"Pentha oil," she answered. "He'll be asleep for an hour or two." She finished reading the cipher. She had always been quick at it after learning the code in the poisoners' school.

The final note stopped her cold.

"Ah, you got to that part," Sir Thomas said, smiling worriedly.

She had. "He was ordered to spy on you," she said, frowning.

"To spy on *us*," he corrected. "He's going to Marshaw as well. To await further orders."

It did not take much imagination for her to make the leap. "Do you think he's there to hurt my mother?"

Sir Thomas looked at her seriously. "I think you were right about the duke, and he wants to make sure you stay loyal to him. Grab him by the boots. Let's get him on the couch."

CHAPTER 15
MARSHAW MANOR

They had left the poisoned Espion on the couch, and in the morning he was gone. Before leaving the inn, Ankarette provided the mistress with a healing tonic and promised it would help subdue her cough and strengthen her. She also inspected the woman's pregnancy and made a mental reminder to check on her in a few months to ensure all was well.

Rain continued to plague them after they left Blackpool, and they arrived in Marshaw soaked and cold. Despite the rain, her mother ran out to embrace her and hurried them up to their rooms.

The reunion between Ankarette and her mother was a mixture of delight, regret, and longing. Ankarette told her mother about her studies at a special school in Pisan, but she did not mention the other skills she had learned there. Her mother had always been a quiet woman, and she'd embraced her new role with dignity, earning respect from the household staff. There were many visitors, she said, and other families who sought out her friendship.

Ankarette was pleased to see her doing so well, but she could not stop thinking about the orders Robert had carried on his person. About the look in Duke Warrewik's eyes when he'd suggested this visit. She kept her concerns to herself, not wanting to make her mother worry. But the problem continued to nag at her.

The day after they arrived, the man they had met in Blackpool—Robert—arrived in the middle of a violent thunderstorm. The guest was not announced to her mother while Ankarette was in her presence, but Sir Thomas whispered the news into her ear. Apparently Marshaw was another Espion hideout, which could hardly be a coincidence.

She gave Sir Thomas an entreating look and asked if he would keep her mother occupied for a moment.

"Of course," he answered.

Ankarette had been stewing over what to do about Robert ever since that night at the inn. After spending some time with her needlework that morning, an idea had sprouted into her mind, followed by a little flush and ripple, which she now recognized as the Fountain's power. Since her conversation with the deconeus, she had been deliberate about her practice and had felt the magic respond accordingly, filling her up inside. It was during these moments when her thoughts were clearest.

She found Robert in the kitchen, drying by the fire. The cook had prepared a plate for him, and he was eating a crust of bread drizzled with honey when he finally noticed her standing behind him. He flinched, his eyes widening with an instant look of panic.

"Are you enjoying the food?" she asked him in a calm, deliberate voice as she circled around to face him.

He suddenly looked down at the bread, his eyes widening with suspicion. His nostrils flared. Then he set it back down on the plate. His dark hair was damp from the rain.

"You poisoned me in Blackpool," he growled in a low voice.

She looked him in the eye. Her voice was low and controlled and sincere. "That kind was rather harmless. It only made you sleep. There is another kind that can stop your heart beating. That death is very painful."

He swallowed the wad of bread that was still in his mouth.

She fixed him with her gaze. "I know you're a brave man. Sir Thomas has told me about you. I know you are not afraid to die, even a painful death."

She watched as he swallowed. He was trying to control himself, but she could see the effect her coldness was having on him. People gave off so many clues without intending to.

Ankarette shook her head slowly. "There are so many different kinds of poison, you see. Ones that can make you itch. Ones that can blind you. Don't cross me, Robert. There are fates worse than death."

He wiped his mustache, his eyes dancing with fear. He was a strong, well-built soldier. It was only natural he feared losing his health.

"You read my mission orders," he said accusingly.

She gave him a dimpled smile. "I only warn once," she said. She put every thought and feeling behind the threat. Her eyes narrowed, her lips were set in a firm line. She stood in front of him, and even though she was the smaller of the two by far, her posture was one of strength and dominance. All these ploys she had learned in the poisoner school. She had practiced them. And she knew what they could do.

There is no pain as awful as that of suspense. It was

a lesson from one of the masters of the school. He had once said that a victim could die *believing* they'd been poisoned even if they'd been given nothing but an innocuous powder. The belief that it was fatal could make it so. A person's mind was a powerful tool that could be used against them.

"I hear you," he grunted. His appetite seemed to have vanished.

Ankarette gave him a courteous nod and turned to walk away. She stopped, looking back at him over her shoulder, but not meeting his eyes—as if he was not worth looking at—and added, "Never tease Sir Thomas again in my presence."

She did not wait for an answer before leaving the kitchen. The cook, who had been watching them but had not heard them, jammed a spoon into a bowl and turned his back.

There were no more problems with Robert after that.

∽

The days spent at Marshaw were a pleasant reverie. Ankarette enjoyed taking rides with Sir Thomas and walking through the lush gardens with him. He commented within a day about Robert's sudden change of behavior, but she said nothing about how she had influenced it. She was pleased that he had noticed the shift.

She spent many evenings in long conversation with her mother, reminiscing about her father and asking for stories of him from childhood. She tested to see if her mother knew about her father's life in the Espion, but as far as Ankarette could tell, she did not. Though he'd kept some unusual habits, her mother did not seem to understand the reason behind it. And so Ankarette decided not to reveal the truth to her mother. She did not wish to spoil any of the memories her mother had of him, and the added intrigue would likely only injure her.

One day, during a garden walk, she shared with Sir Thomas the inner conflict that had been weighing on her. "If the queen does give birth to a son, do you think the duke will truly try to harm my mother?"

"What do you think?" he asked her, glancing over his shoulder to make sure they were alone in their walk.

"I don't think he actually would," Ankarette said seriously. "I think he means to threaten me only. To make me believe I have no choice... but I *do*. We always have a choice, Sir Thomas."

"Indeed," he replied with a small laugh. "I'm also sure it hasn't escaped Warrewik's notice that if he harmed your mother, you could harm *him*."

"That's the conclusion I keep coming to. I don't think he knows me well enough to risk it."

"He's not the sort of man who takes the time for that," he replied. "He trusts the judgment of those beneath him. His wealth puts him in a position to gain the best counsel. He's a crafty man, I'll give you that. But he has no idea our allegiance lies with the king."

She gave him a warning look. "Yet he sent Robert to spy on us."

"A precaution," Sir Thomas said dismissively. "You cannot read the history of Ceredigion without ample evidence that nobles like to betray one another. It's never wise to trust anyone too much."

Did he mean that about her as well?

"I hope you know, Sir Thomas, that you can count on me."

He was quiet for a moment and the only sound was the rustling of the hedges where a bird was either trapped or hunting an insect. The silence unnerved her. She wanted to look at his face to judge his reaction, but she feared what she might see there. If only she could take back the impetuous statement...

He stopped in his tracks, which startled her. She paused and turned to face him. He was very serious, his eyes quite intense.

"Ankarette, you do realize that I've trusted you with my life, don't you? You've known almost since you came to Dundrennan that I was working for Eredur. I've trusted you from the start."

The problem with sincere praise and sympathy, she knew objectively, was how it could make someone feel. His words were like honey to her. They were deliciously sweet and she adored him all the more for saying them. A little heat began to flush her cheeks.

"Thank you," she said, turning away so he wouldn't see her blush. She did not like it when her face betrayed her. Her heart was giddy with feelings, but she reined them in, imposing her self-will on them. It was not impossible for the second son of an earl to marry someone beneath his station, but she was only fifteen and he likely still saw her as a child. She had no intention of marrying. It was not safe for someone with her training.

All this she knew with her head. But her heart felt differently.

The noise of someone approaching caught their attention.

"Sir Thomas!" someone called.

"Aye! Over here!" he answered back. In a moment, a young man came running up with a folded note. "A ship has come from Kingfountain," the lad said urgently. "The messenger just arrived."

Sir Thomas frowned and took the note. Breaking the seal, he read it quickly. His face paled. "The queen is not doing well. The doctors fear her labor may start at any moment."

The queen had not been expected to give birth for another month.

∼

THE FASTEST PATH from Marshaw to the palace was not by horse but by ship. A ship from the royal fleet in the docks of Blackpool was ready to set sail immediately on delivery of the message. Ill weather made the voyage miserable, but the wind was behind them and helped blow the way home. The sudden and unseasonal turn in the weather amplified the anxiety Ankarette already felt.

Ankarette brought her mother with them. An early labor was always perilous. Her mother's experience might prove useful... and Ankarette would also be able to keep an eye on her and ensure her safety.

Even though they made all haste, they did not reach the palace until the following day, and Ankarette feared she had come too late. The duke's men awaited them at the docks and they were rushed to the palace. Warrewik was pacing with the king outside the birthing chamber, his eyes wide with concern, almost frantic. The king was agitated, his face drawn with worry and concern. When the duke saw Ankarette, he seemed utterly relieved.

"There! There you are!" Then he noticed her mother coming up behind her and his eyes went livid.

Eredur stared at Ankarette in near panic.

"What happened?" Ankarette asked. "I got very little of use out of the messenger."

"I will take her in," Eredur said.

"No!" the duke said. "The air is toxic in there. You are the king. You cannot be compromised. She is the best-trained midwife in the kingdom, Your Majesty. Her mother was one of the best in Yuork. Let them do their work." He gave her a piercing look, one that was half-threatening, half-fearful and promised retribution if he was not obeyed.

"I will go," Ankarette said. She clasped the king's hands. "We'll do our best."

"There are thirteen other midwives in there already," Warrewik said, posturing. "Only one is useful... you'll know which. Send the rest out."

Ankarette squeezed her mother's hand and they both went into the birthing chamber. The smell of blood in the air was sickening, but she was used to it. There were indeed thirteen midwives, but most were fretting and pacing and looking helpless. There were linen sheets and bowls of water and wine. The queen was pale, writhing on the bed in nothing but a sweaty shift. A single midwife stood still at her bedside, whispering soothingly to her.

The woman turned as they approached. "I've done all that I know to do," she said, wringing her hands. "The babe won't come. It's too soon."

Ankarette quickly judged the queen's complexion. She was shivering, her lips mouthing incoherent words. She writhed in pain, but her eyelids were sluggish. She looked bloated and swollen.

"How long has she labored?" Ankarette asked,

trying to judge the danger of the situation. It was desperate.

"Almost two days," the midwife said.

Two days like this. Two days and still no progress. The queen was going to die. And so would the child.

Ankarette's mother pressed the flat of her hand against the queen's forehead. "It's not a fever." She squeezed the queen's wrist and let go. The skin remained indented. "I think it's eclampsia. It strikes fast."

Ankarette swallowed. She'd had the same thought. "Did the queen become disoriented and confused?"

"Aye," said the midwife. "She was raving about the babe. Said someone wanted to kill it. She kept calling for Ankarette. Is that you?"

"Send the others away," Ankarette said, nodding curtly. "You stay."

Her mother knelt by the queen, who gripped her hand. The other midwives were rushed from the room.

"Mother?" Ankarette whispered, her throat tugging with emotion.

"It's eclampsia," her mother said with certainty. "I'm sure of it. I've seen it many times. She won't survive."

The other midwife stifled a sob and then nodded in agreement. "It's been my fear as well. I have seen many women die of this. She was so healthy. I don't know what happened."

Ankarette was torn up inside. She was desperate to save the queen and her babe. The fire was blazing in the hearth and still the queen shivered.

Ankarette knelt by her bedside.

The queen's lashes fluttered. "Ankarette?"

"I'm here, Elyse," she said. Her mother and the other midwife stared at her in horror for using the queen's familiar name, but she kept her focus on the queen.

The queen's face relaxed somewhat. "Something's wrong. It feels wrong. I'm ... I'm ... all twisted inside. Eredur. Help. Nnnnggg!" She writhed again, her words becoming unintelligible.

"There's nothing I can do," her mother said. "It may take hours still."

The other midwife started sobbing into her apron.

Ankarette thought deeply. Squeezing the queen's hand, she opened herself to the Fountain's magic, listening for its soft murmurs past the ragged breathing. Her magic was with her, nearly full to the brim. Was there a way she could use it to save them?

Suddenly, the thoughts and images flooded into her mind. And then she knew ... only someone with the dual knowledge of life and death taught at the poisoner school in Pisan could save the queen, for saving her would mean carving into her body. It had been done before, and in rare cases, both mother and child survived. It required stitching and deft hands. Her mother's ability with stitching was unequalled, to Ankarette's mind, so perhaps they had a chance ...

She looked at the other two women. "We need to open up her womb. We need to bring the babe out ourselves. 'Tis our only chance. I've never done this before, but I've heard of it."

The other midwife looked at her in horror. "It cannot be done!"

"It can," Ankarette said with certainty. "Otherwise, she will certainly die. At least this will give them the *chance* to live."

Her mother looked at her sternly. "Did you learn this in Pisan?"

She nodded with determination. "Trust me, Mother. I need your help."

"Show us what to do."

~

HOURS LATER, drenched with sweat and blood, Ankarette held the tiny pink infant in the swaddling blanket. The gray goo of birth had been wiped away, and the piercing squeals from the babe's healthy lungs were like music to her ears. Her mother had just finished stitching the queen's wound. Elyse had fainted from the pain multiple times, but she'd endured the procedure with extraordinary courage. The swelling had begun to subside as soon as the babe was removed.

Ankarette's heart was full as she gazed at the trembling babe. She held the bundle close, breathing in that strange moist smell of fresh life. She cried, her feelings overwhelming her. Tears dropped onto the babe's face and the downy tufts plastered to the little head, starting another round of wailing. Ankarette laughed through her sobs, savoring the delicious sound. She had saved their lives. But it was the Fountain that had shown her the way, had nearly directed her hands. She was exhausted.

The other midwife wiped her hands on her blood-stained apron. "You did it, lass. I've never seen such a trick. Bless me that I was here to see this miracle. Maybe this little one is Fountain-blessed?"

Ankarette nuzzled the babe's cheek with her nose. "Let the king in now."

The midwife grinned and obeyed. Eredur nearly flew in like an arrow shot from a bow the instant the door was opened. His face was full of despair and worry. A storm had raged outside the palace, the rain lashing viciously at the windows. Another unseasonable storm.

One look at Ankarette's face changed the king's expression from utter misery to hope.

"They both made it," Ankarette said triumphantly.

The duke was there next, his eyes taking in the bloody scene with confusion.

Eredur saw the babe in her arms and reached out his arms eagerly and awkwardly. She delivered the child to the father.

"What is it?" the duke asked in desperation.

"She's a girl," Ankarette replied happily. A war had been averted that afternoon. The duke looked relieved, though maybe a little disappointed that both mother and child had survived.

"She's a miracle," Eredur whispered, staring at his daughter, laughing to himself.

"Your wife is the bravest woman I know," Ankarette said, the weariness taking hold of her. "She'll be abed for days, but I have hope she will recover quickly."

Eredur cast his gaze at his unconscious wife and partner. The tenderness in his eyes was touching. He looked like a man brought back from the brink. "Aye, she is," he answered with a catch in his throat. The storm was tapering off and a few gleams of sunlight lit up the droplets on the window. So strange that the storm had ended at that very moment.

The king looked back at the girl. The babe was so tiny, so frail, and she quivered with startled reflexes. When he brushed her hand with his finger, she gripped it, clinging hard.

"We'll call her Elyse," he whispered with tears. "After her courageous mother."

After saving the queen's life and the life of the princess, I spent most of the following year traveling with the duke's family between Dundrennan and Kingfountain.

Isybelle was hopelessly in love with the king's brother. I believed his affection for her was genuine as well, although it was difficult to judge whether he could love any person more than he loved himself.

The hostility between Warrewik and the queen's father grew. Through the spy holes in the Espion tunnels, I witnessed their verbal clashes growing more heated. Eredur did his best to juggle the animosity between the men, but the more he raised up the queen's kin as his allies, the more he threatened Warrewik's position. Warrewik was very popular among the people. His liberality with his wealth ensured this.

I was sixteen when the Duke of Warrewik finally rebelled against Eredur.

— ANKARETTE TRYNEOWY

PART THREE
THE KING'S PROTECTOR

PART THREE

CHAPTER 16
REBELLION

The dance of politics was a delicate one. Delicate and deadly. Or so Ankarette observed as the confrontation loomed between her duke and her king. In the year following the birth of the princess, Eredur and Warrewik had continued to dance against each other. Each turn had increased the power of the queen's family at the expense of the duke's, and yet Warrewik still controlled the largest of the king's armies, the garrison at Callait, and despite all of Eredur's efforts to wrest it from his control, he had been unsuccessful.

Ankarette spent more time at Kingfountain than at Dundrennan because that was where the duke had decided to spend the majority of his time in order to protect his interests. The duchess and her daughters had then taken up residence in the palace, and Warrewik was constantly sequestered in the Star Chamber, issuing orders to the Espion and warning the king that the mad king's wife, Morvared, was once again plotting to usurp the throne.

Every day the palace was filled with tension as uncle

and nephew locked wills. The biggest clash between them was no longer Callait, however—it was Eredur's refusal to let his brother marry the duke's daughter.

Ankarette found the presence of Dunsdworth in her lady's chamber increasingly intrusive, and Isybelle's wits were scattered by her persistent suitor. Ankarette was their chaperone and she felt the need to constantly be on her guard.

One scorching summer day, when tempers inside the palace had grown raw, Dunsdworth suggested they walk the gardens and find some shade. There was one garden that had fledgling magnolia trees interspersed with tall cypresses. A fountain bubbled nearby and the heat and stickiness of the air made Ankarette long to jump into it.

Dunsdworth and Isybelle were talking just ahead, Ankarette trailing behind. They were close enough that their hands frequently touched.

Then Dunsdworth came to a sudden, jarring stop, picked up a seed pod from the tree, and hurled it at the gurgling fountain. The pod landed with a splash and the young duke grinned fiercely at his deliberate act of sacrilege.

Isybelle looked at him in surprise and muffled a laugh. "You shouldn't do that, Dunne!"

"I can't help it," the young duke said, shaking his head and clenching his fists. He was very expressive, very attentive to his own feelings. "Sometimes I am so angry with Eredur that I could strike him. He chose his own bride. Yet he will not allow me to choose my own. I want *you*, Belle!"

The look he gave her was full of heat, and Isybelle's eyelashes fluttered at the bald declaration of love. His words tortured her, Ankarette could see, because she desperately wanted him too. She pined for him when he was not with her. Wrote him love notes, which she then burned in the fire. Some days she was utterly miserable; other days, she was so giddy that Ankarette thought the girl would burst. Ankarette's attachment to Sir Thomas had only grown, so she understood her friend's torment. But she would never reveal her feelings for him to anyone. It was a secret she was determined to keep.

"You know I share your wish," Isybelle said forlornly. "But Papa said we must be patient."

"Hang being patient!" Dunsdworth moaned. "What would Eredur do if we married in secret? Would he send me over the falls? I don't think so. He married in secret to suit his fancy. And look who he chose? A woman whose relations are so grasping, they've snatched up every crumb on the table. It sickens me, Belle, truly. The king treats your father with miserable contempt after all he has done for him!"

"Shhh!" Isybelle said soothingly, touching his arm. She liked to touch him, and her gestures were becoming more and more familiar and tender. "Someone may hear you."

"Who? One of the Espion? I have nothing to fear from them. They're on our side."

"Maybe not all of them," Isybelle warned. She glanced around the garden, but it was just the three of them. Then she looked up at his face with adoration. She was so smitten by his handsome looks, his wavy auburn hair. She'd crafted poems about his features, only to commit those to the flames as well.

They drew near the fountain. Sweat trickled down Ankarette's back. Her gown was so heavy and tight...

She remembered in a rush what it had felt like to jump off that boulder in the North. If only she could return to that moment, standing next to Sir Thomas at the edge of the rock. This time, she would accept his offer to jump together.

Dunsdworth plopped down at the edge of the fountain and leaned his head back. "It's so hot! When will this cursed summer end?"

Isybelle stood by, gazing down at him and hesitating. He patted the stone bench next to him, inviting her to sit, and she smiled with pleasure. But when she turned to lower herself to the fountain, Dunsdworth suddenly grabbed her waist and pulled her onto his lap, startling her.

"Dunne!" she said, gasping with surprise, and started to squirm to get away. He smiled at his trick and held her back, wrapping his arms around her. He pressed his nose against her back.

"That tickles—stop!" She halfheartedly tried to rebuff him. There was a smile of pleasure on her mouth.

Ankarette had seen him take many liberties before, but this was well beyond anything she'd witnessed. She was in a difficult situation. Dunsdworth was a man she did not wish to offend. He was handsome, ambitious, and felt he deserved to be the king. If something happened to Eredur, he was the next in line for the throne. The thought of serving as his poisoner filled her with desolation. She had seen plenty of evidence herself that Eredur's assessment of his brother's cruelty and tendency toward revenge was justified.

"My lord," Ankarette warned softly.

"She's right," Isybelle said, and he let her go. "I don't want any rumors to start." Her cheeks were flushed and her hands trembled as she got to her feet. She gazed at him longingly, her heart in her eyes. Ankarette wished her friend would be more circumspect.

"Hang the rumors." He leaned back and cupped some water in his hand and then splashed her with it. "And hang tradition! We're meant for each other, Belle." The water stained the front of her dress and she backed away lest he become more playful. Ankarette would tell Eredur, as she always did, in the middle of the night. Their flirtations were getting more and more pronounced. It was time to order Dunsdworth back to his duchy.

"I care for you too, Dunne," she said, biting her lip. "As this Fountain is my witness. Let me throw in a coin. A wish."

"Water does not grant wishes," he said with a chuckle. His eyes were burning with feeling. Was it lust? Love? Ambition? It wasn't clear which.

"Don't say those things," she chided.

"I say what I feel," he answered, rising from the bench. She backed away from him with a playful shake of her head.

"Why does he keep us apart!" he said with aching need. "He cannot have you for himself, so his intention can only be to stop me from having what I desire. He does it out of spite." His eyes began to burn with hatred. "Why does he toy with me like this? He shares counsel with our brother, Severn, who is only sixteen. He's not even finished growing yet. And I've seen how close he and your sister are . . . if he asks to marry her when they're older, I think Eredur will agree! I do!"

"He's the king," Isybelle reminded him. "He can do as he wishes."

Dunsdworth shook his head. "He shouldn't be," he mumbled.

"You cannot say things like that," she said. Ankarette agreed. He had already crossed the line of proper decorum. He did it habitually, it seemed.

Ankarette noticed movement and saw Sir Thomas striding toward them, an agitated look on his face. Had he been watching them surreptitiously and decided enough was enough? Ankarette felt a little blush of shame. Should she have done more to prevent it?

"Sir Thomas is coming," Ankarette warned in a low voice.

"Hang Sir Thomas as well," Dunsdworth chuckled, repeating his favorite phrase. He looked in Isybelle's eyes with an almost feverish intensity. "Soon, my love. Soon. I promise you."

"How can you promise that?" Isybelle said. "The king will not relent."

"Have faith in me, Belle," he said with a cunning smile. "Save your coins from rust. Put your *trust* in me."

Ankarette had to give him credit. He was a capable wooer.

Sir Thomas arrived shortly thereafter, slightly out of breath. "The duke needs to see you," he said to Dunsdworth. "A rebellion has started in the North."

Isybelle gasped, but Dunsdworth did not seem at all surprised by the news.

"What has happened?" Isybelle asked.

"Your father will tell you more. There is a man who says that Eredur is not the true king, that the Fountain wants the mad king to reign again. His name is *Robert* Conyers."

Sir Thomas gave Ankarette a knowing look as he said it. Was this the same man they had met on the way to Marshaw? She assumed it was, but what did that mean? Was Warrewik finally making his move?

"A rebellion?" Dunsdworth scoffed. But his tone was unconvincing.

"Aye," Sir Thomas answered. "The king wants you to return to your lands to raise up soldiers to defend the realm," he told him. "The duke will be going to Callait to ready the garrison in case they are needed. The king has called on the Dukes of Westmarch and Southport to help him put the rebellion to rest."

"Not Warrewik?" Dunsdworth said. "He's the most experienced battle commander next to the king."

"He is, 'tis true. The Espion say this plot was hatched by Morvared in Occitania. We have her husband in Holistern Tower and she has few resources where she is. It's a desperate gambit on her part, but Eredur is decisive. He wants to crush the rebellion before it spreads. Some like the idea of playing with fire."

He gave Dunsdworth a pointed look as he said it.

Dunsdworth folded his arms. "If my brother commands it, I will obey."

~

LATER THAT EVENING, the duke's state room was bustling with activity. The duke looked especially agitated. "We're all going to Callait," he told his wife and daughters. "I want you near me during the rebellion. Sir Thomas, tell the king that we will leave with the tide this evening."

"Aye, my lord," Sir Thomas said. "Shall I go ahead and warn Vauclair that you're coming?"

The duke shook his head. "There is no time. I want you with Eredur, Sir Thomas. Stay with the king's army.

There will probably be a battle, and your experience at Mortimer's Cross will be invaluable. I want you to meet up with the Duke of Clare's army and advise him. Go."

Sir Thomas bowed, but Ankarette could tell he wasn't pleased by the prospect of waiting on and protecting Dunsdworth.

After he was gone, the duke turned to Ankarette. "You are not coming with us to Callait, my dear."

Isybelle looked genuinely shocked. "Why not, Father? I need Ankarette near me."

He shook his head no. "You will have to do without her for a short season. Ankarette, I'm leaving you here because I received word that we're expecting the herald of Occitania to arrive shortly. You've met Lord Hux before, so you know what he looks like. You delivered a message to me from him if you recall."

"Very well," she answered, her stomach churning.

He looked at her pointedly. "I don't know why he's coming. But you need to be here to protect the king. This rebellion, if it's being instigated by Queen Morvared, may be more dangerous than it appears. Up until now, King Lewis has not acted openly against Eredur. This might signal a change in that policy. You will stay at Kingfountain and keep your eye on Lord Hux when he arrives. I'll have Sir Thomas leave several Espion for you to command. Now get your things packed, Isybelle. We will be leaving for the docks shortly."

~

THE NEWS of the Occitanian poisoner's arrival put Ankarette in an anxious mood. She found Sir Thomas and shared what she'd learned.

"I hadn't heard he was coming," he said worriedly

as they walked down the main corridor of the palace. He flashed her a concerned glance. "Who would you like to keep with you? You can have the best."

"Are you worried about me, Sir Thomas?" she asked him with a smile.

"Of course. Hux is dangerous. I'd rather stay here and help you than ride north and play nursemaid to Dunsdworth as he wets his sword for the first time." He snorted derisively. "Wait until he experiences his first battle. It'll lose its savor soon enough. Who do you want assigned to stay behind?"

"How about Bennet and Durke?"

Thomas pursed his lips. "Good choices, both of them." He fixed her with his gaze. "If Hux tries *anything*, take him out of the game."

"You're quite agitated, Sir Thomas."

"You noticed that?" he quipped. "Of course. War is a fog, Ankarette. You can't see your hand before your face. Is Warrewik behind this rebellion? Robert Conyers? He fought at Mortimer's Cross too. Is he under orders, or did the Occitanians bribe him? When there's a fire in the fields, it's best to stamp it out fast ere it spreads. Eredur is wise to send Warrewik to Callait. It gets him out of position."

"I agree. But Warrewik is no fool," Ankarette said. "I'm not sure what he's planning, but this doesn't feel right."

"I agree with you wholeheartedly, lass. When nobles squabble and kings fight, there are plenty of daggers that slash. Let me know if you learn anything after I'm gone. I'll do the same for you." He gave her a hopeful smile. "You've got my back, lass. Right?"

"And you have mine," she answered, feeling a flush

of warmth in her heart. "I'll watch the South. You watch the North."

"Back to back," he said as they passed a smoking set of torches. He reached out and patted her shoulder in a friendly way. And she felt her blood sizzle at his touch.

CHAPTER 17
THREAT

With Sir Thomas sent away and one of Warrewik's lieutenants running the Espion in his absence, it was up to Ankarette to keep the king informed. She hardly slept in anticipation of Lord Hux's arrival. Being the king's herald gave Hux unparalleled access to foreign courts. Refusing to let him come could be seen as enough of an affront to declare war. She had interviewed the king's cook, a short and energetic woman named Liona, and was convinced the woman was trustworthy. The cook had vowed to deliver all the royal family's meals personally and not entrust the task to underlings. Her husband was one of the castle woodsmen and he was also put on his guard to watch for strangers or anything untoward.

The Espion had tripled the guard on Holistern Tower, and Ankarette had even inspected the mad king's rooms herself. His unintelligible mutterings always made her feel uneasy in his presence. Ankarette spent her mornings inspecting the royal bedchambers and memorizing where everything was and where it belonged. Her task was to make sure that anything out of place would be quickly identified. She was in the middle of one such inspection when Bennet informed her that Lord Hux had arrived. She hadn't needed to be told. She had sensed his presence herself.

In preparation for Lord Hux's arrival, she had focused on her embroidery, keeping her stores of Fountain magic full at all times. In her year's tutelage to John Tunmore, she had awakened that part of herself that had been dormant before. Her magic would assist her against the Occitanian poisoner. Now that she knew about the power they shared, it would be more difficult for him to act in her presence.

When the news arrived, Ankarette hurried down to the audience hall where the king would receive Lord Hux. As part of her plan, Espion disguised as palace servants had already been dispatched to the hall. She met with Durke just outside the entryway.

"Is all prepared?" she asked, trying not to fidget.

Durke was a handsome man, very tall, and caught the eye of most of the ladies at court. He was a capable spy and quite a charming courtier. "It is, Ankarette. Hux won't be able to use the garderobe without us knowing it. Do you think he will try to assassinate the king in person?"

Ankarette shook her head. "That is not his style. He would never do something so brazen. Where is the king?"

"'Tis as you've planned. He's in the stables preparing to ride out to join the Duke of Westmarch. The queen will meet with Hux."

Ankarette nodded. "Very good. We will watch Hux like a hawk and see what he does. If he goes after the king, we hunt him down."

Durke smiled broadly. "I think your strategy is sound, Ankarette. Hux will be forced to react, which will give us the advantage. The Espion at the sanctuary will notify me as soon as the king has left the city."

"Well done. Let's go inside."

Durke opened the door for her, and Ankarette entered. The room was full of lords and ladies of the realm. Talk of the rebellion was on everyone's mind since Warrewik had left and the hall was unusually boisterous. Ankarette spied the queen talking to Lord Hastings, the king's chancellor, who would ride off later and inform the king about how the conference had gone. Ankarette glided through the hall, sensing that Lord Hux was standing outside the doors, waiting to be admitted. The doormen waited for Ankarette's signal.

After maneuvering through the crowd, Ankarette was within the queen's line of sight. Queen Elyse immediately excused herself from Lord Hastings and mounted the dais to the twin thrones at the head of the hall. Ankarette stayed by the serving table, making it so the queen could see her—and so Lord Hux could not. She nodded to the queen.

"Allow him in," the queen said to Lord Hastings. She fidgeted on the throne just a moment before assuming a tranquil pose. She was very good at masking her disquiet. Ankarette admired her poise—the crown blazed on her golden hair like fire.

The two sentries posted at the door obeyed the order and the doors groaned as they opened. Ankarette counted the Espion in the room once more as she waited for the poisoner to enter. She thought twelve would be enough to overwhelm one man.

Lord Hux strode in confidently with a beaming smile. He bowed respectfully to some of the lords and ladies, addressing them by name as if familiar acquaintances. His hair was combed forward in the Occitanian fashion and he wore a ceremonial saber at his waist. It was more ornamental than dangerous, but it still caught Ankarette's eye. No doubt he sensed her presence, as she did his, but he did not turn to look for her. Instead, he marched up to the queen and made a gracious, formal bow.

"Your Majesty," he said with an elegant accent. "It is indeed an honor to stand before you."

"You grace us with your presence," the queen replied formally. "How fares the Queen of Occitania?"

"Quite well, I assure you," he answered, rubbing his hands together. He bowed again. "You are so kind to ask."

"I pray, forgive me for bearing sad news, but the king has already left to subdue the rebels. He will not be able to hear your message in person, but I am here to preside on his behalf."

Ankarette watched him closely for a sign of reaction. How would he betray his surprise? This would teach her something about him.

Lord Hux bowed again, completely unaffected. "It is only right that the king should disband the rabble himself. He is without peer on the battlefield, they say."

"Some say, Lord Hux," the queen continued, "that this rebellion was instigated by one of your countrywomen. Lady Morvared?" It was said in an accusatory tone. Again, Ankarette was impressed with how well the queen was following her instructions. She was seeing her own plan unfurl before her.

Again, Hux was unflustered. "Idle rumors, Your Majesty. Dame Morvared is not supported by the King of Occitania, my master. She and her young son live humbly with her father in one of his manors in the countryside."

THE POISONER'S ENEMY

The mad king's son, whom many believed had not even been sired by him, was nearly Ankarette's own age. Some still called him a prince of the blood, though, and there was little question he was more fit to rule than his father. He never left his mother's presence.

"If any evidence arises that the rumors are *true*," Queen Elyse said in a warning tone, "it would be an affront to our sovereignty and would yield dangerous consequences."

"Naturally," Lord Hux replied with a pleasant and genial smile.

After a few more exchanges, Lord Hux related his message, which was simply that King Lewis of Occitania offered any assistance should the King or Queen of Ceredigion require it. That there should be no concern whatsoever about Occitania's allegiance with Eredur.

After a time, the conversation ended and the queen suggested the herald spend the night at the palace before returning promptly to his master with her forthcoming response. He bowed graciously, giving her a languid, peaceful smile. Ankarette fumed silently as the hall was once more livened with talk. The man had revealed absolutely nothing about himself or his true aim.

Several nobles tried to engage Lord Hux in conversation, but he dismissed himself quickly, pleading the need for some refreshment. And then he was walking toward her, deliberately and directly. Her pulse began to quicken. She was standing by one of the food tables, and he approached it, gazing at the variety of cheeses and fruit gathered on the trays. She maneuvered herself so that the table was between them.

"It's a pleasure to meet you again, my dear," he said

under his breath, his hand pausing and changing direction many times as he chose what he wanted.

"Welcome to Kingfountain," she answered curtly.

"I find the reception a little cool," he answered, then popped a grape into his mouth.

"What else did you expect?" she replied with a smile.

He turned and faced her, and a smile lit his face. Not his careless, friend of all humanity smile, but a cunning, mischievous one. "Everything, my dear. Everything. You forget how much we Occitanians love the game Wizr. I am always planning my next moves well in advance. I hope you are as well. The offer is still open to join my king."

She controlled her surprise and annoyance enough to give him a noncommittal shrug. "Thank you, but no."

"You might change your mind," he said in an offhanded manner. His gaze met hers. "Once Dunsdworth is king. Imagine taking orders from *him*." He snorted disdainfully.

Ankarette felt her insides crawling with worms, but she kept her face neutral. "I find it an unlikely possibility."

Lord Hux popped another grape down his gullet. "Not as good as what we grow on the vines in the valley of Orle. Well, my work is done. I'll return to Pree with the tide and report to my master that it all went perfectly."

She narrowed her gaze at him.

"Really, my dear. You are so innocent. You have so much to learn. I will be your mentor in the subtle art of deception." He scratched the corner of his mouth with a well-trimmed nail. "Dunsdworth and Isybelle were married in Callait. Your own Espion put him on board the duke's ship ere he sailed. My purpose in coming to Kingfountain was only to keep *you* distracted. By focusing on my arrival as a threat, you blinded yourself to the truth. Warrewik is returning with the garrison of Callait, the largest army in Ceredigion. His forces from Dundrennan are on the march even now. If Eredur thinks Kiskaddon's force will be sufficient to defeat Warrewik's, well then, he is less savvy than he pretends to be.

"Eredur will fight. And he will lose. Threat. Mate. Farewell, my dear. The invitation to you still stands as you watch the board change hands. The King of Occitania would much prefer to see Dunsworth sitting there." He wagged his little finger toward the throne. "Oh, and by the way—there are more ciphers than the formian one. You delivered my little plan to the duke with the letter you brought here for me ages ago. This is how it's done, my dear. Learn the lesson well."

~

ANKARETTE'S HEART pounded as fast as her steed's hooves. She and Lord Hastings rode through the countryside at reckless speed. They changed mounts at every town they passed, going so fast at times she thought they were flying. Ankarette had not even changed her gown or donned a cloak. She'd assumed Hux's worst news was true and urged the queen to seek sanctuary at Our Lady. Then she and Hastings had rushed away to try to avert the impending disaster.

Her insides coiled and writhed, making her sick with dread. She worried about Sir Thomas. He had been sent to join Dunsworth...

Did Warrewik suspect him of disloyalty? She had

every reason to believe that he was faithful to the king, and if he had known of the duke's plot, he would have told Eredur. Would Warrewik have him bound and thrown into the river when he returned?

She wept as they rode, tears flying from her cheeks. At the poisoner school, they had said that most poisoners did not survive the first year of service. Careless mistakes could be costly. She grieved for the king and the queen, for their daughter, for her mother at Marshaw, for Thomas. She would save them if she could. But how? What could she do?

She and Hastings had hoped to catch up to Eredur on the journey, but he was riding just as fast as they were and applying the same technique of switching out his horse. It wasn't until just past nightfall that they caught up to him at an inn in the town of Keens. He was with his household knights and they were just beginning to enjoy the feast that had been provided for his men.

"Tell the king I need to speak to him in his room," Ankarette said urgently to Hastings, her nerves fraying. "You keep his knights distracted. I don't wish to be seen."

"Aye, lass," the chancellor said, scratching his long blond mustache.

Ankarette didn't know which room was the king's, so she waited in the shadows and watched as Hastings found the king and whispered in his ear. Eredur nodded curtly and then raised a quick toast before announcing he needed to use the privy to be able to drink more ale. The banter earned him some guffaws, which followed him as he walked to the stairs and conferred with the innkeeper. Ankarette watched as they mounted the stairs together. Something compelled her to wait, to study the scene before acting, and it did not take her long to realize why. One of the knights rose and started to follow them.

Ankarette pursued the knight at a distance, her heart pounding. Her thighs were a little sore from the saddle, but she was an experienced rider now. The knight walked soundlessly, Espion-style, toward the door through which the king and the innkeeper had disappeared. He paused there, and Ankarette stole up behind him, twisting her ring to expose the needle.

He must have sensed her, for he turned sharply just as she reached him. She gripped his arm and pricked him with the needle. Had he seen her face?

His eyes rolled back in his head and he slumped to the ground. The door of the king's room swung open and the innkeeper pushed out his head.

"What's the racket?" he scolded, and then he saw the slumped soldier and her standing there.

"It's all right, Lamb. She's with me." Eredur's voice was firm and knowing.

The innkeeper dismissed himself, trying not to trip on the body, which he regarded with wide eyes.

Ankarette closed the door and quickly told him everything that had happened and what Lord Hux had admitted to her. His complexion grew pale with fear as she spoke. He was stunned, surprised beyond measure. Eredur began to pace the well-furnished room. It was certainly the best room in the entire place, with a fancy four-post bed and clean sheets.

"I'm sorry to bring these ill tidings," she said anxiously.

"No, no—don't be," he answered. He stared at the floor, horror-stricken. He bit on the edge of his finger. "You told me everything you knew. We all suspected the poisoner was sent to kill me, which was why I agreed to this plan. I knew Warrewik was determined, but this . . . this shows treachery that goes much deeper than I suspected. He intends to win." His countenance fell. "My uncle intends to kill me."

Ankarette longed to comfort him. But what could she say? They both knew the situation was bleak. The duke would ride fast and hard. If his soldiers from Dundrennan weren't almost to Kingfountain, then the garrison from Callait would surely arrive soon.

"How did he keep this secret for so long?" Eredur wondered aloud. "Thomas knew nothing. You knew nothing. Who did he trust? Who did he tell?"

"I don't know," Ankarette said. "Clearly he's been scheming with King Lewis."

"Rather successfully, it appears!"

Ankarette's misery was acute. "I'm sorry. I wish I could have prevented this."

Eredur began pacing again. "I thought . . . I just thought that Warrewik would have done this more . . . honorably. There's a tradition when rebelling against a king. You rise up in arms. You don't use tricks or decoys, like that Robert Conyers fellow. I had hoped to build up enough power to best him on the battlefield. He's always had the upper hand. But this . . . this is knavery. I didn't think he would stoop to it."

An idea began to sprout in Ankarette's mind. "What did you say?"

Eredur looked at her in confusion. "I didn't think he could do it this way. I know he is upset with me for marrying Elyse. But believe me, I don't think his choice of King Lewis's sister would have added to my happiness at all! She would have been spying for her brother the whole time. Where would her loyalty be? I have Elyse's loyalty, completely and honestly. Warrewik's was always in question. Especially after he—" He stopped abruptly.

"After he what?" Ankarette pressed. A secret was trying to wriggle loose.

He pursed his lips and shook his head. "I swore him an oath that I would never speak of it. I've honored my promise, though it's cost me the good opinion of many."

"Will you tell me?" Ankarette asked.

He shook his head no. "I won't forsake my oath. Not even for you."

She felt the Fountain magic stir inside her. It rippled and shivered and her mind began to open like a flower. There was a way out. She saw it, the smallest of chances. The most dangerous of risks. It was as if the pieces had all finally slipped together in her mind. She knew the secret. The Fountain had whispered it to her.

His gaze was intense. "What is it?" he said, touching her arm.

"I think I know a way to escape this trap," she said with conviction.

CHAPTER 18
YIELD

Eredur's eyes widened with surprise, his mouth twitching with suppressed emotion. He wanted to believe her, but his situation truly seemed hopeless. "I'm not seeing it, lass. Even if I fled this very instant, I'd never make it to a port in time. Warrewik's spies would have me. They already have me in their sights," he said, waving toward the door.

She stepped closer to him. "My lord, I don't recommend that you flee. I believe I am a pretty good judge of people and things." She paused, trying to find the best way to express the new ideas that had come into her mind. "The Duke of Warrewik is driven by his ambition for power. And yet he does not crave the kingship for himself. He knows he lacks the right. He is your mother's brother, not your father's . . . which means that despite all his wealth and prowess, he has no blood right to the throne." She gazed at him keenly. "What he craves above all else is for one of his daughters to become the Queen of Ceredigion."

Eredur's face became stony, his eyes narrowing—but not with confusion. She had struck the nerve precisely.

"I believe that Warrewik wanted this so much that he induced Isybelle to . . . putting it delicately . . . put you in a compromising situation. Warrewik may have supposed that you would respond as an ordinary man might in such a situation, only to regret it later. I think his mind was so bent on this outcome that he did not take into consideration your character or his daughter's infatuation with your brother."

She stopped there, not saying anything more. In the silence of the room, they could hear the raucous voices downstairs.

Eredur's voice, when he spoke, was thick with emotion. "No one told you this, Ankarette? Not Isybelle?"

Ankarette shook her head no.

"You are exactly right," the king said softly, entreatingly, his voice edged with suppressed anger. "I have kept silent for several years to protect her honor. It was not her fault. I blame my uncle."

"Which is why I respect you and Sir Thomas so much for keeping silent about it," Ankarette said. "The clues were all there. I just didn't see them all until tonight, until almost this very moment. It's why your brother resents you so much."

"Indeed," Eredur said. "Even though I've told him nothing happened with her."

"He's still not sure he believes you. Sometimes we fear the worst in others to keep from seeing the truth about ourselves."

"You have a gift of insight, Ankarette," he said. "I've not even told Elyse the full truth because of my oath. But you are not so bound."

Ankarette smiled, pleased. "Now hear me out, my lord. Everything Warrewik has done has been in pursuance of his aim. You've been stripping him of power, or at least preventing him from gaining more, because he's proven himself to be untrustworthy. He knows it, and you know it, but the kingdom doesn't."

"He's bought their loyalty," Eredur said angrily.

"So we must use it against him. He's expecting you to flee. He's expecting you to fight. Do neither. Wait for him here to arrive. No matter what news he brings, tell him you wish to reconcile. I don't think he will murder you." She squinted and shook her head. "I don't think he has the stomach for it. He's afraid of you. He's afraid to face you in open battle, but open battle is what he wants and expects because defeating you any other way would be dishonorable.

"Refuse to fight him. No matter what. Seek to resolve the impasse. Give him more power and prominence. He'll likely ask to rule in your name. Say yes. Bide your time until Sir Thomas and I can free you. You'll probably be sent to Dundrennan. Warrewik and Hux think they know what you will do. Surprise them. Make them react to your unexpected move."

He let out his breath anxiously. "You're asking me to trust my life in his hands. He could lock me in Holistern with the mad king."

"I don't think he will. His intention is that you fight and lose, making way for Dunsdworth to become king and Isybelle his queen. According to Hux, they've already married in Callait. But if you are still alive after tonight, each day will improve the odds that Warrewik will face the same troubles you have faced as king, only he lacks your authority to resolve them. Will your privy council listen to him? I think not. Will other kingdoms see our weakness and threaten us? Of course! It all comes down to judging Warrewik's character and then deciding accordingly. I don't believe he will murder you."

A smirk tugged on his mouth. "He may ask *you* to do it."

She blinked at him. Then she looked down at the floor. "If he does, then I will protect you by stabbing him in the heart. And your problem will be solved. I serve *you*, my lord. You are my king."

She felt his hand on her shoulder, so she looked up into his eyes, silently beseeching him to listen. His gaze was full of emotion, of sympathy and tenderness.

"I will heed your advice, Ankarette. I don't think Sir Thomas could have given me better advice. You have wisdom beyond your years. Thank you."

"Sir Thomas has taught me a great deal," she said, trying to deflect his praise.

"He's a good man," Eredur said. "I value you both."

She sighed. "You should give him a command, my lord. When this is done. He'll serve you faithfully."

"I know. And I will." He squeezed her shoulder. "Now we must deal with the body you left outside the door. Best if he is not present when Warrewik arrives."

~

It was an agonizing wait. The night was dark, for it was well after midnight, and when Ankarette glanced outside the window, she saw a light rain coming down. Everything was still, a pent-up breath. Beams within the inn creaked and groaned. Soldiers mumbled in their sleep on the floor down below in the common room.

Ankarette and Eredur stayed up, quietly talking at the small table in his chamber. He told her of how young and inexperienced Isybelle had been that night at Dundrennan. How conflicted she'd been—trying to be obedient to her father's machinations while her heart belonged to Dunsdworth. Eredur had rejected her advances with tact and kindness. He had confronted Warrewik about it that very night and the two men had had a terrible confrontation.

Eredur's promise to keep the indiscretion concealed had calmed the situation. For a time. But the king's generosity had not dampened Warrewik's ambition. He had never lost the determination to achieve his goal, to see his daughter on the throne. The lack of punishment emboldened him. Which was why Eredur had forbidden to let Dunsdworth and Isybelle marry.

Hours passed. The village slept. The night seemed as if it would never end.

Then word came, just before dawn, that the Duke of Warrewik and his army were bearing down on the village. Ankarette hid in the room as one of Eredur's knights announced the disaster with panic in his voice. They urged him to flee, to ride fast for Westmarch and attempt to join Lord Kiskaddon's army. Eredur refused to budge. He would wait for the duke's arrival at the inn.

The only person he told the full truth was Lord Hastings, who had ridden with Ankarette the day before. His response to the king's strategy was bluff and to the point.

"I think you're making a bloody mistake," he growled with disdain.

But Eredur's mind was firm. He dismissed them all and then waited. The duke's horses surrounded the inn. Ankarette surreptitiously glanced through the curtain. Sir Thomas was down below! Puffs of steam came from his mouth. He was gazing up at the room, but he could not see her. His tunic was mud-stained . . . or was that blood? She studied some of the other soldiers around him.

"There has been fighting," she told the king, who was pacing.

"I hope I haven't made a mistake like Hastings said."

She did too. His decision had been made based on her counsel. The awful weight of it oppressed her.

Down below, she saw Warrewik talking to Sir Thomas, both astride their mounts. Thomas was explaining something to the duke, gesturing. She couldn't make out any words and she was too far to read his lips. Then the duke dismounted and started toward the inn, tugging off his armored gloves and tossing them to a squire.

"He's coming," she said.

"I'm ready. Go hide again." He gave her a serious look. "His life is in his hands. If he decides to kill me, he and I may both end up dying here. I'd like to prevent that if possible. I wonder if Hux is down there too."

If so, Ankarette couldn't sense him. She hid under the bed, close enough to hear the conversation and, if needed, to strike.

The thudding of the boots up the stairs and down the hall announced the duke's arrival. He pushed open the door without knocking. From her secret place, she saw Warrewik's face, illuminated by the room's candle, was lined with doubt, his eyes lit with feverish intensity.

"Good morning, Uncle," Eredur said calmly. A tray of breakfast had been arranged in advance. "Would you care to join me?"

"You have the stomach to eat?" Warrewik answered

archly. "I'm impressed. But no, I'll not taste a morsel. It may be poisoned." He said it with a tone of suspicion. "Where is she?"

"Ankarette? She left last night. She warned me you were coming and urged me to join Kiskaddon's army. I saw through her trap and elected to stay here." He lifted a cup and drank from it. "I'll eat if you don't mind. You talk."

Warrewik seemed startled by the news. "I didn't tell her I was coming. Strange."

"No matter to me," Eredur said with a casual shrug. "You've always been good at Wizr, Uncle. Always thinking ahead. Ah, some berries. From Brythonica, I think." He picked up a few and popped them into his mouth, smiling in satisfaction. "We've been at odds for too long. I propose we rectify that."

"And how would we do that?" Warrewik asked condescendingly. "Especially where we stand now. I'll admit, you've surprised me, Eredur. This is not how I thought you'd react."

"I know the game well enough, Uncle. I know when I'm about to lose. Threat and mate." He held up his hands. "But I'd rather not end things this way. I'd like to reconcile with you. These berries are truly divine. You should have one."

"No, thank you," Warrewik snapped. He still hadn't taken a seat, although Eredur had. Warrewik glanced around the room, searching for something.

"So what is it to be, Uncle? It's your move."

Warrewik gave Eredur a wary look. "I don't think we can work together, lad. We cannot be partners. Not anymore."

"Tell me why not? I've treated you poorly. I've humiliated you often. You bear a grudge and rightly so. Can we not mend the breach?"

Ankarette was proud of Eredur's composure. His exhaustion showed in his drooping shoulders, but he had remarkable stamina.

"That depends. I ordered your wife's father to be thrown in the river and sent over the falls for treason. The queen was in sanctuary at Our Lady when it happened." He gave Eredur a wolfish look. "She watched her father perish. So I ask *you*, Nephew. Do you really think we can work together?" His voice oozed with malice.

Eredur's eyes turned to flint. Elyse's father, Lord Rivers, in his new capacity as the Duke of East Stowe, had been wresting the naval power away from Warrewik. Ordering his death was a malicious act of revenge.

The news had rocked Eredur and it showed. His hand slumped onto the table top. "Well, you've had your revenge, Uncle. I know you resented him—"

Warrewik stepped forward. "I don't think you have any idea whatsoever how much I've resented him. How I've bitten my tongue while you advanced the Riverses to positions across Ceredigion, polluting the nobility. I've patiently borne your mistreatment of me, bided my time until now, and now . . . *now* you wish to partner with me? *Now*, you wish to give me due honor and respect? Without me, you would never have become king!"

Ankarette had never seen Warrewik so unguarded, so emotional. If she killed him, it would not end the threat to Eredur's life. No, she was convinced that such an act would all but ensure that Warrewik's supporters, his sworn men, would storm into the room and slaughter Eredur where he stood.

"You're right," Eredur said in defeat. "You are right, Uncle. No king wants to be under subjugation to his vassals. Am I any different?" He rose from the chair. "But by the Fountain, do we not have enemies enough that we must turn on each other?"

"You can forgive me for killing one of your dukes? Without a verdict from the Assizes? I find that difficult to believe. I'm not a fool."

"No! Clearly you are not! *I* have been the fool," Eredur said. "Without you, I would not have become king. I may have won the battles, but I could not have defeated Queen Morvared's armies alone without your support. I've not given you proper credit for your role, and worse, I've humiliated you by spurning the marriage negotiations you made on my behalf. I was wrong, Uncle. Terribly wrong. Please tell me it's not too late."

It was an emotional appeal. Ankarette was amazed at how ably the king performed it. She studied Warrewik's expression, saw the cracks in the stone of his resolve.

"I don't see . . . I just don't see how it can work," he said, shaking his head.

"Name your terms," Eredur said.

Warrewik snorted. "You've prevented them all so far."

"Things have changed. Name them. You wanted my consent for Dunsdworth to marry Iysbelle. Done. I give it."

"The deed is already done," Warrewik said. "They were married in Callait."

"What else can I give you? The duchy of East Stowe?

It's yours. Or put another man there if you would prefer. What about Stiev Horwath? He's loyal to you?"

Warrewik waved his hand. "Are you drunk?"

Eredur shook his head, his eyes blazing with intensity. "No. I just want to live past breakfast."

CHAPTER 19
CAPTIVITY

From the window of the inn, Ankarette watched as Eredur mounted a horse down below, surrounded by knights wearing the badge of the Bear and Ragged Staff. There were grins of victory mixed with looks of confusion and concern. She could not hear the words, but she saw Warrewik talking to Sir Thomas, jabbing his finger at the younger man, then making a dismissive gesture. Her insides were knotted with worry, but at least the king had survived. So far. His unconditional surrender had forced Warrewik to be magnanimous. His sense of honor had demanded it.

Eredur sat stoically, puffs of mist coming from his mouth. The weather had soured considerably and promised sleet as well as rain. How odd. She waited in silence and patience, wondering what her next move should be to rescue the king.

Warrewik had his own horse brought to him and he mounted.

The commotion in the streets was all from the duke's men. None of the villagers had roused from their homes. No one dared to walk the streets when they were choked with soldiers. Then she noticed Sir

Thomas slide from his saddle and march to the inn. She pursed her lips, wondering what he was about.

Her answer came moments later when he entered the room. She had hidden herself again, this time in the shadows in the corner parallel to the door.

He stood in the doorway, his eyes adjusting to the darkness of the room. "Ankarette?" he whispered.

"I'm here," she said, and he whirled, not having seen her. She stepped from the shadows and moved quietly toward him.

He sighed with relief. "Eredur whispered that you were still up here. We don't have much time to talk."

"I did the best I could to save him."

"I see that. My stomach has been in knots thinking I'd arrive too late, that he'd be dead. I'm relieved."

"Where are you taking the king? Dundrennan?"

"Of course. The duchess was sent there to fortify the castle. It's my duty to inform Stiev Horwath about his new prisoner. This is a mess, Ankarette. Truly, this is bad."

She bit her lip. "What happened when you went to Dunsdworth's land?"

He glanced back down the hall, still standing partway in the room. Half of his face was in shadow. "Obviously he wasn't there to advise. I've since learned of his marriage. This is all Warrewik's doing. He's made his move."

"And clearly so has King Lewis."

"No doubt the two of them have an alliance. What can be done? Kiskaddon wasn't willing to risk open warfare with Warrewik, not without knowing what had happened to the king. His army is retreating to Westmarch as we speak." He sounded agitated and angry.

"Did you know that the Duke of East Stowe is dead?"

"No!" Sir Thomas moaned. "By the Fountain, does Eredur know?"

"Yes, Warrewik gloated about it."

"Where's the queen? Did you make sure she was safe before you left Kingfountain?"

"I did. She's in sanctuary at Our Lady. The deconeus will take care of her." While the deconeus was somewhat selfish, she had come to understand him better. She was absolutely convinced that he would follow the Fountain—and equally convinced that the Fountain did not want Dunsdworth Argentine to be King of Ceredigion.

"But what about that poisoner? I've been worried sick that she was his target all along. Or the princess."

"No, they are safe. Tunmore has hidden them on the grounds. Not even the Espion know where they are."

"Are you certain? I would have thought that possible a few days ago, but Warrewik kept this plot from me, and now I distrust everyone." He raked one hand through his hair and squeezed the other into a fist.

She touched his arm. "You can trust me."

He gazed at her in the darkness, wrestling with his emotions. "I believe that, lass. What happens next is critical. We need to free Eredur. Do you have any ideas? My mind is racing like a runaway stallion. I can't keep up with it."

"Warrewik will expect something soon. It will be almost impossible to sneak him out of Dundrennan. So we need to bring help to him."

"What do you mean?"

She dropped her voice lower. "Do you think Kiskaddon is loyal? To the king?"

Sir Thomas scratched his throat. "Aye, lass. Eredur trusted his father-in-law the most, but he's dead and will be replaced by a man of Warrewik's choosing. Southport is run by Lovel, whom Eredur has never fully trusted. He chose Kiskaddon to help put down the rebellion for a reason."

"I will send him word, then," Ankarette said. "The king likes to hunt. Remember that place north of Dundrennan, by the falls? The river with the large boulder?"

"The one you jumped from? I remember it."

"Remember the woods where Hux was hiding? I'll arrange for Lord Kiskaddon to bring some of his soldiers to wait for you in that place. You bring the king hunting. We'll make sure the guards outnumber yours. Then Kiskaddon can bring the king back to Westmarch and they can rally the kingdom from there. I'm sure Severn will support his brother as well."

"Of course he will," Sir Thomas said. "He loves Duke Warrewik, no doubt. But he loves his brother even more. It's a good plan, Ankarette. Your thinking is impeccable."

She flushed at his praise. "You should go. I need to come up with a pretext for going to Kiskaddon."

"I'm sure you'll come up with something." He gave her a tender look, one of approval and fellow suffering. "Thank you."

"Keep the king safe."

"You do the same for the queen. There will be bloodshed ere this is over. It's unavoidable now."

His words made her shiver with dread. She stepped closer to him, so close she could smell the leather and sweat. He'd been riding all night. The furrows of anxiety on his brow were pronounced. She wished she could smooth them away.

"Go," she whispered, longing to kiss his bearded cheek in farewell. *Be safe,* she pleaded silently in her mind.

~

ONCE, Ankarette had observed a servant carrying an unwieldy tray overladen with wine chalices. She'd predicted he would fall the moment she saw him with that tray, and sure enough, the crash had come soon afterward.

She had the same insight about the Duke of Warrewik. The duke had taken on too much.

After returning to Kingfountain, the duke had interrogated her regarding her whereabouts. Her Fountain magic helped her gauge how the duke was reacting to the story she'd concocted, and—much to her relief—he believed her.

Dunsdworth was livid that his new father-in-law had not done away with the one major impediment to his taking the hollow crown. In addition to the verbal abuse of his new son-in-law, the duke had to contend with Lord Bletchley, who refused to answer the summons to Kingfountain for fear of sharing Lord Rivers's watery fate, and the privy council had disbanded.

The duke had long been a man of poise and exuberant self-confidence. Now he was harried with every step. Running the Espion was not the same as running a kingdom. His decrees had all been signed forthwith by the king. But no one believed in them. Trust had been shattered. Only fragments remained.

Six months passed as quickly as a runaway carriage threatening to crash. There was still no council. The new Duke of East Stowe had been named, Lord Countly, but he was weak and ineffectual and would not do anything without Warrewik's express and documented permission. Countly was afraid, of course, that he would be found guilty of treason should Eredur regain his power. Lord Horwath ran the North in the duke's absence calmly and with an unruffled air. The rest of the kingdom was barking mad.

Isybelle had become pregnant almost immediately after the wedding. Ankarette was at her side constantly, helping her understand the various pangs and pains she experienced. The first three months had brought terrible sickness and vomiting. Her husband could not abide the sound of retching and always hastily fled the room when it began. Isybelle was miserable. She had longed for years to marry Dunsdworth. But he was always chafing at the situation, insisting that their problems would all be solved if he were declared king. He railed against Warrewik, even in Isybelle's presence, which upset her.

Another month passed.

Ankarette watched, biding her time. She had made an arrangement with Lord Kiskaddon. He supported Eredur but feared the wrath of Warrewik. Moving too quickly could be fatal to him and his budding family. He had asked her to provide tunics bearing Warrewik's badge for his men to use to infiltrate the North. One by one, she had sewn them, using her skills with needle and thread to fashion badges convincing enough to be used without creating any alarm. Stealing from the duke's stores would have brought suspicion down on them. She had arranged for the tunics to be delivered to Kiskaddon's herald several days ago.

She was in the middle of working on another one, just in case more would be required, when the door to the solar burst open and Warrewik and Dunsdworth stormed in, midargument. Ankarette discreetly concealed the one she'd been working on under a pillow. Isybelle was dozing on the couch across from her, hand resting on her swollen abdomen.

"Can you not give me a moment's peace?" Warrewik said angrily over his shoulder. "I'm doing the best that I can!"

"But you are not doing *all* that you can," Dunsdworth snapped. "How long is this farce going to continue, Uncle? It's been nearly eight months, and he's still hunting and hawking and dancing! Does he even miss his wife or child? Has he even asked for her?"

"I've offered to bring his family to him," Warrewik said, raising his hands helplessly. "But his wife will not come out of sanctuary. She does not trust me."

"You could make her come out," Dunsdworth glowered.

"How can you say that? You know the rules of sanctuary. The people would revolt and I'd be thrown in the river. They're nearly revolting now. As I said, give me a moment's peace, lad! I wanted to come and check on my daughter."

Isybelle, jarred awake by the noise, sat up and rubbed her eyes. She had been very uncomfortable of late, and when she started rubbing her back, Ankarette put a pillow over her own needlework to cover it and went to the other couch and started to soothe the discomfort.

It was as if Dunsdworth had noticed his wife for the first time. He looked sheepish at his failure to greet her and offered a formal bow in lieu of an apology. He had gotten what he had wanted from her. The promise of her lands and wealth and a possible heir.

Now his pleasantries and flirtation had largely faded away.

"I'm fine, Father," Isybelle said. "Ankarette takes care of me."

The duke looked at his daughter, his eyes full of the tenderness that her husband's eyes so distinctly lacked. "Your mother had difficulty with both of her pregnancies. I used to rub her back when it was tender."

Dunsdworth snorted with contempt.

The duke went livid. Rising to his feet, he rounded on the younger man. "Go, if you find this amusing. You're about to become a father. Then perhaps you will understand what it feels to care about someone other than yourself!"

Dunsdworth's eyes glittered with fury at the rebuke. "You promised me," he said, shaking his head.

"And I will deliver it in my own time. You are not yet twenty, lad. For some rewards we must be patient."

Dunsdworth gave him a petulant look, then turned and stormed out of the room, slamming the heavy door behind him.

Ankarette swallowed, disturbed by this further proof that her friend had made a mistake, that she had fallen in love with the wrong man. Warrewik was right. The young duke cared about himself most of all.

Warrewik sighed. He knelt by the couch, wincing a little in pain from his bent knee, but he replaced his vexed look with a caring one and slowly stroked Isybelle's hand. "The Argentines have never been a patient family, have they?" he teased.

"You married one too, Father," she reminded him. "I don't think you regret it."

He shook his head. "No, your mother is a strong and capable woman. I sent for her to come down to Kingfountain. She wants to be with you when the babe arrives."

Isybelle rubbed her abdomen again. "I'd like her to be here as well. And I'm so grateful that you brought Ankarette to us all those years ago."

Ankarette reached out and squeezed her hand, smiling in return.

The duke nodded. "Yes, it was a good idea. I'm grateful for it as well. Your husband is right, as much as it galls me to admit it." He shook his head. "I never imagined the king would surrender. It was against his character to do so. Well, it cannot go on forever. I know he's chafing in confinement."

Isybelle looked at her father worriedly. "What do you mean to do about him?"

"Never you mind, dear." Warrewik stared down at the floor, still stroking her hand. "I will provide the solution to the problem. I'll take care of you. As I've always done." He leaned over and kissed her forehead.

Ankarette could see the ambition still burning in the man's eyes. He was determined to see his daughter married to a king, whatever it cost him.

The door burst open again and Dunsdworth was back, this time with a knight bearing the badge of the North.

"What is it . . . Drackson, right?" The duke pushed himself to his feet, favoring his other leg.

"Aye, my lord. I come from Stiev Horwath directly."

Dunsdworth looked agitated. "Go on!" he pressed.

"My lord." The man swallowed, clearly nervous. "The king has escaped."

Warrewik's eyes went flat with rage. "What?"

The knight bobbed his head. "I rode directly from Dundrennan with the news."

"Tell me what happened," Warrewik repeated, trying to remain calm. His fists were both clenched. His face was turning a shade of purple.

Ankarette felt as though she would burst with giddiness. Her plan, which she had hatched beneath the duke's nose, had worked! She kept kneading Isybelle's back, forcing her own expression to look vague and disinterested.

"The king went falcon hunting, as he normally does," the messenger said. "I was there, my lord. We were north of the castle, by the waterfall."

"Out with it!" Dunsdworth ordered. He was growing paler.

"We were there, all was well, and then suddenly knights wearing tunics with your badges came flooding out of the woods. I don't know where they came from, but they weren't your men."

Warrewik's eyes widened. "Who were they?"

"Duke Kiskaddon was leading them."

"By the Fountain," Dunsdworth groaned. He clenched his fist and bit his finger, starting to tremble with suppressed emotion.

Warrewik was more composed. "How many of my knights died?"

"My lord?" asked the knight in confusion.

"How many of my men died trying to keep the king from being captured? I don't see any blood on your tunic, man."

The knight swallowed, his knees trembling. "No one died, my lord. We were vastly outnumbered. Fifty against ten."

"Fifty!" Warrewik spluttered. "No one in the Espion bothered to mention that the duke and an entire retinue had gone missing?" He was thunderstruck.

The knight shifted from foot to foot. "That's not all, my lord."

"Not all?"

"Sir Thomas . . . he . . . he surrendered the prisoner. He went with the king and the Duke of Westmarch. I don't know how he arranged it, but he did. It's *his* fault the king escaped."

Ankarette felt a thrill of pride in her heart.

Warrewik's face smoldered. "I'll kill him," he vowed.

It wasn't clear which of the supposedly traitorous men he referred to, but by the tone and black look, Ankarette knew he meant the man she loved.

CHAPTER 20
THE RETURN

The palace of Kingfountain went into an uproar when news arrived that King Eredur had been rescued by the Duke of Westmarch. The call to war sounded throughout the land. The Duke of Warrewik summoned his armies and sent for the garrison of Callait to cross the sea to defend the city. More soldiers wearing his badge would march from the North, combining their might with that garrison in preparation to do battle with the king and his ally in the West.

Before Warrewik departed, he called for Ankarette to meet him in the Star Chamber. The summons came as a surprise, and her heart quivered with dread as she left Isybelle to her discomfort and followed the two Espion sent to bring her to the duke. They were both armed with swords and daggers. Should she try to flee?

She'd wrestled with that question ever since hearing the news of Eredur's escape. Although she desperately wanted to join the king, she knew she could help more if Warrewik believed she was loyal to him. No, she would not flee. She would rely on her Fountain magic to help her survive another encounter with the stubborn duke. With it, she could read his moods and judge his level of impatience and mistrust. It also gave her insights, in little flashes, of what she could say to him to overcome his natural skepticism.

The Espion opened the door and joined her inside, locking the door behind them. The duke was wearing his armor and hastily scrawling something on a sheet of paper. His hair was askew and beads of sweat dampened his brow. She summoned her magic, just a teasing of it, to begin flowing. She needed to read the duke perfectly, to anticipate what she needed say to keep herself alive.

He glanced up at her but did not speak until he'd finished with his quill. He set it down and, planting his fists on the desk, faced her.

"Did you know about Eredur's escape?" he asked her pointedly.

An easy question. She'd been expecting it. "No, my lord," she answered, carefully controlling her expression. She'd been taught how to tell a lie convincingly. "If I had known, I would have told you."

Did he believe her? He looked so wary and distrustful, which wasn't so surprising given how drastically his fortunes had changed overnight. The howl of a wolf in the distance was less threatening than the low growl of a wolf right in front of you. Warrewik would face the Sun and Rose banner soon. And he clearly dreaded it.

"What I should have told you," she went on, sighing to imply her inner conflict, "is that I have harbored some doubts about Sir Thomas's loyalty. He was my mentor and trained me in the ways of the Espion. I have respected him and his judgment. But he is ambitious. I wonder . . . I wonder, my lord, if this might not have happened had you given him the captaincy of Callait."

Warrewik frowned in confusion. "You think this is my fault?"

"I'm not saying that," she answered soothingly. She needed to guide his thoughts away from her. "He is very ambitious. I think he has chafed in his current role. He's mentioned to me that he felt he would stay in a subservient state forever. He wants more than that. I didn't think it was my place to encourage you to reward him. I feared you would take that suggestion amiss or question my motives. Maybe the king . . . persuaded him to change sides. It was reckless on Sir Thomas's part, but I do think he would have been vulnerable to temptation. And the king had everything to gain by it."

She kept a close eye on his face, watching to see how he reacted to the news. A lie was always best served with a generous buttering of truth. She knew Warrewik prided himself on his strategic thinking. That he had been caught off guard was humiliating to him personally. Ankarette's excuse could help assuage that feeling.

Warrewik gave her a piercing look. "He's made his choice and must suffer the consequences for treachery."

Ankarette thought it hardly fair to accuse Sir Thomas of treachery or his kinsmen treason considering what the duke had done himself. She wisely kept silent.

"What do you wish me to do?" she asked him.

Warrewik's countenance showed the depth of his anger. "He knows too much, has too much access. I want you to infiltrate Tatton Hall, the duke's manor in Westmarch, and then I want you to find Sir Thomas and kill him." He frowned at her. "This will be *your* test of loyalty, Ankarette. Mind you don't forget that there are consequences for defying me."

The threat was clear. Her mother's life would be the cost if she did not fulfill her duty.

She breathed in through her nose and exhaled. "I thought you might ask this of me. It pains me, my lord. I would be lying if I said otherwise. And yet . . . even if you were to offer him what he wants now, I don't think the two of you could ever trust each other again." She bowed her head submissively. "I will do as you command."

"Good," he said, a bit smugly. "In times like these, Ankarette, the future hangs on a gate hinge. My nephew and I have been avoiding bloodshed for too long. One of us must prevail." Despite his brash words, she could see the anguish battling on his brow. Treachery had not become easier for him. "I wish it were not so close to Isybelle's confinement. This is a wretched moment to fight a war. She needs you, and I need you. Serve me well, Ankarette, and you will rise to great heights someday."

She gave him a pleased smile, the lies still bitter in her mouth.

~

ANKARETTE ENCOUNTERED the king's army camped on the westbound road before the day was through. Part of her had wished to ride North and rescue her mother. But time, she knew, could fly like sparrows and dash away. Eredur was a capable and bold soldier. He would try to strike Warrewik at Kingfountain before his reinforcements arrived. It was the same trick Warrewik had used on him.

She allowed herself to be captured by Eredur's soldiers and was taken to his tent for questioning. Kiskaddon's standard flapped in the breeze alongside the king's. The tent was small, not one of the royal pavilions, but it was spacious enough to hold five or six men standing. The Duke of Westmarch was there, along with Sir Thomas, the king, and the duke's battle commander, whom she did not recognize. He was dismissed, but Kiskaddon was allowed to stay.

"It's good to see you again, lass," the duke said with a smile. She had met him only once before—when she'd journeyed to Tatton Hall to enlist his aid in rescuing the king.

"Likewise, my lord," she offered with a bow. She lowered the cowl of her cloak. She hadn't wanted the soldiers to be able to recognize her, so she had worn a nondescript one. Her gown was much plainer than the court finery she usually wore.

"Well met, Ankarette," Eredur said with a broad smile. The almost broken man she'd last seen at the inn was gone. Hope gleamed in his eyes.

"I was surprised to find you camped," she said. "Why not press for the castle during the night?"

Sir Thomas winked at her astute question and nodded approvingly. That look tugged at her, urging her to go to him. Would he help her save her mother? With or without him, she hoped to ride to Marshaw directly from the encampment.

"Oh, we won't be staying long," Eredur said with a laugh. "I'm only waiting for my brother Severn to join us with the men of Glosstyr."

"You'll be facing superior forces," Ankarette pointed out. "The garrison from Callait has been summoned, and the duke has ordered the armies of the North to come down. You must hurry, my lord." She tried to keep the urgency from her voice and failed.

Eredur glanced at Sir Thomas and the men shared a

knowing smile. There was another element here, something she was missing.

"The person who is out of time," Eredur said patiently, "is my uncle. Stiev Horwath will not be riding south. The messenger failed to arrive." He smiled broadly.

Now Ankarette understood. "He's on your side?"

The king stepped over and put his arm around Lord Kiskaddon's shoulder. "I must give credit where it is due. I had help convincing him. The castellan of Dundrennan has been loyal to my family for years. He's a quiet man. But he is as deep as the ice caves in the North. And so is his loyalty. I could tell during my confinement that he was sympathetic. He did not agree with the duke or what he had done."

"And it's also safe to say," Kiskaddon added with a wise nod, "that *none* of us are in favor of Dunsdworth ruling Ceredigion. He's a petulant, overachieving stripling with no real experience. He'd be Warrewik's puppet. Horwath has seen him firsthand and distrusts his temperament, his ability to lead. Warrewik won't find out for days that his Northern army isn't coming. And the force from Callait will be useless unless they can get off the boat. I think we have enough people to stop them. No, Warrewik is trapped at Kingfountain. His reckoning is past due, and he shall have it at last."

Ankarette sighed with relief.

"And none of this would have happened," Eredur said, nodding to her, "if not for your counsel. I trusted you. I'm glad I did."

She had been trained that praise was a sweetness no one ever lost the craving for. It was best not to be too fond of it. The best way to do that was to share the credit with others.

"Thank you, my lord, for your kindness. But do not forget that Sir Thomas taught me."

He looked at her in surprise, but he seemed pleased by her comment. Then he wrinkled his brow. "I hear someone coming."

The tent door rustled and Ankarette quickly raised her hood.

"My lord, the standard of the White Boar is coming down the road behind us. Your brother has arrived."

"Faster than I supposed," Eredur said with satisfaction. "He's a soldier at heart, Tom. I'll say it now. Defeating Warrewik will be bittersweet for him. He's always admired our uncle."

"I don't want Severn to know about Ankarette," Sir Thomas said. "Best if she's not here when he arrives."

"You don't trust my brother's tongue?" the king asked.

"No one does who knows him," Sir Thomas answered with a wry smile.

"My lord, if you'll permit me to leave the camp and handle a personal matter?" Ankarette asked, though she felt less anxious about her mother now that she'd seen the might the king had behind him.

"Of course. I will see you back in Kingfountain after I've retaken the city. Is my wife still safe in sanctuary?"

"Yes, and in good health," she answered, bowing.

"Well done. Go on." He nodded for them both to leave.

Sir Thomas escorted her from the tent and pulled her aside as Severn's horse rode through the camp, spurs jangling. He wore his armor well, one shoulder slightly higher than the other. The banner of the White Boar joined the mix of the other two banners. Severn glanced at them, his gaze narrowing, but she kept her head and face covered and followed Thomas away.

The sun was fading fast and she wished to get back to her horse to start the ride North. But it was so pleasant being in Sir Thomas's company again after all the months apart, and she wanted to savor it too. Her feelings were so conflicted on so many fronts—it was almost too much to bear.

"Where are you off to?" he asked her curiously.

They were close enough to the tent to hear the raised voices as the brothers met each other warmly. She glanced back at the tent and then looked at him.

"To Marshaw," she insisted. "Warrewik sent me to kill you. It is my test of loyalty." Her throat was suddenly very dry. "I must save my mother."

Sir Thomas's eyebrows crinkled as he held her gaze. "She's not in Marshaw, Ankarette," he said, as if she were being dense. "I recently had her moved to Tatton Hall. She's in Westmarch with Kiskaddon's wife and brood. I told you that I'd make sure nothing happened to her."

Unwilling tears of gratitude sprang into her eyes, and she felt such a surge of caring for the man it threatened to expose her secret.

Ankarette tried to quell the emotions storming inside of her, but she couldn't speak—it was as if her throat were blocked with a wedge. She put her hand on her breast and tried to master herself, only partially succeeding.

"I've never seen you cry," he said softly. "Not even after I took you from your home. You've been worried about her, I can see. I don't doubt it."

But he didn't understand *everything*. He didn't know how she felt about him.

THE POISONER'S ENEMY

"Thank you," she managed, mangling the words. Her nose was starting to run, which mortified her. Unable to bear it, she clutched the front of his tunic and pulled herself against him, resting her forehead on his chest to hide her face, her feelings.

He stood there awkwardly a moment, then patted her back soothingly. "It's all right, lass. It'll be all right. Go to Westmarch and see your mother. Then come to Kingfountain. You'll be needed there."

"I will, Sir Thomas," she said, dabbing her nose on the edge of her cloak. She had mastered herself at last. "I'm sorry."

He shook his head in sympathy. "You've carried a heavy burden these last months. It will be over soon."

"Will the king execute Warrewik and Dunsdworth?"

"Warrewik will go over the falls," Sir Thomas said firmly. "Not Dunsdworth." He sighed. "He could never kill his own brother. It's unfortunate that Isybelle got with child so quickly. That makes the situation even murkier." He shrugged. "Well, it's the Fountain's will. The king promised Horwath a duchy for his aid. He'll become the duke of the North after this is done. The people respect him. I think it's the right choice." There was a hint of jealousy and thwarted ambition in his voice.

"And what will happen to you?" she asked in a half-teasing way. Her fingers were still gripping his tunic. She gave him a playful little shove.

A wry smile spread on his mouth and he shrugged. "Well, I've always fancied Horwath's daughter. Time will tell. We're both the children of earls, so our rank was equal before. Now, she will outrank me."

Ankarette let go of his tunic, impaled by his words like a fish caught in a stream. Of course. She shouldn't have thought it could be any different. When she'd first gone to Dundrennan with him, she'd been a child—Elysabeth, already a woman.

Ankarette recognized that caring for him could only bring her pain.

CHAPTER 21
BLIND

Duke Warrewik had escaped before Eredur and his army arrived in Kingfountain. He'd boarded a ship with his wife, son-in-law, and his two daughters, and no one knew where they'd landed. There was plenty of speculation. But he could have vanished at sea, for all they knew, and been swallowed by the Deep Fathoms.

After returning from a short visit with her mother, Ankarette had spent all her time trying to find news of Warrewik. She was especially worried about her friend and the upcoming birth—a helpless feeling because there was naught she could do.

The tavern on the bridge was boisterous and full of a discontented rabble—many angry men and some who were well past drunk. The roar of the falls was almost blotted out by the shouts and guffaws of customers and the trill of pipes. Ankarette wore a commoner's gown and cloak, her hair braided into coils behind her head. The tavern common room had evil energy to it, and the looks that came her way spoke of hard men in hard circumstances. Her quarry sat alone at a table in the corner, watching as she wove her way through the crowd. He was a cynical man, one of the Espion from the sanctuary of Our Lady, and they had agreed to meet in a neutral location.

A drunken patron careened into her suddenly, nearly knocking her off balance. The man blurted an apology, but his hands were quick to touch. She grabbed his smallest finger, yanking it as she shoved him to the ground. He moaned in pain, shaking his head and wondering loudly how he had fallen. His breath reeked of ale.

She stepped around his fallen body, anxious to get the information she had come here for and leave. A young man with a tray of mugs jostled past her and nearly tripped over the man sprawled on the floor, catching himself just in time. Ankarette dodged him and then joined the man who awaited her at the table. His hair was falling out and a gray-and-black beard bristled his jowls.

"Ankarette," he said warily, giving her a nod.

"Silas," she replied courteously. He looked uncomfortable in the tavern. She had been using her Fountain magic almost every day since Eredur regained power and she felt her stores dwindling. But she needed it now more than ever.

"Are you alone?" she asked him, reaching out with her magic as she glanced around at the patrons. Other Espion could easily be hiding in the crowd. Many were still loyal to Duke Warrewik.

"Of course," he answered gruffly. "That's what we agreed."

He was lying. She sensed it from her magic. He was a gifted liar and controlled his expression perfectly.

"Thank you," she answered. "I need to find Warrewik," she said seriously, dropping her voice. "He fled the city before I could return from my assignment."

His brow lowered suspiciously. "I only agreed to meet you if you made it worth my while."

"I don't have any money. I'm just as dependent on the duke as you are."

The man sniffed and rubbed his whiskers. "I have my own means, my dear. I assumed you did as well. Jewels at the least. You're Lady Isybelle's friend, surely you have something you can barter for information."

"How do I know your information is worth my jewels?" she countered. "I need to use them in the palace among the nobles."

"I could hold them for you," he said with a twisted smile. "Keep them safe."

Every instinct warned her that this man could not be trusted with a single coin.

"Do you know where Warrewik is?"

"Of course," he answered smoothly. "But Sir Thomas has been rounding up every Espion loyal to the duke. You and he were always on *friendly* terms." He gave her a knowing look that made her emotions flare. He was goading her, trying to get her to react.

"I've worked with many," she answered dispassionately. "Where is he? Callait?"

The subtle wrinkle in his brow told her she had struck on something.

"Maybe," he answered with unconcern. "I'm not going to tell you without payment. If you didn't bring something interesting, then this conversation is over."

"I think you're right," she said, pushing back her chair. "It *is* over."

He chuckled darkly. "You didn't think I'd make it that easy for you? Let's continue our chat. Upstairs." His look revolted her. "You'll need to prove you're still loyal to the duke."

"How many Espion are in here?" she asked tightly, rising to her feet, preparing to defend herself.

"Six other than me," he answered smoothly. "And we've all been waiting to meet you."

"That's strange," Ankarette replied coolly. "I had counted seven."

She gripped the table's edge and shoved it into Silas's gut. Then, planting her palms on the table, she spun around and kicked him on the side of the head, knocking him off his chair and landing on the other side. The tavern erupted into violence as the door burst open and soldiers wearing the Sun and Rose stormed inside, throwing the men to the floor one by one.

A ripple from the Fountain announced the presence of another Fountain-blessed in the room. Ankarette had not been expecting that and she whirled about, fishing in the slit of her skirt for her dagger. Silas was scrabbling to get to his feet, blood drenching his face from a cut at his brow. She kicked him hard to keep him down and brandished the dagger. There was Sir Thomas in the lead, plunging through the crowd to reach her at the far table.

Commands to cease fighting were shouted. Some of the patrons tried to wrestle the soldiers and were beaten down. They were completely outnumbered, but she still sensed that presence in the room, and something told her the person was trying to leave. She gazed around, trying to find the source.

"You said it would be a brawl," Sir Thomas called out, punching someone in the face before he reached her. His eyes danced with amusement. He looked down at Silas, who glared at him with undisguised hatred.

"Ah, Silas! Thanks for leaving the sanctuary at last. I have some questions for you."

"You craven traitor!" Silas lashed out. His nose was bleeding and his eye was getting puffy.

"Arrest them all; there are seven more in here," she whispered to him as she charged past. She used her instincts, tried to find the elusive presence with her magic. Angry shouts and curses blistered the air, but Ankarette ignored the fuss, dodging through the melee to try to find the person she sensed. Where was he? If it was Lord Hux, he would not allow himself to be captured. He probably kept a suicide ring to prevent himself from revealing any of Lewis's secrets.

But where was he? She searched the crowd again, trying to follow her senses. The door was still open, and fresh guards were coming in to haul those who'd already been bound out of the tavern. She heard the clacking of wagon wheels and realized that the prison cages were coming to haul off the inmates from the tavern. Still, she could not find him.

Why couldn't she see him?

She sensed the person leaving through the door, but she didn't *see* anyone standing there. The door stood open, and she saw the crowds outside, the spectators who had assembled to watch the goings on. She could feel the presence of the Fountain-blessed person outside, yet she hadn't seen anyone leave. Hurriedly, she crossed the room and gripped the doorjamb and stared out into the crowd, trying to locate the culprit. The crowd was so thick, no one stood out from the rabble. The feeling suddenly faded as the person stopped using the magic. She thought she caught a shock of light brown hair pressing against the crowd. It was just a glance.

She had a sinking sensation. The person had been invisible. She reached into her girdle where she had hidden one of the jewelry pieces she had intended to use to barter with Silas. She'd never pulled it out because of her lack of trust.

It was gone, stolen. Someone grabbed her from behind and yanked her back into the tavern. It was one of Sir Thomas' men.

~

Ankarette was in the solar with the king and queen, Sir Thomas, and Lord Kiskaddon. Eredur had tried to convince the duke to take charge of the Espion, but he had refused. His family was still very young and he had no desire to take up the post that Warrewik had held. No one wanted the job—not even Sir Thomas, who was normally ambitious for opportunities. His concern was that he'd never be trusted again within the Espion after his betrayal of Warrewik.

Queen Elyse watched as her husband paced, her eyes worried. She had lived for months in the sanctuary of Our Lady and seemed pleased to be reunited with Eredur. But her nervous rubbing of her stomach and the slightly queasy look on her face had caught Ankarette's eye, so she'd missed the question the king had asked her.

"Ankarette?"

His words brought her out of her reverie. "I'm sorry, my lord. What was that?"

"I asked if you thought our ruse was successful. Your idea to have everyone in the tavern arrested, yourself included, would lend credence to the thought that you were still loyal to my uncle."

She glanced at Sir Thomas, who seemed to have gained confidence now that he could openly be Eredur's man.

"I hope so," she said. "I thought I saw a man slip away in the crowd."

"I don't think that's possible," Sir Thomas said. "Every man in that tavern was dragged out in irons. And every woman too." He winked at her playfully. "You should have seen her, my lord. She looked miserable and forlorn as she was carted off with the rest. She is a great performer. No, I think word will get out that she was captured today. I'm glad we brought in Silas. I've always detested that man."

With good reason, Ankarette wanted to add.

The king rubbed his hands together and then came to a stop over by his wife. "So we must do our best to speculate where Warrewik went. The most probable destinations are Callait, where he commanded the garrison, or Occitania. He and Lewis have ever been allies."

"Both places are where he would expect us to think he'd go," Sir Thomas added. "He's a cunning man. I had hoped he would stay and fight. With the Callait garrison, he would have been a match for you and Lord Kiskaddon."

"Hardly an even one," Kiskaddon said with a chuckle. "I'm not surprised he fled."

"Nor am I," agreed the king. "If you're not confident you will win a battle, you will lose it. He heard the sounds of the tree cracking and thought it best to flee ere it fell." He rubbed his wife's shoulder and she gripped his hand with hers. She looked worried, pensive.

"My lands are closest to Occitania," Lord Kiskaddon said. "If I hear anything, I will tell you at once. I will leave half of my army, as we agreed, to help defend Kingfountain in case he returns with a fleet provided by King Lewis. The other half will return with me to Tatton Hall and begin securing our western borders."

"What about Brugia?" Sir Thomas asked, wagging his finger. "Do you think he went to Callait and then Marq? The Temaire family is quite duplicitous."

Eredur shook his head and waved off the comment. "Philip Temaire married my sister. I think she would have told us if Warrewik suddenly appeared."

"In talking with Silas," Ankarette added, "I mentioned Callait. He betrayed a look when I said it."

Eredur clapped his hands. "That is good intelligence. Have you gotten nothing more from him yet, Tom?"

He sighed. "He has information we need, but he won't speak unless he knows he's not going into the falls. A few days in the dungeon may soften him."

"Indeed," said the king. Then he sighed and looked at Ankarette. "When is Isybelle's babe due, lass? How soon is it? He may stay in hiding until after the child is born. If it's a son . . ." His words trailed off and he shook his head.

Elyse's eyes tightened with worry and undisguised concern. She rubbed her stomach again, which convinced Ankarette she was right. The queen was with child again. It must have happened quickly after Eredur had retaken the palace. No doubt their reunion had been passionate after such a long forced separation.

There was a loud knock at the door. Sir Thomas frowned and strode over to it. They had asked not to be disturbed. After opening the door, Sir Thomas spoke briefly to the man, someone Ankarette didn't recognize. When he turned around, he was holding a letter. He broke the seal and began reading it. Then his face lit up with surprise and happiness.

"What is it, man!" Eredur said impatiently, eager to hear the news.

Sir Thomas was scanning the words quickly. Was he decoding a message in cipher? It didn't seem so. "By the Fountain," he gasped, shaking his head in wonderment.

"Tell me!" the king insisted.

"Please share the news, Sir Thomas," the queen said, much calmer but no less eager.

Sir Thomas brought the paper down, his surprise still evident. "You will never guess."

"Of course not, you fool. Speak up, man!"

"This letter is from the captain of the garrison at Callait," Sir Thomas said. He gave Ankarette a knowing look. "He's been the duke's sworn man for years. Vauclair. He's a soldier, fought for the duke long ago—well, all of that doesn't matter. What he says," he added, lifting the paper and stabbing it with his finger, "is that he rebuffed the Duke of Warrewik and refused him entry into Callait. He says he is loyal to Your Majesty and has done this as a token of his trust and fidelity. The ships were at anchor for several days outside the harbor. Lady Isybelle went into labor and the duke pleaded with Vauclair to bring her ashore. He refused. He utterly refused." He coughed into his fist. "That is cold-hearted."

Ankarette felt a stab of worry and panic. "When was this letter sent?"

"Last night," Sir Thomas answered. "She may still be in labor."

Ankarette's concern for her friend redoubled. She looked imploringly at the king.

"To prove his loyalty, he bids you to send someone

of your choosing to inspect the garrison of Callait. You'll find all in order and the soldiers willing to obey you. He beseeches you for a royal command declaring that he will still be the castellan if he has earned your favor—just like the writ you so graciously imparted to Lord Horwath in Dundrennan."

"So there was no news about Isybelle's babe?" Elyse asked.

"None," he answered, shaking his head. "But the babe is likely born by now. On a ship. Poor lass. The letter ends saying that the duke's ships sailed westward, allowing the captain to send us this message. There is no cipher on it."

"Indeed. I don't know Vauclair well. Do you think this is a ruse, Tom?"

Sir Thomas shrugged. "I've never cared for him. It's hard to say, but I've no doubt he's a greedy man who wants to keep eating from the plum tree. It makes sense that Warrewik would away to Pree next."

Eredur looked at Ankarette. "You want to go there. Don't you?"

"To Pree?" she asked, still agitated by the news and the thought of Isybelle suffering.

He shook his head. "No, to Callait, where the trail begins. Ankarette Tryneowy, I have an assignment for you. You are my poisoner, after all. I trust your instincts and your judgment. I don't have a fully functioning Espion, so I'm blind to what is happening inside my own borders, let alone outside. It will take time to find replacements and establish new people. I don't have that luxury right now." He looked at her sternly. "Find Isybelle and you will also find my brother. They may have had a son, and if they did, he will be a rival to the throne. I need to know if that has happened."

She dreaded what she thought he would say next. And she knew, deep in her heart, that she could never harm an infant.

"Ankarette, your task is to find my brother. You tell him that if he comes back to me, all is forgiven. He will not lose his duchy or his wife. In fact, I will even take that into consideration for the writ of attainder when we call the Assizes after Warrewik is captured. Dunsdworth may still become one of the wealthiest men in Ceredigion. Convince him to come back to our side, Ankarette. For the good of his wife. For the good of their child. You are my emissary in this and I will honor whatever agreement you make. I know you would never do anything that wouldn't be in the best interest of the realm. But if he will not come, then I won't let Warrewik use him as a puppet against me. Kidnap him if you can. Poison him if you must. We will pluck away Warrewik's supporters one by one. Start with Dunsdworth. If he's not in Callait, then find him in Pree. Do whatever you must. This is my first royal command to you as my poisoner. You must see it done."

Her heart fluttered inside her breast. She was only sixteen years old, and yet the king trusted her so much. She glanced at Sir Thomas, who smiled at her encouragingly. His eyes said, *I know you can do this, lass.*

And because they believed in her, and she in herself, she knew she'd succeed no matter what.

CHAPTER 22
VAUCLAIR

It was a Genevese merchant ship and the cargo was shallots. The smell of the purple root vegetables permeated the ship, including Ankarette's room. In her time at the poisoner school, she had read stories and accounts of political mayhem. In the cold, stale writing of the past, the causes and solutions to problems seemed obvious. But now she was living in her own chaotic times. Yes, Eredur had regained control of Ceredigion . . . and yet something told her Warrewik was not defeated just yet.

A loud thump sounded on her door and she paused in the act of adding poison to her dagger. Before they reached Callait, she wished to be fully equipped with defenses. She hesitated, then quickly set down the implements of death and hurried to the door. She opened it a crack.

The first mate stood there, a bearded Genevese man with long, scalloped locks of grayish-brown hair. "The cap'n wished me to tell you we'll be drawing into Callait soon. Be ye ready."

Judging by the dimness of the light, they were coming in with the tide and it would be dark soon.

"Thank you," she said. The man gave her a gruff look and a wary nod, and she shut the door and returned to the small desk. Before picking up the dagger again, she inspected the area to make sure none of the poison had escaped. Some poisoners, those who were not careful, injured themselves with their own wares.

Most of the voyage had been spent doing needlework, pondering about the situation and her impending arrival at Callait. She would need her Fountain magic in ample supply. Little moths of worry fluttered in her stomach, and she paused her work, reining in her feelings. Sir Thomas had escorted her to the docks, giving her advice and encouragement along the way. She wanted to please him, to make him proud of her. The king's approval mattered too, of course, but she was determined to prove herself on her first major mission.

After coating the dagger with the waxy poison—a fast-acting paralytic called quickworm—she slid the weapon carefully into its sheath and then strapped it to her hip beneath her dress. She wore one of the dresses she had been given in Warrewik's household—a gown that indicated her rank as a lady-in-waiting. She carefully arranged her hair, braiding it in a coil behind her neck, and added jewels to glitter. Next was a necklace, then a poisoned pin for her hair. Most women primped and pouted in front of a mirror. Ankarette readied the tools of her secret trade, including a dose of nightshade should she need to use it against Vauclair. The drug was a powerful, though delicate, tool—too much would kill a man; the right amount would have him singing all his secrets.

After stowing away her things, she went to the round window and watched the sun failing. There were many ships out at sea, each bearing a flag and seeking a distant port. She marveled at the vastness of the world, of the multitudinous lives that came and went. Most would never meet a king or a queen in person. She had been lucky in that regard. Her world, once small, had grown so very large.

That fluttering nervous feeling came again, and she pressed her hand against her stomach. She was going to a foreign land now. And while Callait had been under Ceredigion's control for over a century, she'd been told the culture there still hearkened to its former rulers, the Brugians. She could have arranged for a Brugian dress, for the style was different, but she had chosen to appear to Vauclair as one of Warrewik's servants. She had the badge of the Bear and Ragged Staff sewn onto her cloak. If she ran into Warrewik, she'd report that Sir Thomas had been poisoned as ordered and would be dead within the week. It would take time to prove the falsehood, but she had no intention of lingering long enough to be proven wrong.

The trading vessel arrived at the dock and the captain sent for her again and met her on deck. He was a tall man with a handsome face and long dark hair. "We have arrived, my lady. Do you want me to send a man with you on your errand . . . where are you going again?"

She had the suspicion that his request was self-serving.

"It's no trouble. Thank you, Captain."

"As you insist. We could linger in the port for a while. The shallots will not spoil so soon, I think. Will you need to be taken elsewhere?"

"Where are you bound to next, Captain?" she asked him.

"Genevar, of course."

If she followed the duke's trail, it would lead in the opposite direction. But if Warrewik was going to Pree, then the Genevese vessel could get her there the fastest.

"If you could wait for a few hours," she suggested.

The captain smiled with charm. "It would be my pleasure. We leave with the next tide anyway."

How old did he think she was? He was probably in his thirties, much older than Sir Thomas or the king. In all likelihood, he assumed she was an innocent in the ways of the world. A miscalculation she could use to her advantage.

"Thank you, Captain."

She climbed up on the gangplank and started down. As she began maneuvering through the crowded wharf, she heard the sound of boots coming down the plank behind her. The dockworkers of Callait were mostly from her country, and she recognized their slang as they unloaded the various vessels tied up at port.

Ankarette saw a customs officer wearing the badge of Warrewik stride past her toward the ship. He didn't look at her twice. Sir Thomas had explained the best byway to get to the fortress, and she set off toward it, ignoring the rowdy sailors and dockmen who were already getting drunk in the taverns and inns lining the wharf. The cobbled street smelled pungent with sour wine and yeasty ale from the revelers. Street vendors were still selling their wares, even though the sun had set, and sailors haggled over buns and sausages.

The sound of boots following her reminded her that she was not alone.

She raised the hood of her cowl. She abruptly turned down a side alley, one that was especially dark. Some rangy feral cats slinked in the shadows, mewling and hissing. Rats scuttled amidst the debris. Her eyes flitted quickly to gauge her surroundings and then she pressed her back against the wall. She calmed her breathing and waited. Within a few moments, she saw the first mate duck into the alley after her.

He paused, squinting, trying to see in the gloom.

"If you value your life," she said softly, warningly, "stop following me."

He was startled. "Pardon, my lady, but Cap'n said to follow ye and be sure you arrived safely."

"I'll arrive safely," she assured him. "Wait for me here and we can go back together. But if you follow me farther, the captain will need a new first mate."

He swallowed, looking troubled. He rubbed his hands. "I think I'll get a drink at the tavern yonder. And then wait here."

"A wise choice." She waited until he was gone before she started walking again.

~

THE WALLS of the fortress were thirty feet thick and had low, squat tower ridges with toothlike crenellations and slate shingles. Arrow slits pocked the walls, and sentries and guards manned the tops night and day. Though she had known for some time that this was the largest armed force in Ceredigion, it was quite another thing to see it. Callait was a strategic stronghold, one to be held at all costs because it provided a foothold into Brugia and a place to launch attacks at Occitania's southern borders.

After ensuring that she had not been followed, she climbed the sloping arch that led to the main doors of the interior of the fortress. The bulk of the defenses were pointed outward and ringed the city, but this was the keep, the main interior defense where she assumed she'd find Vauclair.

There were no visitors coming back and forth along the arch and she imagined the gate guards would see her well before she arrived. The noise of the city behind her faded as she made the lonely walk. The briny smell of the sea and the distant cry of gulls filled the breeze. She focused her breathing and tried to appear nervous and concerned.

When she reached the gate, the door was open, the portcullis closed. A few men holding torches waited for her warily, their dark faces twisted with concern.

"It's a long walk to the castle, lass," one of them said imperiously. "What do you want up here?"

"I've come with a message for Captain Vauclair," she answered, deliberately making her voice a little tremulous. "I am Lady Isybelle's lady's maid, come from Kingfountain. Is my lady here?" It did not require much acting to sound concerned.

One of the guards lifted his torch higher so that it would reveal her face. She winced at the stab of light but did not shrink back.

"Open the gate," the man said.

There was a groan as the winches began to pull on the portcullis. Rattling chains sounded and the teeth of the portcullis scraped against the stone insets. In a few moments, the gate was high enough for her to cross, and the officer beckoned her inside.

"Show me your badge?" the captain said, gesturing for the other men to surround her. Her heart began to race faster.

She opened her cloak and showed him the badge of the Bear and Ragged Staff.

"That's it," said one of the others.

The gate captain nodded. "She's one of us," he said, nodding to the others. "Run ahead and tell Vauclair. Wait here, damoselle. Until he sends word."

She breathed in relief through her nose and began fidgeting.

"You served in the duke's household?" the captain asked her. "Where?"

"Dundrennan," she answered eagerly.

"I don't remember seeing you here for Lady Isybelle's wedding," he said. His look lost some of its friendliness.

"Of course not. I was trapped in Kingfountain. Many of us were left behind."

"That is true," the man said, his suspicion fading. "We weren't able to make it to Kingfountain in time, or the false king Eredur would never have seized the throne. It will all be made right, though."

That comment alone spoke volumes. "I thought I might find my lady here. I'm desperate to rejoin her."

"She's not here. Some say the duke sailed to Atabyrion. Some, to Legault. Truth be told, none of us know where the duke be. If Vauclair knows, he's not talking."

Ankarette shivered and bundled the cloak more tightly around her shoulders. A few moments later, the man who had left came back.

"Vauclair will see her straightaway."

"Off with you, lass," the captain said, giving her a respectful nod.

She smiled at him and then followed the man into the most fortified part of the castle. It was immaculately decorated and reminded her of the great hall of Dundrennan. She wringed her hands, gazing at the torches as they passed, trying to come across as a frightened young woman. Meanwhile, she tested the air, trying to sense the presence of Fountain magic, but she felt nothing.

"This way," the man directed, leading her into one of the tower wells that climbed into the heights of the enormous fortification. She brushed her hand on the cool stone, keeping pace with the guard. After turning round and round on the way up, they reached another floor, and she could hear the strums of a harp. The soldier escorted her to a big iron door with huge rivets at the end of the hall. There was a box square already open and a face watched her approach. The door shuddered open, but the hinges were greased.

"Captain, it's the damoselle," the soldier said, bowing formally.

Vauclair was a heavyset, short younger man with dark hair that was puffed forward in the Occitanian fashion and then combed back. He wore an expensive doublet and rings glittered on his fingers. He may have been a soldier once, but he had gone to seed in his time managing Callait. He had dark, eager eyes and an interested, speculative smile flashed across his mouth when he saw her.

"Damoselle, welcome, welcome!" he crooned, bowing graciously and offering her to enter. There was a harp in the room, but the stool was vacant. She glanced around quickly, trying to see if someone else was there. One wall contained a wooden rack that was completely filled with bottles of wine, there were probably fifty different varieties.

"You are most welcome, my lady," he said again after she entered. He gestured quickly for the soldier to leave. The soldier gave a subtle look of disdain to Vauclair's back and then turned away. Vauclair shut the door as well as the spy hole.

"Thank you, Captain," she said, trying to sound sincere. "I came to Callait hoping to find my lady, but I understand that she is not here. I am desperate to find her."

He mopped his brow quickly with a silk kerchief. "I can only imagine," he said with an exaggerated look of sympathy. "Would you care for a drink of wine?" He flashed her an eager smile that said he really wanted one himself.

"Thank you, yes," she replied, not intending to drink any.

"I'm sure, what a dismal journey you must have had. From Kingfountain, yes?"

"I left this morning," she answered, watching as he fetched two goblets.

"I'm assuming," he said, his back to her, "that you stayed behind because of your loyalty to the king?"

She saw him twist something on his hand and subtly shake it, sprinkling something into one of the cups. Her instincts screamed it was nightshade. Then, brushing his hands together, he went to the wall and gazed at the expansive collection. "Let me see. I think some white would go well with the *pouillon* and *crème de mangothe* my cook is preparing in the kitchen. Or would you prefer a red? I have some excellent wines from the Orle Valley?"

He smiled at her eagerly, his eyes brightening with a look of hunger that had nothing at all to do with his cook's delicacies.

CHAPTER 23
DISCERNMENT

"The Orle Valley?" Ankarette said, inflecting her voice to sound impressed. "That's deep in Occitania. What vineyard?"

Vauclair scrunched up his brow. He turned back to the selection and studied one of the bottles.

As he was distracted, she twisted one of her poisoned rings, exposing the cavity beneath the jewel. Vauclair was a portly man. Too little, or too much? She couldn't risk killing him. She shook her fist over the other cup, his cup, and then glided up behind him.

"I'm from Occitania, lass," he said smugly, flashing her a charming smile. "The duchy of Vexin. If you prefer red, then I'd suggest this one. It's from a vineyard in Izzt. Very sweet. Like you." He winked at her and produced the bottle with a flamboyant air.

Although Ankarette was disgusted by his flirtations, she continued to gaze at the wall of bottles. "So many," she sighed.

She heard him grunt as he twisted in a corkscrew and struggled to pop it out. She glanced back at him, saw him wrestling with the bottle unsuccessfully, but as soon as she looked at him, his annoyed look switched to one of grandiosity and ease. "Just a moment," he said gently, then proceeded to wrestle with the bottle in a comical way.

"So you are loyal . . . to the king as well?" he asked again, his voice tightening as he continued to fight the bottle.

She felt an immediate pulse of warning in her heart. Her Fountain magic almost summoned itself to warn her not to answer the question. He was trying to judge her loyalties before revealing his own. He had refused to let Warrewik land in Callait. Or had he? Had his letter been a ruse? It was clear Warrewik still had plenty of men in Callait. Beads of sweat were building on the captain's brow. She nearly offered to help him uncork the bottle. Or was that a ruse too? A distraction from the poison he'd put in her goblet?

Reaching out with her magic, she tested him, knowing full well that she was revealing herself to him if he was Fountain blessed too. He was not. She sensed no magic within him at all. Instead, she sensed someone who was incredibly duplicitous, loyal only to himself and his own best interests. He adored his comforts at Callait and had no desire to come to court or achieve distinction. He was a rake, a drunkard, and he preyed on those who were less powerful than he, using his position to his own benefit.

All this, she discerned in an instant. The man was utterly untrustworthy.

The cork popped out and some of the wine spilled as he scrambled to right the bottle. He laughed playfully at his bungle and continued to stare at her, expecting her to answer his question.

"The king has sent me on a secret mission," she told him in a low, serious voice.

"Aahhh, I thought so," he replied with a winning smile. "How can I be of service? I am completely and totally in support of King Eredur. I forbade Warrewik to land in Callait, after all. Perhaps he told you I did?"

"That's why I'm here," Ankarette replied. "He said I could trust you."

"Of course you can," Vauclair replied gravely. He was eating up her secretive flair with relish. He quickly poured wine into both goblets. "The meal should be here soon. Have a drink. And then tell me all about it. I will help you in any way that I can, damoselle."

He bowed with a flourish and handed her the poisoned wine cup. The one he had prepared himself.

"I must tell you my mission first," she said. "It's too important to delay."

"Yes?" he said. He set down her cup and picked up the other one, talking a quick sip from it. His nose wrinkled, as if the flavor bothered him.

"Captain Vauclair," she said, stepping forward, speaking in a slightly breathless tone. She had to make the lie as believable as possible . . . and she had to distract him from thinking overly hard about the flavor of the wine. "The king has bid me to seek out the Duke of Warrewik and make an overture of peace. There is too much at stake for there to be a rift within Ceredigion. The duke is well loved, especially in the North, and the people are on the verge of revolt. The king thought I would stand a better chance of sneaking through the enemy to deliver his message in person. He wants peace. At any cost. All their past troubles will be forgiven."

"Forgiven, you say?" Vauclair said with a little hiccup. He took another big swallow, his eyes roving across her body. He was clearly thrilled by the news, by the prospect of having such valuable information to exploit. He gulped down another swallow. His eyes swam with tears as the potent powder began working within him.

"Yes."

"But he named . . . he n-named Horwath as duke of the North?" Vauclair's speech began to slur.

"Horwath is loyal to *Warrewik*. Don't you see? He's holding the duke's old position for him until he returns. Eredur wants peace at any cost. But I must get word to him quickly. If King Lewis were to know this . . ."

Vauclair's head bobbed up and down. "He is a wealthy king, of course. Very wealthy. I should think he would bid for Warrewik's loyalty too." His mind was tallying up the coins that were going to exchange hands. He saw that he, himself, could become very rich just from bearing the news.

"I need your help finding the duke," Ankarette said, nodding encouragingly. "Where is he? You must help me find him or Eredur's plan will fail."

She watched as Vauclair's eyes glazed over. He looked liable to drop his goblet of wine, but she snatched it from his hand.

"Sit down," she ordered him. He promptly obeyed.

How long would the poison last? Minutes perhaps? She had given him a very small dose. "Are you in league with Warrewik?" she asked him. She examined the other cup and quickly poured it back into the bottle it had come from. The wine would help dilute the poison. She made sure there was enough residue on the bottom to imply it had been drunk. When he fully revived, his memories of the evening would be spotty.

"No, I'm in league with the Spider King." He smiled absently at her, his mouth spreading wide. He was completely bedazzled.

THE POISONER'S ENEMY

"Are you a poisoner?" she asked him next.

"No. Lord Hux is, though. He taught me the powder. I like the powder. It feels good. It feels like this. Did you poison me?"

"What happened when Warrewik arrived?"

Vauclair stared up at the ceiling and grinned foolishly. She coughed to regain his attention.

"What happened when Warrewik came to Callait?" she repeated.

"I wouldn't let him land," he answered vaguely. "We even shot at his ship. So pretty. You are very pretty. I like you."

"Why didn't you let him land?"

He gazed back up at the ceiling. "He was helpless. Running away. He was vulnerable. My master thought it would be better to refuse him so he would come quickly to Pree and ask for help there. That would be better." He cocked his head and scratched his inner ear vigorously.

"Did Warrewik go to Pree?"

Vauclair chuckled. "No. Shynom."

Ankarette did not know where that was. "Where is that?"

He sniffed and smiled languidly. "Shynom is a palace. It is Lord Hux's estate."

Ankarette's heart filled with dread. "King Lewis wants to use Warrewik as a tool?"

"Of course. He's the Spider King."

He started scratching his ear again, more violently this time. His face was beginning to show signs of confusion and irritation. The poison was wearing off.

"What of Warrewik's daughter? Lady Isybelle? Did she have her child?"

Vauclair's face twisted with pain. He began to look around the room in confusion.

"I d-don't know," he said, stuttering. "She never came ashore. I s-sent a b-bottle of wine."

A bottle of wine. Poisoned, no doubt. Surely King Lewis would not want Dunsdworth to have an heir so soon. Not if he had other plans. Her mind whirled with the news, with the need to act and act quickly. The mad king had a son, an heir, who was being sheltered in Occitania.

And Warrewik had brought *both* of his daughters with him.

"You need to use the chamber pot," she instructed him. "Now."

Vauclair rose from the chair and started walking across the room to the private bed. She opened the door and saw the tray of food waiting on the floor with a silver chafing dish atop. Before she left, she added a poison to the sauce that would give him symptoms of violent dysentery for two days.

When she reached the main street where she had left the captain's first mate, she found him waiting there still, clutching a flagon and rubbing his arms against the night's cold. The streets were full of men who were laughing and singing and staggering with ale.

She did not disguise the sound of her approach. "What is the fastest route to Shynom?" she asked the first mate.

He sniffed and crinkled his eyes. "You can only reach it by horse. The fastest route is through Ploemeur in Brythonica."

"Take me there," she ordered, and started walking briskly back to the ship.

Ankarette was struck by the beauty of Brythonica. The cove was full of ships from every kingdom. Although the Duke of Brythonica owed fealty to King Lewis, it was an independent duchy and self-ruling. The palace was built on a craggy hilltop that would have been a tortuous ride up a series of sharp switchbacks. The Genevese traders deposited her in the harbor and stayed on to barter for some berries, which the duchy was famous for, before continuing to Genevar with the shallots.

The people of Ploemeur were friendly, and under different circumstances she would have been tempted to stay and explore. The hills were vibrant and bedecked with mansions all built above the cove. The calm waters of the bay looked idyllic, and she enjoyed the view and wished urgency didn't compel her to make such a hasty visit. She secured a horse by trading jewels for it and then wrote a letter addressed to Lord Hux in which she congratulated him on his successful operation in securing the Duke of Warrewik's allegiance. She intimated that keeping his allegiance would be a different matter. After dating it for two days before, she hired a courier to deliver it to Lord Hux at the palace of Shynom.

And then she followed the courier from a distance. Her years of hunting with Isybelle and making Espion journeys with Sir Thomas had trained her in the art of managing a horse, so she had no trouble keeping up with the courier's pace.

The lush countryside of Brythonica and Occitania were impressive and picturesque. The wooden signs marking the way made her think the courier was bound for Pree, but he took another road instead, leading deeper into the hinterlands. She had secured provisions for herself on board the ship as well as a bag of coins to provide for herself along the way.

The courier stopped in a village before nightfall. She chose the same one and made sure to stay out of his sight and keep her hood up. Everyone spoke Occitanian, and although she had learned the language in Pisan, it was difficult to understand the dialect. But she used the opportunity to immerse herself in the language and learn aught she could.

Her goal was still Shynom, and she had every intention of avoiding Warrewik once she arrived. Her misinformation to Vauclair had solely been intended as a ruse to sow confusion once the poison wore off. It was her plan to find Dunsdworth and persuade him to come back to his brother's side.

She was desperate to see what had happened to Isybelle and their babe. Had Hux tried to poison the child and the mother? There were tinctures that could halt labor. There were others that would kill the babe in the womb. That thought made her shudder and long for the night to end.

When approached, she ordered very little and spoke even less, mostly pointing to what she wanted to make herself less conspicuous. The room she stayed in that night was cramped and sparse and smelled of dust. The inn was not well used for being along a main road. She awoke before dawn, brushed and braided her hair, and then sat awake listening for the sounds of the rousing patrons. Her courier was not urgent about her business at all and tapped her letter against his chin while he noisily ate a meal of lamb chops. She watched him go and then followed.

The fortress of Shynom had been built on a low hill

below a thickly wooded forest and lorded over an expansive vineyard. It was the height of Occitanian beauty. Several ancient olive trees lined the footpath leading to the huge stone steps going up to the castle proper. It had been built centuries ago and was a mix of square turrets and round ones. It was not as impressive as Dundrennan, but it had been kept in a state of repair and the carved stone balustrade was perfectly symmetrical. She had caught up to the courier within a league of the castle. Though she'd rendered him unconscious and stolen his purse, she'd left him with the note she had written, to be discovered later.

As she arrived, the grounds were full of visitors wearing the high fashion of the Occitanian nobility. Lords and ladies wandered amidst the vibrant olive trees. Some sat on blankets enjoying picnics. There were liveried servants everywhere, and a groom came and fetched her horse. She showed him the duke's badge and he then asked in the language of Ceredigion if she had enjoyed her afternoon ride. There were so many visitors, so many people thronging the castle that one more lady-in-waiting would not be noticed.

"It was quite well, thank you," she answered cheerfully. After handing him the reins, she started walking toward the broad stone steps leading up to the castle's entrance. There was no longer a moat, nor a drawbridge —although there was evidence of the remnant of them. As she walked, she observed that the olive trees were planted in a great lawn that had probably once been a moat but was now filled in. She felt the familiar, eerie feeling of the Fountain's magic. She could hear water pattering in the courtyard ahead.

She sensed the presence of Lord Hux, the master of the castle.

He was there. King Lewis was probably also present. The Spider King had wanted her to serve him. Could she hope to get in and out without being noticed?

Steeling her courage, she started up the steps quickly.

CHAPTER 24
THE HEIR OF CEREDIGION

There were so many servants bustling through the castle that her presence went unnoticed. She walked purposefully past the guards at the door, as if she had come and gone countless times, and since she was wearing the duke's badge, none of them stopped to question her. In one of the corridors, she intercepted a cup bearer and asked in deliberately mangled Occitanian where she might find her lady.

He gave her directions, responding in her own language but with a strong accent, and waved his hand down the hall. She thanked him, and as she walked, she could sense she was going nearer to Lord Hux. Her nerves became as taut as harp strings. Hux was using his magic at that very moment. She dared not use hers, for if he sensed her, the charade would end. Biting her lip, she turned the corridor and found herself staring at a huge heavy door with ceremonial guards holding gleaming pikes on either side of it. A few servants were huddled before the door, some holding trays, talking amongst themselves. The guards stood impervious. No one was being let in.

Ankarette approached warily. From the muffled

noises behind the door, she could tell it was the great hall of Shynom. It was the center of the gathering, which meant Warrewik was likely there. A place to avoid. She did need help navigating the castle, however.

Cautiously, she approached the door. One of the servants looked at her, saw her badge, and gave her a derisive look.

"No one is being admitted," the haughty servant told her with a thick accent. "Not even you."

"Is my lady in there?" Ankarette asked courteously.

"And who is your lady?" the servant said in a snubbing way.

"Lady Isybelle."

The look changed, softened. "Oh, I see. Clare's wife. The duchess. No, my dear. She's still in her room recovering."

Ankarette swallowed and tried a look of helpless pleading. "Can you show me? I keep getting lost here. I don't speak much Occitanian."

The servant pursed her lips, looking burdened by the request, but then she nodded. "Very well. Come quickly. When they open the door, I want to be ready."

Ankarette thanked her and followed her down the hall. She began memorizing the decorations and other features to help her find her way back again. They reached a stairwell and the servant took it, bounding up the steps quickly. Ankarette kept pace, grateful to be heading away from the main hall.

"It is a shame your mistress is so unwell," the servant said, casting a look back at Ankarette as they climbed. "She will miss the wedding revels tonight."

Wedding? Ankarette had to be careful not to be too ignorant. "It is a shame. How do your people feel about the . . . the alliance?" She chose the last word in the hopes it would trigger some reaction.

"The 'alliance'? What a word! Could anything other than the Fountain have arranged such an unlikely union? For certes, it was a miracle."

"I suppose you could call it that," Ankarette sighed. "Though it seems to me more an act of desperation."

The servant smirked at her. "You are honest, for a servant. Yes, I suppose it is true. Queen Morvared is desperate to reclaim her throne. Duke Warrewik is desperate to rule Ceredigion once more. No one thought either would bend the knee and yield. But as we say in Occitania, feeding the wolf is dangerous. Not feeding the wolf, more so. Lest it consider you the next meal."

So it had happened. Warrewik had married his second daughter to the heir of the mad king. Her stomach roiled with disgust. Nanette had always cared for Severn. She had seen the two of them multiple times, engaged in harmless flirting. This news would crush Eredur's brother. And at the same time it would crush Dunsdworth's hope of becoming king . . .

"That's very wise," Ankarette said with a forced smile.

They reached the top of the stairs and then walked quickly down the hall. The servant was very chatty. "For many years I have served Queen Morvared in her poverty after the hollow crown was wrenched from her poor husband's head." Her voice betrayed an inner fury. "Now her son will rule. He is old enough to go to war. And now that he has married Lady Nanette, her father will get what he desires. An alliance, as you called it. But I still think it is one of Lewis's miracles. That is her door, with the filigree trim. Comfort her, if you can."

The young woman gave Ankarette a sympathetic look and then hastily returned the way she'd come.

Ankarette's mind quickly began putting together the pieces and she felt her Fountain magic respond to the situation and the desire to understand it and use it to her advantage. The feeling terrified her, for if she summoned her power now, Hux would be aware of her. She strode to the door, trying to tamp out the burning embers in her scattered thoughts, and then knocked before entering. She did not wait for an invitation.

It was not a grand state room like Isybelle had enjoyed at Dundrennan or Kingfountain. The curtains were drawn, muffling the light. The room was sparsely furnished and there were gowns and doublets tossed around. A set of muddy boots. Her gaze shifted to the bed, and she saw someone sprawled there. For a moment, she was fearful she had caught Isybelle and her husband in bed together. She shut the door and walked in quietly. The air smelled of stale wine. She saw several bottles of it on the floor. Her ears listened for telltale sounds, her nose for telltale smells of a newborn babe. There was no crib. When she reached the bed, she saw Isybelle alone amidst the sheets, still in a nightdress. Still asleep. There was evidence of Dunsdworth in the room, but he was not there in person.

Her heart knew the truth before her mind did. The babe was already dead.

Ankarette's throat tightened. She reached down and gently shook Isybelle's arm. "Belle?"

The tangled mass of hair moved slightly. Her head lifted. "Ankarette?"

Ankarette knelt at the bedside, reaching out and squeezing her hand. "I'm here."

A low groan came from her friend's mouth. "You

came. Oh, you came! Oh, Ankarette!" She sat up and the two embraced. Isybelle's shoulders quaked as she sobbed. She felt feverish to the touch, her skin moist with sweat beneath the nightdress. Tears squeezed through Ankarette's lashes as she held her friend.

"Too late," Isybelle moaned. "You're too late. I lost him, Ankarette. I lost him."

Her own throat was so tight she could hardly speak. She pulled back, sweeping Isybelle's hair away from her face. "The babe?"

Isybelle nodded in misery, her fingers squeezing Ankarette's arms so hard it hurt. "M-my son," she wailed. Her mourning was fresh, the grief raw and oozing.

"What happened?" Ankarette asked with sympathy. "Tell me. Please tell me."

Isybelle used some of the sheet to dab her nose. "It's such a comfort you're here. Even mother . . . has been distant. Everyone is so worried. We were going to lose it all. But father's plan may save us. Or curse us. It is treason, Ankarette. The blackest treason." She sniffed. "When we fled Kingfountain, after Eredur escaped, I was so worried that I started to labor. The pangs were fierce. There was no doctor on the ship. Not a one. We sailed to Callait, but that blackguard Vauclair wouldn't let us dock. Father pleaded with him to let me ashore or to permit a doctor to come to me." She shook her head, her eyes blazing with painful memories. "Oh, Ankarette. He had no compassion, none at all. He said we were enemies of Ceredigion and he wouldn't risk going over the falls to help us. The only thing he did, the only thing, was to send a bottle of wine to ease my discomfort." Her shoulders sagged. "I lost him . . . before dawn. We b-buried him . . . at sea. He's in the Deep

Fathoms now. My poor babe. My little son." She looked at Ankarette in misery, squeezing again. "If you were there, you could have saved him."

The tears were flowing freely from Ankarette's eyes. What could she say? It devastated her that her friend had endured such an awful loss.

Isybelle looked down. "It's not your fault. I know that. It's father's fault. He wouldn't listen to anyone. He sent you away when we needed you most. He doesn't trust you. He thinks you and Sir Thomas are lovers."

Ankarette paled. "We are *not*," she said defensively.

"I know, Ankarette. Of course I know. Do you know what has happened? Did you know there was a wedding?"

She nodded. "I heard it before coming upstairs. Nanette and the prince?"

Isybelle looked anguished. "She didn't want it. She never wanted it." She sniffled, trying to compose her voice. "Nanette tried to convince me to run away with her. To flee Occitania for Westmarch. It's the closest duchy. She's loyal to Eredur. In truth, we both are. If Dunne cannot have the throne, it should be an Argentine. Father has forced us to side with our enemies."

Ankarette gripped Isybelle's shoulders. "It's not too late to return."

"It *is* too late," she moaned. "The wedding is done. They will invade Ceredigion. Once father secures the throne for the mad king, the prince and his mother will set sail for Kingfountain. My father has pledged to risk his life and give Occitania the prize." Her eyes were full of loathing and anger. "And my husband and I get only ashes."

"It is not too late," Ankarette said, shaking her head. "Eredur sent me. If Dunne returns willingly, all is forgiven. There will be no forgiveness for your father. Not after what he's done. But you and your sister can still come home. You will not be disinherited when the Assizes happen. Dunne can retain his lands and stand to gain great favor. Do you think he will listen?"

"He already is," said a voice from the doorway.

It startled her so badly that she whirled away from Isybelle, drawing her knife and holding it up.

There was Dunsdworth. Cold and implacable. Judging by his bloodshot eyes, he was slightly drunk, and his sallow cheeks indicated those empty bottles on the floor had all been emptied by *him*. He wobbled a bit and then shut the door behind him, leaning back against it. Barring her way of escape.

"Or did you come to kill me?" he asked her with a look of distrust.

"I came here to save you," Ankarette said evenly. She would only kill him if he gave her no other choice.

He snorted. "Do you really think I believe that?"

"How much did you overhear?"

"Enough," he said, stepping away from the door. His coppery hair was tangled, and sweat dripped down his brow. "Why should I believe you? I could call the guards and you'd be in chains in a moment."

Ankarette would not let him do that. She stepped forward, but he wasn't afraid of her—even though he should have been.

"Your brother sent me to offer terms of a deal. I am authorized to negotiate on his behalf."

"Pfah," he snorted again. "And who are you? A servant? A poisoner? What are you, Ankarette? What are you really?"

"I'm your wife's friend. And yours if you will let me be. Look at the trap that's been set for you. You are in

Shynom, the castle of Lord Hux, the Occitanian king's chief poisoner! Do you have any idea how much danger you are in?"

His eyes narrowed. He had always been shrewd, always looking out for his interests. She would play on that.

"Just hear me out," she said.

"I'm listening."

She was grateful for that. The Argentines were notoriously stubborn. "The only chance you have of staying alive is if you side with your brother. The only chance you have of prospering is if you side with your brother. Any other road leads to death and failure. I understand that Morvared's son is now wed to Nan. Warrewik had intended for you to get the hollow crown. Not anymore."

His teeth clenched into a ferocious look. "He *promised* me!"

"I know," Ankarette soothed. "But he's broken all of his promises. He gambled and lost. And now he's gambling again, and he stands to lose even more. He no longer needs you. I'm sure you have sensed that here at Shynom." It was a guess, but she saw she'd struck the mark by the way his expression wilted into resentment.

"Everyone looks down at me, talks *down* to me," he said, and began pacing. "I'm a pariah now, but it was mine. It was all supposed to be mine!"

"Let it go," Ankarette said, shaking her head. "Eredur has had a daughter. His next child may be one as well. You never know what the future holds."

"Elyse is with child again?" Belle asked.

"Yes." She gave Isybelle a sympathetic look. "It may also be a son, which would ruin your chance of being king, but there are worse fates than being a duke of

Ceredigion. If you stay here, there is no hope for you. Ever."

He stopped pacing and scowled. "I was told that Morvared would name me heir, in case there is no offspring. Nan is very young. So is the brat prince."

"If you think she will honor that, you're a fool. And I know you are not." Ankarette saw the cogs turning in his skull. He was considering it seriously.

"We're trapped here," Dunsdworth said, shaking his head. "They have people watching me night and day. I'm practically a prisoner. If I could fly, I would go to Westmarch and beg Duke Kiskaddon to intercede for me. I've thought of that, but there is no way to cross the realm safely."

"You don't have to," Ankarette said. She put her dagger away and then, steepling her fingers, began tapping her mouth. She stopped, still trying to quell the Fountain magic that was nearly bursting inside her, begging to be used. "Warrewik will need soldiers to invade. He'll set you loose to gather the men of Clare. You'll march against Eredur as you are ordered to, but when your two armies draw near, send a herald to discuss terms. You can join sides then. Keep your own men ignorant of your intentions until it's too late. Otherwise, someone will betray you to Warrewik."

He looked at her for a long moment, then nodded in understanding. "That could benefit Eredur immensely. I'll know Warrewik's plans."

"Must you kill my father for this to succeed?" Isybelle asked pleadingly. "Cannot he be forgiven too?"

Ankarette turned and looked at her friend sadly. "Your father killed the queen's father without a trial."

"He deserved it," Dunsdworth quipped.

Ankarette turned on him. "He did not, my lord.

Would your brother be a just king if he allowed the blackest treason to go unpunished? He'll go over the falls. If the Fountain declares him worthy, then he will not perish. I think that is the only hope you have."

Isybelle looked downcast, but she nodded.

There was a loud knock at the door. Ankarette froze and Dunsdworth went pale. Casting her eyes around the chamber, Ankarette darted to the changing screen and quickly hid behind it. There were gowns spilled everywhere on the floor, some hanging from the top of the screen. Ankarette yanked them down and sprawled on the floor, covering herself with the discarded ones.

Dunsdworth walked to the door and cleared his throat. "Who is it?"

Ankarette recognized the voice instantly.

"It is I, Lord Hux," he said through the thick door. "Queen Morvared wishes to see Lady Isybelle. May we come in?"

CHAPTER 25
QUEEN OF WILL

The sound of the door creaking made her suddenly still. Isybelle sniffed, and the quiet of the room was invaded by noise from the hall.

"Ah, Lord Dunsdworth!" Hux said agreeably. "After my lady saw you leave the hall, she grew concerned about the delicate health of your dear wife. Lady Isybelle, I bow to you graciously. How are you feeling? Not so well, I should think."

Hux had such an easygoing manner, a voice that dripped sincerity. Ankarette felt his magic sweep through the room and she held her breath and tried to clear every thought from her mind. Ankarette feared even the thought of violence or anger might betray her to Hux's magic.

"I am not well," Isybelle said weakly. "The strain of the journey has been great."

"I can imagine so. I do not think you have been introduced to Her Excellent Majesty, Queen Morvared. The *true* queen of Ceredigion, who has lived these many years in exile here in Occitania."

The swish of skirts announced her arrival. Ankarette

lay still, although she burned to see what the other woman looked like.

"Is it not the tradition in Ceredigion to kneel before your queen for her mercy?" Morvared's diminutive voice came as a surprise. It sounded like the pleasant trill of a songbird, or the dulcet tones of an innocent young woman, although Ankarette knew she was forty years old. But that small, sweet-sounding voice could not disguise the force of will behind it.

"My wife is in a delicate—"

"*Kneel,*" Morvared cut in ruthlessly.

Ankarette heard the order and then she waited. And waited. The room was silent, stiflingly so. She heard Dunsdworth's seething breath. Heard Isybelle's groans of pain. Morvared said nothing, and the moment stretched longer and longer. Pitilessly long. The old queen was having her revenge. She would not be denied even a crumb of it.

Ankarette began to count in her mind. This was not the humble bow as a sign of respect. This was a measure of forced humiliation, a payment owed and due. She could not see what was happening in the room, but the impact of it was palpable. She heard Isybelle start to weep softly. Not in a hundred lifetimes could she imagine Queen Elyse doing this to someone.

The stifling gowns were smothering her and then she heard soft steps approaching the changing screen. Fear surged in her breast. It was Hux, coming to inspect the room and be sure no one was hidden. She wanted to reach for her knife or twist a poisoned ring on her finger. But would doing so reveal her as a threat? While she did not know how his powers manifested, judging from his reactions to her in Dundrennan, it seemed likely he would know. She emptied herself of all hostility and held her breath to keep the fabric from moving.

She felt Lord Hux standing near her head. Even though she could not see him, she experienced his presence as a series of tingling sensations, like her arm felt when someone was about to touch it. She sank deeper and deeper inside herself, wishing she could drop through the stones of the floor, wishing she could melt away into oblivion. She heard a sniff and felt a shoe nudge the pile of clothes just by her head. A fraction closer, and he would have felt her skull. Then he retreated from the changing screen. Sweat had gathered in the hollow of her throat and on her brow. She didn't dare even think.

"You may rise," said Morvared's mellifluous voice.

She imagined Dunsdworth had helped Isybelle rise because she heard a soft murmur of thanks amidst more groans.

"It grieves me that you have taken ill, Lady Isybelle," Morvared continued. "We are going to Pree, and I will make sure the finest doctors attend to you there."

"Pree?" Dunsdworth asked in confusion.

"Yes, you simpleton. King Lewis has promised me an army to invade Ceredigion. I will reclaim my throne and wrest the hollow crown from the head of your usurping brother. I will not be denied this time, putrid duke. After Lord Warrewik has struck his blow, you will be sent to Clare to rally your retainers. And you will do as you are ordered to do. Lady Isybelle will remain with me." Her voice had a malevolent edge to it. "Her sister has dire need of her companionship. I don't think she is taking well to being a bride. And I don't think your wife is up to more hard travel. Poor sweetling." There was not even a speck of sympathy in her voice. "Her presence will ensure your obedience. Am I clear, Lord *Dunsdwick*? You will do as you are told."

The final words were uttered in such a condescending air that Ankarette could imagine the hostile look on Dunsdworth's face as he heard it.

A great yawning silence descended on the room. Ankarette held her breath.

"I understand," he answered hotly. "My brother will never forgive me. What other choice do I have?"

"I'm glad you see it that way," Queen Morvared said. "Now, Isybelle. I know you are grieving for the loss of your child. I have lost babes before in a like manner. I am not without pity. But believe me when I say that I am now grateful for the losses I've endured. They have hardened me to disappointment. They have given me resoluteness of purpose. You are young. You do not even yet know what it means to suffer. Not fully. You are but a child yourself, pretending to be a woman. *I* am a woman. Your father was too lax in the rearing of his daughters. Too indulgent. Too distracted. I'm afraid I have much work to do to correct his shortcomings. But I am a patient teacher. And you *will* learn."

"Y-yes, Your Majesty," Isybelle mumbled.

"Hmmm? Speak crisply. With purpose."

"Yes, Your Majesty."

"Better. Now get dressed and come down to the fete. You are attracting too much pity, wallowing up here in your misery. If you are to become a true woman, you must act like one. Women are strength. I am stronger than Eredur. Not with a sword, but with my will. And I shall bend him until he breaks and then cast him aside as a broken thing. Just as I will do to anyone who defies me." She offered a gay little laugh. "Add some rouge to your cheeks. You are too pale. I expect to see you downstairs within the hour."

"Yes, Your Majesty."

"I knew I would like our little visit," Lord Hux said with delight. "It is all resolved. We will see you downstairs shortly. I'll send my butler to announce you."

When they had left, Ankarette waited several moments and then shed the coverings and emerged from behind the changing screen. Isybelle had sagged to the floor weeping, and Dunsdworth, in an act of compassion, knelt beside her, holding her. His cheek pressed against her hair. When he looked at Ankarette, his eyes were full of hate.

"You must get us both out of here," Dunsdworth told her angrily. "I'm ready to ride for Tatton Hall right now. I cannot endure another moment with that shewolf."

Isybelle looked up, her eyes red and swollen, her cheeks wet. "I c-can't ride, not like—"

"I cannot endure it!" Dunsdworth snarled.

Ankarette wanted to kick him in the ribs. "That is exactly what she and Hux are expecting. He is the chief of Lewis's poisoners. He was trying to provoke you into fleeing. To give him an excuse to kill you. To kill you *both*. They'd like nothing better."

Isybelle shuddered and buried her face in her husband's chest.

"Heed my counsel," Ankarette said, coming up to them. She put her hand on Dunsdworth's shoulder. "Go along with her request. Pretend to be a beaten man."

His mouth quivered with rage and she squeezed the meat of his arm. "I would rather die," he growled. "Warrewik won't let her injure his daughters."

"He will be gone soon and have no way of protecting them. They'll send someone along to make sure you obey their orders. You won't tell your soldiers, nay, not even your captain, what you are really about. Everyone must believe that you are still at odds with your brother. Every word you say must imply it. I will make sure no harm comes to Isybelle." She rubbed her friend's back and stroked her hair.

Isybelle sniffed again and dabbed her eyes. "Thank you, Ankarette. My sister—can you do nothing for Nan?"

The girl's mother-in-law was a formidable foe.

"I will do what I can," Ankarette promised. "Before I sneak away, let me help you get dressed. You must obey the queen as if your life depends on it. Can you do that?" Her words were for Isybelle, but her eyes sought out Dunsdworth's.

The young man nodded stiffly, his lips pressed firmly together. He was shrewd. Hopefully, he was shrewd enough.

~

ANKARETTE'S PLAN worked well until she was nearly out of Occitania. There was no reason to ride for Ploemeur since the Genevese ship was already gone, so she had chosen the road leading to Westmarch, or La Marche as the Occitanians liked to call it. What she had not anticipated was that the border would be closed in anticipation of the impending war. At a small border village called Courbevoy, the inns were all full of merchants who had crossed from Westmarch with goods but were not being allowed to go back. There were Occitanian soldiers everywhere, not a single room to rent, and the tension between the kingdoms was fierce.

Now she regretted leaving the letter for Hux with the courier. The man had probably recovered, which meant Hux was no doubt aware of her presence in Occitania. The letter had come from Ploemeur, but he would not be deceived easily. She had to return to Kingfountain to warn Eredur of the invasion.

Ankarette's horse was weary, and she rested it at a small fountain in the village square. The beast had been pushed to its limits the last few days. Should she steal another horse? No, the beast she had gotten in Ploemeur was used to her. Another animal might not work as hard for her.

She wished she had a map of the area, but maps were the purview of the Espion. Rulers did not wish for their borders to be well documented. Borders ebbed and flowed like the tide. She did know that Westmarch and Tatton Hall were to the east. If she could get into Lord Kiskaddon's duchy, the torture would end. Her mother was still there.

Sitting at the edge of the fountain, she reached in and touched the waters. Bowing her head, she felt the cool water against her fingers and summoned her magic. She needed an escape, a strategy.

The water grew cold against her fingers, and she felt the flowing sensation of the Fountain's power. It was as if, for a moment, she hovered over herself—as if she saw herself resting by the edge of the water. Her horse stamped impatiently and snorted. The swirl of life in the village—the muttering of the angry merchants, the hostility of the Occitanians—all continued in the background. But as she stared at the scene, she thought she saw streams of light emanating from the fountain where she sat. The streams of light were angled like spokes from a wagon wheel and the fountain was the hub. One of the lines pointed northeast like a beacon. A vision opened in her mind and she saw where it led—to another fountain inside the manor at Tatton Hall. She saw it as clearly as if it were in front of her. Something *connected* the two fountains.

There was a strange feeling, as if she were about to jump off the boulder into the river by Dundrennan. It was the anticipation of falling. She sensed a word, a breath was all it would take for her to plummet. But nothing happened and the vision abruptly faded.

A rough hand grabbed her shoulder. "Who are you?"

She was brought back to herself in that moment. Two Occitanian soldiers stood by her, looking at her with suspicion.

"Pardon?" she asked, trying her best Occitanian accent.

"Are you from Courbevoy?" one of them challenged. "Where is your husband?"

Husband?

"She has no husband," the other snorted. "On your feet. Let's bring her to Captain Gallay. I think he'll like this one."

"I was just resting," Ankarette said, but one of them seized her arm and yanked her to her feet. His grip was hard and painful.

"Did you hear her?" the man said. "She's not Occitanian. She's probably the daughter of one of those cursed merchants."

"Let me go," she warned. She tried to jerk her arm free.

The man backhanded her across the face, a blow so stinging and sudden that she had not anticipated it. Her skull rocked with pain. Her eyebrow hurt and she felt sweat or blood trickle down her face.

"Her father's probably getting drunk. Come on, let's bring her to Capt—"

Ankarette kneed the soldier gripping her in the groin. He doubled over in pain and she smashed the heel of her hand into his nose, sending him flying backward into the fountain with a loud splash. The other soldier grabbed a fistful of her cloak, trying to get to her neck, but she kicked the side of his knee and released the catch of her cloak in the same moment, leaving him holding that and nothing else. She twisted her needle ring and then struck him across the face, slapping him hard. The needle left a gash in his cheek that surprised and hurt him. His face twisted with fury before going slack, and he dropped to the ground in a heap.

Ankarette stood over him.

"I said I'm not for sale!" she shrieked at him and his friend in Occitanian. For good measure, she kicked the man who had collapsed in the gut. The crowd roared with laughter, and she witnessed encouraging and delighted looks from many of the villagers. She snatched her cloak from the clutches of the man she'd poisoned with her ring. Then, putting it on with a dignified air, she tossed her head and went to her horse. She only realized her temple was bleeding when she saw the blood on her gown.

Ankarette crossed the border into Westmarch well after sunset by following that beacon of light she'd seen emanating from the waters of the fountain in the village square. There were no soldiers guarding the woods, and to see the way again, she just needed to draw on her Fountain magic to summon that string of light.

She did not know what the lines of light meant. But she was grateful to her magic for showing them to her in her hour of need.

CHAPTER 26
FEARFUL

The roar of the falls faded slightly as Ankarette and her escorts from Westmarch cantered up the road to the fortress of Kingfountain. Duke Kiskaddon had insisted on sending protection with her. She'd told the duke about the merchants who were being kept in the village against their will, and he was preparing a force to retaliate and set them free.

She left her mount with a palace groomsman, then walked urgently into the castle. She recognized one of the Espion she trusted, Bennet, and told him to alert the king that she had arrived and needed to see him at once. Her magic was seriously depleted and she needed to rest, but neither situation could be addressed before she saw the king.

Bennet found her a short while later and said the king was meeting with his war council and wanted her to wait for him in the solar.

While she sat alone in the solar, she couldn't help but think about the ramifications of her mission. Though she felt assured of her success, she worried that making an ally out of the Duke of Clare would only sow seeds for more trouble in the future. Why had Isybelle married such an ambitious, self-interested man? Love was such a dangerous thing...

The sound of approaching steps alerted her of an impending arrival and she backed away from the sturdy table and assumed a formal air. The door opened and Sir Thomas came in first, followed by Eredur and Elyse. The queen's walk showed the discomfort of her pregnancy.

Sir Thomas strode up to her eagerly, his face animated with a look of relief and genuine delight. His eyes instantly went to the sutures and bruises at her eyebrow.

"You were injured," he said in a low, furtive way, the smile melting from his face.

"It was nothing," she answered, a little pleased by his show of concern.

"Ankarette!" Eredur beamed. He came forward and took her shoulders. He too noticed the marks on her face, but his manners were unflappable. "I hope you gave as good as you got."

Elyse approached and smoothed back Ankarette's hair. Her expression was one of friendly concern, and she winced at the signs of violence.

"Who did this to you?" Sir Thomas pressed.

"Some Occitanian soldiers who mistook me for a merchant's daughter," Ankarette answered. "In a border village near Westmarch. There's some trouble there that Duke Kiskaddon has pledged to handle. I just came from Tatton Hall. I am fine, and the news I bring is of far more consequence."

"And timely," Eredur said, tapping his chin. "You are back more quickly than I thought possible. Poor Tom has been moping for days in agitation."

"My lord," Sir Thomas complained.

"I'm jesting, Tom. But only in part. Truly, he's been worried about you. You left for Callait. Did Vauclair tell you where to find Warrewik? Did you treat with my brother?"

Ankarette still felt shaken by the king's words—and by Sir Thomas's embarrassed reaction—but she steadied herself. "Captain Vauclair cannot be trusted," she said pointedly. "He's duping both Warrewik *and* you. He's in the pocket of King Lewis."

"I knew it," Sir Thomas growled in frustration.

Eredur's eyes narrowed. "Are you sure? I was more worried about his loyalty to my uncle."

"I am. The soldiers are loyal to Warrewik, I think, but Vauclair turned your uncle away and wouldn't let him land. I don't think many of his men know what happened. I believe Vauclair deliberately poisoned Isybelle. He and Lord Hux are friends. None of this was done for you, however, but upon the Spider King's orders."

The king and queen both blanched.

Ankarette steeled herself to continue. "Isybelle's son died during childbirth in the harbor outside Callait. Vauclair wouldn't let her in to be seen by a doctor. Instead, he sent a bottle of wine. He tried to poison me as well." She smiled dangerously. "He did not succeed."

"Poor Isybelle," Elyse whispered, shaking her head with a look of maternal sympathy.

Ankarette nodded, grateful for the show of sympathy—even more so because it was clearly genuine.

"I am grateful you realized his duplicity before being caught in his web yourself," Eredur said, shaking his head in wonder. "When I sent you there, I didn't see the risk you were taking."

"I'm a decent judge of character."

"So you poisoned Vauclair instead?" he offered, encouraging her to continue the story.

"I did. I learned that Warrewik has found refuge with King Lewis."

Sir Thomas started. "None of the Espion in Pree have seen any sign of him. I have two men in the palace."

"He's not in Pree. He's at Lord Hux's estate called Shynom."

"That's in the hinterlands of Occitania," Eredur said, nodding sagely. "It used to be one of the Argentine fortresses centuries ago."

"I took a Genevese ship to Ploemeur and crossed to Shynom on horseback. No one took notice of me because I was wearing Warrewik's badge. His people were everywhere. I arrived just in time to learn about the wedding . . . Warrewik has married his younger daughter, Nanette, to the mad king's son, Prince Ardric. Morvared and Hux are in league with each other. Both are undoubtedly doing the will of King Lewis. There will be an invasion, my lord. And soon."

Elyse reached for Eredur's arm. He looked dizzied and baffled by the news. "How could he?" he said to himself in disgust. "How could he stoop so low?"

Ankarette rose to her feet and stepped forward. "You must understand, my lord. Warrewik has always wanted his daughter to be Queen of Ceredigion. It is the driving force behind everything he has done. When *you* would not have Isybelle, he looked to Dunsdworth next. But now that path has failed also."

"But did you get to see Dunsdworth?" Sir Thomas asked. "This new alliance must be bitter wine for him to drink."

"Indeed," Ankarette answered. "Yes, I've seen him and spoken with him."

"Well done, lass!" Sir Thomas said.

"And what did he say?" Eredur pressed. "Do I dare get my hopes up? He is stubborn and ambitious."

"A family trait, I think," the queen offered with a slightly mocking smile. "Judging by her expression, I think she brings good news."

Ankarette had tried to keep her expression more neutral, but the moment felt too heady for her to quite manage it. "I do bring good news with the bad," she continued. "Your brother recognizes that his position is even more diminished than before. He sees this new marriage as a betrayal, and the Occitanian court has treated him with derision. He and Isybelle are pariahs now. I told him all would be forgiven if he supported you. He agreed to do so."

Eredur squeezed his fist and grinned broadly. "You didn't manage to smuggle either of them back with you, did you?"

"No, that was beyond my ability and resources," she confessed. "But I did give him instructions. Their plan is for Warrewik to reclaim the mad king's throne while Queen Morvared waits in Occitania with her son. Only once his position is assured will she cross the border. Isybelle is to be kept in Pree as a hostage for Dunsdworth's obedience. I advised him to follow every command given to him, telling not even his captain that he has switched sides. He will approach your army while appearing to obey Warrewik's orders, and then you must send an emissary to him. He will then fall in with you. It's as if a white piece is masquerading as a black one on the Wizr board. When the time comes, I will save Isybelle and her sister."

THE POISONER'S ENEMY

Sir Thomas scratched his head. "It doesn't offer much by way of support, but it's a success any way you look at it."

Ankarette beamed. "Thank you, but the mission did not go perfectly. Lord Hux may have known I was there. He and the queen came to see Isybelle and Dunsdworth while I was in the room, although I did hide."

Sir Thomas started pacing. "What do we do about the prisoner in the tower?" he asked Eredur with a meaningful tone.

Eredur stood stone-faced. "I'll not hurt that harmless man," he said. "And it wouldn't do any good, besides. It would only make Prince Ardric even more valuable."

Sir Thomas nodded. "Certainly, but should we move him? What if Warrewik strikes at Kingfountain? You could have Stiev Horwath take the prisoner to Dundrennan."

"A good topic to discuss in council," Eredur said. He turned and faced Ankarette and then stepped forward and took her hands. "I cannot tell you how helpful you've been. You have served me well, Ankarette. Thank you for your loyalty."

"You are welcome," she answered.

Eredur went to Elyse and offered his arm to help her stand. The queen smiled kindly at Ankarette. "You are appreciated more than you know," she said. Their gratitude made every risk worthwhile, and she had the thrilling feeling of knowing she'd helped the king and queen.

The royal couple left the solar, but Sir Thomas lingered at the doorway, watching as Eredur and Elyse went down the hall. He sighed and butted his head against the doorframe.

"Are you all right?" she asked him, coming closer and touching his arm.

He had a sheepish smile. There was a mix of feelings in his eyes and he gave her a strange look. The roil of emotions she sensed baffled her.

"I've been a wreck since you left," he said softly, carefully, deliberately. He twisted his neck and gazed at her. "I've been worried about you. Sick with worry, actually. I knew you were capable. It wasn't that. And I can't say how relieved I am that you made it back safely and with useful intelligence." His lips pressed together. He was wrestling with something inside, and she felt her heart beat faster.

"I'm proud of you, Ankarette. I hadn't prepared myself before you left. Prepared myself for how I would feel if something happened to you. I've been in the Espion a long time. Missions fail. They don't always end in success." His gaze was tender as he looked at the bruise on her brow and the stitches. "Who did the sutures? Your mother?"

Ankarette nodded, suddenly unable to speak.

"I should have known," he said, smiling smugly. "I'm sorry you took a blow. If I had been there, I would have killed the man for touching you."

His look frightened her, and yet it filled her with sunrays of hope. He felt something for her after all . . . her departure had pained him. It was a delicious moment, one that she would think on multiple times when her heart was no longer afire.

"They thought I was a merchant's daughter," she said simply. "That they could do what they wished with me."

"You could pass for someone much older," he said,

folding his arms. "A merchant's *wife*, mayhap?" He shook his head. "An awkward jest. I'm sorry."

What was he trying to say? What was he implying? She felt vulnerable in that moment, looking into his eyes. The ground between them had shifted during her journey. She was in unfamiliar territory.

She wanted him to kiss her—and she suddenly feared that he would.

The noise of bootsteps came down the hall. Ankarette stepped back, realizing they were standing very close together. It was Bennet the Espion.

"Come quickly," he said, his breath harried.

"What has happened?" Sir Thomas asked with concern.

"Word just arrived. Atabyrion has invaded the North."

CHAPTER 27
INDECISION

I n the days that followed, the uncertainty in Kingfountain became more pronounced. King Iago of Atabyrion had landed troops in the North and was attacking villages in the hinterlands. The king's council decided to send Stiev Horwath to drive the invaders away, lest Iago's presence create a foothold for Warrewik's force. Atabyrion and Occitania had a long history of uniting their forces against the might of Ceredigion.

The news about the Atabyrions' attack was followed shortly after by word from Duke Kiskaddon that a large Occitanian force led by the Duke of Brythonica was assembling at Averanche. It seemed poised to strike at Westmarch, or possibly Kingfountain itself.

Ankarette felt the mounting tension of the conflict grow day by day. Her health was returning, and she had been feverishly stitching to restore all her lost Fountain magic. She wanted to be useful again, to lend assistance to her king. After days of not being summoned, she made her way through the Espion tunnels to the Star Chamber, where she found Sir Thomas poring over correspondence from the many new Espion recruits scattered through the kingdom. His eyes were bloodshot and he looked as if he hadn't slept in days.

He glanced up from the desk, midway through a letter, and then tossed it aside and leaned back in his stuffed chair.

"Ankarette," he breathed with a weary sigh. "You're looking much recovered."

"And you're looking much worse," she said, shutting the secret door behind her. "What news, Sir Thomas?"

He rubbed the stubble on his chin and then shook his head with helpless frustration. "None of it is good. The Atabyrions are hitting hard. They've avoided a pitched battle, preferring to stay on the move. Horwath's men are stretched thin and he's asked for reinforcements, which we can ill afford to give." Another sigh escaped his mouth.

"And Westmarch?"

"Duke Montfort is a mystery," he said. "We've never had any Espion in Brythonica before. Your quick trip through Ploemeur has been our only source of intelligence from that land. Kiskaddon is skittish. He's expecting the brunt of Warrewik to hit Westmarch first, and he's asking the king for reinforcements too. Which side to aid? Or neither?" He frowned. "The king is racked with indecision. And so he delays, and the people are growing more concerned day by day."

Ankarette went to the desk and stood over his shoulder, looking at the mass of papers strewn across the surface.

"Has the king chosen a new master of the Espion yet?"

"It's me for now," he said, gesturing toward the heap. "As little as I care for it. There is so much to read and decipher. I crave action, not words. But without these scraps of paper, we are totally blind. With them . . . we're confused. I'm not sure which is worse."

"When did you last sleep?" she asked, feeling the urge to rub his shoulders. He looked so weary, so miserable, and she longed to comfort him.

He let out a small chuckle. "I've stolen a snatch of time here and there. It's all so insufferably vague. It's like playing Wizr, except one cannot see the moves in play. And there are multiple hands guiding the pieces."

"You need to get some rest," she said. "Your mind is spent. Let me help. I can read letters you haven't. Maybe I will see a connection you do not."

He turned his head and looked up at her, a relieved smile twitching his mouth. "I would be grateful. I haven't dared to sleep for fear that some bit of vital news would arrive the moment I took some rest. Most of the reports are mundane and useless. But I have to read each one. It's true, you might see something I've missed."

She smiled at him. "Show me where to start."

He stood and began to sort through the massive heap, explaining which of the letters he had read already, which he had postponed reading, and how an Espion courier would soon return and add more to the stack.

"Bless your heart, Ankarette," he said, smiling in relief. "I wouldn't trust any man to do this work for me. But I trust you."

In the hours that followed, Ankarette immersed herself in the wayward world of spies and deception. Some of the reports she read were responses to inquests Sir Thomas had made of Warrewik's past servants and allies. Some were reports overheard in taverns throughout the realm. She enjoyed the work immensely. Each message was a sign of life from the kingdom, like the ragged intake of breath, the throbbing pulse of a heart. It felt as if Ceredigion was some breathing, living thing.

There was one letter she wished she had *not* found. It had been tucked beneath a stack at a crooked angle. The handwriting was different from the rest, a woman's hand.

Sir Thomas,

I must beg you not to importune me with further letters. My mind is quite fixed on marrying your brother.

I have waited and waited for news of your promotion, only to have my hopes continually dashed. For years, I have waited to see your promises fulfilled. I have been patient, or tried my best to be. It was too much to hope that your connection to the king would result in you receiving a title or lands of your own.

Things have changed. I wish you well. But in doing this, I must please others before myself. I am fond of you, Sir Thomas, and always will be. When father returns from crushing these knaves from Edonburick, I will ask him to settle the arrangement with your brother. We must remain friends apart.

Elysabeth Horwath

• • •

Ankarette gently folded the letter and carefully put it back where she had found it, wedging it beneath the stack of discarded correspondence. No wonder Thomas's spirits were so depressed. He had fostered ambitions for years of becoming a noble in his own right. It was apparent that Elysabeth would only have him if he succeeded. A snip of disappointment cut into Ankarette.

It was impossible not to brood on the letter. She had always been jealous of Elysabeth, or rather of Sir Thomas's feelings for her. The girl who'd helped her dress with such boredom and disinterest on her first night in Dundrennan was a beauty, no doubt, but she did not appear to have great depth of mind. Still, she was a duke's daughter now. Her prominence in the world had risen greatly. She was an eligible match for any young man in Ceredigion, and she knew it.

The letter said too much, and Ankarette wished she had never seen it. Her feelings for Sir Thomas roiled inside her, more conflicted and confusing than ever. She was disheartened that his attitude had begun to change only after his advances—and it was clear from the letter they were *recent* ones—had been rebuffed once again. Ankarette had not been his first choice. But that feeling was mixed with a degree of sadness and tenderness for him and a desire to ease his pain. There was also a small feeling of relief that the haughty girl from the North had rebuffed his advances. He deserved someone better than her.

The courier arrived later with another stack of letters. He was short, with a pudgy face, a dark goatee, and wavy dark hair. "Another pile," he apologized. She took them from him and quickly began to read again, trying to maintain her focus.

Her heart pined after Sir Thomas much like his did for Elysabeth.

Should she tell him how she felt?

The mere thought of it made a flush creep to her cheeks.

It was at that moment that he appeared in the secret doorway, looking more rested. "Are you cold?" he asked her, glancing at the brazier, which had burned low.

"Not at all," she hastily replied, rising from the chair.

He gestured for her to remain. "I need to go see the king. I can't tell you how much I appreciate this, Ankarette. You're a jewel. What news?"

He came and stood over her shoulder, as she had done with him, and his nearness made her ache inside. "I've organized them all and tried to straighten up your desk."

"I can see that. Thank you."

"These two you should read on your way to the king." She said, handing them to him. Turning to another small stack, she snatched it up and said, "These you should answer and seek more information. What happens with this pile after you've read it?"

"The courier burns them," he said. "This room generates more messages than you can possibly imagine. Even more than the royal correspondence. Thank you again, Ankarette. I could not bear this task alone for much longer."

"Of course. I only wish to be useful."

The next few days passed in a like manner. They took turns reading the correspondence in the Star Chamber. She would fill him in on the latest news, which he would use in his reports to the king, and he would inform her of what he'd read while *she* was resting. There was no fixed schedule, and sometimes they would talk for hours to compare what they'd learned. Neither of them could see what Warrewik was doing. Neither of them could deduce his plan. As the days stretched on, the tension in the palace grew and grew. But she savored the partnership they'd formed, and the frank discussions they had fed her mind and her heart.

And then the letter came that changed everything.

It was a short letter, one hastily scrawled line from an Espion in the southern town of Lawness.

Warrewik has landed.

Ankarette gripped the letter, her heart racing as she leaned forward. She felt the pulse of her Fountain magic respond to the note, bearing witness to the truth of it. It was dated one day ago. She pushed away from the desk and, grabbing a lantern, swiftly entered the Espion tunnels. It was the middle of the night, but the catacombs were familiar to her.

As she walked, she saw someone approaching her. Assuming it was Sir Thomas, she held the lantern higher.

"There is news," she said urgently and then suddenly stopped. She didn't recognize the man. Then she heard the soft tread of boots behind her.

Someone smashed a rag against her mouth from behind.

The instinct to breathe in was strong, but she had learned to fight that instinct in Pisan. Dropping the lantern, she jabbed her elbow back into the ribs of her assailant. Then, gripping his forearm, she twisted and hoisted him onto her back, then flipped him down so that he landed on the lantern, squelching the flame. The man barked in pain and surprise and the tunnel was

THE POISONER'S ENEMY

smothered in darkness. The rag had left gritty residue on Ankarette's face, and her mind began to swarm with dizziness. It was *morgrith* powder.

She heard the noise of bootsteps coming toward her. She unsheathed her dagger and threw it, hearing the hiss of an indrawn breath as it hit her target in the heart, followed by the sound of a second body slumping to the floor.

The other man, still moaning in pain, tried to scramble away. Ankarette grabbed his sleeve and then jammed the edge of her hand into his neck. He struck back at her, flailing, but she encircled his neck with the crook of arm, ignoring the spots dancing in front of her eyes. He tried to grab her face, her hair, but she leaned back, twisting away from him, fighting the weakness weighing down on her.

The man twitched, losing his strength as she choked the air from him. Then he collapsed. She sagged against the wall of the corridor, feeling lightheaded and dizzy. No longer able to stand, she began to crawl away in the dark. She moved past the two fallen opponents and made her way to Thomas's room. Was she lost? Her mind was a fog...

The terrible urge to vomit struck her and she sprawled forward, purging herself onto the ground. But after the spasms ended, she felt her wits returning, along with her strength, and she managed to make it to her feet. Soon, she was at Sir Thomas's bedroom. She didn't bother being quiet and he awoke instantly.

"Ankarette?" he asked in a worried voice. She heard the rustling of his bed sheets, and he quickly lit a taper from the coals in the brazier.

He stared at her in shock.

She looked down and saw blood smeared on her

gown. Her throat was still burning with bile. She thrust the letter into his hand and he read it quickly.

"I killed two men in the corridor," she croaked. "They were Warrewik's men."

"Lawness is a day's ride from Kingfountain," Thomas said, scrubbing his hand through his dark hair. He looked at her in grave concern.

"Which means he'll arrive by dawn," she answered, having come to the same conclusion. "He already has men in the palace."

"Are you injured?" he asked her worriedly.

She shook her head. "The blood is theirs." Then she looked at him fiercely. "Warrewik doesn't want a pitched battle. His honor demanded one before, but now he's too afraid he'll lose. Everything else has been a deception, an attempt to lure our attention away and keep Eredur undecided. We have to assume he's known our movements better than we've known his. Somehow he knows Eredur is still in Kingfountain . . . and that he's sent away most of his knights. He'll attack swiftly, and he won't grant quarter this time."

"No, he won't," Thomas said. "I must get the king out of here. But where? Warrewik probably has people watching the bridge night and day. We'll have to cross the river."

"No," Ankarette said, shaking her head. "You'd be playing into his hands. Eredur must leave Kingfountain. He must leave Ceredigion completely."

"What are you suggesting?"

Her mind was awhirl with ideas, plots and plans fitting together. "He must do the same thing Warrewik did. The tables have turned. He must flee. To Brugia."

"You said yourself that Captain Vauclair cannot be trusted!"

"I didn't say go to Callait. Didn't the king say his sister is married to the King of Brugia? He must flee to Marq."

Sir Thomas looked appalled. "I wouldn't trust that man with the king's safety. He's treacherous. He could hold him for ransom, and Warrewik would pay."

"In times of crisis, we turn to our families," Ankarette said. "And right now, being unpredictable may be the only thing that saves Eredur's life."

Sir Thomas looked at her seriously. He took a deep breath. "All right, but I'm not telling him this on my own. You're coming with me."

CHAPTER 28
THE CISTERN

T he logs added to the hearth were beginning to snap and flame, which brightened the royal bedchamber considerably. Eredur paced back and forth, his countenance fallen with worry and despair at the news they had brought. Elyse sat in her robe on a small cushioned sofa, one hand protectively over her swollen abdomen. Her eyes were tracing her husband's frantic stride. This was the worst kind of news to receive in the dead of night.

"I don't want to abandon the palace," Eredur said angrily. "Do you have any idea how difficult it will be to win back Kingfountain? If we summon my knights, perhaps we can hold Warrewik off for a few days, give Horwath and Kiskaddon a chance to interrupt the siege?"

Sir Thomas sighed wearily. "You're risking more than just the castle. Warrewik will throw you in the river."

The queen looked imploringly at her husband. "He will, my love. I think Thomas and Ankarette's plan is wise. You must flee to Brugia while you can."

Eredur brooded, walking to the hearth with clenched fists. "I should have kept an army near me. I want to fight him. With a hundred sworn men, with a hundred *loyal* men, I could defeat him."

The queen rose shakily from the bench and went to him, wrapping her arms around his middle, pressing her cheek against his back. "No, you could not. Sir Thomas, if Warrewik's spies have already infiltrated the castle, there will be a trap for us on the bridge. They'll expect us to flee."

"Yes, we've already considered that," Sir Thomas said, nodding to Ankarette. "I'd suggest rousing your knights and Severn right now while I fetch the palace woodsman. He knows the grounds even in the dark and can bring us through the wall. No torches or lanterns. We flee to the village of Lindower and bribe some fishermen to row us to Brugia. We could get away before they leave with their nets this morning. The docks will be watched."

Eredur turned angrily. "Elyse is in no condition to march that far! Not to mention the danger of a sea crossing. The babe is due in another month."

"My other sons are with my brother," Elyse said. "What will happen to them if Warrewick seeks more revenge on my family?"

"I know this is difficult," Ankarette said, stepping forward, acutely aware of the queen's condition. "She cannot flee. She and your daughter must remain behind in Kingfountain."

Eredur was grief-stricken. "I cannot abandon them again!"

Elyse's eyes were wet with tears, but she held herself bravely. She leaned against him, clinging to him as a pillar. His arms wrapped around her.

Ankarette looked him firmly in the eye. "I will bring them back to the sanctuary of Our Lady. They will be under the care of Deconeus Tunmore. Not even Warrewik would risk the wrath of the Deep Fathoms by dishonoring the privilege of sanctuary. Tunmore is a powerful ally, my lord. And your step-sons can be taken to another sanctuary if you fear for them. St Penryn's for example."

Sir Thomas put his hand on Ankarette's shoulder. "Listen to her, my lord. Every moment we waste convincing you, we run the risk that this plan will fail. The chance is slim enough as it is."

"But you just said that the bridge would be guarded and the Espion tunnels may be crawling with Warrewik's lackeys. I don't mind taking risks for myself, but this is straining my trust and confidence to the utmost."

"I understand," Ankarette said. "I would need to hide the queen and your daughter in the castle for a few days. A place where no one would come looking for them."

Sir Thomas turned to her. "What about the cistern beneath the palace? No one ever goes down there."

The queen looked worried. "I don't know where that is. Is it very small, like a well?"

"No, my lady," Thomas soothed. "It runs the length of the palace. It's like a huge catacomb. It stores the rainwater for the palace each year so we don't have to haul it up the hill in barrels. I think there's even a boat down there the servants use to inspect the far ends. Even in the daylight, it's pitch dark down there. You could hide easily."

The queen brightened.

"Just long enough," Ankarette said, "for Warrewik to seize the castle. I could take your daughter to the sanctuary first—in disguise, of course—and then come and fetch you. People will expect to see you in royal robes and gowns. A peasant woman and her daughter will be unrecognizable."

"Love?" Eredur asked, stroking her cheek with the edge of his finger. "I don't want to be parted from you. Not again."

The queen cast her gaze down and then looked at him with determination. "We must think beyond ourselves. The time has come for us to break your uncle's dominion once and for all. Go to your sister and beg for aid. Promise whatever you must. But return with an army and claim what is yours. This castle is yours. The hollow crown is yours. What will happen to the land if we are put under the rule of a mad king? You must set us free, my lord husband. My dearest friend." She leaned up and kissed him on the mouth. Then she turned and approached Sir Thomas. "I trust you with my husband's life, Sir Thomas. Do not fail me."

He swallowed at the solemnity of the moment. "I won't, Your Majesty."

She stood on the tips of her toes and kissed Sir Thomas's cheek. "I hold you to your vow." Then she turned. "Ankarette. Let's awaken Elyse."

~

THE PREPARATIONS WERE ALL UNDERWAY. Everything was done in profound silence. The knights had been roused. So had the king's younger brother, Severn, who wore a black tunic and stood by the hearth in the king's chamber, his eyes brooding darkly. Ankarette saw him gripping a dagger handle in his belt. He slowly pulled it partway from the sheath before slamming it back into the scabbard, as if he were plunging it into Warrewik's back. News of Nanette's forced marriage had thrown him into a fury. Lord Hastings, the king's chancellor, was also with them. He had no desire to remain behind and risk the consequences of Warrewik's disfavor.

Drew, the palace woodsman, stood there warily in the midst of the royal company. Ankarette did not know him well, but the menacing axe strapped to his back gave him a dangerous look despite his being soft-spoken. He had a backpack full of food and provisions for them to eat along the journey, hastily assembled by his kind-hearted wife, Liona, the castle cook.

Sir Thomas brushed his hands together. "Everything is ready," he said. "We must go, and quickly. We must be like the shadows. We're taking no armor, to avoid the noise, and you're to keep your swords in their sheaths. If I catch anyone muttering above a whisper, you'll be left behind. Is that clear?"

All the men nodded. The queen and her daughter were both wrapped in cloaks, as was Ankarette herself. The child Elyse rushed up and hugged her father fiercely. He crouched down to squeeze her, pressing bearded kisses against her cheek. She sobbed quietly, and it was clear to Ankarette that she would have braved the long walk in the woods at night if she'd been allowed. She did not beg her father to stay, but faced the situation with courage.

After hugging her father, she walked up to her teenage uncle, Severn, and hugged him as well. Her kindness touched him, melting past the seething anger. He too bent down and hugged her, patting her head tenderly.

"Keep Papa safe," little Elyse told him.

"Loyalty binds me," he said.

"We go," Eredur said curtly. He had already bid his wife good-bye. Their looks were full of sorrow and concern, the one for the other. The sight of their mutual affection pricked Ankarette's heart. They were the closest, deepest of friends and allies.

The men began filing out of the room into the dark corridor, the woodsman leading the way. Sir Thomas waited by the door, making sure everyone was accounted for, and finally he and the king were the only ones who had yet to leave.

Eredur gazed at his wife one last time.

"Come back to me," the queen pleaded in a whispered voice.

He nodded in response and slipped into the hall. Sir Thomas let out a heavy sigh and then gazed at Ankarette. Her heart churned with emotion. She walked up to him and withdrew a folded letter from her girdle.

"I went by the Star Chamber," she told him, offering him the letter. "You had set this one aside. I thought you might want to keep it . . . or that you wouldn't want Warrewik or anyone else to discover it."

It was the final letter he had received from the woman he'd loved. His eyes widened with surprise as he took it.

"Did you read it?" he asked. He didn't look offended or concerned, just curious.

She worried her cheeks would flush, so she hurriedly nodded, preferring to reveal herself through her words.

His lips pursed. "Well, thank you, Ankarette." He stuffed it into his pocket and raked his hand through his hair. His cheeks reddened a little with embarrassment. "That was very good of you. I'm not sure I want to keep it now." He glanced backward into the corridor. "Well, I must go. I wish there were time to say more—ah, but there isn't."

There was much she wished she could say to him as well. There was something in his eyes, that new look she'd noticed. If only...

"Good-bye, Sir Thomas," she said, her chest aching.

~

Ankarette had never been inside the cistern before, but it fascinated her. She marveled at the stone buttresses overhead that were burdened with the enormous weight of the castle. Little Elyse was nestled in the prow of the small boat, holding the lantern to help them steer. Ankarette prayed the girl wouldn't be careless and drop the lantern into the water, plunging them into darkness. The queen sat with a cask of jewels on her lap, shivering with cold and fear. Ankarette held the oar and gently pushed them deeper into the massive expanse, eyeing both sides as they went.

There were pillars coming up throughout the cistern and she noticed markings etched into the stone showing the depth of the water. It was the middle of autumn. The scorching summer heat had long since ended, but the winter rains had not come to replenish the stores. Ankarette had tested with the oar and felt the paddle scrape the stone bottom.

"What are those sounds?" little Elyse asked, and her voice echoed and rippled off the stones.

"Shhh," the queen urged her in a whisper. "It's just the rippling of the water against the pillars."

There were other noises as well. Some commotion was going on above them in the palace. It had to be past daybreak already. They had gone as quietly as they could, but their speed was limited by the queen's delicate condition.

When they reached the end of the cistern, Ankarette spotted a stone portcullis higher up on the wall, hanging from a series of chains and pulleys. She guided the boat toward it, but it was too high for her to reach.

"Let me see the lantern, please," she asked, and little Elyse handed it to her.

Shining the light at the door, Ankarette saw a small catwalk leading up to it. Steps led from the bottom of the cistern to the catwalk. She asked the queen to hold the light and steered the boat toward the steps.

"Keep the boat here," she said to the queen. Elyse handed her the lantern, and Ankarette climbed up the steps. There was a metal grate at the top of the portcullis and she was able to see outside. Beyond the stone door, she saw a gentle sloping ramp and quickly deduced this was the drain of the cistern. If the water filled the cistern too much, the excess would spill through the grate down to the ramp, which fed directly into the river. The winch system was rigged with counterweights so that if the lever was pulled, the entire stone door would be hoisted open and the water from the cistern would be drained into the river.

Craning her neck, she tried to get a view downriver to see how close they were to the falls. A feeling of hope began to swell in her chest. The ramp faced the rear of the sanctuary of Our Lady. If a boat were put into the river at the end of the slide, there would be time to steer it toward the back of the sanctuary. It was, indeed, the most direct route possible, but missing the sanctuary would be disastrous. The current would surely rush the boat directly down the falls.

Ankarette gripped the grate bars and thought about it. Yes, it seemed that the design had been deliberate. The system allowed for the cistern waters to be purged, but it also provided a secret way of escaping the palace. It was possible that Warrewik didn't even know about it.

It would definitely be a faster way to safety. Ankarette pondered it again, but she didn't want to risk the life of the queen or her unborn child recklessly. While squeezing the bars, she bowed her head and sought to summon her Fountain magic. She plunged deep into herself, listening to the muted rush of the river behind the thick stone wall. The power came to her, invited in gently. In her mind, she saw the small boat gliding down the ramp and splashing into the waters. She felt a thrill of wonder, a sense of peace and certainty. The presence of the sanctuary seemed to draw her to it, compelling her to bring the queen there to seek the protection they offered in such times.

And yet, in that moment of certainty and assurance, the Fountain magic inside her also warned her of the presence of another Fountain-blessed who was inside the castle that very moment. Lord Hux was searching for her and the royal family.

A spike of fear shot through her chest when she realized that she'd revealed herself to him. Now that she had invoked her magic first, she sensed him respond immediately, like a flare of flame striking pitch.

He was coming for them.

CHAPTER 29
THE DREADFUL DEADMAN

Ankarette tightened her grip on the bars as her heart began to batter inside her chest and her throat went dry. Controlling panic was never easy. But panicking led to mistakes, and mistakes were fatal in her profession. She gazed down the ramp, looking at the angle, and clung to her magic, trusting it with all her thoughts. The river's turbulent waters thrummed against the stone.

"My lady, I think I found a way for us to escape," she called down.

"Where?" asked the queen.

"There is a ramp that leads down to the river. Once the lever is pulled, this portcullis will grind open and the current will push us down the ramp. We could make it to the sanctuary this way."

"But what about the falls?" asked the queen with worry.

"We are far enough upriver."

"I don't like the thought of going into the river," the queen said worriedly. She clutched her daughter tightly.

A noise reverberated from the far end of the cistern.

The door had opened, and the sound of boots marching echoed throughout the vast chamber. Voices grunted and called, sounding eerily close.

"He said they were hiding down here," muttered one man. Torchlight illuminated the distant side.

"What does he know?" carped another soldier. They were too far away to be seen, but Ankarette presumed they were Warrewik's men.

The queen pressed her daughter even more tightly to her bosom. Ankarette tiptoed down the stairs.

The men's voices echoed throughout the chamber. "How deep is the cistern?"

"Look at the notches. Not that far. Go in there and test it, Beannon."

There was a splashing sound. "Only up to my waist. Come on, spread out."

Ankarette reached the edge of the boat and pitched her voice softly. "Lord Hux is coming. He's Lewis's poisoner. We must go."

The queen flinched. She bit her lip and nodded.

"Do you see anyone? Could be hiding behind one of these pillars."

"Shush, man! They'll hear you."

"I don't care. Do you really think she's down here? Warrewik would pay us well if we find her."

Ankarette stepped into the waters to direct the boat. Her skirts were quickly soaked up to her waist, tangling around her legs.

Then she heard Lord Hux's voice. "You're making enough of a racket," he said angrily. "Be careful. Do you see anyone?"

The light from the torches was getting closer. The queen's daughter began whimpering with fear and the queen hugged her close, trying to soothe her. The queen's eyes went wide with panic. Waves generated by the advancing soldiers sloshed against the hull of the craft. Ankarette positioned it prow-first against the stone portcullis.

"Come, Ankarette!" Lord Hux's voice ghosted. "I know you're down here. We both know it. Come into the light."

"I think I see something," one of the soldiers grunted.

"Where?" Hux demanded.

"At the far end. There's a little boat. Oy! I see them!"

"Get them!" Hux ordered.

The soldiers began charging through the cistern waters, making loud splashes.

Little Elyse started to sob, and the queen quailed with fear. Ankarette felt a peaceful tug at her heart despite the commotion. They would make it. She reached up and caught the end of the lever that held the counterweight. Pausing, she waited until the soldiers were closer. Anxiety knifed her stomach, but she kept her eyes on the closest man. She could see the hunger in his eyes as he approached his prey through the water.

Ankarette yanked on the lever and the stone door began to grind open. She felt the tug of the water immediately, sucking at her legs as the pent-up waters burst down the spillway. She hoisted herself into the boat, rocking it violently, and then felt it rush forward. The queen and her daughter screamed as the tiny craft pitched down the ramp. Ankarette swung her legs inside, and fear and excitement battled inside her as they careened into the river. The force jolted her, nearly capsizing the boat, but it righted itself and began to plunge down the river. Ankarette grabbed the oar and began to steer toward the island sanctuary.

Another splash sounded behind them and she whirled to see one of Warrewik's men had tumbled into the river behind her. He splashed frantically, trying to swim against the avalanche of water. His head bobbed up and down, and his screams for help were cut off when he was dunked by a dip in the current. Ankarette worked at the oar, not trusting her strength as she watched the river carry the man away in its deadly embrace. It was a stark reminder of what could happen to them if she was not successful. The boat sliced through the current and headed for the dock. Ankarette summoned her strength and continued to row hard. She felt the presence of Lord Hux behind her, and when she turned, she saw him standing at the top of the rampart, gazing down at them. His fury was almost a palpable thing, but she could not watch him. She needed to give the river all her attention.

As they approached the dock at the rear of the sanctuary, she sensed the presence of another Fountain-blessed. The deconeus, John Tunmore, and his sexton came hurrying down the wooden ramp to meet them. The sexton threw her a rope, which she caught, and the boat was secured. The deconeus helped the daughter out first and then the queen.

"You are safe, Your Majesty, thank the Fountain," Tunmore said, helping her up the steps. "The duke's men have blockaded the gates of the sanctuary, searching every person who comes to visit. I have told them they are not permitted within the grounds for now, but they are looking for you and your husband. Where is the king?"

Ankarette heard the soldier's screams again as he went over the falls.

Queen Elyse shivered at the sound and the deconeus wrapped his arm around her shoulders and started leading them down the pier. The sexton reached down and helped pull Ankarette up.

"He is gone, Deconeus," the queen said. "And this I promise you. My husband is the rightful king, and he will return to claim his throne."

The deconeus nodded worriedly, glancing up at the sky. "He must. Before it is too late."

∽

THE SHOUTING from the confrontation in the chamber echoed across the stone walls and tiled marble floor. Ankarette stood concealed behind a pillar to watch and listen. Warrewik had come to face Tunmore two days after learning that the queen had taken sanctuary there. His men patrolled the exterior of the grounds day and night, though the queen was hidden deep within the sanctuary in a private cell. The thieving sanctuary men had found their trade disrupted and tensions ran high.

Ankarette watched as the two men faced each other in postures of defiance and authority. The sanctuary was the deconeus's domain. His was the ultimate authority there.

"My quarrel is with Eredur, not his peasant wife! You think I would harm a woman?"

"I think you are capable of any deed if it suits your ambition, my lord," Tunmore shot back. "I am not keeping her here against her will."

"She's with child and due imminently. Let her come back to the palace where she may receive all due care and attention."

"The queen does not wish to leave."

Warrewik exploded with rage. "She is *not* the Queen

of Ceredigion! Morvared is the queen, duly anointed by the sacred chrism. Your rightful king has returned to power. You can be *replaced*, Deconeus!"

"Your false king cannot replace me," Tunmore said with bravado. "And I find it the height of hypocrisy that you support him now that your daughter is wed to his son. You are the one who overthrew him in the first place!"

Warrewik's cheeks were purple and quivering. "Your service ends with your life, Deconeus. Must I remind you of that?"

"Are you threatening a deconeus of the church?" Tunmore said hotly. "Mind yourself, my lord. There is a crowd gathered at the gates. They know you are here and they will gladly obey my will and throw you into the river should I denounce you. The people of Kingfountain love Eredur now, not you. Your fame has waned since you usurped control of the throne. Mind your tongue and don't you dare threaten *me*."

The words proved effective. The Duke of Warrewik stepped back away from the deconeus. A look of fear muted the rage in his eyes.

"You've made an enemy of me," Warrewik said. "I thought you were wiser than this, John. I'll not forget this betrayal. Wherever my nephew went, my men will find him. He will not be coming back."

"But his wife is great with child, a child who will be born in this very sacred place. Who knows. The child may be the Dreadful Deadman."

Ankarette wrinkled her brow. It was a prophecy from the ages about the return of an ancient king, a ruler who would unite all the kingdoms in peaceful harmony. A worldly man like Warrewik would consider it superstitious.

Warrewik sneered. "I don't think so."

Ankarette heard the soft clip of boots and turned to see Lord Hux approaching her in the alcove. His eyes were guarded but respectful. Her worry intensified a thousandfold.

She turned to face him, surreptitiously twisting her ring to expose the needle.

"No need for that, lass," he whispered coaxingly. "I'm very aware of how resourceful you are."

"Thank you," she answered, not feeling at all at ease. She knew he was dangerous, that every part of him could kill her.

"Your king does not have many pieces left on the Wizr board," he said with a conniving smile. "The game is almost over."

"I will not tell you where he is," Ankarette said. "You will get nothing from me."

He smirked. "I don't need you to tell me what I already know. He arrived today in the city of Marq."

It was an arduous journey to Marq. There was no possible way that a spy could have traveled so quickly. Was he simply guessing in the hopes of making her reveal the truth? She kept her reaction neutral.

He took a step closer. "You have no idea the game you play," he whispered. "Or what the rules are. Someday I will teach you. There is much that I could teach you." His eyes smoldered at her with heat. She saw just a little hint of teeth.

Suddenly Warrewik was standing next to Lord Hux. The duke saw her in the shadows and her stomach lurched with even more foreboding. His eyes narrowed and his cheek twitched.

"Ah. There you are. I'm not surprised to find *you* in the shadows," he told her.

She inclined her head to him, keeping her poise and dignity.

"It's because of you that Isybelle's babe died," he said with acrimony. "You betrayed her as well as me. She was your friend."

It would have been easy to fling something back at him. To defend herself and justify what she had done. To tell him about Vauclair's wine or the way Morvared had mistreated Isybelle. But no words from her would ever convince him that *he* was the one who had betrayed himself. And so she did not answer at all, but met his look with one of defiance.

"We must go," Warrewik finally said, nodding to Lord Hux. "I cannot trespass against Tunmore's goodwill any longer. It would be a shame if he died suddenly, Lord Hux. Life is so fragile. Isn't it?" Although his words were addressed to Hux, his eyes were glaring at Ankarette.

"As you will," Lord Hux said graciously. He bowed to Ankarette and turned to leave.

Warrewik kept her fixed with his dark look. As he turned to leave, she finally spoke.

"One of your men went over the falls, my lord. It will not be long before it's your turn."

~

A MONTH after taking sanctuary at Our Lady, the queen's pangs of childbirth began. It was late in the day when they started, and Elyse had experienced the precipitous sensations before. There were no servants present, only Ankarette and the queen's daughter. Light came from oil lamps, which helped dispel the gloomy shadows of the windowless cell. The queen was brave during the pangs, her teeth clenched as she strained against the stuffed pallet that had been brought in to comfort her. Sweat drenched her skin.

The queen gasped with the strain, the beads of sweat trembling before dripping down her cheek or her nose. The hushed groans grew more urgent. Ankarette applied some oil to her hands and helped minister to the queen's comfort as best she could. The deconeus stood guard at the door, gazing in periodically to check on the progress, only to leave immediately with a look of grotesque disgust on his face.

The daughter tried to comfort her mother through the pangs, whispering assurances. The queen was exhausted, but there was still work to be done. Somewhere far away, her husband was a fugitive, unaware that she was giving birth.

Ankarette's mind wandered, as it often did, to Sir Thomas. Her heart ached to see him. Winter was poised to begin and there would be no war during those months. The treacherous seas or the Deep Fathoms would prevent the situation from progressing. And so, a mad king sat on the throne in Kingfountain. Some said he mostly played on the floor like a child, humming to himself. Queen Morvared waited in Averanche with her son and Warrewik's daughters and an army of Occitanian knights ready to invade. Horwath was besieged at Dundrennan by an army from Atabyrion and Warrewik's remaining loyalists. She wondered how the siege would affect the upcoming marriage of Horwarth's daughter to Sir Thomas's older brother. She knew Sir Thomas was heartbroken. But she was good at mending things ...

"I'm ... I'm so tired," the queen panted, lying back after the spasm had passed. The contractions were coming closer and closer together. It would not be long now.

"How old were you when you first went through childbirth?" Ankarette asked as she performed her examination. Questions always helped people think through the pain and discomfort.

The queen smiled weakly, her eyes closed. "I w-was, let me think, I was eighteen. You'll be that age . . . next year."

"How old were you when you married Lord Degriy?"

"Fifteen. I was . . . .*nghhh!* . . . so young. Too young, maybe, but it was a good alliance. I loved him well enough. These cursed wars. Will they never end?" She panted, gasping for breath. "If only it were true, and a king would come to end such feuding."

The pain started again in earnest and she sat up, arching her back and straining with agony.

"You can do it, Mama," said little Elyse.

Ankarette was ready when the babe came. It was an easy birth this time, with no complications. The gooey infant was wrapped up in a towel and Ankarette's heart was thick in her throat. A surge of happiness filled her with such sweetness. Little Elyse began stroking the soft, feathery hair atop the babe's scalp.

"There there, wee one. There there," she said softly.

The queen looked utterly spent, exhausted to the point of insensibility. The babe's squeals brought Tunmore into the room anxiously, his eyes wide with anticipation.

"The babe's come? It's come?" he gasped hopefully. "What news! Tell me!"

Ankarette rocked back and forth, humming softly to the babe.

The little boy.

"He has strong lungs, don't you think, Deconeus?" Ankarette said, feeling tears well in her eyes.

The look of relief on Tunmore's face was palpable. "A son. An heir. Thank the Fountain! May it be praised forever. We are safe. We are saved!"

His words were incongruous to her. Although it was good news an heir had been born, the little infant could do nothing to solve their immediate predicament. Did he mean something else? Something more?

Ankarette brushed her lips against the pink forehead.

The queen roused herself. "Is it done? A boy? Did I hear right?"

"Yes, my lady," Ankarette said, smiling, bringing the bundled babe to his mother. "Your son is hale and strong. Like his father."

The queen smiled sweetly, the pain forgotten. "I was going to name him that. Eredur—after his father. He will be a mighty king."

There was a soft whisper from the Fountain. It sounded in her ear.

He is not the Dreadful Deadman.

She blinked in confusion and turned to the deconeus. Tunmore's face had reacted—as if he too had heard the words. The two looked at each other.

No one else had heard the whisper.

CHAPTER 30
MARQ

S unlight flooded the diaphanous curtains of the deconeus's chamber. Ankarette parted them, gazing out at his private garden. She saw clumps of ash-colored snow in a few of the shadowed nooks, but the barren trees were beginning to bud. A leathery gardener dragged a bucket of tools to a corner where he would begin to furrow the soil.

The deconeus's voice was ominous. "Your Majesty, if we do not send word to your husband soon, it may be too late."

Ankarette let the curtain fall back into place and turned to face her queen, who cradled her infant son in her arms and jogged from foot to foot. The babe had grown much in the months since his birth. There were no palace attendants here, no ladies-in-waiting save Ankarette herself. The Espion named Burke was stationed at the door, and it was his latest news that had cast a pall on the conversation.

"What can we tell him that he does not already know?" the queen asked in a tired voice. "Surely Philip Temaire keeps his own spies."

"Indeed," Tunmore said, "but he likely shares little

information with your husband. The situation grows more dire by the day. The snows are nearly done melting, and while spring was late this year, summer is coming on winter's heels. One need not be the Wizr Myrddin to predict what happens next. The North is lost if we do nothing. Horwath has had the advantage of the ice and snow to protect the passes leading into Dundrennan. My informers within the sanctuaries say that Warrewik has gathered an army sizeable enough to break Horwath's grip on Dundrennan. While Warrewik reclaims the North, you can be certain that Lewis will invade Westmarch. If both or either fall, Eredur will fail. The king must return to claim his throne. Or the mad king will hand over Ceredigion to Occitania and it will destroy us all."

"Surely it is not that dire," the queen said with concern.

Tunmore planted his palms on his desk, looming over her. "Believe me, my lady. I've never known the situation to be graver. Eredur must be told."

"You are suggesting," the queen said, glancing at Ankarette, "that I send *her*."

Tunmore nodded. "I am. It's the wisest course of action."

"But where is Lord Hux?" the queen asked with concern. "We are blind to his movements. I need Ankarette near me, to protect my children."

Tunmore glanced at Ankarette. "You are already protected, my lady. Hux would not dare violate sanctuary. The city of Kingfountain is loyal to your husband. If he were to return here, the populace would rise up in support."

Ankarette disagreed and said so. "I don't think it would be prudent for him to come to Kingfountain," she said. "The people may be loyal, but Warrewik controls the city. It is just what the duke expects him to do."

"But he needs those who will fight for him," Tunmore countered. "Horwath is trapped in his own castle while Atabyrion runs amok in the North. Kiskaddon is trapped between Warrewik and Occitania. He can't defeat both alone. The garrison at Callait, as you've already told us, is in the pay of an Occitanian sympathizer. The king has been gone for six months already. His choices are few."

Ankarette turned to Burke. "Can you wait outside, please?" she asked him.

He was her supply of information from outside the sanctuary. Many of the Espion were still loyal to Sir Thomas and Eredur and provided information discreetly from the gates, passing notes under the very noses of Warrewik's guards. Some messages had even been baked into muffins. The Star Chamber might still be sequestered in the palace, but it was also operating from the sanctuary, and Ankarette was the center post holding it up.

Burke obeyed and ducked out of the room.

Ankarette came forward and dropped her voice lower. The queen leaned in eagerly.

"I have been giving this much thought," she said. She'd spent hundreds of hours at her needlework, trying to pull together a plan that would help Eredur reclaim his throne. The stitching had given her time to think, time to replenish her Fountain magic, sort through the ideas and facts, and try to put together a series of actions. The obstacles were significant.

"I know you have," the queen said. "You've kept it to yourself."

Ankarette smiled. "There wasn't much to say until

now. I agree with the deconeus that we must act. Your husband cannot read our thoughts, cannot know all the troubles he's facing here. He needs to be warned. I think I should go to him in Marq. Let me explain my strategy."

"I'm anxious to hear it," Tunmore said, furrowing his brow.

"I would advise the king to land in the North, at Crowspar."

The deconeus looked perplexed. "That's Warrewik's domain. I don't understand."

"I'm from the North, Deconeus," Ankarette said. "My father was a lawyer in the city of Yuork, and my family was loyal to Eredur's father, the Duke of Yuork. He told me an obscure story when I was a child, and I've since found the tale in one of the histories I read while living in Dundrennan. One of Eredur's ancestors used a certain ploy to regain power, and I believe it could work for him. In the North, there are many there who are still loyal to the memory of Eredur's father. I suggest that Eredur return to lay claim to his ancestral title. He can say he accepts the rulership of the mad king and seeks only to maintain his heritage as Duke of Yuork, not as King of Ceredigion."

Silence pummeled the room. It was audacious. Tunmore blinked in surprise, looking at her as if she were either brilliant or mad.

"The mayor of the city of Yuork would never open the gates to him under such a pretext. Who but a fool would believe him?"

Ankarette stared at Tunmore. "That is where you come in, Deconeus. You will *make* them believe him."

His eyes widened as he realized her meaning. She nodded. "For this to work, the queen must know your secret. I've never told anyone. But I think it should be revealed at last. And that is why I dismissed Burke."

"What does she mean, Deconeus? What secret?" the queen asked in concern.

Tunmore straightened, his expression somber as he weighed Ankarette's words. "And this is your entire plan?"

She shook her head no. "It's only the beginning of it. The mayor of Yuork will not open the gates unless he's convinced Eredur is telling the truth. You are the only person I know who can do that."

"Tell me what is going on," the queen insisted.

The deconeus sighed and scrubbed his scalp vigorously. "You're right, of course. I can no longer keep my secret. Your Majesty, Ankarette is not the only Fountain-blessed in your service." He breathed in through his nose. "I was blessed with the gift of convincing. I can create a letter, forge it—if you will—and whoever reads it will absolutely believe what I have written to be the truth, even if it is a blatant falsehood. This ability led to my success at a young age. I've kept it carefully concealed, and I would ask Your Majesty to safeguard it if I use it on behalf of your husband."

A delighted smile brightened the queen's face. "We have *two* Fountain-blessed?" she whispered in awe.

Tunmore nodded sheepishly.

Ankarette was pleased. "Starting in the North will throw Warrewik off balance and it will relieve the strain on Horwath, allowing them to combine forces. And there are many supporters who will flock to Eredur's banner of the Sun and Rose once he lands. Our plan will trap Warrewik between Westmarch and us. And who will Warrewik call to aid him in such a dilemma?"

The deconeus gazed at her in confusion. "I'm assuming you mean the Duke of Clare, his son-in-law. But how does that help Eredur?"

Ankarette looked at the queen knowingly.

The queen smiled. The strategy was perfectly clear to her now. "You see, Master Tunmore, my lord husband and his brother are already reconciled. Thanks to Ankarette."

The deconeus stepped backward, reeling from the information. A grin quirked the corner of his mouth. "Oh, I see. I see what you are doing. But if Warrewik still controls Kingfountain, he can escape as he did last time. He needs to be trapped in the middle of the realm."

"Exactly," Ankarette said with a smile.

~

ONE OF ANKARETTE'S favorite parts of studying at the poisoner school was learning about other realms. Now, she was dressed in the traditional style of Brugia, in a white chemise that was puffy at the sleeves and had garter bands at the wrists and elbows. In another nod to Brugian fashion, she wore a jaunty velvet cap. She had arranged for the Espion to bring the disguise to the Genevese ship she had used for passage. Sneaking out of the sanctuary had been simple enough, for visitors came in and out of the grounds daily to worship at the fountains, and the guards could not keep track of everyone.

Now that the queen knew Tunmore was Fountain-blessed, it had eased her concerns about temporarily losing Ankarette's protection. Tunmore would be able to sense if Lord Hux used his powers in the sanctuary, and he'd vowed to toss the man into the river if he dared enter the grounds while she was gone.

The ship dropped Ankarette off at one of the headwater cities, and from there she took a barge upriver to Marq. Burke had assigned another Espion to accompany her to Eredur's hideaway in Brugia. She was grateful for the escort, and also that she would not have to discover his location on her own. The Espion who accompanied her, a man by the name of Hawkins, was in fear and awe of her. He refused to use her given name, referring to her instead by the title of the *Queen's Poisoner*, or *Her Ladyship's Poisoner*.

The city of Marq exceeded the size of Kingfountain in terms of population. The outer walls were massive and the interior was all interconnected waterways, arched bridges, and tightly clustered buildings. The air was humid and had a mossy smell to it. Fleets of gondolas scudded along the placid waters, delivering passengers from one quarter of the city to another.

"My lady, the king is staying at a small manor house at the inner rim of the city," her guide told her in a small, nasally voice. "I have been there several times to deliver intelligence to Sir Thomas Mortimer. The only way to access it is by these strange boats. I've heard that King Philip keeps an eye on those who come and go, but no one has ever troubled us."

He arranged for a gondola to take them to their destination, and she found herself growing more anxious to see Sir Thomas again. She had expected to see him, of course, but she'd forced herself to keep her focus on the plan, not on what Sir Thomas might say to her after so many months apart. Somehow, she maintained a calm dignity as the boat glided on the waters and the poleman sang a humble tune to himself to pass the time.

She watched the people on the roads and overhead

bridges, reminded of her studies and fascinated by the accuracy of the information she'd learned at the poisoner school. Marq was so different from her land, but she was enamored of it already.

The gondola turned a lane and began approaching a row of houses that faced the water. There was no street access, only a small wharf before each one. The places all looked similar and were in a state of disrepair. The dock posts were black with slime and the waters were stagnant and stale smelling.

The poleman reached the dock of a two-story dwelling with curtained windows facing the waterway.

"This is it," Hawkins said, wiping his nose. A man came out to interrogate them, and when he made the Espion hand sign, her guide responded with the correct return signal. The newcomer nodded and then looked at her. It was Bennet, and a broad smile lit up his face when he recognized her.

"Ankarette!" he said in welcome. His hair had grown longer and his clothes matched the fashion of the Brugians, including a ruffled collar. It had taken her a moment to see through his disguise.

"Hello, Bennet," she said. He reached for her hand and helped her out of the gondola.

"We were not expecting you!" he said in surprise. "Let me bring you to Sir Thomas. He and the king will be overjoyed to see you."

"Thank you," she said, giving him a fond smile. Her companion tipped the driver a few extra coins.

She was ushered through a small gate, which led to a tiny walled courtyard. So this was where the king had found refuge during his exile? She had expected to find him at the palace in the center of town.

The sturdy wooden door of the manor opened before they reached it, and then she was face-to-face with him once more. Sir Thomas had a rakish beard and he too had grown out his hair to match the style of the country. A sword and dagger were belted at his hips and he wore a dark jerkin decorated with slashes of green and little ruffs at the cuffs but not at the neck. She could see his desperation in the new worry lines on his forehead and around his eyes, the desperation of a man fighting to swim while sinking.

And then he saw her.

He halted as if he'd struck a wall of glass. The worry lines melted away, and the look he gave her—the warm smile, the brightening of his eyes—filled her with warmth and happiness.

"Ankarette Tryneowy," he said in disbelief, his voice throbbing with pleasure.

Bennet coughed into his hand and tried to conceal a knowing smile. "Well, I see we've found him already. If you'll excuse me." He shook his head and ducked past Sir Thomas into the manor.

Sir Thomas stood there, gaping at her. "No one said—"

"There was no—"

They'd both attempted to speak at the same moment. Her cheeks began to flush at the way he was looking at her. It was more than a look of just friendship.

An awkward quiet stretched between them.

"Look at you," he said, chuckling softly, shaking his head. "You're not that young waif I was sent to fetch from Yuork all those years ago. Have you come to bring us home, lass?"

Her throat was suddenly thick, but she still managed to speak. "Yes. It's time to go home, Sir Thomas."

He shook his head and took a step closer, reaching for her hands. When his fingers touched hers, she felt a lively jolt go up her arms. Her skin tingled. He looked a little shy, very uncertain of himself. "Just Thomas, lass. Thomas will do from now on."

Standing alone with him in the small courtyard, her heart began to burst open.

CHAPTER 31
THE KING'S GAMBIT

King Eredur received the news of Ankarette's arrival with warmth and appreciation, and soon she was sequestered with him and Thomas in a private room, seated around a small table. Voices were kept low, for secrecy was essential. The king listened with keen interest to her strategy and the news she had brought from Ceredigion. There was no doubt he realized his kingdom was perched like a precarious boulder—one false shake would send it crashing down with no chance of recovery.

After she finished her explanation, Eredur rubbed his mouth, his intent gaze showing he was deep in thought. "Can I see the letter that Tunmore wrote? Everything depends on it, for if the mayor does not believe it, we'll be trapped outside Yuork and vulnerable to Warrewik's army."

"Of course," Ankarette said. She removed the letter from the hidden pocket in her gown and handed it to him. Thomas got up and stood behind his shoulder to read it as well.

She felt the rippling of the Fountain as they began to read.

Moments later, Eredur's hand dropped and the letter tumbled onto the table. "By the Veil," he said, shaking his head, "I'm convinced it is true and I *know* it's a lie! I had no idea the deconeus was Fountain-blessed. He's kept this secret carefully guarded."

"Indeed he has," Ankarette replied, glancing at Thomas over the king's shoulder. He was giving her that look again . . . the one that said he truly saw her. Her emotions bubbled over inside and she nearly grinned like a foolish young woman.

"You need to see Philip," Thomas said, putting his hand on Eredur's shoulder. "Right away. This instant. He must provide you with some boats and some men. We cannot let this opportunity pass. If he will not agree to help, then you must convince your sister to assist you behind his back."

"He's not been very supportive thus far," Eredur brooded. "He's provided us a run-down manor to live in, far enough from court so that he doesn't have to see me every day and be reminded of my plight."

Ankarette looked the king in the eye. "Then you need to remind him what will happen if Warrewik wins. His daughter will sit on the throne alongside a puppet king from Occitania. Our three kingdoms have always challenged one another for land. With Occitania and Ceredigion united, Brugia will be in a weak position. It would be best for King Philip to have you on the throne."

"It's the only reason he's supported me thus far," Eredur said, grinning. "But Warrewik and Lewis have the upper hand right now."

She shook her head vehemently. "They do not, my lord. You have never been defeated in battle. You've been tricked and duped before. But this conflict will only end on the battlefield. Your uncle fears you. And so does Lewis. When you land in the North, it will terrify them both."

Eredur rose from his chair and began pacing. "I risk all with one throw of the dice. I don't want to be wrong."

"Horwath can aid you," Thomas said, trying to help persuade him. "If you lose Dundrennan, you will have no further defense. Kiskaddon cannot stand alone. He'll capitulate to save his duchy. Horwath is staunch. He'll fight to the end."

"I'm counting on that," Eredur said. "I've always respected that man. He does what he says he'll do. And he was loyal to my father from the beginning." He sighed and tossed up his hands. "What else can I do? I'm not just fighting for my throne. I'm fighting for my son's future as well." He gave Ankarette a fond smile. "I'm grateful you were there to bring him into the world, lass."

"He's a handsome babe," Ankarette said, dimpling at the praise. "He'll need you to teach him how to be king."

"Then I cannot waste a moment," Eredur answered. "We go to the palace."

∽

ANKARETTE KNEW the powers of every type of poison. Some could leave your insides wrenching in pain. Others could create a dreamy sense of euphoria. But she knew of no substance that could counterfeit the feelings she experienced while walking hand in hand with Thomas Mortimer in the gardens of the Temaires' palace in Marq.

Eredur was meeting privately with King Philip and his wife, Eredur's sister, so Thomas and Ankarette had started strolling through the grounds. They had started off walking close together—Ankarette sharing the latest news from Kingfountain, and Thomas telling her about the subterfuges and politics of the Brugian court. And then he had stopped and taken her hand.

"Look around us, Ankarette. Couples walking together, hand in hand. I envy them at times like this. Some days I'm so weary of the deception, the frustration, and the injustice of the world. Do you ever long for simpler days?"

"Has it ever been simple?" she asked teasingly.

The feeling of his hand in hers made her giddy inside. *Finally,* she found herself thinking. *Finally.*

"Not in a long time," he answered with a chuckle. "Sometimes I think about the falcon hunts. You and Isybelle riding ahead. I was your protector—not that you needed it! Those were quiet and simpler days. Or maybe it's just that I'm looking at them in a different light now." He gave her a covert look and a private smile. "Thank you for sharing the burden of the Star Chamber with me. I was hopelessly overwhelmed by the flood of messages. Thought I'd drown in them. You made the impossible task . . . enjoyable."

"It wasn't so bad to me," she confessed.

"That doesn't lessen my gratitude for it. And if you don't mind, I'd like to savor this little haven a trice longer." He breathed in deeply, casting his eyes around the park.

But he didn't release her hand, and soon they were strolling the waterways, watching the herons and swans, and relishing each other's company. There was no feeling in the world to describe it. They had been friends for so many years, and somewhere along the way, he had stopped looking at her as a child and started to see the woman she'd become. It was a heady feeling, and she knew she would savor this moment forever.

"There is a little place," he said with a sly voice, glancing at her, "by the bridge leading to the only sanctuary of Our Lady in Marq. There are little tables and chairs outside where you can watch the people come and go. Everyone owns a pet in this city—many of the dogs are whip thin and better groomed than the people. The food there is really quite good. Would you care to join me? We'd need to take a gondola to get there."

"If you think we'll have time," she said.

"I'd like to take you there," he said, squeezing her hand.

The gondola ride was idyllic, but Thomas had her full attention, and they continued their talk of Brugia.

"Everyone carries a sword," he explained, patting his own, "because the youth are hot-tempered and quick to insult and challenge one another. There are feuds among the nobility that have lasted for generations. All the wealthiest families have a manor home here in Marq and squabble over their holdings throughout the realm. There was a riot a few weeks ago caused by some disturbance or other."

"What do they fight about?" she asked.

"Everything," he teased. "They're not very different than we are in Ceredigion. Are we not also fighting over land and squabbling over insults? Contention seems to be the sport of the nobility."

"Would that have anything to do with excessive ambition?" she asked, giving him a pointed look.

He smiled, cocking his head to one side. "There's

that too," he conceded.

After the boat arrived at the small dock, he got out first and then helped her out, not surrendering her hand as they walked. They looked like any of the Brugian couples along the lane, and she had a momentary fancy that they could melt into the crowd and remain in Brugia forever, forsaking the troubles and the perils of their lives. A strong part of her hungered for that, to lay down the burdens of a kingdom and simply be this man's wife. They made it to the little bakery, and he ordered a variety of local fare for them to sample.

"A strange combination of spices," he said about the drink she'd just sampled, "but I do believe it is my favorite."

"What is it?"

"It's made from some kind of root," he said with a shrug. "I don't remember the name, but we do not have it in Ceredigion. It has a unique flavor, does it not? And the rice pottage is excellent too." He took her spoon and stirred the little bowl with the pottage. "There is some egg, some green onion, some poultry, I think." He pitched his voice a little lower. "Maybe it's swan—there are so many of those abominable birds in this city."

She laughed at his joke. "It's wonderful," she answered, setting her hand on the table close to his. He stared at it a moment, and she saw his brow wrinkle slightly, altering his expression.

"What's troubling you?" she asked.

He looked abashed by her question. "You're too clever, Ankarette. I feel there is nowhere I can hide where you cannot ferret me out."

"What do you mean?"

"Are you toying with me?"

She arched an eyebrow.

He sighed, leaning back in the chair. He stared at her hand on the table and put his own hand on top of it. "I wasn't expecting . . . I didn't think that when I saw you again . . ." His voice trailed off and he fidgeted, then gently stroked the top of her hand with his thumb.

"Is there something you're trying to say?" she asked gently.

His eyes met hers. "I've never been clever at speaking my heart. I try, in my own clumsy way, but I'm too much a soldier. Or maybe too much a spy. I always worry too much about what the other person is thinking, how they are taking my words. Then my thoughts get jumbled together and my tongue unloosens from my jaw and I make a botch of it all." He smiled at her, but she could see his worry, his fear. "I don't want to *ruin* this moment. I'm afraid that I will."

Ankarette gazed down at the pottage bowl. "Just speak from your heart, Thomas. Speak the truth."

"The truth? Only it's not very simple. Not very tidy. The truth is that more than once I've made a fool of myself in the eyes of the girl I thought I loved. You handed me her note, her rejection, before I left Kingfountain. That was very kind of you to give it to me. Look at me, Ankarette."

She obeyed, though it terrified her to look at him just then.

He clasped her hand. "I've chased after someone for years to satisfy my ambition. But all this time in Brugia . . . it has given me time to think. I realized that if we were forced to stay in exile, I would never see Elysabeth Horwath again. And that thought didn't trouble me." He sighed. "What did," he whispered, "was that I might never see *you* again."

Her throat was dry, so very dry. He was on the verge

of confessing his feelings for her. She had never dreamed it would be possible, although she had hoped for it.

"Here I am," she said, giving him a kind smile, willing him with all her soul to lean over the table and kiss her.

"What a surprise it has been to see you here," he said, shaking his head. He raised her hand and pressed his mouth to her knuckles. "I'm still afraid I'll discover this was all a dream. I would be happy if I never awoke from it."

"This isn't a dream, Thomas," she said, sidling a little closer. "But we must go back to Kingfountain. We are both loyal to Eredur and Elyse. What will happen then? I would never want to lose your friendship."

He set her hand down in mock surprise. "That's not even possible, Ankarette. You have been a true friend to me ever since we met. No, I'd already decided this before you came. When this is over, I'm going to ask the king to let me manage one of his hunting lodges in the North. Maybe Marshaw?" he added with a wag of his eyebrows. "I'm done chasing my ambition. What has ambition gotten Warrewik? It has turned a man I once respected into a shell of himself."

As Ankarette listened to him, she couldn't help but wonder if his fatigue of politics and intrigue would last. It thrilled her to be part of the machinations of power, and she believed it thrilled him too.

"I don't think becoming an earl could make me happier than I feel at this very moment," he continued. "I know the king will use you. That he must use you. You are his poisoner." He said the last part in a very quiet voice so as not to be overheard. "But you are dear to me, Ankarette. And ever will be."

She saw the look in his eyes change. Saw the warmth in his eyes freeze over. He let go of her hand as Severn Argentine arrived at their table.

"There you are, Sir Thomas," Severn said coldly. "Flirting with one of the local lasses, I see. Make your excuses to the girl, if you will—my brother wants to see us back at the palace. He's been promised boats and a few hundred men." He snorted. "Not much of an army, but it's better than fighting with spades and shovels. We'll be departing this city of bird droppings on the morrow." He looked sternly at Thomas, saw the flustered anger in his eyes. Ankarette said nothing, but she did not have kind feelings for the king's brother at that moment. His sharp tongue was unwelcome.

"What?" Severn chided. He wrinkled his nose and looked around coldly. "You like this place? I'd sooner limp with a tack in my boot than stay in his muck hole a day longer. Let's go, man. On your way."

Severn was a duke of the realm and had the right to command.

Thomas rose from his chair, offering an apologetic smile to Ankarette. Severn had not even recognized her. Her attire and manners had deceived him without any effort.

Thomas pitched his voice low for her. "I'll meet you back at the manor. Let me go back to the king with Severn."

She nodded, feeling disappointment well up inside her.

"Come on, man!" Severn growled. "Leave her be. You're never coming back here again."

Thomas straightened, trying to curb his anger. Then, in defiance, he grinned at her, leaned down, and kissed her cheek before he left.

CHAPTER 32
CROWSPAR

Ankarette and Hawkins returned to Kingfountain aboard another Genevese trading ship. Many mercenaries come to fight for the Duke of Warrewik traveled with them. Ankarette poisoned their supper so that all the would-be fighters would suffer from a bowel disorder during the night. Her escort, Hawkins, was even more afraid of her after she told him what she'd done.

She had exchanged her Brugian disguise for a commoner's frock and walked purposefully to the bridge leading to the sanctuary of Our Lady. She and Thomas had not been able to say good-bye privately prior to her departure. In exchange for the small show of support Severn had mentioned, Eredur had agreed to support his brother-in-law, King Philip, should he decide to wage war on Occitania. Eredur had been in no position to deny him anything.

"There are many of Warrewik's men guarding the entrance," Hawkins said worriedly in an undertone as they approached the sanctuary. Indeed, there were at least a dozen soldiers milling around in the street before the gates. Some of the riffraff on the inside of the grounds were jeering at the guards wearing the badge of the Bear and Ragged Staff.

"Let's split up," Ankarette said to him as they maneuvered through the bustling crowd. "You enter from the left, and I'll go in from the right. One of us needs to get through to tell the queen her husband is returning."

"Very well," Hawkins said nervously. The two of them separated and Ankarette lengthened her stride. She adopted the manners of a fretful woman, rubbing her hands and sighing like a penitent come to throw a coin in the fountain for a prayer. She kept her gaze on the spire of the sanctuary and even managed to summon enough emotion to wet her eyes. As she fidgeted with her hands, she twisted her poisoned ring and exposed the needle.

As she tried to pass one of the soldiers at the side of the gate, a firm hand grabbed her shoulder, stopping her.

"Hold up, lass," the soldier said, turning her. It was one of Warrewik's men. She recognized him from Dundrennan, though she couldn't place his name. He scrutinized her face, his expression guarded and wary. "What's your name? Do I know you?"

She was almost a footstep from being within the sanctuary. Another soldier stepped up, blocking the way.

The longer she delayed, the more soldiers would come. Without responding in word, she grabbed the first soldier's littlest finger and yanked it hard, snapping the bone. The soldier's face crumpled with pain and he jerked away from her, howling, his face contorting with surprise and agony. She backed away from him, right into the man who had come up to block her way. As soon as she felt his body, she pretended to be startled and then dropped her hand and jabbed the poisoned ring into his thigh.

"What the . . . ugh!" he said, feeling the sting of pain. She turned in time to watch him crumple to the ground. Looks and stares began to come from those around her. Other soldiers were turning, looking angry and confused. Ankarette stepped inside the gate as the soldiers clustered around. Some of the sanctuary men began laughing at the soldiers, and soon apple cores and rubbish were being hurled at Warrewik's men.

Ankarette saw Hawkins trying to argue his way in through the gate, but the sentries had blocked everyone from coming in or going out. He was on his own. She walked away from the scene of the confusion and felt the ripple of Fountain magic behind her, following her. Her stomach clenched with dread. It didn't feel like Lord Hux, but she couldn't be positive. Instead of going into the majestic structure, she went to one of the large mirror pools outside of it and stood there, head bowed, thoughts running wild.

The presence of the person drew closer to her, stealing up behind her. A ripple of distrust and awareness of danger coursed through her. She continued the posture of prayer but surreptitiously reached for her dagger. When she felt the person nearly behind her, she suddenly whirled, brandishing the weapon in anticipation of a duel.

She saw no one, but she heard rapid shuffle steps backing away. Her eyes darted quickly to each side, realizing that the person who had stolen up behind her could not be seen.

"Who are you?" she said in a dangerous voice. She had sensed this person, this invisible man before—the day she and Thomas had staged the scene at the tavern.

There was no reply, just the vague feeling of retreat.

"Come near me again, and I'll kill you," she said. "I'm the Queen's Poisoner."

The feeling continued to wane. But then she heard a reply. "My mistake," said the raspy, cunning voice. A man's voice.

Had there not been so many bystanders in the general area, she might have chanced throwing her dagger. But without a visible target, she did not dare take the risk. She sheathed her weapon again and her heartbeat slowed to a more bearable rate.

~

DECONEUS TUNMORE WAS the first person Ankarette saw upon entering the sanctuary. He had come to investigate the conflict at the gate. When he saw her, his look changed to one of understanding.

"This explains the commotion," he said. "I was warned that the duke's men were starting to riot."

"One tried to stop me from entering," she answered.

"Is anyone dead?"

She gave him an arch look. "I only do that when there is no other choice. I wounded two. Take me to the queen. There is news. But a question for you, if you will."

"Yes, what is it?"

She watched his expression closely. "There is someone Fountain-blessed on the sanctuary grounds. I just sensed him over by that fountain."

Tunmore nodded. "That would be Dragan."

"Who is he?" she asked. "His power . . . it's invisibility, isn't it?"

"Yes, and it fits his choice of profession quite well.

He's one of the sanctuary men, a thief. He steals from people in the city during the day and sleeps in the sanctuary at night. He's a coward, but as slippery as a fish drenched in oil. I've never revealed to him that I know the truth. He's a pickpocket. And he sells information to the Espion. If he saw you slip through the gate, he was probably trying to earn some money by reporting you to Warrewik."

"I should have killed him, then," Ankarette said. "He's stolen from me before."

"He's a coward. No doubt he will stay away from you now. But that is inconsequential. There is news, Ankarette. Queen Morvared has returned to Ceredigion."

Ankarette stared at him. "She's at Kingfountain?"

"Not yet," Tunmore answered. "She crossed the border into Westmarch with an army. Kiskaddon is hunkering down at Tatton Hall and isn't opposing her. She could be in the city in days. Where is the king?"

"He'll be landing in Crowspar today," she replied. "We must tell the queen."

Tunmore nodded vigorously. "The war begins. Follow me."

When they arrived at the queen's private quarters, they found little Elyse cooing and playing with her baby brother, who was in a wooden crib.

The queen had been writing at the small table and came to her feet, rushing to Ankarette and embracing her. Her eyes were alight with hope. "You are back sooner than I expected. Have you seen him?"

Ankarette smiled warmly and nodded. "I left him just this morning." The queen's fingers squeezed into Ankarette's shoulders almost painfully. Tunmore secured the door and came closer to hear the news.

"Did he accept your plan?" the queen asked.

"He did," she answered. "King Philip gave him several hundred soldiers and a small fleet. They would have landed in Crowspar by now. Then they will proceed to Yuork."

The queen turned away, entwining her fingers together, and started to pace. "How long will it take for news to reach Warrewik?"

"As early as midnight by my reckoning. Dawn at the latest. His Espion are efficient."

The queen nodded. "So few men. So few."

"He has his brother, Lord Hastings, and Sir Thomas. The men of the North will be loyal. And once Dunsdworth joins their ranks, it will put Warrewik on the defensive."

The queen nodded, closing her eyes as if in prayer. "So much hinges on Dunsdworth." She sighed. "Hope is all that we have. Warrewik cannot be allowed to escape. This conflict must see an end."

"I know," Ankarette said soothingly. She breathed deeply. "That is why Eredur sent me back to you in Kingfountain. I'm going to the palace. If Warrewik tries to escape with the mad king, I've been ordered to stop them. And kill them if I must."

The queen blanched. "You could be killed trying."

Ankarette felt her insides flutter. "I accepted that risk when I chose to serve His Majesty. Others are risking their lives as well." She was already worried about Thomas. So much could happen in a battle, and there would likely be more than one skirmish. Her feelings collided with her duty.

The queen came and took her hands. "Deconeus, would you make sure you have men watching the palace for signs that Warrewik is leaving with his knights?"

"Yes, my lady," said the deconeus, bowing. "My understanding is that he is currently still there. I'll watch for signs of his herald as well."

"Thank you. Ankarette, rest a moment before you go." The queen gave her a concerned look.

After the deconeus left, the queen steered her to a small couch and sat beside her. "You look different, Ankarette. Did something happen in Brugia? Something you're not telling me?"

The queen was so observant to the moods of others. She touched Ankarette's shoulder with sympathy, entreating her to confide more about her visit.

"If you're worried about Eredur, he is in good health," she said. "Marq is a beautiful city, but he's been undeniably restless to leave. No one feels as much urgency to act as he does. He's worried about you and the children."

"That is comforting," Elyse answered. "But there's more. I can see it in your eyes."

Ankarette looked down at her hands in her lap. Her throat bulged and she felt tears prick her eyes. She did not wish to burden the queen with her private concerns —and yet she *did* wish to talk about it. To confide her dearest thoughts and worries to someone.

"It's nothing," she said softly.

"Tell me," the queen pleaded.

Ankarette tried to rally herself, tried to subdue the conflagration inside her. "I learned while I was there that Thomas—*Sir* Thomas—has harbored some feelings . . . for me. I wasn't expecting it."

The queen nodded in understanding. Then a pleased, relieved smile spread across her mouth and she enveloped Ankarette in a hug. "I've long suspected it," the queen confided after pressing a kiss on her cheek.

Ankarette pulled back in surprise.

"I've known that you care for him for some time," the queen said, stroking her shoulder. "But I've seen hints of his feelings as well. I might have guessed it before he knew it himself."

"Does the king know?" Ankarette asked, feeling her heart swelling again to outsized proportions.

"We've never spoken of it," she said. "Men usually aren't that observant. But Eredur values you both. He's confided to me that he would like to put Thomas in charge of the Espion permanently. Only Sir Thomas doesn't want the charge. The two of you work very well together."

Ankarette felt the blush creeping on her cheeks. "I wasn't intending to trouble you."

Elyse took her hands and patted them. "You have done so much for my family, Ankarette. I know there are many obstacles. But you could do much worse than Thomas Mortimer. He has been Eredur's friend for many years. We will both be worrying about the ones we love in the days ahead." She closed her eyes and let out an anxious breath. "So much uncertainty we have to endure. If my husband fails, I have nowhere I can go. I worry that I'll be trapped in this sanctuary forever."

Ankarette felt a throb of compassion. She touched the queen's sleeve. "Whatever happens, I'll do my best to serve you."

Elyse offered a resigned smile. "We will not pretend. Not with each other. This could end badly. I'm frightened, Ankarette," she added in a very low voice, glancing at her daughter and infant son. "But I must be brave for them. And so must you. Thomas is probably worrying as much about you as you are about him. War is the great uncertainty. It's not always a matter of who has the most soldiers or the most loyal followers. Warrewik is rich, and yet people distrust him now because of what he's done. Once you've sold your integrity, you cannot buy it back."

She looked down and then over at Ankarette. "Part of me is tempted to ask you to intercede now. Our troubles might end with Warrewik's death. But Eredur wishes to win his victory on the field, to prove to all that his claim to the hollow crown is legitimate. He feels he must fight his uncle. So we will obey his command because he *is* the king. This must end, one way or another."

~

AFTER NIGHTFALL, Ankarette made her way back to the palace of Kingfountain. As she surmised, the duke was short on Espion at the moment, for he was trying to run a kingdom through his spies. She made it to the secret tunnels and walked in them without any source of light, having long since memorized the layout. The cook, Liona, had offered her food and shelter in her own room during the remaining daylight hours. As the night stretched out, Ankarette roamed the interior of the palace. She found herself outside the king's council chamber, watching Warrewik from the spy hole as he made his way through the huge stack of letters on his desk.

She waited patiently, listening to the sound of his breathing, his snorts of disgust as he read certain missives. His scribe was busy scrawling letters and issuing orders. He had no idea she was watching him.

It was midnight when the courier arrived. Ankarette held perfectly still.

"He's landed," the man said breathlessly, wiping sweat from his brow.

Warrewik flinched but otherwise kept his composure. "Where?"

The man was gasping for breath. "He's in the North. Landed at Crowspar and then went to Yuork. He claims"—he took a big swallow of air—"that he only seeks what is his, the right to the duchy of Yuork. The mayor opened the city gates."

Warrewik was on his feet then, his face white as cheese. "How did—what did you say?"

"Eredur's claiming to be the Duke of Yuork. Nothing more. He concedes the throne."

"And the mayor *believed* him? He's not a fool. How could he fall for such a blatant trick?" He whirled and scattered the letters from the top of the desk with a sweep of his arm. "He betrayed me! Fetch my herald. It's time to summon my son-in-law from Clare. We have to stop this. Eredur cannot stay in Yuork another day. I said get my herald!"

Ankarette smiled and watched as the courier bolted out of the chamber.

CHAPTER 33
THE BRIDGE

There was fear in Warrewik. It shone in his eyes, in his sallow skin, and in the nervous pacing that Ankarette observed through the spy holes as he prepared to confront Eredur in battle. He knew his soldiers and knights outnumbered his opponent's Brugian mercenaries. Queen Morvared was coming from Westmarch. He had dispatched Espion immediately to hasten them to Kingfountain, to hold the capital while he dealt with his rival. For Warrewik had no illusion that Eredur had truly abdicated the throne. Both men knew that only blood would heal the breach between them.

The next morning, Warrewik prepared to depart. He left his duchess in charge of the palace and charged his lieutenant, Robert Conyers, with keeping her safe. When Ankarette saw Sir Robert through the spy hole, she remembered how he had been sent to Marshaw to ensure Ankarette's obedience. He had the same ruthless expression in his eyes, the cunning that had made him so useful to a man of ambition like Warrewik.

"I'm bringing the bulk of the army with me to the North," Warrewik said, planting his hands on the table.

He tried to project confidence, but Ankarette could hear the tremor in his voice. "This is Eredur's last gambit. He knew he would lose Ceredigion if he didn't strike before Morvared's return. Once she is reunited with the mad king, everything will change. I want you to make sure that her people do not infest the palace. Keep an eye open for Lord Hux, Lewis's herald. I'm expecting him after Morvared hears the news. She'd better not tuck tail and run back to Occitania with her brat."

Robert chuckled. "He hasn't wet his sword yet," he said, shaking his head. "It doesn't matter what she says—he's itching for a fight. In fact, he won't want you to defeat Eredur without him. The lad wants the glory for himself."

Warrewik snorted. "I don't care what he wants. The longer Eredur is ashore, the more of a threat he becomes. More and more of the disaffected will rally to him. I've sent orders for ships to throng the coast by Crowspar. I don't want him escaping this time."

"Like you did before," Sir Robert said snidely.

Warrewik bristled. "I had no choice. You are the temporary castellan of Kingfountain. Serve me well, Sir Robert, and there are more honors in store for you."

The man's eyes lit up with greediness and he bowed with as much respect as money could buy.

"Now I'm off to the North. Dunsdworth hasn't wet his sword yet either, and he'll be chafing for the chance. I can't tell you what a relief it's been not to have him nagging me constantly like he did in Occitania. I miss my eldest daughter, but I've grown weary of his complaining."

"You can't expect a dog robbed of a bone not to howl," Sir Robert opined. "Dunsdworth will learn soon enough that honor is won through blood. The kind that is shed, not the kind that flows in his veins. He wanted to be a king, but he did nothing to earn it."

Warrewik stared down at the table, conflict raging in his expression. He squeezed his fist and looked as if he'd hammer the table with it. Instead, he butted it against his mouth, nearly trembling. "We can do this, Sir Robert. Once Eredur is dead, our problems are ended. Morvared won't find me a weak-willed pup to command at her whim. *I* will decide who wears the hollow crown." His eyes shot to Sir Robert. "She will learn that soon enough. They will *all* learn that."

Ankarette was impressed at his capacity for self-delusion. He didn't see the trap about to be sprung. She had the conviction that he would never step foot in Kingfountain again.

"Aye, my lord," Sir Robert said, nodding. He smiled with the look of a man ready for the violence of war. His eagerness was palpable.

Ankarette loathed him.

~

THE PALACE WAS IN AN UPROAR. Ankarette had hunted Warrewik's loyal Espion down, one by one, rendering each man into a helpless state of misery. She had enjoyed poisoning Sir Robert in secret and watching as it took effect. He had begun acting the part of the tyrannical overlord the moment Warrewik left, even going so far as to make inappropriate comments to the duchess. The poison she had administered to him had given him the bloody flux. Not enough to kill him, but enough to make him lose fluids from every orifice. Some were fearful he had the plague. Without his leadership, the palace staff went into anarchy.

And then word arrived of Dunsdworth's betrayal. Ankarette relished the news of how the Duke of Glosstyr and Duke of Clare had met each other as if to battle, only to fall into ranks with each other and swell Eredur's army to an impressive size. It still left Isybelle in danger, but Ankarette planned to remedy that and set her friend free. The shock of the turnabout was on the lips of every servant. People were astounded. There was cheering in the streets and at the sanctuary of Our Lady. The true king would return and depose the mad man who gibbered in his rooms and spoke to the air and giggled at nothing.

It was midafternoon and she was eating in the kitchen with Liona when she felt the presence of Fountain magic enter the palace. Ankarette had been expecting him to arrive eventually and she had rallied several of the Espion loyal to Eredur to help her in case it happened. She'd left some at the sanctuary and some watching the bailey.

None of the Espion had warned her of his arrival.

"What is it, lass?" Liona said, noticing her change of countenance.

Ankarette's stomach churned with dread. "Lord Hux is back," she said softly. "Bolt the doors of the kitchen until I return. Do not let him in here."

Liona hurried to the door while Ankarette slipped into the secret passageway. Though she still feared Lord Hux, she was determined to capture or kill him. It would remove a valuable piece from the Wizr board.

As she traversed the tunnels, she tried to discern his position. She was so tempted to use her magic to help her, but knew that doing so would reveal her presence to him. Was he deliberately alerting her to his presence?

Or was he in too much of a hurry to interfere in the conflict?

His presence had stopped moving, and she found herself approaching the royal chambers. It was the place where the mad king was confined. She gritted her teeth. He could not be allowed to free the prisoner and escape with him.

When she arrived outside the chamber, she carefully opened the spy hole. She sensed Lord Hux in the room, his power jabbing at her senses in a way that increased her fear. Her palms were sweating. She had already readied a dagger with poison on the tip.

Squinting, she gazed into the room and saw Lord Hux kneeling before the mad king, whose wispy hair was more gray than blond now. "I cannot bring you with me, my lord king," said Lord Hux in a reverent voice. "Her Majesty, the queen, bids me tell you that she has ever loved and cared for you. That your rightful son and heir will rule this realm in your stead. She is sorry it must be this way."

Ankarette's magic flared within her. It rose involuntarily. She sensed Hux's intention of poisoning the king —of laying the blame for his death on Eredur's shoulders. It would give the prince the rightful title and remove the mad king as an obstacle. She felt the fiery certainty rise inside her in a surge of magic.

Lord Hux turned to the wall, his eyes narrowing, his gaze as cold as ice.

Ankarette opened the door and entered the room. She didn't have any of the Espion guards with her. She was alone with him. It had come to this.

"I thought you would come, my dear," he said with a glimmer in his eye.

The mad king turned and looked at Ankarette in confusion. "Mumble voth? Zands!"

His words were always gibberish to her.

"The Espion are closing in," Ankarette said, bluffing, striding forward. "You are not getting out of the palace alive, Lord Hux."

The quirk of a smile twitched on his mouth. "I came here alive. And I will leave here alive. I don't wish to harm you, Ankarette. Or the ones that you care for. You've taken a fancy to Thomas Mortimer, I know. I can arrange things to benefit you both in Occitania. Otherwise, I promise you, he will die in the battle that is coming. And so will your king."

"The Fountain takes who the Fountain wills," Ankarette said, shaking her head. "You offer me something you cannot give. I serve Ceredigion. And I always will."

"Alas for you," Lord Hux said.

Ankarette threw her dagger at him. She watched it go straight for his heart, but the poisoner grabbed it midair, clenching it in his fist. She gaped at him, wondering what kind of practice he had endured to be able to do that.

He glanced at the blade. "So you *were* intending to kill me," he said in a dispassionate tone.

Ankarette twisted her poisoned ring to expose the needle. Her heart was racing, but she continued to let the magic course through her, making her stronger.

"I don't have orders to kill you," he said. "But if *he* must die, best it come from your hand."

He raised her dagger and prepared to plunge it into the breast of the mad king. Ankarette rushed forward, closing the distance. With one hand, she shoved the mad king to the floor. She blocked the thrust with her

THE POISONER'S ENEMY

other forearm, and the two poisoners began fighting in earnest.

There was no time for a plan. She could rely only on her instincts, honed at the poisoner school in Pisan. She had done well in knife fighting and hand-to-hand combat. But Lord Hux was a more skilled fighter. She tried clawing at his face, only to find the edge of his palm at her throat, crushing her windpipe. She choked in pain, unable to breathe, but still she fought, thrashing against him with arms, legs, and fingers. There were no more subtle jests, no provoking. She wanted to kill him. She did her best to defeat him.

And she failed.

She ended up facedown on the floor, his knee in her back, her arm twisted painfully. The mad king was cowering, weeping openly at the violence, and the worst part of her suffering was the knowledge that she couldn't save him. She couldn't save herself. Her mind scrambled for a strategy, but her Fountain magic was ebbing fast.

"I didn't think you'd be easy to tame," Hux said, panting. She watched him remove a vial from his doublet. "Truly, you are an exceptional poisoner."

The hand with her poisoned ring was the one he was torquing behind her back to control her. She tried to bring her elbow back to knock away the vial, but he only increased the pressure on her arm, which made her gasp in pain.

"No, not yet. I'll let you go in a moment. Here, drink this one. It's one of my favorites."

He let go of her arm, then grabbed the hair at her forehead and jerked her neck back, exposing her throat. He did it so quickly and violently that she opened her mouth to scream—

JEFF WHEELER

And that was when he splashed the liquid inside. It tasted bitter, terribly bitter. He quickly adjusted his hold on her and triggered her swallow reflex with his fingers. The liquid burned down her throat. She didn't recognize the poison. It was unlike anything she'd ever smelled.

Then Lord Hux was off of her. Her body started to tremble, the feeling of burning reached her stomach. She clutched her abdomen, looking up at him in misery.

He backed away, wiping sweat from his brow. "I would have killed anyone else for daring to strike me, my dear. But I've fulfilled my orders, and now I will go."

The pain in her stomach increased. She was going to be sick. She wanted to be sick, to purge the poison from her stomach.

"What is it?" she demanded. "What did you do to me?"

He smiled pleasantly. "Oh, it's not something from our kingdoms. There are plants all over the world, you know. This particular one is from the East Kingdoms. It won't kill you, Ankarette. Not right away. With the right antidote, you will live a little while longer, as long as you keep drinking it. I'll send some to you after I've gone." His eyes narrowed coldly. "If he chooses to let Morvared live, then so will you. Tell your king this. When she dies, you will die. Farewell."

She rose to her knees, cradling her stomach. "What have you done to me?"

"What I came here to do," he replied blandly. "I needed some way to control you." And then he left, abandoning her and the mad king.

Her stomach hurt so much she couldn't stand straight, but she tried. She needed to summon the Espion to chase him down. She crawled toward the door, not comprehending what had happened. Her insides burned from within, as if she'd swallowed a hot coal. The convulsions grew worse.

"Ankarette!"

She turned her head. Thomas stood in the doorway of the secret passage, gaping at her in open horror. He rushed to her side and lifted her up.

"Hurry," she said, shaking her head. "Lord Hux is in the palace. Don't let him escape. He has the antidote."

His eyes were frenzied. "He poisoned you?"

She nodded. "Quickly, Thomas!" With a quavering hand, she touched the side of his face. "Be careful. Be careful, my love."

He set her down on the king's bed, looking anguished. He gripped the pommel of his sword. His hair was disheveled. She saw the chain hauberk beneath his tunic of the Sun and Rose.

"I'll kill him," he vowed.

Ankarette nodded. "Be careful," she pleaded.

He bent down to kiss her mouth, but she held up her hand and stopped his lips from touching hers. A wounded look filled his eyes. Her magic was draining from her—spilling, wasting. She didn't have much left.

"There's still poison on my lips," she said.

His jaw clenched in fury. Pulling the sword from its scabbard, he marched to the door and kicked it open.

CHAPTER 34
THE BATTLE OF BOREHAMWOOD

It was difficult to decide which pain was worse—the one from the poison spreading through her belly or the suspense of wondering whether Thomas was even now facing off with Lord Hux. She was cold from the inside of her marrow. Breathing was a challenge. In all her experiences as a midwife she had seen women suffer the pangs of childbirth in different ways. She was determined to endure her suffering with dignity.

She lay clenched in a ball on the bed, knees up to her middle, and did her best to stifle the soft moans. A face loomed above her. It was the mad king. He stared down at her with a look of pity.

"Gromph," he said. It was gibberish still, but he wasn't menacing or threatening. With the back of his hand, he gently smoothed some of the hair from her brow. Then he patted her shoulder and began to hum.

The room was soon disturbed by knights bearing the emblem of the Sun and Rose. The mad king quailed and began shouting at them. He seized a pillow from the bed and hurled it at one of the soldiers before spluttering more nonsensical words.

One of the knights looked at the bed, at her. "Sir Thomas said we'd find you here. We're to remove the mad king to Holistern Tower before the king arrives. He's at the sanctuary greeting the queen at the moment, but will be here presently. Can I offer you any comfort? Are you wounded?"

The other knights wrestled for control of the mad king, grabbing him by the arms. He tried to cling to one of the bedposts and wailed in anguish. The sound made Ankarette's soul shudder and shrink. He was so helpless. Powerless.

She wanted to speak but couldn't even properly think through the pain. The knight gestured for the others to remove the man quickly. Her eyes locked with the mad king's gaze and he seemed to be entreating her to save him. The noise from the conflict continued out in the hall.

"I'm sorry, my lady," the knight said, standing guard over her. "Can I fetch you some wine perhaps?"

"Just a little, thank you," Ankarette whispered, stifling a groan.

He quickly made arrangements and then brought her a cup. She tried to sit up, but the pain inside her stomach made her shrink back down. The knight was helpless to lessen her discomfort. With his help, she managed a few swallows before the flavor made her want to retch.

"Thank you," she said softly. Her head was swimming with dizziness and she sank back down on the pillows.

"Is there anything I can do for you?"

"Help Sir Thomas," she said. Spots began to dance in her eyes and her vision retreated into a dark tunnel. She collapsed on the bed.

ANKARETTE FELT a gentle arm cradle her head and lift it. She was as weak as a newborn, unable to resist. She felt the lip of a small vial pressed against her mouth. Instinctively, she tried to resist, to turn away her head and repel the arm.

"Sshhh," Thomas soothed. "Drink this, Ankarette. I think it will help."

As her eyelids fluttered open, she smelled Thomas's scent, felt him pressing against her. She obeyed and parted her lips. The liquid from the vial was a pungent ichor. She took a little sip and winced as it went down her throat.

"Is it awful?" he asked. "It smells awful."

The pain in her belly immediately began to ease. Her vision cleared and she saw Thomas hovering over her anxiously. Her eyes darted around and she saw Eredur and Elyse standing at the foot of the bed, also concerned. They held each other tightly, the king's arm wrapped around the queen's shoulders.

The soothing feeling spread through her.

"The pain is ebbing," she said in a quiet voice. Then she noticed the vial in his hand. Thomas was holding a silver bottle, about the size of a perfume bottle. The silver was ornamented with little curves and embellishments around a glass interior. She saw the deep purple liquid inside and blinked in fear. She'd seen such vials before in Pisan. It was one of the accoutrements of a poisoner.

"What is that?" she asked him worriedly. "Where did you get it?"

"Lord Hux left it behind," he answered. Then he tilted the bottle and showed her the cap. Her name had been engraved there in delicate letters done in exquisite script.

"Are you feeling better?" the queen asked Ankarette worriedly.

She was and so she nodded.

"I'm so relieved," the queen said, leaning her head on Eredur's chest.

"As am I," said the king. "Tom says you faced Lord Hux on your own." He shook his head. "I'm grateful you're still alive."

Their concern for her meant the world. She tried to sit up again, and although it made her dizzy, she had the strength.

"How did he escape?" she asked, looking into Thomas's eyes. He was sitting on the bed and helped her straighten. Her body felt as if she'd been thrown from the tower and landed violently on the ground. Something within her was broken.

"We don't know," Thomas said. He looked perplexed. "I saw him, Ankarette. I saw his doublet, his hair. He went into the chapel by the audience hall. There is only one way in and out of that place—that private little chapel with a fountain. You know it?"

She nodded, squinting at him.

"When I arrived, I thought he'd demand sanctuary, and I was ready to spill his blood for hurting you, despite the sacrilege." He chuckled to himself. "But he wasn't there. There was only this vial of poison with your name on it waiting on the edge of the fountain. He left it there." He shrugged. "I stood guard and summoned soldiers to help me search the room. There is no place to hide in there. We even dipped our swords into the water of the fountain. There was no trace of him."

"He is very good at deception," Ankarette said. "I don't blame you."

"I blame myself," he said angrily. "I smelled the vile thing. It had your name on it. We saw you lying there, twitching and trembling. You were dying."

"It was awful to watch," Elyse said with a shudder.

"The pain is diminishing," she said. "But I still feel something is wrong. I don't think he gave you the cure. Just something that will prolong my life."

Thomas's eyes widened and his face crumpled. She reached out toward his hand that was holding the vial and placed hers on his wrist. She squeezed. "You did the right thing, Thomas. He gave me a message before he left." She swallowed, still tasting the ichor. "He said that as long as Queen Morvared lived, I would live. My life for hers."

Eredur's face glinted with anger when she looked at him. "Did he think I was going to take revenge on that woman?"

"I don't know what he thought," Ankarette answered. "I think he was just being sure that we got the message."

The queen scowled at the news. "It's not a fair trade. Ankarette is worth far more than that false queen."

"Indeed," echoed her husband. "Tom—we must go. How far away is Warrewik's army? He's at our heels."

"He'll be at Borehamwood before nightfall. That gives us tomorrow to prepare Kingfountain for his attack."

The king shook his head, his look stony. "No, Tom. No more hunkering behind walls. He's expecting me to hide in here and throw his soldiers against the walls. We're going to face him."

Thomas looked surprised. "His army is double our

size, even with Dunsdworth's force added to our own. We need time for Stiev Horwath to come down from the North and even the odds!"

Eredur was grim faced. "We don't have time to wait for Horwath. We won't get another chance like this. Morvared's forces will be here within a day or two, and if we wait for them to come, we'll all be dead. We've got the city. They'll hold for us. Now we face my uncle and end this."

A throb of worry clenched Ankarette's heart. Her hand tightened on Thomas's wrist.

He stared at the king, the conflict evident on his face. Thomas had served Warrewik for years before betraying him. There was no doubt his future and his fortunes rode on the outcome of this battle. If Warrewik won, Thomas would be sent over the falls. Of course, he could also be killed in the chaos of battle. Ankarette could not bear either outcome.

Eredur gave his friend a hard look. "I need you, Tom. So much can happen. I need your wits. I need your courage."

Thomas looked away as he rose from the bed. "Let's get this done, then," he said with a sigh. But he paused at the door to look back at her. "Good-bye, lass."

∾

IT WAS after midnight and few in the palace were asleep. Little Elyse was curled up on the royal bed, exhausted. The prince fidgeted in his cradle, restless. The queen was pacing, repeatedly casting anxious looks toward the door every time the sound of bootsteps approached and faded. Ankarette sat at the window seat, a blanket spread over her lap, her fingers working quickly and deftly on the embroidery of a fleur-de-lis, the flower of Occitania. As she worked, she felt little trickles of Fountain magic returning to her. Her stores were hollow within her, a cistern that had drained like the one beneath the castle.

There was a soft tap at the door and the queen ceased her pacing. Ankarette was about to set down her needle when the queen flashed her a gentle smile and gestured for her to keep at her work. Ankarette hated feeling defenseless. She was determined to find out what poison Hux had used on her—and more importantly, she needed a permanent remedy.

The queen answered the door and discovered Liona standing there with a tray and some steaming mugs. "I thought you might care for something at this late hour," the cook said tenderly. "I'm afraid none of us are sleeping this night. Have you heard any news, my lady?"

"You are so thoughtful, Liona," the queen said. She gestured to the small table near the couch and the cook came in and set down the tray. "The two armies are facing one another north of Borehamwood. The battle will be in the morning, I fear."

Liona clucked her tongue. "Then tomorrow we know. But assuredly, my lady, the king is blessed in the arts of war. He's never lost a battle. He's fighting for you, for your sweet ones. I can't count how many coins we've all thrown in the fountains. He's sure to win."

The queen smiled and hugged the cook. "Thank you, Liona. You are very thoughtful. I treasure your friendship."

Liona smiled and looked pleased. "You're kind to say it, my lady. I've affection for your little ones. And you too. The duke is a proud man. He never gave us much notice."

"His error," the queen said sweetly. "Good night. Rest if you can."

The cook shook her head. "Not tonight, my lady. May the Fountain bless you and yours."

"Thank you."

The cook turned and left, shutting the door quietly behind her. Ankarette worked quickly with the needle. It was no longer her turn to play a role in the events. Somehow the waiting was even more agonizing.

The queen tightened the shawl around her shoulders and stared out the window into the dark night. "Both sides prayed to the Fountain tonight," she said, her gaze far away. "It has always been so. The night before the Battle of Azinkeep, the King of Ceredigion knelt and prayed to the Fountain for victory. After his success, he swore he would kill any man who boasted of the accomplishment, who denied the Fountain its due praise." She sighed deeply. "Somewhere they are out there, Ankarette. They are not sleeping either. The die has been cast. It is still rolling." Then she looked at Ankarette. "Will we win or lose? I don't know. Only the light of day will reveal that to us. We must have hope, even when there is so little to cling to."

Ankarette said nothing, working at her stitches. She thought of Thomas and it made her want to weep.

∽

News came the next morning, but it was not decisive. It only added to the strain.

Lord Hastings was seen riding across the bridge with a motley band of soldiers who had been routed in the Battle of Borehamwood. The queen waited for him in the audience hall, wearing her crown and a regal dress, standing with the patience and fortitude of a solemn mountain. Ankarette was nearby, though the other servants and nobles had been hurried out of the room.

Lord Hastings had blood and dirt on his armor as he came and knelt before her, his face flushed and mired, his hair askew. The dents and gouges in his armor attested that he'd seen heavy action. There was a cut on his left cheek.

"What tidings, Lord Hastings?" the queen asked him, her voice shaking slightly.

He sighed and looked up at her. "The battle isn't over yet, my queen."

"Then why are you here and not with my lord husband?" she asked him angrily, gesturing for him to stand.

He groaned and then made it to his feet. "Eredur asked me to command the left flank. He gave Severn the right. He and Dunsdworth took the center. He charged me with defending the road, to prevent Warrewik from getting past us and striking at the city . . . at you." He sniffed and exhaled roughly. "During the night, the king ordered us all to march closer to Warrewik's ranks under cover of darkness. Not to engage them, but to draw closer. It was wise that he did so, because Warrewik's archers shot volleys at our tents with their longbows in the dead of night. We remained quiet all the while, the arrows sailing over our heads. They had no idea we were so close. Eredur thought they'd attack, but they didn't. They were confused by the stillness."

Ankarette clenched her hands, smiling at the king's foresight. Or had it been Thomas's idea?

Lord Hastings began pacing. "During the night, a thick mist fell across the army. It was difficult judging friend from foe. We readied for battle, and my soldiers were immediately outflanked. Our lines were overlapping," he said, holding out his hands to demonstrate it. "The Earl of Oxgood struck us from behind. My men started to flee and scatter. I knew we'd be cut to pieces if we tried to join ranks with Eredur's part of the army, so I ordered my men to retreat to the town so we could hold the road and stop the rout. Oxgood's men then swung back and attacked the king. There was nothing we could do, my lady. My men were scattering, fearful. It was too much commotion. I took what few knights as would stay loyal and came to defend Kingfountain. I know not what has happened to your husband."

Ankarette's insides twisted with horror. Warrewik's forces had already outnumbered Eredur's. With Oxgood rejoining the fight after the cowardice of Hasting's men, she didn't see how they could succeed.

The queen kept her composure. "Thank you, Lord Hastings. Prepare the battlements. If my husband loses, we are all that protects the prince."

Tears streamed down Hasting's face. "Aye, my lady."

Fear overwhelmed the inhabitants of the castle. Servants were crying openly, whispering about what would happen to the queen, to her children. Ankarette was walking upright, but she felt something wrong in her core, a faint queasiness that would never leave. Could it be the lingering effects of Hux's poison?

Within the hour, another rider was seen. It was Bryce, one of the Espion, and he rushed into the palace, his tunic stained with grime from the battle—and yet the look on his face said everything . . . His smile broke through the clouds of despair and filled the great hall with radiant sunshine.

"It is finished," he said breathlessly to the queen. He

lifted his head in triumph, and his enthusiasm crushed the dying embers of their fear. "Your husband prevailed. Warrewik is dead."

The queen bowed her head solemnly. When she opened her eyes again, she looked relieved yet maintained her poise. "You bring good tidings, messenger," she said with gratitude.

"By the stars!" he exulted.

"What happened, man!" Lord Hastings bellowed. "How can this be?"

Bryce turned and bowed his head to the nobleman. "The mist and confusion wreaked havoc on both armies, Lord Hastings. You were flanked, but so was Warrewik. The Duke of Glosstyr commanded the right and he met no opposition. He attacked with all the viciousness of a . . . of a boar!" He laughed in jubilation. "He tore through Warrewik's army. The king and Dunsdworth met the rest in the middle. And then lo! Soldiers arrived carrying the banner of the North. It was Duke Horwath and his frostbitten men. They had put the Atabyrions to flight and then marched day and night to reinforce us. We were more than a match for Warrewik. He was struck down whilst trying to flee the battle. I saw his corpse myself."

"How many notables did we lose? How bad was the carnage?" the queen asked hopefully.

"We gave worse than we got, Your Majesty," Bryce said with iron in his voice. "But many of our men gave their lives for their king. The most notable was Mortimer. He died on the field this day. Sir Thomas, bless his soul, died fighting for his king."

Ankarette's world began to tilt and sway.

CHAPTER 35
PREMONITION

Ankarette's stallion plunged down the road that was full of soldiers hobbling toward Kingfountain. Some hung their heads in defeat and humiliation. Some held heads high in triumph. But all were aching, bloodied, and exhausted. The Battle of Borehamwood had tested their mettle. These were warriors of Ceredigion. The men tilted their heads to look up at her, a cloaked apparition riding a pale stallion toward the carnage they had left behind.

Her heart thrummed with suppressed pain. She was still achingly weak from her fight with Hux. But nothing could stop her from coming. The news could not be true. It *must* not be true. She would not believe it unless she saw Thomas's shattered body on a pallet with her own eyes. Just the thought of it unloosed grief unlike any she had experienced. But she clenched her jaw, held the tears at bay with sheer force of will, and rode like thunder toward the battlefield.

Her mother had warned her that the most dangerous kind of childbirth was the expectation of twins. A mother, exhausted by the ordeal of childbirth, would still have to deliver the second babe. As she neared the chaos of the camp, she saw that the pangs of the second birth had already begun. The soldiers she had seen trudging to Kingfountain were the ones deemed too injured to fight. Those who remained at the battlefield were now preparing to face Morvared's army. The ousted queen knew this was her final opportunity to seize the throne for her son. Her army was fresh, and Eredur's was battered. Though Warrewik was dead, the crisis was not over.

Reaching the picket lines on her lathered stallion, she was halted by sentries wearing the stained tunics of the Sun and Rose.

"This is no place for a lass," one of them said, holding out his hand and grimacing darkly.

She met his gaze with ferocious intensity and showed him her Espion ring.

One of the sentries nudged the man stalling her. "I know her," he muttered. "She's the Queen's Poisoner. Let her through."

The soldiers backed away and she kicked the horse forward. The smell of battle hung in the air. The road was mired, and makeshift tents had been thrown up everywhere. Everywhere there were signs of the cost of battle. A pile of ripped Bear and Ragged Staff tunics had been discarded in a ditch. Their duke had fallen, and his symbol was no more. Now that she had reached Borehamwood, her resolve began to wilt. There were so many dead . . . The scene defied belief. If Ankarette had not already been hardened to blood, she would have fainted.

The roads were clogged with people, everyone begrimed and with the same haunted look in their eyes. There was little order in the ranks, and she felt out of her ken.

"Ankarette!"

She recognized the voice and whirled in the saddle. The tall, flaxen-haired Espion named Bennet was shoving through the crowd toward her. "This way!"

She tugged at the reins and pressed through the crowd, which parted around her steed like water, and followed him. The day was waning quickly. Finally, she caught sight of the command pavilions at the center of the maelstrom. The king's banner fluttered above the main one, and she saw the standard of Duke Horwath as well, the lion with an arrow piercing its mouth. Some men stood at guard with pikes, while others rushed to and fro doing the king's bidding.

Ankarette slid out of the saddle.

"He's in that one," Bennet said, taking the reins from her and pointing to one of the smaller tents.

Ankarette nodded her gratitude and mustered her courage. Every step caused her heart to throb with agony. What would she do when she saw his corpse? Was there a way someone who was Fountain-blessed could revive the dead? She didn't know. She only knew that she would willingly give her life to save Thomas.

Unable to bear the suspense, she rushed into the tent. It was darker inside, and for a moment she could not see. A body in armor lay on a pallet on the floor, cold and still. She could sense the absence of life, the void of breath.

As her heart began to break, she heard a familiar voice from the shadows.

"Ankarette? Is that you?"

She looked up in shock, and there he was—Sir Thomas. *Her* Sir Thomas. He gave her a baffled look and then his mouth melted into a delicious smile as he walked forward.

In an instant, she understood. It was a mistake. Thomas's older brother, the Earl of Mortimer, had died in battle. In the confusion of the moment, people had confused the matter and assumed the dead man was Eredur's friend. She nearly staggered.

Overcome with relief, she rushed to him and hugged him close, pressing her nose against the links of his chain hauberk. She squeezed him tightly, relishing the feeling of his arms around her.

"You're alive," she gasped. "You're alive!"

She looked into his dirty face, his exhausted brow. Then she lifted onto the tips of her toes and kissed him on the mouth, kissing him as she had always wanted to, surrendering her heart and her feelings to this man she loved so dearly. He seemed startled by her show of affection, but then he kissed her back with equal intensity. The world was spinning. The world didn't matter to her. She clung to him, feeling a thousand different things all at once. There was a strange ache inside her stomach, a reminder of the poison that lingered within her. She had not felt herself since taking the antidote—the one that delayed the poison's effects. She had brought the vial with her, not knowing when she would need another sip from it.

Thomas's hands touched her cheeks, and she realized he was brushing away her tears.

"Ankarette," he breathed, a weak smile on his mouth. He kissed her nose, then her brow. "I hadn't expected you to come, not when you're so weak. You rode all the way here?"

"Of course I did," she said, shaking her head, trying not to cry. "Bryce told us you had died in the battle. I couldn't believe it, not until I had seen you for myself."

He grunted. "You're not the only one. Everyone who

sees me thinks I am a spirit," he joked. "No, it was my elder brother, Stillman, who fell. I'm heartsick over it, truly. So many died." He rubbed his forehead and she longed to soothe and comfort him.

"But I am grateful that you came," he continued. "Eredur ordered me to round up a hundred knights and half the Espion and flank Morvared's army. We're going to ride to Beestone castle to cut off their retreat and warn Kiskaddon that we won the day. She's trapped between both of our armies right now and doesn't realize it. Once she does, she'll try to flee."

"Or fight," Ankarette said.

Thomas shook his head. "No, she's a mother. She'll protect her son first, even if he's eager to fight. I had wished there was time to go by Kingfountain and get you and see that you were well, but here you are. You're coming with me if you're up to it."

Her eyes brightened. "I'll go anywhere with you." The relief was so immense her strength was draining.

He took her chin gently and then lowered his mouth to hers again.

It was a delicious kiss. She wanted more.

"I'll tell Eredur you're here. He's meeting with Dunsdworth, Horwath, and Severn. The Espion couriers tell us the queen is a day's march away. If she had reached Warrewik in time, things would have ended very differently."

"How many men do you have now?" she asked with concern.

Thomas smiled wryly. "The king offered a pardon to all of Warrewik's men who will fight with him, come what may. Most of them have torn up their tunics and willingly joined the king's ranks. Our army has swelled considerably and we have the advantage of momentum on our side. The king has never lost a battle. He doesn't intend to lose this one either. Come, lass. Get your horse and let's ride out together."

He gazed down at his dead brother, his look darkening. "I'll see you in the Deep Fathoms, Brother," he murmured.

~

ANKARETTE HAD NEVER BEEN to Beestone castle before, the royal castle in the region of Westmarch. Thomas had convinced the castellan that Warrewik was dead at Borehamwood, leaving Eredur in power once more. The castellan, genuinely relieved by the news, had opened the gates to let them in.

She wandered the inner courtyard now, watching the wind whip the banners, which would soon be changed to the Sun and Rose. Her stomach was growing queasier, so she perched on the edge of the well in the middle of the courtyard. She rubbed her hand on the smooth stone and listened to the gurgle of water far below. Her Fountain magic was still coming back and her reserves were low, but she sensed something special about the place where she sat. A premonition that made the place seem familiar despite the fact that she'd never been there. She cast her eyes around, trying to understand the source of her feelings, but there were no clues. Only men walking around and soldiers talking animatedly about the battle they'd fought and won.

She closed her eyes, trying to listen to the ripple of the waters. Was the Fountain trying to communicate something to her? She couldn't hear it above the din of voices and steps. Perhaps the well led to a cistern like the one she and the queen had used to escape Kingfountain? That made sense because Beestone was built on a hill.

The sounds of someone approaching brought her attention back to the present. Thomas strode up to her, looking quite pleased with himself.

"I just sent someone to Tatton Hall," he said, "with a message to Kiskaddon that Beestone castle is ours. We'll need him to bring all his force to face the queen."

"Won't that leave his lands unprotected?" she asked.

Thomas shrugged with unconcern. "If Lewis is foolish enough to invade Ceredigion with his own army on the heels of two decisive victories for Eredur, I'd be surprised. He doesn't have anyone close enough to help him, and Eredur promised that if the Occitanians encroach on Westmarch, the entire Ceredigion army will come to defend it and then march on Pree itself. King Lewis is cunning. Not stupid."

Ankarette smiled at his words. She rose from the edge of the fountain. "I'm glad the castellan opened the gates. A hundred men might not have been enough to take the castle."

Thomas laughed. "Oh, I wasn't worried. Even if he had said no, this castle is riddled with secret passages. There's an inn at the base of the hill that has a tunnel leading to this very spot, actually." He gestured surreptitiously to the well. "There's a fountain down there where the water is stored. 'Tis an Espion secret. No, we would have taken Beestone either way. I just learned that the queen's army has turned northward after hearing about Warrewik's defeat. They know Kiskaddon is blocking the way back and Eredur is closing in. Now that the message has been sent to

Kiskaddon, we'll use the garrison horses and ride in pursuit."

"Do you think they'll go for Blackpool?" Ankarette asked. "It's on the coast."

He tapped his nose. "We think alike, you and I. Yes, that's where she will go. She'll abandon her army if she must. If we ride all night and refresh our mounts, I think we will get there first."

Ankarette agreed.

He gave her a curious expression. "How are you feeling? Do you want to rest here a while longer?"

"We should not delay," she said emphatically.

∽

THEY APPROACHED Blackpool from the southwest. They rode without torches, knowing they were in enemy country now, and outriders went ahead to ensure they wouldn't unknowingly stumble upon Morvared's army. As they neared the coast, she could smell the scent of the sea in the air.

The journey had indeed wearied Ankarette, and she feared she might topple from the saddle. Although she was exhausted—they all were—they continued to hasten forward, carried by the wish to see this through. They did not want to miss the final battle and their share of glory.

As the sky began to brighten, they reached a hill overlooking Blackpool and the sea. The waters stretched off into the horizon, filling her with a sense of wonder. The trees rustled and swayed and the ruckus of the sea birds overcame the snorting and stamping of the horses. Thomas rode to the front and she followed.

"One of the Espion just got back from Blackpool," he

told her, his voice pitched low. "Morvared hasn't reached the town yet. Word has it their army is camped less than a league from here. The king sent Severn ahead to hold the town and prevent her from taking it. There will be battle today right in the plains yonder." He knifed his hand in the air. "Morvared's army is betwixt ours and Eredur's. If we keep riding, we can probably make it around before the action starts." He rubbed his mouth thoughtfully.

Ankarette summoned her Fountain magic, trying to sense for the presence of danger or unseen trouble. Just smelling the sea made the magic come more easily to her. It was quiet and peaceful. Her eyes fixed on a grove of trees.

"What if we position ourselves there?" she suggested. "Neither side would see us. Morvared might try to send soldiers through it to attack the flank. We'd be waiting for them if they try. If they don't, we can use the same tactic on them."

Thomas's eyebrows raised. "Ankarette, that is bloody brilliant. Are you going to don armor and sword as well? Are you the Maid incarnate?" He grinned at her and rubbed his hands together. "The trees are certainly dense enough to conceal us and our horses. Either way, it benefits the king. We can watch the battle progress and intervene when the moment is right." His smile filled her with pride. "Good thinking, lass."

"Do you have an extra sword?" she asked with a wry, joking smile.

He laughed and shook his head. "I was only teasing. I'll lead the men there to wait and watch."

"And I will find the queen's hostages. Lady Isybelle and Nanette." She knew Morvared to be excessively cruel and was anxious to find them.

"Their father may be dead, but Eredur does not hold them accountable for his actions. Severn cares for the youngest daughter. And if you find the former queen too, I wouldn't object to you capturing her."

He gave her a knowing smile.

CHAPTER 36
REVENGE

When Ankarette Tryneowy was a child growing up in Yuork, her father had often described the scenes of battle to her, and she had always been entranced by them. As she stood atop a small hillock, surrounded by a group of mounted Espion, and watched the Battle of Hawk Moor unfold, she felt sick and ashamed of the brutality of Ceredigion. But the courage the soldiers demonstrated also inspired her. The view also gave her the perfect vantage point to search the enemy's movements and to try to discern where Morvared was skulking.

Queen Morvared's army, trapped on all sides, did not surrender. They fought. From Ankarette's vantage point, the size of the forces were pretty much balanced. Eredur's men were weakened from their previous fight. Morvared's were fatigued from the hasty march to escape. It was a battle of wills.

During the thickest part of the fight, it was not clear which side would win. She gripped the reins of her stallion, occasionally glancing at the wooded glen where Thomas's soldiers lingered, holding back. She was grateful he was not in the midst of the bloodbath on the fields below. Strangely, the sounds from the battle ghosted in and out of her hearing.

"The king is in the thick of it," Bennet said with respect shading his voice. "No one can stop him. It's as if the spirit of King Andrew is with him today."

He was visible amidst the flurry of banners bearing the Sun and Rose. Many of the banners were spattered with mud, some stained with crimson. She watched and she hoped and she prayed that the Fountain would yield victory.

"Look!" one of the other Espion said fearfully, pointing. "Over there! A fresh wall of troops! Morvared must have sent in a reserve. They're rushing to strike the king!"

It looked like the flooding of a river, the mass of soldiers riding out from concealment to join the battle. Eredur's men were nearly cut off from the other portions of the army led by his able lieutenants.

"That's the prince," Bennet said with a hushed tone. "That's the mad king's heir! He's joined the fight."

Ankarette straightened in her saddle, gazing at the woods. This was the moment. This was what Thomas had been waiting for. It was the final pang of birth, the scream before the squealing of a babe.

Sir Thomas and his hundred knights swarmed out of the forest, as if her thoughts and his had been sewn together by thread. She thrilled inside, so proud to watch as his riders emerged from the grove, brandishing swords and swooping down to join the fray. A cheer went up from Eredur's army. It was a cry unlike anything earthly. Tears swelled in Ankarette's eyes as she watched the soldiers and the man she loved sweep down on the enemy like hawks, scattering the Occitanian soldiers. Her mount snorted and tossed its head, anxious to partake in the violence below. She soothed it, eyes fixed on the scene. The battle unraveled in that moment, the energy spilling out of it.

"It's time," Ankarette said to the Espion. "If the reinforcements came from the concealment over there," she said, pointing, "that's where we will find Morvared. Hasten."

They gave curt acknowledgment of her orders and then charged down the hill, sweeping around the flank of the battle in the rear. Her escort blocked her on all sides, although she didn't fear being attacked. Few of the soldiers had mounts now, save for hers and Thomas's men. There were corpses all around. The defeated soldiers were running now, scattering to the winds.

Whoops of victory and cries of despair began to fill the air as the resolution of the battle was finally acknowledged on both sides. Ankarette ignored the jubilation, focusing her attention. This would be dangerous. Morvared would have armed knights with her, but she had nowhere to flee. The ports were all blocked now. All she could do was hide.

They slowed their mounts as they reached the small woods from which the enemy soldiers had emerged. Weapons were drawn, and the noise of the scraping scabbards made her edgy. They pressed deeper into the copse, passing soldiers who were slipping and hiding behind trees trying to escape Eredur's men. As they passed a larger bush, she saw an Occitanian man, hair swept forward, cringing there, holding up his hands in the sign of defeat.

"Where is the queen?" she asked him in his own language.

The man blanched and pointed the way. His eyes were full of terror, his skin white as milk.

The defeated soldiers were straggling away and being rounded up by Eredur's men. Ransoms were being pled for and accepted. Knights were taken into custody. She looked down at the cringing man.

"Show us. Now."

The man, anxious to have his life spared, rose on trembling knees and walked ahead of their horses. Soon, the trees parted and the makeshift camp of the Occitanian army spread before them. Breakfast fires were guttering out. Blankets had been left in the dirt. Spears and cook pots were unattended. There was no one left.

Ankarette summoned her Fountain magic, feeling for threats and the presence of others. Bennet cast her a worried look as she nudged her stallion forward. Then she heard voices, the noise of people arguing. Motioning for the Espion to follow, she pressed onward. The voices were speaking in a frenzied rush of Occitanian. They came from the center command tent. Three horses were tethered outside.

"You must come, Your Majesty!" implored a man's voice. "The fighting is over. We're defeated, yet again, by these dogs of Ceredigion! We must fly, my lady! Now!"

"Where is my son?" said the high, trilling voice she recognized from Shynom. Ankarette knew it was the queen. "You promised he would be safe at all costs."

"I did, my lady. I know of my oath. But he is slain. I saw it happen with my own eyes. Duke Severn struck him down in cold blood as he pleaded for mercy. There was no pity in Glosstyr's heart to move him. He said the prince was a coward for trying to sneak away from the battle. Your husband won't survive a fortnight. We must away, Your Majesty. All is lost. All is in ruin."

"Bring me his corpse, then!" Morvared snarled. "Bring it so that I may weep over it. Bring it to me!"

"We cannot!" said another man. "There's naught more we can do. Come, my lady! Leave these two here."

Ankarette realized that Morvared wasn't alone. Warrewik's daughters were probably with her.

"No!" the queen said fiercely, her voice throbbing with tears. "My son. You promised me that he would live. He would live!"

"She won't listen to us," said one of the others as Ankarette's cadre approached the tent.

"Shhh! I hear horses!" The voice was panic-stricken.

Two knights rushed from the tent, swords drawn, to face Ankarette and her dozen Espion.

"Lay down your arms," Ankarette said in their language. The two men looked at each other, then at the number of foes. They tossed down their weapons, their faces crumpling with misery.

Ankarette nodded for Bennet to subdue them and then slid out of her saddle. She walked swiftly to the tent and heard these words before she entered.

"Your husband's brother killed my son," Morvared said in a strangled, tear-stricken voice. "A life for a life, then. We can all join them in the Deep Fathoms!"

Ankarette parted the curtain, drawing her dagger. Queen Morvared stood there with a knife in her hand, and Isybelle and Nanette cowered before her, their eyes wide with terror.

She remembered Hux's warning. If she killed the queen, then she herself would die.

"Ankarette!" Isybelle cried out in desperation, seeing her.

Morvared turned toward the tent opening. When she saw the poisoner standing there, she raised the knife and prepared to plunge it into Isybelle's chest.

Ankarette stepped forward and hurled her own dagger. The blade pierced Morvared's wrist, impaling it. Blood bloomed from the wound, and the former queen dropped her own knife from the spasms of pain. Ankarette strode in and subdued the older woman swiftly, bringing her to her knees before she slid the dagger out of her wounded wrist. Morvared groaned in agony, shuddering with tremors. Ankarette snatched a linen napkin from a small camp table and squeezed it around the wrist, watching as the blood began to soak it.

"You dare deny a queen her vengeance?" she said savagely, her eyes full of hate.

"You are not a queen that *I* serve," Ankarette answered coldly. She had made an implacable enemy. One who would never forget or forgive her. So be it. The wound in Morvared's wrist was not fatal, but it would pain her the rest of her life.

Isybelle and Nanette hugged each other, sobbing from the close brush with death. Isybelle looked at Ankarette with warmth and gratitude as she kissed her sobbing sister's hair. The next moment, Bennet burst into the tent, looking concerned and confused.

"Take them out of here," Ankarette told him, nodding to the two young women. "They are not hostages to ransom. They are noble daughters of Ceredigion. Take them to the king."

Bennet grinned triumphantly. "And what of her? What of *that* woman?"

"I need a healer!" Morvared spat, shuddering. Even in defeat she was proud.

"Leave four men with me," Ankarette said. "I will take her to Blackpool, to the Arthington. Tell the king to find us there."

"I know the place," Bennet said. "And I'll tell Sir Thomas as well." He gave her a wink.

~

NEVER HAD a meal tasted so good. Never had a fire felt so warm. Never had a couch been so comfortable. Ankarette had fallen asleep at last, for the first time in days. It was pain that awakened her, pain in the pit of her stomach. It was a gnawing, cruel poison and it poked at her insides like liquid fire. She opened her eyes, wincing, and realized how dark the room was. She had sat down on the couch in the common room and fallen asleep without realizing it. She jerked awake, trying to rise.

"Shhhh," Thomas whispered. "No need to fret, lass."

He was sitting at the edge of the hearth on a small stool, his elbows propped on his knees. He looked haggard and weary and there was a look of deep sadness in his eyes.

Her heart began to tighten. "What's wrong?" she asked him, covering her burning stomach.

He tried to smile. "I didn't want anyone to wake you," he whispered. "You looked so peaceful . . . until the end." He bit the edge of his knuckle, trying to compose himself. "This victory, Ankarette, should be yours. Eredur is so grateful. We have Morvared in custody and she'll soon be taken back to Kingfountain. Are you . . . are you ill? Do you feel the poison again?"

"My stomach hurts," she said, wiping sleep from

her eyes. "What's wrong, Thomas? You don't look the same."

He sighed heavily, sitting up more. "I can never hide anything from you. It's not fair."

She straightened on the couch, feeling her worry grow like a wildfire. She rested her arms on the edge of the couch and laid her head on them, looking at him sideways. His demeanor had changed. Why hadn't he awakened her with a kiss? He was chafing, wrestling within himself. It did not take long for her to realize why.

And once the suspicion reared up inside her, she recognized it to be true. A spike of pain jabbed her heart.

"I see," she said, her voice raw. "Tell me."

He looked at her in misery. "I don't want to tell you," he whispered hoarsely.

"I already know what it is," she said, sitting up. "Just say it." Her heart was turning blacker and blacker as the thoughts gripped hold of her.

He looked up at the ceiling for help. "Ankarette, I did not ask for this dilemma," he said. "It was thrust on me. As much as it pains me, I have a decision to make."

"Just tell me, Thomas," she said softly, gazing down.

He tried, starting once and failing. His breath came out slowly as he tried to subdue his feelings. "Eredur has given me leave to marry Elysabeth Horwath. It would make me the heir of Dundrennan."

She wasn't surprised by his pronouncement. Only pained by it. She bit her bottom lip. "So he has he made you the Earl of Sur, then? Your brother's earldom?"

"Yes," he answered flatly. He laced his fingers and stared down at them, looking absolutely miserable.

Thomas had always been ambitious. He had wanted

to serve in his own right, not run around doing the bidding of others. His role in the battle would be spoken of for years to come. He'd be a hero to the people, a favorite of the king's. He'd been in love with Elysabeth Horwath for years and, until now, had always been rejected by her. He was getting everything he had ever wanted.

And yet his eyes were full of remorse because he cared for someone else now. Someone more like him in temperament and loyalty. A truer friend. She knew his feelings for her were real and powerful, but she could tell he'd already made his decision. Much of him *still* wanted those old dreams.

That was why he did not hold her. That was why he looked so wretched. An earl did not marry a midwife's daughter without infamy.

She could make this easy for him. Or she could ruin his heart. If she loved him, could she deny him his ambitions? After all, she had ambitions of her own . While Thomas had spoken about leaving the subterfuge and politics behind, she thrived on it. It *fed* her Fountain magic. And in her current state, with Hux's poison destroying her from the inside, she might not even live long enough to discover the cure.

"Thank you for telling me," Ankarette said, barely able to master herself. "I think it is the right thing. You will be an excellent leader. And the kingdom needs you."

He stared at her in disbelief. "How can you say that?" he whispered in pain. "I *love* you, Ankarette Tryneowy. It feels as if my heart is being wrenched out of my chest. Would that I had died on the battlefield instead. Would that I could go to the Deep Fathoms in my brother's place."

She savored hearing the words, his profession of love, but she shook her head. "I wouldn't wish that, Thomas. We both knew this might happen. I think we were willing to content ourselves with dreams of what might be otherwise. Back in Brugia, anything felt possible. But not now. Not anymore."

"Is it that easy for you to walk away?" He looked hurt.

"None of this is easy," she answered, wincing with discomfort at the pain inside her middle. "Remember how people looked down at Queen Elyse when the king chose her? She had pedigree I will *never* have, even if the king were to grant me a title. You would be the object of ridicule. I couldn't bear that, Thomas." She sighed, forcing herself to speak it, to make it easier for him to leave her. "There's another reason. I don't know how much longer I have. My stomach hurts because of the poison Hux gave me. I'm going to try and find a cure. But it is likely to be fatal, I know that much . . . and I fear I will never be able to carry a child because of it. You must become a duke. A father. You must support Eredur's fragile throne. He needs you. Just as he needs me, only in a different way. That is why he is giving you a choice. It's up to you." She paused, her heart pounding fast in her chest. "But it is truly for the best if we remain as friends. It will be painful, but in time . . . most wounds heal."

His cheek rested on the edge of his knuckles. A tear streaked down the side of his face. He stared at the wall, anywhere but at her.

"It will be all right, Thomas," she said comfortingly, trying to help him endure his feelings. Trying to endure her own.

He turned his face and looked at her with a longing that almost made her reach for him.

"I'm glad I met you, Ankarette," he said. "I will never forget what you have done for me, for my life." He wiped away the tears. "Look at me, I'm a wreck and you haven't even cried!"

"I will, Sir Thomas," she said gently. She reached out, took his hand, and squeezed it, trying to fill him with strength. "Just not now."

He squeezed her hand back, his eyes glistening. The smile he gave her was full of both warmth and pain. "If I ever have a daughter, I'm going to name her *Victoria*. People are saying this victory is mine. But truly, Ankarette, it has been yours."

EPILOGUE
THE MAD KING

Ankarette climbed the stairs to Holistern Tower, her heart heavy with the duty she had to perform. Part of her had died that day at the Battle of Hawk Moor. Perhaps it was the sense that all life was sacred. For how could that be so when death came so swiftly, indiscriminately, and in such massive numbers? When one duke's ambition had led to such carnage?

After the battle had ended, the king had pronounced his younger brother Severn and Duke Horwath as the chief justices of the Assizes to determine the individual guilt of those who had fought in the battle. Ankarette had enjoyed seeing Isybelle again at the palace. Dunsdworth had been officially pardoned and would inherit half of Duke Warrewik's vast wealth. The duke's other daughter, Nanette, the prince's widow, would inherit the other half. There was talk that Severn had been seen in the palace garden with her, holding her hand.

Eredur had asked Ankarette if she would go back to serving Isybelle for a time, to make certain that Dunsdworth's ambitions remained in check. He would call on her, on occasion, for her skills as a midwife—or at least that was his ruse. She had agreed to continue being his poisoner so long as she was allowed to save the lives of five people for every person he asked her to kill. He had agreed without hesitation and promised her that he did not intend to use her abilities maliciously. Queen Morvared was being held for ransom in Kingfountain. Eredur never wanted to see her face again. He would not release her without extracting a heavy price from Occitania. In fact, he didn't intend to release her at all. But he kept her alive, and samples of the antidote continued to arrive.

As Ankarette reached the top of the steps, the Espion guarding the mad king's room nodded to her. They knew her well. Without being asked, one unlocked the door and opened it.

She heard the raving noises within, the screams and frightened cries of a man completely mad and wild. One of the Espion guards twitched his nose with revulsion at the sound.

As Ankarette walked inside, the mad king quieted. He looked worried, fretful, his hands chafing each other. His eyes were guiltless. Innocent.

She took a deep breath and steadied herself. "Good evening, my lord," she said. "I've heard you weren't feeling well. Would you like a cup of tea? It will help you sleep tonight."

AUTHOR'S NOTE

I have enjoyed immersing myself in the world of Kingfountain, but it is time to take a break from it for now. Last night, I learned that a fan named his newborn son Owen after the Duke of Westmarch, and he even sent me a picture of the little guy. What a sweet experience! I'm completely humbled by his decision.

As I've said in the past, Ankarette was born in my mind decades ago when I was working on my history degree in college. The events of this novel are pretty much factual. Sir Thomas and Ankarette are invented, but nearly everyone else is based on real players during the famous War of the Roses, my specialty.

Back when I was studying this era, I didn't know why this particular part of history touched me so deeply. Was it because I loved Sharon Kay Penman's novel *The Sunne in Splendour* so much and felt that Richard III had been maligned by historians? Who could have predicted that his bones would be discovered and put to rest in Leicester Cathedral within my lifetime! But perhaps the tie was more personal. Years ago, as I was perusing some family history that my Aunt Donna had provided for me, my eyes fell on the death

AUTHOR'S NOTE

date of one of my ancestors: August 22, 1485. I knew that date because it was the date of the Battle of Bosworth Field where Richard III was killed. That ancestor, I discovered, was John Howard, the Duke of Norfolk (aka Stiev Horwath, the duke of the North). I stared at the page, dumbfounded, realizing that one of my own ancestors had fought for Richard III in that battle and had died.

So when I rewrote history in creating *The Queen's Poisoner*, I not only changed the fate of Richard III but also his most powerful defender, John Howard. I kept the duke of the North alive and instead killed his son —Thomas.

Evie's father.

There is still a little more to Ankarette's story that needs to be told, and I plan on writing it as a short story or novella and publishing it in my e-zine *Deep Magic*. How did Eredur die and where was Ankarette when that happened? Let's just say, it involves our friend Lord Hux.

Next, it's time to start working on my new series.

I'm excited to bring you something new.

ABOUT THE AUTHOR

Jeff Wheeler is the Wall Street Journal bestselling author of the Kingfountain series, the Muirwood series, and the Mirrowen series. He took an early retirement from his career at Intel in 2014 to write full-time. He is a husband, father of five, and a devout member of his church. He lives in the Rocky Mountains and is the founder of Deep Magic: The E-zine of Clean Fantasy and Science Fiction. Find out more about Deep Magic online atwww.deepmagic.co, and visit Jeff 's many worlds at www.jeff-wheeler.com.

ALSO BY JEFF WHEELER

The Kingfountain Series

The Poisoner's Enemy (prequel)
The Maid's War (prequel)
The Queen's Poisoner
The Thief's Daughter
The King's Traitor
The Hollow Crown
The Silent Shield
The Forsaken Throne

The Legends of Muirwood Trilogy

The Wretched of Muirwood
The Blight of Muirwood
The Scourge of Muirwood

The Covenant of Muirwood Trilogy

The Banished of Muirwood
The Ciphers of Muirwood
The Void of Muirwood

Whispers from Mirrowen Trilogy

Fireblood
Dryad-Born

Poisonwell

Landmoor Series

Landmoor
Silverkin

Milton Keynes UK
Ingram Content Group UK Ltd.
UKHW041025071023
430065UK00003B/21

9 781648 393938